Grover Square

Grover Square

Waverly Fitzgerald

GENESTA PRESS

First published in hardcover in 1984 by Jove Press.
This edition published in 2018 by Genesta Press.
ISBN: 978-0-9835714-6-9

Genesta Press
1211 East Denny Way #187
Seattle WA U.S.A. 98122

For my friends & teachers

Stephen Lacey
Marv Chernoff
& Jean Young

who helped me learn about myself
and thus about all the characters
in this book

Contents

Every man takes the limits of his own field of vision for the limits of the world.

Schopenhauer,
Studies in Pessimism

PART ONE

Jenny's Prologue

~ ~

What are your historical Facts;
Still more your biographical?
Wilt thou know a Man,
above all a Mankind,
by stringing together beadrolls
of what thou namest Facts?
The man is the Spirit he worked in;
not what he did,
but what he became.

Carlyle,
Sartor Resartus

Prologue

You may recall (or may have at least heard) the rumours that swept through London Society like brush fires during the Season of 1844 regarding Arabella Farraday, the young and beautiful heiress to a substantial fortune who had married a well-known and respected London solicitor only two years before. At first, the rumours were mere sparks that flared as a result of her sudden disappearance but then died as quickly as they were kindled for lack of fuel. Later, fanned by malicious gossip, they became a full-scale conflagration that threatened to destroy the lives and happiness of Arabella, her husband, and her child. The scandal slowly died, but long afterward the cinders remained, scorching and painful to those who disturbed them. Even now, there are times when a conversation stirs the ashes of memory and I am taken aback to find the embers still glowing after all these thirty years.

"You knew her then. What was she really like?" they ask me, eyes glowing hotly. Among other tales, they had heard that Arabella had borne a child from a liaison with a common foot soldier. This was, of course, arrant nonsense and shows the degree to which the details of the case were perplexed. I suppose that the inquisitive confuse the roles played by Lieutenant Philip Vandeleur and Daniel O'Connell, the man with whom I was walking out at the time. He met Arabella only once, assisting in her flight from her husband to a reunion with her long-lost mother, and he never saw her again.

I have heard still others speculate that Arabella inherited the depraved constitution of her mother, who had vanished from Society twelve years before and was thought to be incarcerated in an asylum, irretrievably mad. Well, I will let the reader judge for him or herself on that point.

It is strange to relate that now, more than thirty years later (thirty-three to be exact), my husband and I own the house at 19 Grover Square, the very house that was the scene of Arabella's debut and her marriage and should have been the setting for a happy domestic life. Instead its walls witnessed only misery—her misery and that of all those who became involved with her, including myself.

When I first came to 19 Grover Square I was just fourteen, as skittish and as wild as a homeless cat. I had just come from a twelve-month of training at an Academy for Domestic Servants, an education my mother, a cook, could ill afford but which was provided for me by the charity of her employer, a Mrs. C—. I think Mrs. C— had planned to offer me a position in her household, but when she saw the changes that year had wrought on me (I had developed from a gawky, withdrawn girl into a spirited and attractive young woman) she thought of her eighteen-year-old son, gave me a guinea, and wished me luck in my search for employment.

As my luck would have it, my first application was to Mr. Walter Farraday at 19 Grover Square, and I was engaged immediately. It was the worst possible position I could have chosen, but not knowing any other profession, I remained and found too late (when Daniel, the scoundrel, finally asked me to marry him) that I was too attached to my mistress to leave her alone at such a critical time in her life.

In some ways she was a sister to me and I to her, despite the great gulf that usually divides a lady's maid and her mistress. We grew up together, we dreamed together, we intrigued together, we clung together for comfort. Though I saw the worst of her—and she was a great deal more cruel and arbitrary than most people realized—I saw also the best of her, a side that even she was incapable of viewing, since her picture of herself became so distorted.

I suppose you are wondering how it is that a mere lady's maid could become the mistress of a house at such a fashionable address and how I acquired the education to be able to phrase this prologue so literately. Those questions will be answered in the course of my story, and I shall leave the exact details to be revealed at their proper time.

Suffice it to say that I have had the good fortune to marry a gentleman, in every sense of that word, a man who has the compassion and courage to support me in my endeavours as I do him in his.

When Sir Henry Warder-Mull's estate was sold off after his death, we purchased 19 Grover Square, thinking it the appropriate situation for the private Shelter we planned to establish. I had not realized a house could be so alive, that the mute furnishings could speak so eloquently, that a portrait could haunt me, that a humble object, such as a candlestick, would become animate and harry me so. I think these feelings may indicate what it means to be mad. It was as if I were walking on live coals; everywhere I turned for comfort, there was something lying in wait to sear me.

It was my husband who suggested that I gather together the personal papers that had come into my possession and add my own account of the events of those years. At first, I was reluctant, thinking the blaze of memories might overwhelm me, but he pointed out that often when a fire is raging, whole streets of houses are burned before the holocaust, finding it has no fuel for its savage appetite, falters and dies.

So I began piecing together this narrative, and when I had finished I realized that I should seek a publisher and present this full account before the public. None of the principals is now alive to be harassed by a rekindling of interest in the case, and indeed in the final reckoning I believe they would have wished to see the ashes stirred and the fire extinguished at last. How else can I explain that at one time or another each of them consigned to my care his or her own very personal recounting of the events gone by?

Arabella gave me her diary long ago, upon her marriage; she was unable to bring herself to destroy it, but likewise could not bear rereading the accounts of happier times. Miss Finch also confided her journal, which she wrote partially at my suggestion, to my safekeeping. The letters of Mr. DeWinx came to me from his friend, and now mine, Mr. Charles Lindley, to whom they were written; they helped greatly in my understanding of the change in Mr. DeWinx, which previously puzzled me. Finally, and perhaps most strange of all, Sir Henry Warder-Mull bequeathed to me his own analysis of his marriage in his last will and testament I wonder if he hoped it would thereby reach Arabella, a sort of posthumous apology; unfortunately, if this was his wish, I was never able to show it to her.

I realize there are parts of this story which may offend the sensitive reader, but I trust that we are now better able to examine these topics frankly than we were more than thirty years ago when they took place, for it is only by looking at our own capacity for deception and cruelty that we can make conscious moral choices.

Be assured these original papers and letters were not arranged in "chapters" by their original craftsmen, but by me in order to give the story they reveal more shape, and the truth, a greater chance for airing.

So without further ado (though I will interject a note of explanation or clarification here and there as necessary), I give you selections from the diary of Miss Arabella Farraday, beginning in May 1841.

Jenny Steward
19 Grover Square
18 June 1877

PART TWO

Miss Arabella Farraday:
Selections from Her Diary
May 1841–August 1842

~ ~

March has its hares,
And May must have its heroine.

Lord Byron,
Don Juan

Chapter One

May 1841

The first thing I did directly after my father's funeral was to move into Mama's old room.

It had been left exactly as it was the day she eloped. I don't believe my father ever entered the chamber, though the housemaid, Katie, cleaned and dusted it every day as she did the rest of the house. Still it retained an air of dejection and regret, a mood of indefinable *tristesse*. Sometimes I fancied I could hear Mama sobbing behind the closed door; other times, I thought I discerned the sweet rising trill of her laughter. (Finch, if she read this, would say I enlarge too much; she has long accused me of having an overactive imagination.)

None of Mama's personal belongings remained. I never learned whether she had taken them with her. I picture her fluttering about the room, her eyes dancing with excitement her slender fingers curled about a framed miniature—Oh, it's a likeness of me!—pressing it lovingly to her bosom before tucking it away in the secret recesses of her portmanteau) or perhaps my father had them all destroyed. Afterward.

Being only a child of eight at the time, my memory of Mama is somewhat indistinct. I was forbidden to have any pictures of her; the gold locket she had given me was taken away. Whenever I spoke of her I was shushed, and my dear nurse, Mrs. Anthony, who took me on her knee every evening and told me my mama loved me and would come back for me, was dismissed suddenly without explanation.

I was forced to honour Mama's memory in the secrecy of my heart, and the relics I had with which to create her image were those I found in the quiet sanctuary of her forbidden room. Evidence of Mama's sweet, cheerful character was everywhere. The striped lavender-and-white silk hangings with tiny floral medallions—my father had them especially made up to please her when we moved into the new house in Grover Square. Alas! She left a fortnight later. Likewise, the imported lace curtains at the window and the brass canary cage before it are mementos she never enjoyed.

Poor Dodo! He was forgotten during the excitement and died of starvation. I buried him in the garden beneath the tallest lime tree in a velvet-lined jewel casket my father had given me to hold my pearls. For a few weeks, I would adorn his grave with flowers every day. He was all that I had of Mama to bury and mourn.

I told Finch I wanted a canary. She responded, "I don't believe you have demonstrated sufficient responsibility to be entrusted with the life of a poor, dumb, feathered creature." That's the way she speaks. A stern, austere, solemn old woman. What my father saw in her I do not know.

She had similar words for me when she emerged red-eyed and sniffing from her room, where she had closeted herself after the funeral to find me directing Jenny and Katie in the removal of my clothes and other personal items.

"May I have an explanation for this extraordinary behaviour, Arabella?" she asked, dabbing at her eyes with her sodden handkerchief.

"Perhaps I shall tell you," I said, tossing my head. I saw the maids watching wide-eyed. They dislike Finch as much as I do.

"I demand an explanation immediately," Finch cried, her voice becoming shrill and her back stiffening.

"I shall consider your request," I replied graciously. "As I am now mistress of this household, I must determine how best to deal with unnecessary and impertinent questions from the staff."

Katie gasped. At least, I think it was Katie. Jenny would never gasp. Nothing I do surprises her. She's my very own personal maid and has been with me for over three years now. It's true she's some-what unreliable. Finch often threatens to dismiss her, but I put my foot down.

"I shall never find anyone to dress my hair like Jenny," I said. And really it is most unfair that now the fashion calls for straight hair when I have such lovely, glossy dark curls. It requires an hour every morning for Jenny and me to tame them into submission.

Finch's lower lip was quivering. I merely smiled. I know just how to manage her. Like the time I pretended to poison her.

What a lark! I purchased some arsenic from the chemist by saying that I needed it for my complexion. Then I left it out on my dressing table, at the same time putting some nasty medicinal powder into Finch's evening chocolate. She came into my room in her nightdress, with a ragged old nightcap on her head, holding her stomach, and then she saw the packet of arsenic on my vanity.

I thought I should die laughing! She was such a funny sight! Rolling around on the carpet in hysterics, screaming and tossing her head from side to side. The doctor was called in, and he adminis-tered a purge. I could hear her retching and moaning in the next room, all the time insisting that she had been poisoned. I, of course, feigned complete innocence. The arsenic was merely a complexion wash, which Jenny had recommended to whiten my hands. Why Finch should take it into her head that I was trying to murder her I did not know. That was my story.

I had hoped her wild suspicions would prompt her dismissal. Faugh! I was not counting on how besotted my father was with her, though a rift did occur. He was displeased that she should even dwell on the possibility of poisoning, and I know he paid Dr Steward three times the usual fee in the hopes the embarrassing incident would not become widely known.

I don't suppose it was Dr Steward's fault that the story got out. Poor man! He really suffered quite enough, what with having to minister to Finch while she was being sick as a dog, and then never being called back again. Afterward my father, even in the throes of his last-illness, called upon Dr Mitten from all the way across the Park, though Dr Steward lives right around the corner and serves the medical heeds of all the other occupants of Grover Square.

I think it was John Footman (who at the time was courting the under-house parlour maid at number 11). Or maybe it was Tibby, who told Small Thomas, her admirer, the footman to Mr. and Lady Elizabeth Tuttle. At any rate, the word was out all over the Square by the following day. I hear that it was the main topic of conversation over luncheon at the young ladies' boarding school.

Finch never lived it down. Why, my father wouldn't have her in his presence for several days. I never saw her so frightened. She kept pleading with him, trying to convince him I was to blame, not she.

"Mr. Farraday," I remember her saying one of those times, her voice choking. I was listening at the keyhole. "I cannot remain silent. I would if I thought in all conscience it was right, but it is my duty, as the guardian of Miss Arabella's moral well-being—"

"Nonsense," spoke up my father. "I will not hear another word of such drivel about my own daughter."

"But, Mr. Farraday," she continued, "I do not think it was undeliberate. There was something in my chocolate. I—"

"Damme, woman!" he shouted. "I will listen to no more of this. Remove yourself at once from my presence and do not return until you are able to remain silent on this subject!"

"But Mr. Farraday—" She cried like an old ninny. I withdrew from my post near the door at that point, but he must have continued in the same vein, for she came scurrying out of the room a minute later, gasping and sobbing, and didn't even notice me standing in the shadow of the stairs.

Still, within two days she had wheedled her way back into his good graces. Jenny doesn't believe that she was my father's mistress, but I am convinced of it.

"What would he want with her?" she asked. "She has as much passion in her soul as a snail."

"Jenny, I tell you," I replied earnestly, "I saw her scuttling away from his door in the small hours of the morning, and she was behaving most suspiciously: darting up the stairs, glancing around furtively."

"Bella," Jenny says. "You know she was his nurse throughout his last days. The hired nurse kept swilling down his brandy and falling asleep at her post."

12

Jenny makes me cross whenever she speaks in that manner. I took the brush out of her hand and rapped her across the knuckles. I knew too she was protecting the Old Snail, for surely she too had witnessed those "episodes" and was simply holding back for some perversely unselfish reason. So after delivering her due punishment, I cried, "Go away and leave me alone!"

She shrugged her shoulders and went off. Disappeared, I should say. I suspect she went to meet her handsome soldier. Daniel is his name. Very handsome. Six feet four in his stocking feet (so Jenny tells me). Fair hair, the most delightful blond side-whiskers, blue eyes. I've seen him walking with Jenny around the Square. She tells me everything that passes between them. Well, nearly everything. Sometimes I suspect there are certain more intimate details held back from me. I know when I have a lover we shall be able to share even those things.

Once I asked her to introduce me to one of his brother soldiers.

"Oh, no, Miss Arabella!" she gasped. She calls me Miss Arabella when she's angry or upset. "That wouldn't be proper at all. You must meet a young man of your own station."

Alas, how was I ever going to do that with my father and old Finch watching me like basilisks?

But I am straying a long way from the day of the funeral. Finch says I do the same thing when. I am required to write a composition.

"I fear, Miss Farraday," she says with a sigh, "your mind is like a butterfly, flitting from one subject to the next, alighting briefly but never settling on any one thing for long."

I shall prove her wrong. My father's funeral. The fifteenth of May 1841. We had just removed from Pittlesbury Hall to come to London for the Season. It was raining heavily, and my father took ill, first a fever, then pleurisy. He had just turned fifty, and he had always anticipated a long life so that he could "guide me" as he said when I was called to his deathbed, "in the fulfilment of your destiny as a woman of wealth and in the development of a sober and industrious character, which up to the present has been lacking." He did not call in his solicitor until the day before he died, so determined was he not to relinquish his hold over me and his fortune. If

I had known then what I know now I would have given Sir Henry Warder-Mull some arsenic in his brandy.

The funeral was lavish, and I looked quite fetching in black— thank Heavens, for I shall have to wear it for a year. Jenny fitted the ugly woollen dress to me most tightly so that it really set off my tiny waist, and I thought the long veil, which covered my face, neck, and bosom, gave me quite an air of mystery. I kept my head bent and my shoulders bowed, and everyone supposed I was wracked with sorrow. Sir Henry supported me throughout the service as if he thought I would collapse without his plump, fleshy little hand beneath my elbow and then saw me into the feather-trimmed carriage with the greatest solicitude.

Once back at the house, he retired into the library to straighten out my father's papers, whereupon Miss Finch, who had been snivelling throughout the ceremony, retreated to her room to be alone with her sorrow, that is, until she surprised me in the midst of transporting my belongings.

"My dear Miss Finch," I said politely, seeing that she was unable to speak. "Now that my father is dead, I shall occupy my mama's room and, in general, live entirely as I please."

"We shall see about that, miss. We shall see," she said abruptly and, going back into her chamber, slammed the door.

If only I had known how soon I would understand the dreadful truth of those words.

Chapter Two

But I did not know. I was still to have a little time to revel in my visions of freedom. I was full of plans for the future.

"What do you suppose Finch meant?" I asked Jenny innocently as we filled Mama's pretty wardrobe with my dresses. A faint hint of her lavender perfume still scented the air.

"I'm sure I don't know," replied Jenny with a puzzled little frown, shaking out a crumpled white muslin frock.

"You may have that gown, Jenny," I said, waving my hand graciously. "Heaven knows, by the time I can wear white again, I shall have completely outgrown it." Though she is a year older than I, her figure is not as well developed as mine. Sometimes when I am in a teasing mood I call her the Board, for she is as flat as a board and just as thin when viewed from the side.

"Thankee," said Jenny, with a little curtsy, clutching the dress to herself possessively and looking ridiculously thankful.

"Now leave me. I wish to be alone," I commanded, and off she ran. I heard her light footsteps hastening up the stairs, doubtless on her way to her little attic room to try on her spoils and preen herself before her looking glass. Jenny is a little vain, I fear, but that's all for the good where I am concerned because she always knows the latest fashion and insures that I am dressed up to the minute. Not that anyone ever sees me except the young ladies at the boarding school, who always "ooh" and "ah" over my gowns.

It was Jenny who informed me that the crossover bodice was all the rage this Season. Alas, she had just put the finishing touches on a lovely rose-coloured shot silk, which was open from the waist to the hem to reveal a pearl-grey silk gown beneath, when my father died!

I wouldn't want you to suppose that I did not love my father. It was a horrible shock to see him lying in bed so pale and weak he could barely keep his eyes on me for long. He had always been a strong and Spartan individual. Though I saw little of him when he was well—a perfunctory five-minute visit to discuss the progress of my studies (and he was usually displeased) after dinner (he ate alone or with Finch, while I dined in the schoolroom)—I knew he was always there. His presence permeated the household. The maids, even my Jenny, were all terrified of his displeasure. I think none of us quite believed he had gone, and if ever a man was likely to come back from the grave to see that all was going as he ordained, it was my father.

Still, my primary sensation was one of relief. Imagine if you will, that you are a lonely, affectionate, and motherless child. Your father has decreed that from the age of seven you should spend every minute of your day in doing lessons. My only day of leisure was Sunday, at which time I was allowed to read the Bible and other religious works rather than my school books. This regime continued whether we were in London or at the sea in August or in residence at our country house outside Pittlesbury, the only variations being that nature walks along the sand or through the fields were then included in the curriculum.

Of course, I could not ride. My father claimed that he was safeguarding my life, that the thought of my suffering an accident tormented him. I think he really wished to deny me what he knew would bring me pleasure. He never rode himself, having a real fear of horses. On the other hand, Mama loved to ride. She was an excellent horsewoman. I remember how she looked when she came back from one of her many solitary rides, her mount dancing skittishly along the cobbled courtyard, Mama sitting so straight and composed on his back, her cheeks glowing pink and her blue eyes shining from the exercise.

Peter, the stable keeper, said that I reminded him of her once I finally convinced him to teach me how to ride.

"You've just her way with the beast," he said.

I must say I had always the finest attire. My father liked to see me well dressed, particularly on Sunday, particularly when we attended services at St. George's in Hanover Square. He wanted me to out-shine the daughters of the aristocrats who looked down their noses at a man who made his fortune in trade, and so I usually did. Sometimes that wasn't enough. He complained if I appeared before him with a spot on my glove or a torn flounce on my dress, and whereas he was close-fisted about everything else, he was extravagant in this area. "Throw those out, daughter," he would say, or, "Give that gown away," and next morning someone would arrive from the Farraday and Company warehouse with bolts of material fresh off the mills. For a few days, Jenny and I would pour over fashion plates, and when we had made our selection, the dress-maker was called in for fittings. You can be sure that I often chose my shabbiest gown to wear before my father, and sometimes even deliberately spilled a little wine upon my skirt or caught the hem in a buckle, but this stratagem could not be employed too often, for my father's temper was formidable.

I always felt that I was at fault around him. I don't know if you've ever been in the company of anyone like that. He was always telling me that I was irresponsible, lazy, childish, frivolous. When I did something correctly, there was no praise; it was just as it should be. Sometimes I ventured to express my opinions; at one time, I was most outspoken about Miss Finch. He would not even respond. He would stare at me coldly until I was covered with confusion and certain that in some way I had revealed something horrible about myself.

After he died (he died during the night with Finch at his side), I felt only an enormous release, as if I had been underground for a long interval and was only now emerging into the fresh air. Those last few days had been the worst. To sit quietly by his bed as he gasped for air, the breath catching in his chest and his mouth opening and closing spasmodically, his face contorted as he struggled to breathe. I shudder still at the memory. And every time he spoke, his words strung apart by pauses wracked with wheezing, it was the same terrible request.

He wanted me to swear that I would do my duty as a true Christian and a lady. Well, that was certainly easy enough. My conscience could allow some liberal interpretation as to exactly what those words entailed. But, in addition, he begged me, with tears in his eyes, clutching my hand with his own slippery one, that I would never have any intercourse with my mother's family.

I asked him if my mother still lived, and I thought for one awful moment that I had killed him. His eyes rolled up in his head so that only the whites showed; he jerked around on the bed like a fish that has been caught on a hook. Finally, he managed to say (I give it to you the way I thought I heard it): "She...she...she (hands twisting the bedclothes convulsively) is (laboured breathing, glazed eyes) *dead* (his voice suddenly gaining strength; his visage terrifying, as if he had murdered her) to (wheezing, his tongue protruding from his mouth) me." He fell back and closed his eyes. Only the tortured sound of his breathing signified there was still life within him.

Of course, this told me nothing, but then it did give me hope that she might still be alive. Surely, he would have said she was dead if she was, or perhaps he did not know. I should make it my business to find out.

But that was when he reiterated his request.

"You must never..." he said. (I will spare you the description of the sufferings he endured as he endeavoured to speak—they still live vividly in my mind.) "...You must promise me never to have any intercourse with anyone in your mother's family."

What could I do? I could not lie to a dying man, my own father. And yet I could not swear never to do the thing I most desired, the goal of all my young life, my only reason for living since my mother's departure.

I lied. It was my only course. I think he knew I lied. He asked me over and over again, and every time I repeated, "Yes, Father, I promise never to contact anyone of my mother's family." His eyes under those glaring brows searched my face as if he could peer into my soul and see my stubborn determination to do exactly as I pleased once he was gone. I think that is why he called in Miss Finch and Sir Henry and had me swear in front of them. How humiliating that scene was! But I played the dutiful daughter, on my knees, with tears in my eyes, my words broken and muffled by sobs. Sir Henry told me in the hall how brave I was. Why couldn't he have told me that my father's request was unreasonable, that I did not have to consider myself bound by it? He's a solicitor and knows the legal aspects of these sorts of things, but he was called back into the room immediately to help my father draw up his will.

A few days later, as I was setting my new room to rights, I peered out the window and saw what my mother must have seen in those few days she spent within these walls: the Square garden with its wrought-iron fencing and the little walks curving through the shrubbery; the gardener's lodge devised to look like a Greek temple; the façades of the houses on the other side, barely visible through the tall lime trees; the street below, up which she might have watched the carriage of her lover come rolling, signalling her release from bondage. How I longed to have someone coming for me, a handsome, passionate man who would take me into his arms and kiss me until the world and all my cares disappeared!

I moved away from the window with a sigh. It was time at last to provide my greatest treasure with a fitting shrine. From the deep pocket of my old mantle I removed a miniature in a gilded frame, my only portrait of Mama. No one knew that it existed. Somehow, I had discerned that I must hide it as soon as I learned of my mother's elopement. I used to study it at night by candlelight, conning every line of that lovely face as I never learned my Greek or history. Now she could see the light of day! Now I could have her always before me!

I placed it proudly on the dressing table behind my silver toilette set. Mama's gilt-framed mirror hung above it, and I scrutinized my own face in the glass, trying to trace the resemblance. We are really very much alike. Her face was smaller than mine, and her chin more pointed; I have inherited some of the plumpness of my father, especially through the cheeks. I tried to starve myself to acquire that haunted, thin look of Mama's but to no avail! I am too fond of food, I fear. Our hair is exactly the same, only in her day, when the portrait was painted, curls were fashionable and her dark ringlets fell in gay confusion about her ears and neck. I look even rounder and more moon-faced with my hair pulled straight back into a chignon.

Her eyes are blue, and even though her mouth is curved in a be-guiling smile, almost a pout, her eyes show infinite sadness. Distant, as if she were seeing something no one else saw. Mine are dark, so dark they are almost no colour at all, my father's eyes. Still the like-ness is there in the straight, small nose, the flawless white complexion (my father was ruddy), and the smile: I practice my mother's smile: lower lip thrust out slightly, corners turning up in a playful smile.

I was practicing it when Katie came plodding into the room. She's a country girl from somewhere up north, not at all pretty and quick like my Jenny. She's slow and big and plain. Jenny and I sometimes call her the Ox, which is quite a fitting appellation because she's strong—she does all the heavy work for the entire house—and dependable. "Really, if she was a cow, she would moo quite nicely," Jenny once said.

"Miss Bella," the cow said now in her low, unexpressive voice. "You're wanted in the library."

"Oh, for the reading of the will!" I declared, springing up from my seat before the mirror. "Tell them I'll be there in a moment." She nodded and left, her eyes downcast as usual.

I really had nothing to do, but I once read a novel about a lady who enhanced her public image by always making late entrances, so I have adopted the habit. Besides, Sir Henry believed that I had been weeping uncontrollably throughout the funeral, so I rubbed my eyes vigorously with my fists until I looked suitably red-eyed. Finally, I kissed Mama's smiling face for luck, went downstairs, and crossed the hall to the library.

Sir Henry leaped up as soon as I entered the room.

"My dear Miss Arabella," he said in his prim, fussy voice, clicking his tongue against his teeth, a mannerism I detest. "Allow me," and he guided me very carefully, as if I were an invaluable piece of china, to the seat directly before my father's desk. Such a prig! While he watched me closely, I kept one hand over my eyes—the hand with the amethyst ring—and sniffed slightly a few times, but all the while I was glancing about to determine who was present.

All of the servants. Probably they had all been honoured with small bequests. They were huddled in a group at the back of the room in their makeshift mourning garments, a black apron for Tibby and Katie, black armbands for John Footman and John Groom. Jenny stood out defiantly in the white gown I had just given her, but she looked sullen. I believe Miss Finch must have taken her to task for her unsuitable attire.

Miss Finch was seated in a chair to my right, sobbing violently into her handkerchief and gulping and gasping in an effort to stifle her tears. She would be quiet for a few moments and then, the effort proving too much for her, fall to wailing and sniffling all over again.

Sir Henry, standing behind the desk, his plump hands playing nervously with the papers before him, was plainly annoyed. He kept clearing his throat and preparing to begin only to be besieged by a fresh barrage of grief from Miss Finch's direction.

At length he spoke up impatiently in his thin, pompous voice. "My good woman," he said, fixing her with his beady blue eyes, "if you cannot calm yourself, pray leave the room."

Finch took one final gulp, dabbed at her eyes, and said brokenly, "I am composed now. Please proceed."

"My good friends," Sir Henry intoned, crossing his fingers upon his waistcoat and then undoing them to play with the gold chain of his watch. "We are gathered here today for a most solemn reason. I am sure you have all been saddened, as I have been, by the passing of a great man, and none of us, perhaps, can feel the pain as deeply as she who knew him best, our brave and courageous Miss Arabella."

As he nodded at me, the balding patch on the top of his head gleamed in the gaslight, for though it was only afternoon, it was a dull day outside and the lamps were all lit inside.

"She requires our greatest support and unflinching devotion," he went on with another nod.

There was a murmured assent from the servants' group. Finch said nothing.

I bowed my head as he droned on about the need to make the best of this unpleasant business, the sad adjustment ahead for all of us, a man in his prime, so unexpected, *et cetera, et cetera.* I was already planning how I should use the money.

I knew there must be some sort of trust, for I was not yet of age, but my father's fortune was vast, and even the annual interest would be enough for me to redecorate the house, dismiss Finch and replace her with some kinder and more biddable companion, buy several attractive mourning costumes, locate my mother's family, and with their assistance, begin building a select circle of acquaintances. Until the year of mourning was over, I could not come out, but oh, the parties 19 Grover Square should see next May!

In fact, Grover Square is a most unfashionable address, out in the middle of market gardens and empty fields. Perhaps I shall sell it (Sir Henry can advise me) and purchase a little *pied-à-terre* in Mayfair instead.

So my thoughts were racing when I heard the words:

"…do hereby bequeath all of my assets, both the real property, including the house in and the estate known as Pittlesbury Hall in Sussex, as well as the invested capital with the exclusions mentioned below—" Ah, here it was! "—to be held in trust for my only child, Arabella…" I sighed, audibly, I think. For a moment, I feared he might have designated some absurd charity. Not that my father was a charitable man, far from it, but you know how the mind plays tricks with you at a tense moment. "…To be at her disposal for life, subject to the following conditions and, after her death, to the heirs of her body, lawfully begotten."

Well, it was evident he trusted in my good judgment no more in death than in life.

"The trustees to be Sir Henry Warder-Mull, my solicitor…" Now there was a puzzle! But he was my father's closest, and only friend, and a man of business who could manage the financial and legal aspects of the trust. I knew I could twist him around my little finger; indeed, he was already there. "…And Miss Tirzah Finch, my daughter's governess and companion—"

"This is outrageous!" Dear God, I had spoken aloud. But it could not be helped. It was outrageous! That woman, that odious, smirking woman, to be placed over me in such a manner. Oh, how she must have cozened and bewitched my poor father! She was not snivelling now.

"Arabella, please!" she said firmly. "Pray, continue, Sir Henry."

"During the period of the trust, my daughter, Arabella, is to have an annual income of one thousand pounds from the interest on the capital—" But that was nearly nothing! "—to be administered by

Miss Finch, who is to continue managing the household affairs as she has demonstrated her competence to do so in the past."

To have her always watching over me as if I were still a child! Oh, the mortification of it all!

"When is the money to become mine?" I spoke up in my agitation. I must know the limits of my servitude, for surely no human being could endure a year in bondage to Miss Finch. Dare I hope that the money became mine on my eighteenth birthday, only a year and a half away?

"That is next, Miss Arabella," the solicitor said with great sympathy. "Please be patient. I know this must be distressing to you." He could not know how distressing, the pretentious little humbug!

"The bulk of the trust to be settled upon my daughter upon her twenty-fifth birthday—"

My mouth fell open. How could he consign me so casually to eight years of abject slavery!

"—Or on the day of her marriage, provided she marries with the written consent of both executors."

To have a dried-up old spinster and a priggish bachelor decide whom I should marry! It was an unbearable thought!

"In the case that my daughter marries before the age of twenty-five and without the written consent of the executors, she is to receive only a legacy of forty thousand pounds, to be raised from the invested capital, with the bulk of the assets, including the real property, to become the sole and exclusive property of Farraday and Company, to be sold or used at the discretion of the board of directors of that enterprise."

I arose to leave. I could not tolerate any more, but there was more humiliation to be parcelled out!

"Finally, an income of five hundred pounds a year for life to be derived from the interest on the capital to go to Miss Tirzah Finch, to be revoked if my daughter makes an unsuitable match or in any manner disgraces herself or my good name."

Chapter Three

"...I do hereby sign in the presence of witnesses, *et cetera, et cetera.*"
Sir Henry was racing through to the end of the will. I stopped him
with a scream. I screamed until my ears were ringing and all I saw
before me was red.

Jenny told me later I was pounding on the desk and shouting,
"He cannot do this to me! He cannot do this to me! That she-devil,
that witch, it is her plot against me! This will is a forgery. It's a fraud!
I'll have it thrown out! I'll find the real will! My father loved me! He
would never do this to me!"

Finch came at me to calm me down. and I kicked her—viciously.
She bore the marks for weeks, as she constantly reminded me by
wincing and sighing whenever she sat down. I pulled her hair, I
scratched her face. That was evidence I could see for myself later,
never once feeling remorse for the deeds. Instead, I wanted to attack
her again.

Sir Henry cowered behind the desk. Jenny said he shrank back,
holding up his soft, ladylike hands as if to ward me off. It required
the combined efforts of John Groom and John Footman to hold me
down in my chair until the rage passed and I was left sobbing bitterly.

"I told you this would be too much for her," said Finch sharply
from my right. "A private reading would have been preferable."

Sir Henry sounded uncertain. "She has been through a great deal,"
he ventured timidly. "The terms of the will are highly unusual, though

perfectly within the law. Yes, perfectly legal. There should be no problem with the probate."

"What is the probate, Sir Henry?" I asked innocently, in my choked, tearful voice.

"Oh, my dear," he said, coming round the desk and patting my head. "You must not trouble yourself with such complicated matters. That is the purpose of the race of solicitors, you know. If young ladies concerned themselves with such things, why, we might all be out of business, you know. Ha! Ha!" He laughed joylessly at his own joke.

"But I wish to know everything about the handling of my father's affairs," I said sweetly, looking up at him through tear-soaked lashes, "for, after all, these things affect my future happiness—greatly."

He bent down and took both my hands in his own hot ones. Was there some sort of secret message in his doglike brown eyes?

"My dear," he said patiently, "probate is merely a term that applies to proving the validity of a will."

"Then there is a possibility this will can be declared invalid?" I asked triumphantly.

"Oh, no! Oh, no, indeed!" He shook his head emphatically. "The court merely concerns itself with the form, the proper affixation of signatures, the correct number of witnesses, *et cetera.* Oh, no! Everything about this will is letter-perfect. And legal-perfect, you see. Ha! Ha! Why, I drew it up myself, my dear Miss Arabella."

"Yes, you did, Sir Henry," I said, pressing his hand gently. "And you must come back tomorrow afternoon and explain it all to me in great detail. I am afraid my poor, muddled head could not take it all in today. The shock of my father's …" I allowed the tears to come at last, "and the funeral and everything…" My voice trailed off brokenly.

"My dear Miss Arabella," he said sympathetically, clicking his tongue again, "you must rest and not fret yourself so. We will talk of this another time There are many matters we must discuss, yes, many matters." Did he have the insolence to return my hand-squeeze? Yes, he did. There it came again. I fluttered my eyelashes in confusion.

"May I assist you to your—ahem—room, my dear young lady?" he asked, his voice hot against my ear. I blushed.

"You are too good to me," I murmured. "My maid can assist me. Jenny! Jenny! Will you help me?"

Jenny detached herself from the knot of servants who were discussing the whole scene in the back of the room.

"Off with you and be about your work!" said Finch harshly when she noticed their excitement. "If any word about what has transpired here passes beyond the walls of this house, I assure you the culprit will be found out and summarily dismissed."

It was an idle threat. Finch would never learn of any gossip about what happened, because no one in all of Grover Square ever spoke to her, not even the governess at the Tiffins or the teachers at the boarding school.

It was with difficulty that I concealed my desire to be away from the library. First, I had to allow Sir Henry to extricate his fingers from mine, then I had to remind him of his promise to call upon me, and finally, he had to proffer again his condolences on the loss of my father: "a fine man, a great man." I wept a little, and he dabbed at my cheeks with his handkerchief.

"Oh, Jenny!" I exclaimed when the door was safely closed behind us. "What am I to do?" And I flung myself upon my bed and cried passionately.

It was the nadir of my existence! The defeat of all my hopes! Like a phoenix I had been struggling to rise beyond the boundaries of my dreary existence only to fall back into the pyre and be extinguished! I could see no ray of hope in the blackness that overcame me.

Jenny knew better than to make idle promises or paint rosy pictures of the future. She never spoke to me when I was in one of my dark moods, by mutual consent, I suppose. The first time she attempted to do so, she had been in my service only one month and I threw an inkwell at her. She still bears a small white scar on her temple, which in my penitent moods I kiss lightly, murmuring apologies for my unmanageable temper. Instead, she has learned to cosset me like a sick child, and on this the most wretched day of my life, she carried out these tasks silently and competently. She held me in her arms as I wept, she dried my tears when I had done and washed my face and patted it with powder, all with the utmost concentration, her lower lip bearing the marks of her teeth as she tried to restrain her own emotions. One devastated young woman was unbearable enough. She brushed my tangled hair, leaving it loose about my shoulders, and while I sat lifeless upon the bed, she removed my gown and petticoats and corset. She brought my morning robe, my favourite robe with the blue ribbons threaded through the lace, and pulled it on over my head, adjusting the folds and doing up the ties in back. She begged some broth from Cook and fed it to me by hand. Having done all this, she helped me into bed, plumping up the pillows behind my back so I lay semi-upright like some abandoned doll, then drew the curtains and left as quietly as a mouse.

I lay like that for nine days, barely stirring, taking only broth and some Madeira. Finch came in several times daily and upbraided me for my surrender to my feelings.

"You must try to rouse yourself," she advised. I merely stared at her as if I had no notion of whom she was. She sent for Sir Henry Warder-Mull. I heard them whispering outside the door.

"She must not be allowed to indulge herself any longer," Finch was saying. "She will make herself even more ill. She requires fresh air and exercise."

Sir Henry seemed to scoff at her suggestions. I heard him say, "Nonsense!" The door opened, and he halted, as if petrified, at the threshold.

At one moment he had his usual capable, controlled, even slightly annoyed expression, his small mouth pursed up, his eyelids blinking rapidly. The next moment his pale, waxy face was suffused with colour; his eyes were opened wide and had assumed a peculiar glazed look. They were somehow softer and yet more piercing. His mouth was agape. I saw Finch's dour face looming behind his shoulder; she had to prod him to advance into the room.

I was not a little pleased to see the extremity of his reaction, especially since he's always such a prim and proper little man. I knew I was a fetching sight, my curls like a dark cloud on the pillow behind me, my pale face and long neck rising from the ruffles of my gown.

"My dear Miss Arabella," he said in a strange, choked voice very different from his usual high-pitched, thin tones. He approached my bedside, and I lowered my lashes, extending one languid hand.

He clutched it convulsively and patted it rapidly with his other hand, never taking his eyes from my face.

"My dear Miss Arabella," he repeated in great agitation, "if there is any way I can be of assistance, any way…"

I merely dabbed at my eyes with my lace-edged handkerchief and then pressed it to my mouth as if I could not speak for sorrow. He remained for several minutes more all the time babbling about his sympathy, his distress to see me so, *et cetera.* I never spoke. When the door closed behind them, I crept out of bed and listened at the keyhole.

"Miss Finch," he said peremptorily, "the dear child has just lost her father. Is it any wonder she would be so affected? Why, her extreme sensibility is most touching. Most touching."

"I know Miss Farraday quite well," Finch began. "If she is permitted to remain indolent, she will sink further into despondency. She must be encouraged to rouse herself. Perhaps a carriage ride around the Park. At least, the windows must be opened."

"I beg to differ," he said coldly. "Your regime might kill her. Miss Arabella must be cosseted. I believe I ought to call in the doctor to be sure there is no fever or weakening of the constitution."

Finch was properly squelched, and it was no more than an hour later when Dr Mitten came and prescribed a horrid dose of Epsom salts in senna tea (which I made Jenny take in my stead) and three hot baths a day. Sir Henry visited daily and brought little gifts: bunches of lilies (Finch had them removed as "irritants in the sickroom"), a shawl to ward off drafts," and some lovely oranges. All this while I was in a very peculiar frame of mind. And it was only when my desperate thoughts settled upon the notion of turning to the Dowager Countess of Evershire for aid that I decided to recover my good health.

Writing down an account of my malaise does so little to convey the suffering that I was undergoing at that time. The worst of it is not the pain nor the boredom nor the sleeplessness, but the lack of understanding. When I try to speak of the helplessness, the futility I feel, even to Jenny, she simply nods and says she understands, but I can see she does not. For how else could she add so blithely, "You must think of the future a little, Miss Arabella, and stop dwelling on those ills that can't be remedied"?

Does she fail to see that I cannot?

Chapter Four

It may seem odd that I knew nothing about my mother, not even her name or her age, but how was I to know? I always called her Mama or Dearest Mama; my father addressed her as Mrs. Farraday. I remember seeing her wince at this; he seemed to stress the fact that she belonged to him. He nearly always called me Daughter, which is the same sort of statement, a belief that others exist only insomuch as they are connected with him. Of course, I thought of the family Bible. When I was fifteen and my father was away from the house inspecting the fences with the land agent at Pittlesbury, I escaped from Finch and locked myself in the library. Alas, having mounted a chair and coaxed the heavy volume off the uppermost shelf with my fingertips, I found that the page that should have recorded the marriage had been torn out.

What child of eight knows the age of her mother? To me she was simply Mama. But now that I am grown I can see by her portrait that she was quite young. She must have married my father shortly after she came out. I can imagine the scene the beautiful young girl forming an attachment with someone unsuitable perhaps a penniless soldier as handsome and as madly in love as she. Her parents, discovering this would then insist on her marriage to an older man of substantial wealth and sober character. Heartbroken, separated from her lover forever, she agrees. Would the soldier return several years later to reclaim his love? Perhaps only her love for me, her child, prevented her from flying to his side for those long, dreary, loveless years.

For though my father loved her in his heavy-handed way, I knew, even as a child, that she did not love him. She feared and avoided him. He never understood her gentle and affectionate nature, much like the discord that existed between Indiana and her brutish husband in George Sand's novel of the same name. (My friend from the girls' school, Chloe, loaned it to me.) Perhaps, like Indiana, Mama was so crushed by my father's want of sympathy that she turned to others for shelter.

I remember a scene that occurred between my parents when I was very young. Mama often had visitors. She played the piano. She sang. I recall her sitting behind the tea service in her lavender satin gown, smiling and pouring out tea for several dashing young gentlemen. It was in the red drawing room at our old house in Bayswater. I was brought down to make my appearance. I curtsied and was petted and coddled. Then suddenly my father burst into the room. He wrenched Mama to her feet so that the cup she was holding was shaken out of her hand and fell, splashing her gown and crashing to the floor. My father ground the delicate cup—at this point still intact—beneath his heel. One of the strange gentlemen protested, whereupon my father turned without warning and smashed the man's nose with his fist, Mama screamed, "Stop it you bloody fool!" He slapped her and for a moment the world seemed to stand still. Now they shall see your vulgar character!" he shouted. Mrs. Anthony snatched me up and hurried me out of the room, so I knew no more but the details still live in my memory vividly; the blood on the white shirtfront; the dark stain on Mama's gown; the cream-and-brown striped waistcoat of the fair-haired gentleman; his friend's words, "Let the lady alone," and my father's reply, "She is no lady."

I did not see my mother again for many days. She was ill much of the time afterward, and I was taken up to visit her as she lay in bed, full-eyed and immobile. She would rouse herself a little at the sight of me, and then suddenly a curtain would fall over her eyes and it would be time for me to leave. There were always many doctors in the house, and my father was insufferable even to them. Up on the nursery floor we would suddenly hear his gruff voice from below loud with anger. "Damn you, man. Get out of my house and away from my wife!"

Then there was the horrible scene after she left...but no! It is yet too painful. I cannot force myself to relive it.

I know Mama was of an excellent family. That was one of the major bones of contention between them. My father would accuse her of putting on airs, of thinking herself better than he, of adopting the immoral and frivolous conventions of the upper classes. Then he would forbid her his permission to attend whatever social event it was to which she was pleading to go.

Sometimes she went anyway, braving my father's wrath upon her return. Those were the quarrels that awoke me in the middle of the night. I would climb into Mrs. Anthony's bed to shiver in terror beside her as I listened to the sounds of my parents' voices raised in anger, the shrieks and scuffles, and inevitably my mother's sobs.

I recall one visit to my maternal grandparents when I was very young. A grand old house on a wide street near the Park. A pack of dogs in the hallway yipping and biting at our heels. Mama's nervousness. A sharp-voiced, hook-nosed old gentleman who peered at me closely through a monocle. I was prompted to address him as Grandfather, but in my terror could not find the words. He announced sharply, "Looks but no wits, like her mother." I recall the butler called him my lord. Then upstairs to visit an old woman lying upon a daybed in a froth of lace and flounces, an old woman with skin like paper and dreamy eyes. I was not able to speak in her presence as she could not abide noise or commotion of any kind. We were not there five minutes before she waved us away declaring she was quite exhausted. She had a nasty-tempered little lapdog lying across her legs and a box of chocolates on the table beside her. How I longed for one, but not once was one offered. An ugly young woman downstairs, who I think was my aunt, set my mother to crying after a short interchange, and we left abruptly. Perhaps that was my only visit to them. At any rate, I do not recall ever seeing them or that house again.

It was after I remembered this visit that I first thought of the Dowager Countess of Evershire. If my mother's family was at all well known then there must be someone who would know her parentage and the events of the past, and I fancied that Lady Evershire might be that individual. She was the oldest resident of Grover Square and the most titled, though Jenny has told me that she was only a singer at Vauxhall before she married the elderly Earl of Evershire.

Determining to call upon her at once, I rang for Katie and bade her to help me dress: It was a sorry experience. Her big, clumsy fingers fumbled with the buttons, and when she had finished dressing my hair it resembled nothing so much as a bird's nest. Still, the black bonnet would conceal the monstrosity. I was trembling for fear Finch should take it into her head to check up on me, but at last I was ready.

"Now you must come with me, Katie," I said.

"Oh, no, miss. I cannot," she replied in alarm. "I've still the dining room to do and only a half hour before dinner."

"It can't be helped," I answered briskly. "I require your presence. I'll give you a sovereign for your trouble." This was generous of me considering that I had as yet received no allowance from Finch.

"But who is to do the dining room, miss?" she asked desperately. "Jenny's out, and there's no one but me to do it."

"Never mind the dining room," I said. "Fetch your bonnet. We must be off at once."

Katie was evidently still worrying about the neglect of her duties as we set off, for her brow was furrowed and her mouth set. Although still weak from my prolonged bedrest, I rather enjoyed the sensation of being out in the world taking in all the sights. It was a fine spring day—white clouds scudding briskly through the blue sky, a sharp wind nipping at the tender leaves of the trees. The nursery governess was pushing the youngest Tiffin in a perambulator along the gravel paths, followed by a troop of other Tiffins of various ages. A young girl (we believe she is the daughter of the notorious Gabriella Edwards, who lives at number 15) was reading quietly on a bench. The two outlandish-looking mulatto children, the daughters of the former slave from Jamaica and his English wife who occupy one of the smaller houses near the entrance to the Square, were playing a noisy game of tag around the sham Greek temple.

Katie appeared to take no notice of any of this. She kept her eyes to the ground except when she occasionally turned to glance apprehensively back at number 19 Grover Square, from whence I suppose she feared Miss Finch would issue forth bent on vengeance. But we reached our destination without any obstacle and were soon within a dim drawing room furnished in the style of the past century. All the furniture was small and delicate and classical; the colours were subdued blues and greys. Tall mirrors stood between the windows, reflecting back the silent splendour of the room.

The dowager countess, when she finally swept through the door after the butler informed her of our presence, furthered the impression of silent splendour. Though she is nearly eighty, she carried herself erect and moved with the grace and surety of a much younger woman. The beauty that had captured the heart of the Earl of Evershire while he watched her sing at Vauxhall was still evident. Her snow-white hair was piled high upon her head; her eyes, though sunken somewhat, were still dark and direct in their gaze. Her long neck, circled by frosty diamonds, was yet unlined, and her hands, glittering with rings (an enormous sapphire, a cluster of blazing diamonds, a large opal) were nearly as white and soft as mine. She wore an old-fashioned silk gown of ice blue with a narrow skirt and a high waist, similar to but much prettier than the dress I remembered my aunt had worn. I was surprised at her height; she stood a good foot above me.

"Miss Arabella Farraday," she said in a low, melodic voice, as if she had known me all my life. "What a pleasure this is. Pray, be seated. I've sent Robert for some light refreshments."

"Thank you," I said coolly, trying to remember what I had learned of etiquette from my novel reading. I took up a seat in the middle of a sofa and spread out my black skirts. How like a crow I must look in that sparkling room!

"Mrs. Trevilian," said the dowager countess, indicating a middle-aged, dark-haired woman with a sad expression and a plain purple gown who had followed her into the room.

"My maid, Katie," I said quickly, nodding my head toward the corner where the awkward girl stood nervously wringing her hands.

"Be seated, Katie," said the dowager countess gently. Katie brushed off her skirts and sat gingerly on the edge of a graceful Greek chair. I could have screamed with vexation at her gaucherie.

"Now tell me about yourself, my dear," said Lady Evershire, settling herself across from me. "I have heard of your father's death. May I offer my condolences?" And we proceeded to exchange those pleasantries so essential to the continuation of civilization and the growth of friendship. All the while my mind was distracted by rustlings and sighs from the wretched Katie behind me, but once I began on the topic of my mission I forgot all else.

"So now that my father has passed away and can no longer be saddened by the presence of those who must remind him of my mother, I wish to re-establish the ties severed so long ago," I concluded, allowing a note of sadness to enter my voice.

"Dear me," said Lady Evershire, setting down her cup. A handsome footman had brought in a tray laden with little cakes and a tea service while we chatted. "Then you really have never had any contact with them. Perhaps you should let them seek you out."

"Oh, I should die of impatience!" I blurted out.

Lady Evershire smiled, a broad smile that revealed all, her teeth. "You are very young, she said. As if that made any difference whatsoever. "It may be that they will not welcome you," she went on, "for, after all, they have made no efforts to see you during these many years."

"I do not know so," I pointed out. "My father may have repudiated them."

"True," she sighed and was silent for a long while. I felt my future happiness swinging in the balance. At length, she sighed again and said, "Well, I suppose it does no harm to tell you what I know. It is little enough. Mrs. Trevilian will recall the details better than I. Let me see, Walter Farraday married a young woman of high birth. She was just out—a Beauty. I was not invited to the wedding. Once Frederick died, you see, people thought they could drop me from their invitation lists. Did you attend, Alice?" She turned to Mrs. Trevilian, who sat silently all this while before the fire.

"I was sixteen at the time," Mrs. Trevilian replied in a flat voice. It was hard to imagine that mournful woman ever having been sixteen.

"But then you do recall it!" said the dowager countess. "What was the young woman's name?"

Mrs. Trevilian turned her gaze upon me, and for a moment I felt I might be levelled by those piercing brown eyes.

"Lady Perdita," she said. "Lady Perdita DeWinx."

"Of course!" exclaimed Lady Evershire. "The DeWinxes. Her father was, is Duke of Drumland. His son—that would be her eldest brother—is the present Marquis of Calverley."

"Do you know any more?" I asked breathlessly. To think I was so highly connected!

Lady Evershire deferred to Mrs. Trevilian.

"She eloped," intoned that woman solemnly, "with her cousin, Geoffrey DeWinx. He later married Lady Harriet Bendle, the daughter and heiress of the second Earl of Gammage."

"Did my mother die?" I asked, horrified.

Mrs. Trevilian shrugged her shoulders, a graceless gesture, I thought. I turned away from her raking gaze. Lady Evershire was more sympathetic.

"Poor child," she murmured. "I have not heard of your mother since that time, but neither have I heard that she died."

It was little enough, but still I might have the opportunity of speaking to my maternal relatives face to face.

"Is Lord Drumland in residence in London this Season?" I asked.

"Most likely so," replied the dowager countess. "Let me see, that would be—"

"Number 5, Park Lane," put in the mysterious Mrs. Trevilian.

"Quite so," agreed Lady Evershire amiably. I liked her more and more. "You must call upon us again, dear Arabella," she said as I arose to go, "and let us know the fruits of your inquiry."

"You can be sure that I will," I replied, kissing her on both cheeks. But, alas, in the excitement of my quest, I quite forgot this promise!

Naturally, you would have supposed that I would go immediately to 5 Park Lane, but I was more circumspect than that. I must give Finch no cause for suspicion, and to be truthful, I was exhausted after so much exertion already. As it was we were very late for dinner, and Finch did not seem to believe my story that I had conceived a sudden fancy for fresh air and exercise. Poor Katie was soundly scolded, and except for her pointing out that Miss Arabella required a companion on her walk for propriety's sake, I believe she would have been dismissed on the spot. Of course, this gave occasion to questions about Jenny's whereabouts, but she claimed to have been sent out on an errand to purchase some black crepe for altering my bonnets. So all was smoothed over for the while.

I had a plan, though. It involved my friend at the Seminary for Young Ladies in Grover Square, Chloe, whom I have mentioned before. We had conducted a long and secret correspondence, via Jenny, until Miss Finch found one of the letters describing an imaginary lover of mine and marched over to wave it under the nose of Miss Roman, the headmistress there. I knew from our long acquaintance that Chloe went to visit her brother and father every Saturday afternoon, and so I made arrangements for her to take me along with her on the following Saturday. I told her that Miss Finch had finally consented to let me go out socially, which of course was a lie; once in the carriage, I told her I was required by courtesy to return a visit paid me by my mother's relatives, which was equally false. Chloe is very timid but also easily persuaded, and soon we were driving, in a pouring rainstorm, through the gates of 5 Park Lane.

"I don't know," whimpered Chloe when the carriage halted in the drive. "Perhaps they aren't at home. Perhaps they will refuse to admit us."

"I don't care," I replied, hopping down out of the carriage with the assistance of a footman in the gold-and-purple livery of Chloe's family, the Shales. "I shall go in myself if you choose to remain."

Chloe seemed to weigh the assets and debits of remaining behind, alone, in the carriage and decided against it, splashing along behind me through the quagmire of the road that lead to the shelter of the portico.

An elderly servant dressed in black answered my knock and suspiciously left us in the hall while he went to find out what to do with his unexpected visitors. I had thought my grandfather was a man of wealth, but I was disappointed by what I saw so far. The exterior of the mansion was imposing enough, but within everything was shabby and neglected. The heavy oak tables were scratched and without lustre; the paintings on the walls were so grimy with smoke and age that one could not discern their subjects. An arrangement of roses that had died some days—or even weeks—before sat in a vase of stinking water. I tried mentally to compare the present surroundings with my childhood memory, and as if on cue, a pack of ugly little spaniels came scuttling down a passage and began sniffing at our feet. Chloe is afraid of dogs. She clung to me, burying her head against my shoulder.

"Chloe, compose yourself immediately," I snapped. She only clung to me more tightly and began whimpering. I took her by the shoulders and shook her soundly. She looked like a wax doll, her eyes rolling about in fear, her head limp. I thought, what if my grandfather, the Duke of Drumland, should make his entrance at this moment? But it was my aunt Portia who broke the tension by hobbling awkwardly down the stairs, preceded by her sharp, nasal voice.

"What is this commotion?" she asked querulously.

I whirled around to face her, loosening my hold on Chloe, and she halted, her foot hovering in the air, and grasped the banister with both hands. She was plainly terrified at the sight of me. Her eyes were wide, her face pale, and the fingers clutching the rail were bloodless, so firm was her grip.

If anyone should have been frightened, it was me or Chloe, for the woman before us was—there is no other way to put it —hideously ugly. Her nose was long and hooked; her lips pale and thin; her eyebrows dark and looming; her hair drawn up tightly, giving her pallid face a pinched look. In short, she had every feature that renders a woman unpleasant to behold. But worse, as she gathered her wits and descended the few final steps, we saw that her strange gait was due to a deformity. She hunched toward us like a witch, like a crone, with a huge lump above her left shoulder; she was bent nearly double, as if burdened by its weight.

"You are not welcome here," she said insistently. Chloe hovered behind me.

"I wish to see my grandfather and my grandmother," I said clearly.

"Your grandmother died in 1830," she said in the voice of a Greek oracle. At that time, I did not understand the significance of that remark.

"Well, my grandfather, then," I insisted.

"Let's go, Bella," Chloe whispered from behind my shoulder. I felt her rapid breath against my neck.

"He does not wish to see you," intoned our prophetess of doom.

"That is ridiculous," I replied with dignity. "This is my family, and I do not intend to leave until I have spoken to my mother's relatives."

"You are speaking to one. I am her half sister," answered the woman, coming toward us like a black crow. Chloe whimpered again.

"Be so good as to tell me where I can find my mother and I will not trouble you further," I suggested pleasantly. Really, one would have supposed us to be actors in some Greek tragedy were it not for my efforts to inject some realism into the scene.

"She is dead to us," pronounced her half sister, my aunt. "Now be on your way and do not bother us again." She thrust her hideous face near mine, so close I could smell her rotting teeth.

"Come along, Bella," urged Chloe, tugging on my waist. I hesitated for a moment, uncertain of what to do, and in that moment, I was lost. The course of my future was irrevocably altered.

For the front door opened behind us and two persons entered. One was a small, ineffectual woman, dressed in a childish blue cloak inappropriate to her years and carrying one of the frivolous new parasols of coloured silk, which of course had been quite spoiled by the rain. I gave her barely a glance, for my attention was riveted on her escort. A young gentleman, slightly older than myself, with fair, waving hair, revealed when he removed his top hat, was shaking out the rain. He had a smooth, almost austere face, a firmly set mouth, a stubborn chin. He was of medium height, medium build, a form evident in all its masculine breadth and strength when he stripped off his brown frock coat with its deep burgundy velvet collar. His eyes were angel's eyes, azure and warm and commanding, and as they met mine they assumed a look of appreciation rapidly altering to adoration.

We belonged to each other from that moment forward. Our two souls had met and mingled in a clime rarely known to man in this life. It was as if the clouds had opened before me, vouchsafing me a glimpse of Heaven. It was as if the ocean had rolled over me and I was gladly succumbing to its siren spell. It was suddenly a summer's day, and the birds were singing, the wind rustling in the trees, and the whole world crying out with mad joy.

I had met my true love, my cousin, Franklin DeWinx.

Chapter Five

I cannot convey in words the utter bliss of the next hour spent in his company, that sweet certainty that settles upon one's soul when one has at last met one's other self. Perhaps other women have had this experience. Perhaps there was one moment when, as they strolled down the street, they saw the face of the one they loved in a carriage passing by and felt the pang of Destiny. Perhaps there was a time when as they sat conversing at a crowded party, the music and the strangers faded around them, their words becoming mere symbols for the magical, indissoluble link being forged, a sensation so intense, so powerful, that the woman felt she would soon swoon without a respite. But still she could not bear to tear herself away for fear she would die.

If those women should hear me now, they would either thrill in the secret place of their hearts, my words evoking a frisson of that wondrous passion, or they would not. If it is the latter, I pity them. They are one of those individuals who, from lack of courage and lack of faith, settle for a comfortable companionship; a sedate alliance, a contract written in ink and not the heart's blood. Women like that choose their husbands as they choose their gowns. Cynics would scoff at my words and term me a foolish schoolgirl, a believer in fairy tales. But then they have long ago put away their dreams of mad, heedless romance. And I have not.

Franklin and I were meant for each other. That much would be clear to any reader of romantic novels. While I am dark, he is fair.

While I am below medium height, he is tall. While I am incautious and prone to easy enthusiasms, he is circumspect and thoughtful. While I retained little of my childhood lessons at the hands of Miss Finch, he is the consummate scholar, always thinking and probing. But reviewing these words, I find them inadequate. It is not the coincidence of our appearances, nor the complementarity of our accomplishments, but something that I cannot describe, a sense of urgency, a feeling of being more alive than ever before, a heightened awareness of my own femininity. Oh, blast it! If one could know love by writing and reading about it, well, there would be no need to experience it.

You may notice I don't dwell upon the particulars of our first encounter. I barely recall the words we exchanged; it was as if I were wrapped in a dense fog, and yet, while the whole was lost, small details I will never forget. The way a drop of tea gleamed on his blond moustache while he spoke. The sudden weakness in my knees when he kissed my hand in farewell.

Even my sweet Jenny was annoyed by my vagueness—mooning, she called it—when I tried to impart to her my intoxication.

"Calling him an angel is not a sufficient portrait, Miss Arabella," she complained as she helped me repair the ravages the rain had wrought to my costume and hair. "Who is he anyway? How is it that he stays at your grandfather's house?"

"He's my cousin, Jenny, I breathed with shining eyes. I had only to glance at my mirror to see the transformation of love. There were roses in my pale cheeks, my eyes danced, an irrepressible smile played upon my lips. My eyes fell upon the portrait of my mother, and I realized, with a small shock, that I looked exactly as she did. So that was her secret! She was in love!

"A cousin," sighed Jenny, tugging at my hair with a brush. "Who are his parents? Is that old terror you described his mother?"

"Good God, no!" I exclaimed, sitting up on the vanity seat. "No, I understood that she—that is, my mother's half sister, Portia—never married. Who would have her? No, his mother was present. Didn't I mention her?"

"You did not," was the exasperated reply.

"Ah, well, she's easily forgotten. A timid, unremarkable little woman. She kept whispering to herself and shaking her head to and fro whenever my aunt Portia frowned at her."

"But is she also a sister to your mother?" Jenny wanted to know.

"Don't be absurd, Jenny," I said, becoming annoyed with both her obtuseness and her clumsy wielding of the brush. I snatched it out of her hand. "A characterless mouse like that a DeWinx? Bah!"

"So then, it is his father who is a DeWinx?" Jenny continued imperturbably, plopping herself down upon my bed and chewing on the frill of her lace cap.

"Was a DeWinx. He was the second son," I replied. "I understand he died in India some time ago while doing research for a book. His wife and son came to Lord Drumland while he was abroad and have remained ever since. A case of poor relations, I fancy." I smiled at myself in the mirror. "Not any more. Franklin's the member of Parliament for Dartonhampton, though he expects when the Whigs go, so will he. He's also published a volume of poetry and was a clerk for a short time in the Home Office but found that too much beneath his capabilities."

"There is still the military and the Church," suggested Jenny in a somewhat sarcastic tone, which I did not like.

I propped my elbows on the dressing table, put my chin in my hands, and studied my pose in my reflection. How I wished that my hands were Franklin's and he was drawing my face closer to his for a kiss. What would he be wearing in this romantic scene? I saw him outfitted in a dashing scarlet uniform, a blue cloak slung over his shoulder and a sword strapped to his hip.

"My Franklin would look splendid in a uniform," I mused "Perhaps I shall suggest it to him. What regiment is your Daniel in, Jenny?"

"The Foot Guards," she replied with a quiet blush. "But he is not my Daniel, Miss Arabella."

"Jenny!" I whirled about and studied her with genuine fondness. I felt a sudden surge of affection for her; she was the only woman with whom I could share my dreams. I dismissed Chloe and her feeble attempts to ensnare the Hon. George Grasston as a mere schoolgirl in the throes of an infatuation. And Finch? Well, sometimes I wondered if Finch was a woman—a saint, yes, but a woman?

"Jenny, I'm a woman in love also now. You don't have to pretend indifference with me. We can share everything."

"I don't pretend indifference," she said, wriggling a little. "It's just that we have *no* understanding."

"Well, neither do I," was my airy comment. "Not a mutual one, at any rate. Yet I know exactly how it shall all begin…" Visions of Franklin and me, holding hands, talking in low whispers, his moustache brushing my cheek, filled my mind. We'd be walking on the Downs near Pittlesbury. I would show him my secret hideaway, a small bowl of green on which I could lie and watch the clouds passing overhead. And what would happen in those stolen moments as we sat on the soft grass, my head nestled on his shoulder? Would we speak of our dreams? Would he take me in his arms and kiss me until I could no longer breathe? I had a vision of him, his blue eyes darkening, his sword drawn from its scabbard, his deep voice saying, "I cannot bear living if you will not have me. What will it be? Shall I kill us both?"

"Really, miss." Jenny's plaintive voice intruded on my dreams. "Nothing that happens between me and Daniel would be of any interest to you."

"Everything is interesting to me!" I declared, flinging out my arms as if to embrace the world. The blood pounded madly in my veins and sung in my ears. "Do you know when I see Franklin again?" I asked.

"No, I don't, miss," she said, her eyes downcast, bustling about my new room, putting things to rights, always the quintessential lady's maid.

"Neither do I," I laughed. "But see him I shall. And soon. I know it. He cannot resist. He is drawn to me as moth to a flame."

"Surely an unfortunate simile," said Jenny wryly.

I was constantly surprised by the quickness of her wit. Once she began to do lessons with me she rapidly surpassed me, although we both pretended not to notice.

"Do you know how I have arranged to meet him—and secretly, without Finch's interference?" I asked, ignoring her rejoinder.

"To be sure, I don't, miss," replied Jenny, spreading out my waterlogged black dress on the clothes rack before the fire. I was wearing an old grey shot-silk gown and intended to inform Finch that I would not wear full mourning again until she had purchased several new gowns for me. Besides, I rather fancied that if Franklin should arrive in the dark of night, flinging pebbles up to my window (How would he know it was mine? I must contrive a signal—perhaps a handkerchief!), I wished to look my best.

"Well, I said with pride, "we spoke of my quest for my lost mother, and he seemed quite intrigued, despite the gloomy glances of Aunt Portia and the worried little sighs of his mama. He vowed to become my *preux chevalier* and come to me as soon as he had gleaned the smallest particle of information with which to guide me in my search. I explained that I was guarded by a loathsome dragon by the name of Finch, whose claws he must be most careful to avoid, and he declared that in order to escape such a fate, he would send a message first through my handmaiden—that is you, Jenny—designating a secret tryst. Is that not excellent?" I capered before the mirror.

"Somewhat compromising," was Jenny's grim reply.

"Oh, pooh! I suppose your meetings with Daniel are not."

"A different matter altogether, Miss Arabella, and of that you are well aware," she snapped.

"My dear Jenny, whatever have I done to put you into such a foul temper? Never mind, we can discuss it later. I must go down to dinner or Finch will throw the soup at me. Give me a kiss. There. *Pax?*"

And barely heeding the coolness of her kiss, I danced my way down to the dining room, unconcerned as to the likelihood of a reprimand from Finch about both my attire and my tardiness, so full of goodwill was I. And it seems that my good angel was with me.

As I came flying into the sombre dining room, still hung with the funeral decorations (would Finch mourn him forever?), Sir Henry Warder-Mull rose from his chair across from Miss Finch. His eyes glistened at the sight of me, and he rubbed his palms together, moistening, his lips with his pink tongue.

"My dear Miss Arabella," he said softly, "how wonderful to see you in good health once again," His brow creased a little as he took in my grey silk gown and my bare shoulders rising out of the frothy lace at the neckline.

"Oh, Sir Henry," I said pressing a kiss upon his waxy cheek. I was extravagant with my good spirits. "Please excuse my attire. I would not like so soon to forget my poor papa and the respect due him."

I glanced up at the portrait of my father, which hung above the mantel. Finch had draped black crepe all around the frame. He sat in his chair, pushed back a little from his desk, his stern eyes staring off into the distance the way they did when he called me into the study and inquired about the progress of my lessons. Once there had been a companion portrait of my mother in a crimson velvet train, a pendant ruby gleaming on her forehead. I remembered it from our first London home. It had not yet been hung when Mama eloped. I wondered what had been its fate—the dust heap or the fire?

"It is just..." I began, settling into the red plush armchair at the head of the table. Sir Henry was to my left, Finch to my right. The expanse of the remainder of the empty table was beyond the circle of light cast by the two candles in their silver holders. "It is just that I have worn my only black gown every day for the last fortnight because—" I glanced triumphantly at Finch "—for some reason, the new mourning costumes have not yet been ordered. I do think Papa would prefer me to be fresh and neat, even if in grey, than soiled and shabby in black."

"Why, this is shocking, Miss Finch!" Sir Henry was quick to take on my appeal. "Surely the amount for such a trifling expenditure can be gleaned from the very generous allowance granted for the maintenance of this household and Miss Arabella's needs."

Finch bit her lip. "It was simply that with Miss Farraday's illness and then her sudden, rather unexpected, recovery, I—"

"No excuses. No excuses. We will brook no excuses, will we, Miss Arabella?" laughed Sir Henry. He, too, seemed in rare good humour; he had an air of boyish bonhomie. He even winked at me.

"They shall be ordered tomorrow," murmured Finch, bending to her soup.

I winked back at Sir Henry before falling upon my own vermicelli soup with gusto. I never understood the notion that lovers lose their appetites. I found that romance increased my desire for food as it did all my appetites.

Conversation throughout the meal was desultory. Finch pouted under her reprimand and seemed chastened by the presence of Sir Henry. Hurrah! Ordinarily I was subject to long dissertations upon the nature of man or the history of popular delusions with frequent digressions on my table manners. Of late I had suffered through eulogies upon my father, often punctuated with sobs. But tonight Finch was silent.

Sir Henry, in turn, exhibited a lively interest in his meal that precluded any other topic. Perhaps he, too, was in love, I thought, and giggled with my mouth full of rump-steak pudding, an indiscretion I hid quickly by touching my napkin to my lips.

I did learn that Sir Henry had called that afternoon to inquire after my health and, hearing of my recovery, had requested a private conference with me in the evening regarding some very important matters.

I was all agog to hear his mission explained, hoping against hope that the will had been declared invalid, and so, after the gooseberry tarts had been consumed, I followed him eagerly into the back drawing room, the one we called the music room because it contained the piano and the harp. No fire had been lit, despite the chill of the spring weather, and the room was cold and a little bit damp. Heavy magenta draperies crisscrossed by gold braiding concealed the fine view of the garden, and I pulled one aside only to discover that night was falling fast, the little daylight that remained being quickly obscured by banks of black clouds moving solemnly over the horizon. The leaves of the elm trees seemed grey in the strange light, and as our garden had a tendency to flood in the rain, the grass was concealed beneath a sheet of dull silver water.

A wave of ineffable sadness swept over me as I gazed on this melancholy scene. It was the first evening of my life since I had known Franklin, and he was not here with me. I sighed, my breath forming a little cloud on the cold pane.

"Come away from there, my dear," said Sir Henry, affably enough. "Now that we have you feeling more yourself, it wouldn't do to expose you to a chill. No, no, it wouldn't do."

Well, I could fill pages with Sir Henry's soothing small talk. I used to think of him as a sort of substitute father, a benevolent gift-giver. He was, after all my godfather. But then some years past he had dared to suggest a change of roles, and since then we had grown distant. I thought he had given up his foolish fancies when they met with no response but alas, I had overlooked the unyielding obstinacy of his nature. Once a notion entered his head, it was, apparently, irrevocably fixed there.

And, oh, it will make you laugh when you next hear the foolish dream he cherished!

Chapter Six

He wanted to marry me! I declare, I can barely hold the pen for laughing. It was all I could do to prevent myself from laughing right in his face. The absolute audacity of that pretentious little man, passing himself off as my responsible and concerned guardian, eager to take care of me and—oh, incidentally—my vast fortune, all with the benevolent benediction of my dear departed papa. It seems they had spoken of this during my father's last days. It had been my father's wish to see me united in matrimony with his closest friend. When illness threatened to put a period to my father's existence (and I am sure he never thought that he was mortal), he had pressed Sir Henry to lay violent suit to me and have the wedding performed before his sickbed!

Well, Sir Henry showed what little good sense he possessed by convincing my father that such a rapid courtship would frighten a young and inexperienced girl such as myself, but he assured Papa solemnly that he would be at my side to guide me as I blossomed into a comprehension of his great love and a marriage contracted with mutual respect and choice on both sides could be rendered. There was no doubt in his mind as he calmly laid out these visions of the future before me.

Of course, this was not the first time I had to listen to his amatory fantasies. He had hatched this preposterous scheme when I was very young, and I fear my father had humoured—him in it. Well, I had never given it a moment of serious thought, and now, following the vision of true love granted to me with my first sight of my cousin, it seemed even more absurd. He is twice my age with no personal charm or accomplishment to recommend him and apparently little poetry in his soul. I felt called upon to respond as if I were yet a child, his explanation seemed so reasonable and irrefutable. I listened solemnly, promising to consider the matter, which was his request, and stifled my fit of the giggles until he had bowed his way out of the drawing room.

If I had been able to share this ludicrous scene with Jenny perhaps I would not have squandered so much valuable space upon it in my diary. But she has vanished, doubtless for a rendezvous with Daniel.

Katie just poked her head in my door with an urgent message from Finch requesting a conference. Doubtless she wants to know what passed between me and Sir Henry. Well, she is not to know. Sir Henry, in another surprising burst of good sense, advised me not to discuss his proposal until the engagement became fact.

Oh, the unbearable smugness of these men who think that they have only to tell me how they wish me to behave and I will at once fall at their feet in obeisance! Sir Henry will certainly be surprised; I wonder if my father can be, too? I had a sudden vision of him, wrapped in a snowy tunic, clutching onto his cloudy perch in astonishment as he bends over to see me walking down the aisle with Franklin by my side. And my mother beaming proudly from her place of honour in the foremost pew.

I shall put down my pen and go to sleep to dream of my beloved holding me in his arms.

> *A sizable gap appears at this point in Arabella's journal, partly, I believe, because she became more able to live her fantasies in her day-to-day life, without need of the journal. There is another and more prosaic reason, which Arabella cites when she once again takes up her pen. —Jenny Steward.*

5 April 1842

How strange to be back in this house in my room—I had almost forgotten that it was once my mother's. Sitting before her writing desk, my fingers curled about one of her pens, holding it poised above the pages of this neglected book, which I concealed beneath my mattress last July and only just this minute retrieved, I find my gaze straying out past the purple brocade hanging at the window and through the lace curtain to the Square garden, barely visible through the thick London fog. Only the tops of the elms can be seen here and there as the fog shrouds them momentarily in clouds of swirling mist and then is blown onward by the fitful breeze. The sounds of the street, the traffic on the high road beyond, are muffled. It is as if I were alone, the only person in the world, wrapped in solemn contemplation of my solitary state, my uncertain future, my paltry accomplishments. The dampness of the fog has penetrated even into the room, despite the cheerful coal fire burning in the grate; my muslin dress is too thin for this weather, and I have to secure the gorgeous Indian shawl that Sir Henry brought me as a Christmas gift more tightly about my shoulders.

Another forty-one days and I can shrug off this drab mourning and be done with it forever! Jenny and I spent the tedious time during the carriage ride from Pittlesbury pouring over the latest copies of *The Gentlewoman's Domestic Magazine*, deciding upon my new gowns. Oh, there are such plans afoot for me!

I can hardly credit that it has been a year since my father died. So much has happened since then, and yet so little—no wonder, considering the stern surveillance of Finch, still my most insidious of watchdogs.

And yet there are certain battles that I have won over her, the formerly invincible. No more lessons! Let the trumpets sound and the mountains rejoice, for I am delivered from the heavy hand and the watchful eye of my implacable foe!

It was a juxtaposition of happy necessities that brought this about. A series of illnesses under which I suffered last summer rendered it impossible for me to write or hold a book at times. Finch wanted Jenny to read to me. Jenny was only too willing to do so to improve her reading, but I told Finch that Jenny's stumbling over and mis-pronunciations of words (somewhat of an invention, for Jenny reads creditably) pained my very soul and made such practice a torment rather than a pleasure. Then, especially at Pittlesbury Hall, Finch

51

found it impossible to maintain the household in good running order and supervise my lessons at the same time.

When we arrived in August, one of the housemaids, Sally, was far advanced in a somewhat indelicate condition considering her unmarried state. The gardener, who is also our cook's husband, had become a debilitated drunkard who never put in the vegetable garden. Sally had to be dismissed—not before I got all the details of her fall from grace from Jenny; more of that anon—and the gardener had to be graciously pensioned off, so generously that he would feel charitably disposed toward the family, and yet so parsimoniously that his wife would be required to stay on as cook in order to support them. These delicate negotiations and the excursions into the market towns to get the produce that we could no longer boast was homegrown, along with countless other details of the estate, kept Finch busy from dawn till dusk, leaving her delicate nerves so shattered that she often retired before dinner today in her darkened room with a cold cloth over her eyes.

Never had I such freedom! Twilight rides alone on Parvenue, my filly, racing across the Downs, watching the sun set over the hills. Rambles along village lanes, peeks into the houses of cottagers I didn't know, or glances at the swarthy silent sons coming in from the day's labour, the interested askance looks of the daughters. There were picnic lunches with Jenny by the side of the Cuckmere carrying a hamper we filled ourselves with food pilfered from the larder and berries we picked along the hedges as we walked.

I suppose in some fashion I was enjoying the innocent gaiety I had missed in childhood. Oh, the practical jokes I played upon Miss Finch! They ranged from salt in the sugar basin and the bucket of water propped over the transom to the more grisly rabbit's head on her nightstand. I had begged an old man returning home from haring to give me the severed head of one of his prizes; I put it right where the light from Finch's candle should fall upon it when she set it on her washstand to perform her nightly ablutions. Her scream was heard all over the house, and I was afraid for some little time that we would be unable to revive her Of course, I concealed the ghastly trophy so that when she regained her senses she was only able to babble about butchered heads to no one's enlightenment. They thought her quite mad!

I recall one picnic with Jenny. I brought along a bottle of my father's favourite claret. We were delightfully obfuscated by the time we had done with it. This, I believe, was the occasion when Jenny confessed to me the fleshlier details of her liaison with her handsome soldier. They had not actually done It—that mysterious It that was the secret at the very core of my dreams of love and marriage—but they had done every seeming approximation of the deed. Tentatively, blushing, sighing, she described furtive embraces on dark streets, her body crushed up against the iron railing and he fondling her as if she were unclothed. A few meetings in the Square gardens; she had stolen my father's Grover key, which was never used. During these she had almost surrendered to his will but was always providently recalled to her senses by the sound of the footsteps of a passer-by. She spoke of scrambling up from the wet grass, shaken and trembling, and he, angry, pleading, refusing to let her go until she satisfied his desires.

"Then what?" I wanted to know.

"Oh, Bella." She smiled a woman's secret smile and turned her head away. "It's not for such as you to know."

"Now, Jenny," I applied a remorseless pinch to her elbow. Everyone says I am most strong, particularly Jenny. "You cannot go so far and then refuse me the rest."

Jenny wriggled in my grasp. "Well, leave go of me then," she said. "You remind me of Daniel. Those are his words exactly." And she giggled. And proceeded to tell me that there are ways to satisfy a man besides the mysterious It. Her explanation necessitated a thorough course in masculine anatomy and physiology.

"So that is what is underneath the fig leaf!" I said with amazement, thinking of the engraving of Adam and Eve that hung in the parlour.

"Oh, I should ask Finch to teach me this," I roared, rolling about in the sweet-smelling grass, clutching my stomach, weak with laughter, "as a necessary part of my studies in biology. Do you suppose she knows men have such things?"

We clung to each other, crying with amusement, picturing Finch's horror, her pale, thin face drawn with her struggle to maintain her composure while discussing such subjects.

Afterward I was consumed with curiosity and went through my father's library, finding to my great satisfaction a few medical texts and old engravings that showed the problematical organ in all of its strangeness. Finch commended me on my studiousness; little did she know the object of my research.

I looked at men differently, too. When Sir Henry came to stay over Christmas I was aware that even he bore this enigmatic instrument and evidently thought to employ it with me. Rather than disgusting me, I felt strangely exhilarated. My knowledge gave me a power over men of which I had heretofore been unconscious.

Jenny was much chastened the day after our frank talk. That morning I lifted my aching head from the pillow to see Jenny, pale and tight-lipped, setting down the breakfast tray.

"Oh, Jenny, take it away. I can't bear to look at it!" I cried.

"I want you to know, Miss Arabella," she said primly, folding her hands under her apron, "that I am truly ashamed of my behaviour yesterday. I told you something that should have been reserved for your husband, things that no well-bred young lady thinks on, much less speaks about. I completely forgot my station and—"

"Nonsense, Jenny!" I said wearily. "I can't even move, much less concern myself with your remorse. Leave me alone!"

It took me weeks to coax her out of this sudden attack of scruples. She called me Miss Arabella, and pleaded household chores when I asked her to accompany me on walks. Because of her desertion I spent a great deal of time on solitary rambles, and it was during one of these that I first saw the blacksmith's apprentice. He was standing before the forge, and the blaring light of the fire illuminated his muscular frame, glowing in the darkness of the shed. I had no need of my engravings or Jenny's timid description, for every lineament of his masculinity was evident in the harsh light cast by the fire.

I began to haunt the forge and soon was laughing and joking with him as I plied him with questions about his work. One day, in the course of our conversation, my glance fell and lingered below his waist. He noticed the downward drift of my gaze, and after that his manner changed. He remained deferential, but there was a new element of challenge, even of danger. I was suddenly in the presence of real male vitality and virility and I felt a little like a flower apt to be trampled upon by a bull. It was not the same thing at all to study anatomical sketches or to entertain the thought of stimulating Sir Henry's fancy, for he would be as courteous and careful of my fragility as Society dictated he should. But this strange creature of the earth, so large and so unschooled—what might he do?

I murmured some feeble excuse and turned to go, but it had begun raining heavily as I spoke to him and I paused for a moment, drooping at the thought of sloshing home in my thin dress through that wild downpour. He came up behind me so silently (he had the ability to walk as quietly as a cat) and said gruffly, "I can leave off my work and see you home, miss."

Without waiting for my assent, he went off and retrieved an ancient black umbrella from a pile of rubbish in the corner, and brandishing it with pride and a wide smile, which revealed all of his teeth, he ushered me out into the storm.

I still recall with horror the wildness of that walk. We went along the towpath beside the Cuckmere, which was swollen and roaring like some great beast. The umbrella offered little shelter from the onslaughts of a rain propelled by a biting wind, and I was soon soaked through to the skin and shivering. The trees sighed and swayed about like fitful candles tossed hither and thither. It was as dark as night.

He whistled in a tuneless fashion, seemingly unconcerned by the tempest, and occasionally put out one of his large, coarse hands to guide me when I stumbled along the path. At last we came in sight of Pittlesbury Hall and, leaving the towpath, cut across the great sloping expanse of lawn that led up to the house. It was like trudging through a swamp; my feet were thoroughly cold and wet, the rain having gotten into my boots, and I was hampered by the heaviness of my wet skirts. The wind blew my straggling hair across my eyes.

My companion bypassed the front entrance to the house and led me by way of the neglected garden to the cobbled courtyard off the kitchen.

"I am sorry. I have nothing to give you for your trouble," I babbled with relief as my feet finally gained a firm foothold and I removed my elbow from his sure grasp. "I have left my reticule within. If you will wait, I will have my maid bring something down."

"Aye, money is naught to me," he said roughly. "A kiss is all the payment I require," and he drew me to him remorselessly. His breath was foul, and despite the drenching he had received, he still reeked of sweat and smoke. I had only a moment to notice this, and then his mouth was clamped upon mine and his big hands were fastened upon my back, drawing me even closer to him. I struggled, but to little avail—his strength was prodigious—and yet even through my panic I was aware of a certain wild excitement at the proximity of that strange organ, which I could feel burning against my thigh through a dress that felt thin.

Chapter Seven

It was Finch who saved me. She had seen us from the pantry window as we passed by, and now she came running out of the green-painted kitchen door, hissing with outrage, and flapping her arms like a black crow. She pulled me away from him with her thin, talon-like fingers and, with the other hand, slapped him soundly across the face. He, that great, hulking brute of a man, turned red, doffed his cap to her respectfully, and went scrambling off, disappearing immediately into the sheets of rain.

Of course, I could not expect that Finch, for once having done me a service, would behave with any humanity. She called me a Jezebel and a painted woman and, when I tried to protest that it was not my fault, informed me that I could not play with fire without being burned. She hoped I had learned my lesson well and that this would help tame my unholy curiosity for all things worldly. As punishment, I was to remain in my room, reading the Bible and meditating upon my sins with only bread and weak tea for nourishment.

This regime lasted as long as the storm, which blew over two days later, leaving the grass sparkling under the sun and dappled with the shadows of the serene white clouds passing overhead. Unable to stay inside, I slipped out and went down to the river, my arms around my waist. I needed to reflect on my sad adventure.

When I made my appearance for dinner, Finch soundlessly directed me back upstairs and—oh, most unspeakable of atrocities!—locked me into the room like a wicked, irredeemably lost child. I spent the night screaming fitfully, for she slept in a small room directly across from me where she stayed during my most "fitful" nights, and I knew she would be unable to get any rest. But in the morning, there was no release, only a tray of bread and tea, brought up by a sullen housemaid who was watched by Finch, as she followed behind, rattling the keys that she wore around her waist.

Screaming was of no avail during the daylight hours for Finch was always engaged downstairs. That is, I thought my screaming was of no avail, until I saw the carriage belonging to our parson's wife coming up the drive. I began screaming again, throwing open the window as soon as she was within hearing distance, and though she actually entered the house, peering up all the while to see whence the noise came, she made a hasty retreat. Finch was soon at my door, shaking me and berating me but nonetheless granting me my freedom. This only with a new stipulation: Jenny must go with me everywhere.

The next time I went by the forge—and it was many weeks, for neither Jenny, who had heard the rumours flying about the village, nor I had the slightest inclination to wend our way in that direction—my rustic Hercules was gone. He had been supplanted by a sickly, wizened youth. I wondered if Finch had somehow maneuvered his dismissal, though I refrained from inquiring as to his whereabouts. For in truth I was relieved that he was no longer in the neighbourhood. His swarthy face still haunted my dreams and soon wouldn't be soon enough to forget his touch.

Finch had also discharged in turn each of the three maids who had replaced the hapless Sally; it was their duty to clean her room, and money was frequently missing. Jenny pleaded with me to confess that I had been the one to take it. I don't know how she had guessed, but she was right. Finch had refused to give me any pin money unless I accounted for how I spent every halfpenny in a gloomy black ledger that she had presented to me as if it were a gift. The figures troubled my head, and I had finally given it up as a bad attempt and took to helping myself, having found Finch's secret cache and feeling that I was, after all, only helping myself to what was rightfully mine. Jenny argued that the girls turned out without a character could not find employment elsewhere and often could not return to their families, where they were looked on as a burdensome expense. Of course, as soon as Jenny enlightened me, I discontinued this practice, though fear of Finch and cowardice prevented me from confessing my transgression. Instead I turned to Sir Henry.

We had been in frequent correspondence, and now I began making allegations against Finch, first charging that I was sorely troubled by our poverty after the luxuries of life with my father. Actually, the opposite was true. I had to give Finch credit: She was a consummate housekeeper. She could purchase all of our provisions for half the cost that Cook had previously spent and, by insisting on greater attention to recipes and timing in the kitchen, manage to have delicious and hot meals on the table night after night instead of the burned, overcooked, and tasteless offerings that had satisfied my father.

When Sir Henry at last inquired about the monetary difficulties to which I had alluded, and these inquiries were a long time in coming—I believe he was as parsimonious as my father, reluctant to lay out more of the money under his disposal than necessary—I made little of them. It did not trouble me, I insisted, to go without a fire in my room, and this in a chill November. Nor did I mind walking everywhere like a simple village girl, because Finch said we could not afford to repair the ancient carriage. When he waxed a little more indignant, I dropped the topic completely, saying only that I thought it best not to refer to the matter we had been discussing, he could understand, a friendless girl, *et cetera, et cetera.*

Sir Henry demanded a conference with Finch as soon as he arrived at Pittlesbury Hall in December, and I heard his prim, precise little voice raised in a thunderous rage as he deplored her parsimony. Finch abhorred conflict of any sort, and though the allegations against her were only partially true, she came away from this meeting chastened and shaking and willing to put a generous monthly allowance into my hands the next day.

This stratagem of mine had another pleasing effect. Sir Henry came down from London in a spanking new black barouche with orange trimming, which he had purchased for me with money from my trust, and this fine carriage was further loaded with costly gifts of all sorts to ameliorate the austerity under which he believed I had suffered. There were gloves and a little Pomeranian puppy, a complete leather-bound set of the works of Sir Walter Scott and a heart-shaped locket set with pearls and diamonds, which had belonged to his mother. Within this last I found a scraggly lock of grizzled hair.

It was Christmas afternoon, and we had just returned from the morning services. After a round of hot punch and kisses, compliments of the season, Finch excused herself to go check on the dinner: I was alone with Sir Henry when he handed me this gift, and I opened it to discover the strange contents. I could barely hide a laugh; he had so little hair to begin with that this token represented a considerable personal sacrifice.

"Might I be so bold as to request a lock of your hair in return, my dear Miss Arabella?" he said, stopping the restless pacing that he had begun when he put the velvet jewel box into my hands.

"Why, Sir Henry!" I blushed. "What a lovely token of friendship!"

"Surely more than friendship," he said abruptly. "I have been very patient, Arabella. It is nearly six months since last we spoke of this matter and even longer since I first raised it. Might I hope that your feelings have deepened, as mine have, into something more than friendship?"

He seemed quite agitated, and I felt benevolent toward the singular little man.

"I am certainly very fond of you, I replied quite truthfully. I had only to name something I wanted, and he would produce it with all the pride of a conjuror at a fair producing flowers from a tall silk hat. And our correspondence had been most warm. I called him my good Caleb Balderstone, after the trusty butler of the Ravenswoods, who was so loyal to the family and so unflagging in his efforts to please them. He had taken to naming me his Little Angel or his Provoking Pet. The greater part of his letters was given over to comments on the weather (miserable) and concerned inquiries as to my health, while I confided descriptions of the countryside and increasingly pointed condemnations of Finch. I cherished at first the hope that he would find some means of uprooting her from her position, but I later realized that as a man of the law he would do, nothing to interfere with the stated wishes of my father.

Yet without concurrence on this matter, I needed him as my ally for the battles with Finch that lay ahead and I had no wish to lose his goodwill.

"I think of you as my dearest friend," I said gushingly. "Can that be enough for now? I fear that young as I am and with so little experience of life, I can go no farther."

Sir Henry, usually so timid and afraid to pursue this topic, would not stop at this. Perhaps it was the effect of the punch and the imminence of Finch's return.

"No, my sweet angel," he said, going down on his knees before me, "that cannot be enough for me. I need some assurance that I can expect a more definite contract in the near future. You cannot know how much you mean to me. I adore you and want to ensure that you live in the style and with the respect owing to one of your great birth right, by which I mean your fortune, breeding, and personal charms." He was perspiring—I could see the beads of sweat gleaming on the top of his bald head—and his eyes glittered.

"Sir Henry." I removed my hands from his, my maidenly dignity offended. "This is yet a painful subject to me, recalling as it does my poor dear father's illness. Only this last year we were celebrating Christmas together in this very room and now…" I sighed. "You understand"—I fixed him with my imploring eyes— "that I would gladly give you an answer, but lacking any wise adviser, any motherly spirit who could help me see the way to my own heart, I am afraid to make such a solemn promise."

"My sister, Phoebe," he put in quickly, "would be more than happy to serve as such a mentor to you. May I suggest to her that she write to you?"

I was vexed at this suggestion and went on to propose a new objection. "Sometimes I wonder, not ever having moved in Society nor met anyone of position, if my poor girlish ways would suit for someone who must serve as your wife, your hostess, your helpmeet. If only I could be presented, but Finch says it is impossible, and she must know."

There was a natural enmity between Finch and Sir Henry, which I did my humble best to cultivate. I think Sir Henry felt demeaned by sharing the important position of executor with a woman who was a mere governess, and she disliked his peremptory way of making decisions that never included her suggestions. I had only to hint that one of them wished things to be done a certain way, and the other would countermand the order. Now I planted the idea that Finch wished to see me remain a young girl, inexperienced and socially gauche, in order, I speculated, to divert my monies to her own benefit.

"I fear," I confided in a letter written shortly after his departure,

> that she intends to see that I never marry so she may continue to exercise control over the bulk of my income. She will raise a great outcry if I inform her of your proposal and spread stories that you have abused your position as my guardian and prevented me from forming any other attachment in order to gain for yourself control over my monies. Of course, she could refuse to give her consent to the marriage, and if we contested her decision the rumours might affect your reputation, which is surely the most valuable asset of your trade. It is a sad spell under which I languish, for; of course, I cannot disprove her theories and yet I am sure that if I met *tout le monde* I could not find a man as precious to me as my darling Caleb Balderstone.

I added a postscript that seemed sure to hook my fish in case my previous words did not.

> P.S. I must inform you, my dear, that I cannot allude to my suspicions again. Finch insists on reviewing all of my correspondence before it leaves the house; I am having this smuggled out, but I dare not do so again. I am mortally afraid of her. Today she hinted to a caller that I am too unstable to receive visitors or go out. How am I to refute these charges if I am kept immured like a madwoman? I do apologize for burdening you with my petty troubles, but you have ever been my best consolation through great ordeals.

> Your own,
> Arabella

His response was immediate. In a letter to me and another to Finch he related his intention to see that I made my debut in London after, of course, the anniversary of my father's death. I guessed how deeply this decision must have troubled him by the careful, even awkward phrasing of his note. I would spend hours in the company of handsome and virile young men, all aware of my personal attractions and my great wealth. Would I still retain a place in my heart for a balding, middle-aged bachelor? Little did he know that my heart was already promised and not all the men of London could touch it, for it was not mine to give any longer.

I wrote immediately to Franklin. He was in Florence that month as the tutor to a young gentleman whose conduct was the despair of his family and who had been sent abroad for their peace of mind. "My dearest of all dear creatures," I wrote,

> I have news that even under the brightest Italian sky should bring an extra portion of sunshine into your life. I am to be presented next summer in London! We will be able at last to meet, to speak, to share our confidences face-to-face, even to dance together—oh, sublimest of all bliss! And once we have been introduced somewhere, it would be beyond the cruelties of even Finch or Sir Henry to forbid our further meetings. Oh, my love! How I wish I could see your face when you read this! Are your eyes as blue as the sky above and is your smile as broad as the miles that separate us?

And so forth. His reply was characteristically formal. I had become used to the reserve and moderation with which my true love expressed his heart. He thanked me for the lock of hair I had sent, saying only that he kept it where he could gaze on it often. He said he anticipated the prospect of seeing me in London with pleasure and added with his usual modesty that he did not consider himself a dancer.

Franklin was a lazy correspondent at best. Often I wrote five letters to his one. Of course, there were several explanations for his lackadaisical response: He was traveling all the time, moving about from place to place, sightseeing and visiting while I had all the leisure in the world, provided by the isolation and quiet of Pittlesbury Hall. I had dedicated my entire mornings to correspondence and applied myself diligently to this task, heedless of any other distractions, managing to keep up my literary output even during my brief acquaintance with Philip Vandeleur, while Franklin seemed put off easily, often pleading fatigue or the necessity of keeping a watchful eye on his charge, who was always on the verge of some new catastrophe. Then again, whereas my notes were short and effusive, his letters contained long descriptions of the landscape, cathedrals, and museums he had visited, quaint depictions of various local customs, and some rather remarkable sketches of the people he had met. He must have spent long nights composing these lengthy epistles whereas I could dash off a letter to him within an hour. My letters to Sir Henry, because of the care I took to convey the proper attitude of growing affection and maidenly modesty, required a great deal longer to write.

Alas, the magnificent romance I had dreamt of had not blossomed! Looking back now, I can view this sad fact with some detachment and calm, but during the summer months I was often frantic and wild with grief, contributing I think to the fragility of my physical health. Some mornings I was unable to rise from my bed, so grey did the world seem that would not bring my lover to my door. Some nights I could not sleep, tormented by my longings, fraught with fear that Franklin did not return my love, convinced that others were plotting to see that he never entered my life again. On some of these terror-filled nights, I found myself roaming the house like a somnambulist, certain that it was on fire and I must escape or die. The others in the house would find me screaming and beating on the locked front door, and only after such violent episodes would I be able to sink into an exhausted sleep, which sometimes lasted for days.

Dr Steward, who was consulted by courier, felt that such attacks were to be expected in a young girl who had just lost her father and was not yet able to take part in social activities that would distract her mind from morbid fantasies. Finch hinted that these were all manifestations of my wayward and ungovernable temper, which could only be cured by a total surrender to God's will and an absorption in His works. Sir Henry, I think, saw my sensitivity as evidence of the great depth of feeling experienced by a passionate nature and was accordingly humbled and solicitous.

But I knew that my enormous love for Franklin was nearly too powerful for the fragile vessel which contained it. Unless I could find some way to be at his side forever I would languish and die from yearning. And yet the very intensity of my feelings kept us apart.

Because of my frequent illnesses, we had been able to meet only twice in the Square garden. The first time was an unforgettable June afternoon. When he told me that he believed my mother was still alive, I wept with relief in his tender embrace. We were both left trembling. The second meeting took place the after-noon of our departure from London. It was a torrid August day, and I felt faint in my black wool gown in the abominable heat and dust. I had been crying all night at the thought of leaving my Franklin, and I hid my red, puffy eyes with a veil. He did not touch me but stood a little apart from the bench on which I sat, the sun glinting off his fair hair, his blue eyes kind and troubled.

I began to weep, and he stood watching me helplessly, torn, I think, by a desire to comfort me and a reluctance to touch me.

"Miss Farraday," he said desperately. "I am at your service, with all my heart." And with a clipped and formal bow, he took off down the gravel path, almost at a run.

This had been his only open declaration of his feelings for me. Only mere suggestions surfaced in his letters. And to remain even-tempered, I had to resolve to be content with so little for a while longer. But now it is April, and within a month I will be dining with him, flirting with him, dancing with him! Let him try to run away from our love then!

Of course, the mystery of my mother occupied a great part of my energy. I explored every nook and cranny at Pittlesbury Hall, took down every book from the library shelves hoping to find a letter, a diary, even an inscription. But I found nothing. Every evidence of her existence had apparently been obliterated. I questioned the servants, but they had all been hired after her disappearance. In fact, it seems my father had dismissed all of the old servants *en masse* the autumn after her elopement. He wanted nothing to remind him of their life together—or was it that they had witnessed something he wished to conceal? Jenny, at my request, inquired of the farmers' wives and the villagers at Pittlesbury, but they were ignorant of the goings-on at the Hall.

The only other source of information would be the County families who might have called upon my mother. Unfortunately, Finch was always present as my chaperone when they made their initial calls and would not permit me to return them, giving as excuses the lack of a carriage, my mourning, the unavailability of anyone who could accompany me. Gradually the invitations to teas, to musical afternoons, to dinners trailed off, and I was left as Finch wished me to be, utterly alone.

One of these ladies was more persistent than the rest, perhaps because she herself was lonely from not being visited by the other neighbourhood ladies. She had been a music-hall actress with three young sons when she married a retired military gentleman twenty years older than she. He adopted her boys, and when he died he left her a charming and brand-new villa with sufficient income to maintain it. This was Mrs. Vandeleur, a pretty, soft-spoken woman with a weakness for conversation and frivolity. She was still plying me with invitations when Sir Henry declared his intention of seeing me make my debut, and I cajoled him into allowing me to experience County social ways before being plunged into the maelstrom of London manners. He, in turn, advised Finch of his wishes, and so one afternoon I setoff in my new barouche with Finch at my side on our way to Mrs. Vandeleur's for tea.

Finch was horrified by her scandalous conversation—she related an anecdote about the later misadventures of Sally, who had been recognized by her son walking the streets in the garrison town where he, was stationed—and by her irreverent attitude toward religion and convention. I ignored Finch's vicious censures and soon was spending many afternoons laughing and chatting with Mrs. Vandeleur in her pretty bower of a drawing room.

All would have been fine had I not me her son, Philip, the soldier, who had only recently arrived home on leave.

Chapter Eight

I don't intend to discuss Philip Vandeleur in this journal. It is an episode in my life of which I am deeply ashamed.

I was still devoted to Franklin, and wrote him every morning. But Philip was inexorable in his attentions and so irresistible in his scarlet uniform. He managed to place himself in my path whenever I took an afternoon walk. In the evenings, he stood under the trees at the edge of the lawn, watching my window. He was present every time I called upon his mother, and she often left us completely alone.

Well, what was I to do? An inexperienced and passionate young girl, newly aware of the fascination she exercises upon men, consumed with curiosity about the mysteries of the relations between men and women, and bedevilled by an unscrupulous and handsome soldier.

I did not love him. My heart belonged to Franklin. I avoided him whenever I could without offending. When I was strolling along the towpath that ran beside the Cuckmere, and he suddenly appeared on the bridge ahead of me, I walked past without speaking to him. I never let him know that I watched him from my window just as he watched me. I never replied to the fervent notes he smuggled to me through Jenny. I had her open them over the tea kettle in the kitchen, read them aloud to me, and then seal them up to be sent back, apparently unopened. We laughed together over his atrocious penmanship, faulted his grammar and spelling, and teased each other by reciting particularly torrid passages from his epistles.

One I remember read:

> Cruel maiden, your eyes are like black pools within which I
> drown, yet you lift not your pale white hand to rescue me.

Alas, familiarity and flattery have a way of winning over even
the most determined of young ladies, and as the winter gave way to
an early spring and his attentions rather than slackening redoubled
despite my disinterest, I felt myself yielding.

Oh, Franklin, I was never untrue to you! My heart and soul have
belonged to you since first our eyes met! I live only to be your wife
and to serve you, to be yours for an eternity, to make our way through
this life hand in hand, inspiring each other to a truer devotion and
affection than ever before until the bond between us is so strong that
even Death cannot sever it. I feel myself to be your wife already; we
have pledged ourselves to each other with our minds and spirits, and
it wants only for Society to acknowledge this alliance.

So how can I explain the intimacy that grew up between me and
Philip Vandeleur? It was nothing, the merest of nothings! A baga-
telle! A whim!

You must never believe anything you hear to the contrary. Philip
and I were friends, only friends. If by chance he should ever meet
you (which I doubt, since he is just a lieutenant in an infantry regiment, and I pray to God that they will soon be ordered abroad)
spurn his vile accusations as the infamous deceits of a man whose
suit has been rejected in favour of one more worthy. Could anyone
believe the stories of a man of his sort, a dissolute, depraved, inconse-
quential, conceited, illegitimate son of an actress?

Every day I pray for forgiveness that I ever thought of sinning
against our love and curse the fate that sent the Devil in the shape
of Philip Vandeleur to tempt and torment me.

Philip Vandeleur is vile to me. Henceforth I shall never speak his
name nor inscribe it. He and all his works shall be as if they had
never been.

The ascendancy of him who shall remain nameless marked
another change in my relations with Jenny. As she guessed that I
was no longer so scornful of his scribbled requests for secret meetings, she became as prim as Finch. I believe that caution is the

foundation stone—of Jenny's character. Though she can be as reckless and impulsive as I, though she enjoys gossip and joking as much as I do, though her spirit of adventure is as marked as mine, beneath it all is a fundamental caution. I think that this, and not the possibility of discovery by a passerby, is the reason she never consummated her love for Daniel.

Caution is not a part of my nature. Perhaps because I was dominated by the cautiousness of others for so long, it repels me.

Jenny would expostulate with me. She told me that it was well known that Philip had been Sally's seducer and that she had not appeared in his regimental town by mere chance but in order to plead with him to support her and their child. Little did Jenny think that this piqued my curiosity rather than dampened it. What sort of man would do such a thing, and what would he want with me when he could satisfy his baser appetites with any simple country lass?

The times I asked him he said it was my beauty and my spirit that beguiled him.

But I said I would not write of this, and I will not except to note that Finch also has changed her attitude toward me.

One night I finally acquiesced to his demands and promised to admit him to Pittlesbury Hall after everyone had gone to bed. He expressed an immense curiosity to see my chamber ("The shrine in which my goddess resides," he called it), and I must confess I wondered what it would be like to be alone in my bedroom with a man. I waited until the servants had all retired and then flashed him our prearranged signal, a candle held up to my window twice in succession. When I had finally undone the massive bolt on the front door, he was waiting impatiently on the portico, blowing on his hands to warm them in the chill night air.

I led him up the backstairs, as I had planned, my feeble candle illuminating only a fitful circle about us. Whenever I glanced at him, his fine dark eyes were fixed on me with a brooding intensity and his hand was always on me, about my waist, beneath my elbow. I trembled with fear and anticipation of what he might do.

As soon as the door closed behind my back, it was evident what he understood by my invitation. He advanced upon me, muttering something about how we should not fear interruptions now, referring, no doubt, to the foolish liberties I had permitted him previously. He was so very charming. I backed away from him, but he stalked me, cleverly maneuvering me until I was up against the bed, whereupon he snatched the candle from my hand, placed it on the night table, and fell upon me.

I struggled at first, but there was a magic in his caresses and soon I realized, to my amazement and terror, that I did not want him to stop. Something had awakened in me that I had not dreamed existed. I wanted to dissolve, to drift away altogether in the tide of sensation. I felt drugged, indolent and unthinking. I saw a blaze of light.

Then I realized the blaze of light was not a product of my feverish passions, but a fire! The candle, so carelessly set down, had caught the bed-curtains on fire. I sat up; I screamed at Philip; I shrieked, "Fire! Fire!"

Probably he saw in the fire the total destruction of his desires. At any rate, he would not let me rise, but renewed his assault upon me. Thus, Finch found us, me almost completely undressed, in the desperate embrace of a man, the silk hangings flaming away.

I think she must have staggered or hesitated, for Jenny pushed past her and tore down the fiery curtain, flinging it upon the ground and stamping it out quickly. I managed to push Philip aside, and he sat on the other side of the bed, putting his clothes to rights. Finch recovered herself and, taking up the poker from the grate, shook it at Philip and shouted something hysterical about killing him if he did not leave at once. He rose and contemptuously wrenched the poker from her grasp, throwing it upon the floor. Then, with an inscrutable look for me (I was sitting on the bed sobbing with relief and frustration), he stalked out the door through the ring of excited servants.

A horrible scene followed. Finch raging, almost babbling with incoherence, speaking of the sins of the flesh, the perversion of love, the desecration of a temple of the spirit. I sobbed bitterly, unable to defend myself, for had I not admitted this man into my bedroom at night, and with what purpose?

When Finch at last was through and had locked me in my room, I fell into a troubled sleep and woke near dawn, having dreamed that the Devil had set fire to my bedclothes and was standing at the foot of my bed, sneering at me as I writhed on my pyre and my flesh crumbled away.

It was a fever, the return of brain fever, said the country doctor. I lapsed into incoherent delirium. Jenny would not even tell me afterward the things of which I spoke; she was ashen-faced, her eyes troubled and dark. I awoke after several days to find the fever had broken. I was cold for the first time, the sweat lying clammy on my skin. Jenny was asleep in the armchair, curled up like a kitten, her hair lank, her breathing fretful. The fire had almost died down. The grey light of early morning was filtering into the room. I could hear the cows lowing in the fields, the rumble of thunder in the distance.

"Jenny," I moaned, and she looked up with a start, crying a little as she felt my forehead and saw that the fever had left, helping me to sponge off and change my nightgown for a fresher one. I lay all day, hearing the sound of the rain, feeling weak and penitent. Oh, I had sinned, and no one was so conscious of that as I! For what business had I consorting with a man of his sort, a man of the worst moral character, whose hand had undone the bolt that kept closed the citadel of my virginity? I vowed never again to let the weaknesses of the flesh assail me, and when Finch came to feed me, I asked her to pray with me for my immortal Soul.

She informed me that Sir Henry would arrive on the morrow from London, very concerned about my health. I dared not ask her about Philip, but I inquired timidly for news from Jenny. Finch sent her in, but all my friend would say was that Finch had gone over there to upbraid him and his mother and that there had been no message from him at that time.

I don't know what it was. Perhaps the Devil is really within me. Perhaps it was a recurrence of the brain fever. But as the evening drew near I was in an agony of doubt over Philip. Why had he not called to inquire what had become of me? Why had he not confessed his seduction and absolved me from any blame? What had happened to all his fine words of love?

When Jenny had been sent away to get some much-needed sleep in her own bed, I struggled to get up and dress myself. Finding the effort too great for me, I pulled on my heaviest cloak over my nightgown and stumbled downstairs and over the fields to Vandeleur House.

The rain had ceased, but the grass was heavy with moisture and a light mist lay upon the meadows, lifting every now and then to give me a vista of silent groves and low hills, the weight of the dark storm clouds heavy upon their crests. In my ultra-sensitive state, every stone beneath my foot was a little Purgatory, every slight incline an unbearable obstacle. There was the place Philip had showed me the wild violets and had tucked them gently into my hair. That was the stile over which he had lifted me and let me linger in his arms a little longer than necessary. And this—oh, bitterest of all—was the grove where we had lounged at twilight and he had kissed me fully and solemnly, telling me that no one had ever so moved his heart.

It seemed an eternity before someone at Vandeleur House finally answered my feeble knock. I was left, sodden and miserable, in the hall while the maid went off to fetch Mrs. Vandeleur. She came out, her pretty mouth fixed in a thin line, her white forehead creased. She did not invite me into the drawing room, but stood contemplating me as if I were some sort of insect.

"What is it *you* want?" she said.

"I wondered if Philip was here," I said miserably.

"May I—could you give him a message from me?" I asked.

"He has rejoined his regiment," she said, "and now, if it is quite all right with you, I have guests for dinner and I would like to rejoin them."

"Without a word of explanation or apology to me?" Why did I make myself so unhappy?

"Pray, tell me why he should explain himself to a wanton girl who invites him into her bedroom and next moment sets the whole neighbourhood about his ears so that he dare not show his face anywhere? Your so-called guardian had some fine things to say about my son when she called. I told her she was mistaken, she was confusing him with *you*." And without a further word, she turned and went off down the passageway.

For some reason, I fancied that it was Philip with whom she was dining and that he had asked her to deny his presence. Within a moment I had thrown open the door to the dining room, screaming I know not what, only to meet the astonished gazes of two male strangers. There was an extra place set, before which no one sat, and thinking that it belonged to Philip, I picked up the plate and hurled it at the wall. I had smashed two of the wineglasses and had the goblet in my hand when the gentlemen subdued me and I was ushered, shaking and weeping, back home. I suffered a relapse of my fever, brought on by the damp and the excitement. When I awoke again it was to the sight of Finch's drawn and troubled face.

"Sir Henry is below stairs," she said with great consternation. "He insists on seeing you immediately."

"You haven't told him!" I started up from the pillows in terror.

"Hush yourself. Lie back down," she said, pushing me back and stroking my hair. "Be calm, Arabella. No, I haven't *told* him. How could I?"

This last was in an undertone, spoken as she turned away from me. I little guessed at the time the import of those words. It was many days later, when Sir Henry was assured of my recovery and had bid his fond farewell, that I realized what her words had meant. He said he hoped that he would soon be able to protect me and my fragile health.

At that moment, all my shackles fell away from me. I was free at last of all my demons! Finch could not tell Sir Henry of my mis-adventures, for in so doing she would, under the terms of the will, thereby lose her annual income and possibly her position. She had changed, all in an instant, from my jailer to my accomplice!

Chapter Nine

I am waiting for the man from Farraday and Company with bolts of the latest brocaded silk for me to inspect. Looking back on those last pages I fear that I have been guilty of great indiscretion. If only I could find my penknife I would excise them, but it is missing. I wonder…yes! the letter opener is also gone. It is that Finch! Poor woman! She is doubtless tormented by guilt and fear lest I repeat my crimes. She never lets me out of her sight for a moment. What does she fear I will do? My threats to put an end to my miserable existence were only that, threats. Why should I die when there is Franklin to live for?

I caught Finch with Dr Steward in the drawing room the other day. Though my father dismissed him not long ago, he is still consulted by that woman! She insists that he is the most competent London doctor we could engage, knowing my family history and everything, and that if my father had lived, he would have eventually come to his senses, and reversed himself. I don't argue; I have always been fond of the man myself.

But you should have seen Finch's reaction when I walked in. Most peculiar! She jumped up, and said in the feeble, apologetic tones of a lie that Dr Steward had dropped by to inquire after me having been in the neighbourhood after hearing about my ill health. He then proceeded to ask me the oddest questions! Did I hear voices? Do I feel people are plotting against me? Was I dwelling on any one subject to the exclusion of others?

Well, though I told him no, the truth would have been that I am. I just received the dearest letter from Franklin. He is on his way back to London, and he should be here within a fortnight. He writes:

28 April 1842
Sir Henry brought his sister, Miss Warder-Mall, to see me. He acts as if our betrothal is understood, when all that I said was that I would agree to marry him after I had a Season in London. Surely that's ambiguous enough.

Miss Warder-Mull does not seem to care for me. I daresay she recognizes the feeling is mutual. Imagine having to live in the same house with her sour face! Miss Finch would be preferable.

There's little reason to even dwell on such gloomy possibilities except that it makes the prospect of gazing upon Franklin's dear face for the rest of my life even more delightful by contrast.

29 April 1842
He is here! Though I have not yet seen him, my heart beats faster at the thought of his presence just a mile away from where I sit at this moment! The strange lassitude of the past weeks has lifted, and I find myself playing the piano again, having Chloe in for tea, taking up my beadwork.

I even asked Finch if I might learn something about the management, of the household. Fortunately, I remembered to bring the volumes Miss Warder-Mull sent me and have been totally absorbed in them. How much there is to learn about how one deals with servants, the cost of provisions, the care of plate and silver, the planning of a menu if I am to provide a happy home for my Franklin.

Finch seemed surprised by my request but several hours later returned and asked me if I wished to accompany her to the kitchen while she supervised the preparation of dinner. How fascinating, it all is! I've been down there only twice before and never at mealtime. I watched Tibby shape the dinner rolls, inspected the layout of the larder, saw how the plates are kept warm on the heating tray, and watched with admiration as Mrs. Glover wrestled with the stove, trying to maintain an even temperature for the meats that were cooking in huge stew pans. And how complicated, too! The ham from two nights ago is minced to be used in the forcemeat for tonight's stuffed veal. And yesterday's fowl has become the base for the soup stock. I wonder how one keeps it all in mind!

Two of the gowns came back today: a pink changeable silk with an overskirt of black lace and a white muslin trimmed with pale blue ribbons and Valenciennes lace. I have yet to get the slippers or gloves I will need. Finch refuses to let me out of the house to do any shopping. I fear I shall be required to turn to Sir Henry once more.

2 May 1842

Sir Henry took me himself! He said that he could take the afternoon off, and so out we went in my new barouche. He seemed enchanted by the world of feminine finery in which he found himself and kept urging me to purchase more and more. We went to Swan and Edgar in the Regent Street Quadrant for the gloves, stockings, and other trimmings, and then, passing a bonnet-maker's shop after our exit, I stopped to admire a cunning little bonnet in the window that would just match the fawn-coloured carriage outfit I have ordered. He insisted on buying it for me.

The shop assistant remarked, while helping me adjust the bonnet, that my papa seemed very young to have such a grown-up daughter.

"Oh, he is not my father," I said, all innocence. "We are to be married at the end of the Season." I wanted to see the effect of this news.

A little smirk crossed her lips. "How do you like this angle, miss?" she asked quickly, adjusting the bonnet. Well, let her scorn me all she likes. She little knows the handsome young man whose admiring eyes I bought the bonnet to please.

Another note from him saying that he is busy with certain business arrangements.

Where is my penknife? I must find it!

7 May 1842

I am downcast today. The sun is shining, but the day seems common and horrid. The chirping of the birds in the elm trees only grates on my nerves. I struck Jenny when she brought in the break-fast tray, and she went away in tears. Since I cannot dress myself, I decided to remain in bed.

Franklin has not yet arrived. And yesterday Sir Henry informed me that Lady S—, who had promised to present me to Society, has had to fly to the side of her married daughter in Kent, whose infant son has just died of pneumonia. He does not know how he is to find someone else who will do.

If I had some poison, I believe I would take it. Life simply isn't worth all this struggle. And Finch, thinking that I am ill, brought up a cup of beef tea. I threw it at her instead.

8 May 1842

Franklin was in church today! He stood immediately behind me, and if I turned my head ever so slightly I could see his warm blue eyes fixed upon me and his soft smile lifting his moustache so that it, too, appeared to smile. Oh, how I love him! I could not concentrate at all on the lessons, though I remember one passage:

> Arise, shine; for your light has come,
> and the glory of the Lord has risen upon you.
> For behold, darkness shall cover the earth,
>   and thick darkness the peoples;
> but the Lord will arise upon you
>   and His glory will be seen upon you
> And nations shall come to your light,
>   and kings to the brightness of your rising.

I have no need of nations and kings, for the Lord has sent me my beloved!

Finch was so rapt in her own spiritual world that I hoped she had not noticed him, but afterward she wanted to know who that impertinent young man was who stared so. I pretended total oblivion and teasingly chided her on her inattention to the divine worship.

He spoke to me briefly on the steps of the church and asked if he could call upon me this afternoon. Oh, my love, I tremble with eagerness at the thought of your eyes on my face, the sound of your voice falling like music upon my ears, the touch of your hands!

Will he never come? It seems likely to rain at any moment. Oh, where is he, the dearest of the dear, my Soul?

. . .

He has been here. It was an inspiration for him to choose Sunday, for Finch was shut up in her room reading sermons. We met in the back drawing room, the music room. He seemed as entranced as I. We were both speechless. We sat on the rose love seat, holding hands, gazing wordlessly into each other's eyes. When we began to speak it was both at once. Oh, there is no bliss like true love!

I told him that I lived only to be worthy of him and asked him to advise me what to read that I might be conversant on his pet, topics. He laughed and said he hardly thought that I could get through Schopenhauer. He kissed my hand when he rose to leave.

Oh, I am desolate! When will I see him again?

9 May 1842

I awoke with the image of Franklin in my mind. It was so irresistible I could not bring myself to rise and allow the more mundane details of the day to cloud the vision of him granted by Heaven.

So I stayed in bed despite Jenny's puzzled looks and Finch's discomposure. I stayed abed and indulged in further fantasies regarding my Franklin. I imagined us sitting before the fire in our own snug little drawing room, holding hands and gazing alternately upon the bright flames and our own bright faces. We would speak of our dreams of the future—perhaps a parliamentary career for him, the plans contingent upon our removal to Pittlesbury Hall for the autumn. And then I would impart to him the joyous news:

"I wonder if we should choose a Pittlesbury girl for a nurse," I would say, and his hand would start in mine, his blue eyes growing dim with tears.

"My darling—"

"Yes, it is true. I had the confirmation from the doctor just this morning: I wanted to be certain before I raised your hopes. We are to have a child in May. I pray he is a handsome man of genius like his father."

"No, a lovely, laughing little girl with your eyes and your charming ways." And he would bury his head against my bosom, he was so immersed in wonder.

By afternoon I had named all of our children: There was a Perdita for my mother and an Arabella after me; a Franklin, of course, a bonny, healthy, loving little boy with his father's fair hair and mesmerizing blue eyes; and a Frederick for his father; and then perhaps a Lucy and an Isabella, a Roland and a Guy.

But though our nursery would be full to overflowing, my dear husband should never be neglected. No, we would be alone together every evening at the close of our busy days, lost in a world of marvels of our own fashioning. At parties, we would dance only with each other and he would never flirt with pretty, dashing young women, and people would say of us: "So old-fashioned, but so charming." Each year we would go abroad, climbing the Alps together, visiting the ruins of Pompeii, floating through the canals of Venice in a gondola, an Italian moon above and a serenade softly flowing over the water. And with each moment together, our love would deepen and grow more sparkling and alive, a force stronger than the two of us together.

10 May, Tuesday

Sir Henry just left. I am so upset I can barely hold this pen. My hand is shaking. He said my entrance into Society will have to be delayed a year. He said that with the defection of Lady S— he does not know whom to ask to present me. Is it my fault he knows so few people in important positions? And this is a man who wants me to become his wife! What dreary circles I would have to move in if I did so. I asked him what about some one of my mother's relatives. He became quite agitated.

"Why, my dear Arabella, that would go expressly against your father's wishes," he said, and his eyes seemed to roll, his face to flush. "Oh, no, that would not do."

And though he shook his head fiercely, I should still like to know why not. I remembered Lady Evershire saying that my mother's eldest brother was now Marquis of Calverley. That certainly sounds impressive. Why shouldn't his wife present me? Particularly since they are relatives, that would lend a greater propriety and a finer feeling to the whole affair.

I reminded Sir Henry of how much he had to lose if my debut was delayed, and he, seeing that I remained quite firm in my decision not to make any definite announcement until I had been presented, promised to canvas a few more of his acquaintances.

Our conversation ended there, abruptly.

11 May, Wednesday

I hate her! I despise her! I spit upon her! She, that she-beast, that lying, sneaking little hussy, has the audacity to call herself my friend! I should have known when she kept asking me about my cousin that she held some evil designs in her seemingly vapid mind. No friend of mine would come to visit as she did a fortnight ago and prattle on about her presentation at a Drawing Room, the ball given for her debut, the fancy dress ball to be given by the Queen, the gowns that she had ordered, knowing that I might never experience these pleasures. Oh, the treachery of women! And I used to call her my bosom friend!

Chloe saw Franklin at a ball last night! She danced with him!

"I had to persuade him," she said a sly, cunning tone in her voice that had never been there before. "He vowed he could not dance, but really, Arabella, your cousin is a delightful waltzer! I felt absolutely transported to another world! And he is so charmingly sincere, unlike the other men one meets everywhere!"

"Oh," I said with disinterest.

"He told me all about his travels in Italy and Greece," she rattled on. "He is a very fascinating conversationalist. I actually sat out two dances that I had already promised. We went out on the terrace where we could hear each other speak. But Aunt Caroline, of course, came after me and told me I must not show so much attention to one young man or people would start to talk."

"What of George Grasston?" I asked to conceal the pain from the knife that I felt sinking into my heart and remembering Chloe's *tendre* for that gentleman the previous summer.

"Oh, he has no sense!" she declared, tossing her head. "I have quite given up on him."

Not a word, not one word, not any mention of me? Surely, Franklin spoke about me. In any case, I sent him a sharp note. That makes the fifth in two days, and only one brief reply, saying he was very busy. Busy attending the Gammages' ball, doubtless.

12 May, Thursday

It is clear that I must take matters into my own hands. I cannot endure another night like the last. When I blew out my candles, all the demons that had been hovering around me crowded upon my bed, their ugly faces sneering at me. There was Doubt, its tremulous pale face shifting into a thousand different forms. There was Temper, swollen with blood and venom, side by side with Violence, who stood poised with claws dripping scarlet. And Pride gloating and Envy slit-eyed and green-faced, and all the others. Even Madness loomed out at me from the corner, a slavering, babbling, lunatic form.

I rang for Jenny and made her sit up with me all the night. Even with her presence the demons only retreated to the corners, where they giggled and chatted amongst themselves. I did not tell her about them. I read to her all my precious notes and letters from Franklin and described in detail all the words that had passed between us, the tokens of affection, the way I felt.

And then Jenny, my closest companion, the only one I can trust in this shifting morass through which I try to wend my way, struck the mortal blow.

"It seems to me," she said, letting go of my hand and going to stand by the fire, "that perhaps you place too much emphasis upon the return of his interest in you."

A chill descended over me. I could not speak. She turned and probably guessed by the pallor of my face and my immobility what had happened.

"Oh, Bella, forgive me!" she cried, running back to the bed, kneeling and pressing my hand against her cheek. "I am tired and thoughtless tonight. Let us pretend I never said that."

"Nonsense, Jenny," I said in a strange voice that seemed to come from quite far away. I felt an odd desire to torment myself. "Pray tell me, what makes you think so? You know how I value your opinions."

Jenny sighed and was silent for a long while.

"I don't know quite what it is," she said. "He is certainly warm and communicative, but there is so little on how he feels about you. I grant that when he describes how he looks forward to seeing you, one might conclude there was some romantic spirit moving him, but might it not also be seen as mere politeness of a friendly sort?"

She had made her point so well and with such delicacy and feeling that I felt a surge of love for her. And yet there was pity in her voice, which I could not abide.

"Perhaps you are right," I said coldly. "I shall have to think on it. At any rate, once I am presented, I shall meet many gentlemen. Let us talk about something else for now." And we took up the subject of my gowns, two of which needed extensive alteration, and the dinner dress, which we decided to trim differently.

Finch must have been awakened by our voices because very close to dawn she came and knocked upon my door and thrust her pale, sleepy face through the crack.

"What is it? What is wrong?" she asked with some disorientation.

"Never mind, Finch," I said sharply. "I could not sleep, and Jenny kindly consented to sit up and talk to me."

"How is she to do her work in the morning if she stays up all night?" Finch wanted to know.

"I am doing it now, Miss Finch," put in Jenny quickly, holding up the gown on which she was working. "I will be able to sleep once Miss Arabella falls asleep."

"And if she does not?"

"Oh, one can hardly help but sleep," I said, annoyed. "It's not of one's own choosing."

Finch rubbed her eyes sleepily, seemed to consider this a moment, and then, with a murmured "Very well," shuffled off down the hall.

But I was wrong. I could not sleep. Though we continued to converse on topics of indifference, my mind formulated a new plan: I would approach the Marchioness of Calverley personally and ask her to bring me out. Poor Jenny was to get no sleep.

She did not like this idea, but I think she feared to discourage me because of the pain she had previously inflicted when she doubted Franklin. So she said nothing, merely helping me put on the black brocade gown with the white lace collar and cuffs, brushing off the black velvet mantle and muff and bonnet, waiting with me on the front steps for the carriage. Fortunately, Finch had set off on some errands and she always walked.

Of course, we did not know where Lord and Lady Calverley resided, but John Groom asked some of his fellow coachmen about the Square until Miss Peacock's man said that he recalled hearing they had leased the old Fountain House after Lady Fountain's tragic death.

It was in Grosvenor Square, a graceful house of stone with many-paned windows. Inside, everything was exquisite: a marble entrance hall hung with splendid Venetian scenes and lined with statues and potted palms. Chairs of gilt, a gold candelabra at the foot of the stairs. The hall table had a marble top inlaid in intricate arabesques of pink and gold and black.

The butler ushered us at once into a magnificent drawing room. "Her Ladyship," he said, "was just going out, but could spare you a few minutes of her time." He evinced no surprise when I said that I was her niece and continued exhibiting the most scrupulous courtesy toward both me and Jenny—who, oddly enough, seemed quite at ease in these elegant surroundings.

And, oh, were they elegant! My heart pounded with pride every time my eyes swept the room and I realized this was the home of my uncle. Pale-blue Aubusson carpets scattered with flowers lay upon the gleaming floors. Striped silk curtains, heavily swagged and fringed with gold, draped the windows, which looked out upon the street. The window itself was a bower of plants: tall palms, ferns, and aspidistras on marble pedestals. All the furniture was delicately carved, lined with gilt, and upholstered in various shades of rose, purple, and blue silk and brocade. Of the various tables, some were inlaid with mother-of-pearl, some were marble-topped and others trimmed with gold. Everything sparkled: the crystal chandeliers descending from the coffered ceiling, the huge pier glasses on the walls, the priceless china behind the glass-fronted cases.

Jenny and I had a good opportunity to admire these treasures since Lady Calverley took her time, and when she finally swept into the room—all ruffles and lace and flowery scent—I could understand why. She was far advanced in that blessed condition that would soon provide an heir to her husband, Lord Calverley. I doubted that she had ever intended to go out —perhaps this was an excuse the butler offered so she could cut short unpleasant calls— for she was in the most fetching morning dress I'd ever seen. It was of a soft cream-coloured muslin, embroidered all over with small floral bouquets and trimmed with yards of costly lace and many pink ribbons. A lovely little boudoir cap, trimmed with the same lace and ribbons, framed her undressed brown hair. She was little more than a girl and quite evidently delighted at having someone with whom she could talk.

After the introductions, she sat down gingerly on one of the fine gilt sofas and rearranged her draperies.

"Oh," she sighed, "you have no idea how tired I am of this condition. I hope you won't be offended by my being rather frank."

I murmured, "No," fascinated by being admitted to this new aspect of what it means to be a woman. (Oh, if only I had a mother!) She, however, didn't wait for approval but went right on:

"I am positively drooping with ennui! I can't go out anywhere— the carriage is absolutely too jolting for me at this stage—and no one will call," she complained sorrowfully, "for not having gone out at all I don't know any of the latest gossip. I shall be so glad when this is all over. I vow George shall not come near me again for a year. I will not miss next Season's parties. Can you imagine, I was unwell from the first moment! I knew I had been caught directly afterward. I just felt different; really, I can't explain it any other way. I suppose it must be fascinating to be a mother, don't you? But to have to go through this each time?" She shivered delicately. "But I am boring you, am I not?"

Both Jenny and I were quick to demur, but she went on in her light, breathy voice: "George says I talk too much. It has been his major complaint. Not having known each other very long before we were married and then only at parties, where one is supposed to talk, I guess he thought I went about thinking all day and speaking only when necessary, like him. Oh, was he surprised! He kept asking me was I never going to run out of things to say!"

She seemed not the slightest bit discomfited by her husband's evident displeasure.

"What I can't understand is his silences. How can someone keep to himself so much? He must surely drive himself mad! I know I do when I think too much!" She stopped, ruefully; one pale beringed hand flew up to her lips. "Oh, you will think me the greatest rattle-brain! You know, I do like to hear others talk, not just myself. Tell me about yourself!"

She was an expert at evoking conversation and soon had me rattling on about our estate at Pittlesbury, my lessons, the house-hold, my father's death. I had not meant to ask her to present me, once having realized the impossibility of such a request, but I slipped and had confessed my loneliness, my lack of a chaperone, and my hopes under her subtle guidance.

"Oh," she made a wry face, "I would have so loved to present you, too. Oh, the wretchedness of this child, interfering with my life so. You know, we haven't even been married quite a year. It will be a year in August. Already I am condemned to the restricted life of a matron. I thought I had a few years of parties and balls left in me. And it would be such fun to bring out such an attractive young lady."

"Oh, but I wouldn't ask it of you, in your present condition," I said, blushing a little.

"Well, there must be something else that can be done," she said. "Let me inquire of some of my friends. Perhaps my sister. She is Lady Throttle, and she's not expecting this Season. I would like to see something done for you, and then you could tell me all about the receptions and dances and all the handsome young men you meet and the latest scandals." She was wistful, lost in a reverie for a brief moment. "But, tell me, how are you related? What is your name again?"

"Arabella Farraday," I said, "but my mother, Perdita DeWinx, was—rather, is—a sister to your husband."

"How odd!" She put her head to one side. "He has never men-tioned her. I thought I knew everyone of his family. He does not like to speak of them; he says they mean nothing to him. Of course, I don't believe this. My greatest sorrow is being separated from my mother and my sisters." Tears welled in her eyes. "They are all still in Hampshire, yet George says I must be confined in London so I can have the best medical attention. Still, I have to visit them— George's family, I mean. What a gloomy house! That sick old man and his poor deformed sister—"

"Then you have met my cousin Franklin and his mother," I said eagerly.

"Oh, yes, one of those perfectly useless and charming young men," she said lightly. I did not care for this remark; it seemed unworthy of her. "It was his father, the brother, who died in India. George has spoken of him. And then there is a sister married to a rector in some outlandish country village. But he has never spoken of your mother. What was her name?"

"Perdita. Lady Perdita DeWinx, then Farraday."

"What a lovely name!"

I smiled with pride as if I had had something to do with her christening.

"Well, I will ask George! How provoking of him to conceal it from me. Why does she not bring you out? Is she dead? Oh, how thoughtless of me. I declare this baby has completely deprived me of my wits. Pray forgive me!"

I forgave her and told her a little about my mother's disappearance. I left out the elopement, merely saying that she had left my father.

"Oh, a mystery!" Lady Calverley's, eyes were all aglow. "I do so love a mystery. Why, you have certainly given me a pretty puzzle on which to ponder." She started suddenly and laid a hand upon the front of her gown. "Oh, the spiteful little beast is kicking me again!" She wagged her finger at her stomach playfully. "Now, stop that, you monster! Mama doesn't like it." She looked up at us apologetically. "I fear I must retire," she said with a sigh. "I become fatigued so easily. I have enjoyed this so very much. Do you think… could you call again? I would be so grateful for the company. I feel almost as if you were my sister, and really, I suppose we are related."

"I would welcome the opportunity," I said taking her hint and rising to go. "I shall return as soon as it is convenient."

"Now, don't be too long!" we heard her call out as the butler showed us back down the gleaming hall. "One never knows when this inconvenient child will make his appearance." I thought I saw the butler wince a little at the candidness of her remark, but really it would have been surprising to see any hint of human feeling in that impassive face. I may well have been mistaken.

Chapter Ten

13 May, Friday

I am sorely vexed. Franklin is not behaving as he should. I sent him a note indicating that I would be in Bond Street in the afternoon today and might it not be fortuitous if we should see each other. Well, Jenny and I wandered up and down that wretched street for literally hours before he at last arrived. He had been at his Club, he said.

I suppose my temper was short from being made to wait so long. I foolishly upbraided him about his attending the Earl of Gammage's ball. He became quite cool. His manner, if not his words, indicated that he thought I presumed upon our friendship.

Then he let fall the most astounding news. It seems the Duke of Drumland, in very poor health and accustomed to having his every whim satisfied, never came down to London for this Season but decided instead to remain on his estates in Yorkshire. Since Franklin's mother is with the duke, and since she wishes to see Franklin soon, she insisted he quit London at once.

"Then how are we to see each other?" I asked, matching him for iciness.

He seemed unconcerned. "Oh, as to that I have many things in progress in London at the moment that I should hate to let go by the way," he said blithely, "so I imagine having once seen Mother, I shall return."

Am I one of his works in progress, I wonder? In any case, I sobbed all the way to the carriage and was the object of many curious stares.

And he looked so handsome in his lilac waistcoat and white trousers with a light-blue frock coat, a cornflower in his buttonhole just the colour of his eyes.

I was still weeping when I descended the carriage in front of the house. There Sir Henry was waiting for me. He had a preoccupied air about him, though he was most attentive, declaring that I had tried to do too much in my delicate state of health and should be resting at home rather than rambling about Mayfair. Not a word did he say about my coming out, and I was feeling far too dejected to ask for any news.

I suppose knowing that the Marchioness of Calverley is asking about for me made Sir Henry's feeble efforts unimportant.

15 May, Sunday

Franklin was not in church today. He sent a formal note taking his leave of me yesterday, and ever since then the world is grey and totally devoid of meaning. I could not sing out with joy, and why should the heavens rejoice when my true love is in Yorkshire and his absence lies on my heart like a nine-ton stone?

I am not a strong person despite what the world thinks of me. I am like a vine that must creep and crawl around a sturdy oak for support. Since Franklin is the person God has chosen round which for me to entwine myself, I must be patient and abide these trials a little longer.

The anniversary of my father's burial. Finch has been crying all day: She still wears black from head to toe. I wonder what was the true nature of her relationship with my father? Despite what Jenny says I am certain he must have been more to her than a mere employer. My God, how she idolizes him! His picture in the hallway is still swathed with crepe. His name is spoken only with a reverent hush, followed by a moment of silent meditation.

Why is my life so difficult, so fraught with obstacles and disappointments? Others seem to live calm, moderated lives with a few judiciously enjoyed pleasures and some trifling, though heartfelt sorrows. I suppose I am more sensitive than the others.

16 May, Monday

The last day of mourning! My room is a clutter of hatboxes, trimmings, gowns, feathers, and flowers. Jenny has been stitching from
dawn to dusk, finishing up the dress that I will need first. I think I
shall celebrate my liberation by calling upon the Marchioness of
Calverley to get the news of her researches.

17 May, Tuesday

Sir Henry found someone to present me! Her name is Lady
Molliton; she is the widow of a brigadier.

He was so proud of himself, he was nearly bursting out of his
vivid orange waistcoat, his round face glowing with triumph when
he came to tell me the glad news. I agreed to meet her; there seemed
no harm in allowing the events to proceed. So he took me to tea at
her house in Half-Moon Street. I wore my new visiting costume, a
charming confection of coral silk trimmed with white lace and roses.
Falling open over an ivory underskirt, it finished at the bottom with
flounces trimmed with thin piping of the coral silk. With it I had a
little white parasol, trimmed with coral ruffles; a straw hat with
coral ribbons, red roses, and white lace; and straw-coloured gloves.

Sir Henry said I looked fetching. He fussed about me as if I were
the Queen, helping me spread out my skirts in the carriage so that
they wouldn't be crushed, handling my little parasol with an ardent
awkwardness. As he handed me down before Lady Molliton's tiny
town house, he held onto my hand a little longer than necessary and
I pretended not to notice.

What can I say about Lady Molliton? Nothing good, that is certain.
She lives in the most cramped and cluttered of dwellings. Perhaps
because she rents out the upper floors she has had to crowd the
accumulation of a lifetime into a few rooms. The effect is overwhelming. The walls are plastered with pictures, as close as flag-
stones on a pavement, their frames jostling other frames. There are
silhouettes, paintings, portraits, engravings, mirrors, and miniatures
lined all the way up to the ceiling. Only one path exists among the
jungle of fragile chairs and little tables leading to the sofa set before
the fire. My gown was almost too full for this tiny path, and I had
to hold up my skirts to prevent them from sweeping away a whole

display table of porcelain figures and a papier-mâché tea tray crowded with a china service. The rest of the room is a morass of furniture: *chaise longues* blocking the display cases, a massive bookcase backed against a little cottage piano, circles of chairs drawn up facing each other and separated only by a crowded *étagère* in the centre.

But I have become distracted from my subject, which is the mistress of this domain. She is one of those tall, angular women with an impossibly erect carriage. One fancies she would have been a good brigadier herself. She wore a black gown, very plain, with only a gold watch chain for ornament. Her only concessions to femininity were a little bit of lace on her black cap and her lace mitts. She has stern, piercing black eyes, which studied me as if I were an insect on a collection table, a classic Roman nose, and thin lips set in a grimace of disapproval and displeasure. Or was this simply her response to me?

I could just imagine her thinking: "Frivolous. Showy. Extravagant. Immodest. Fast. Useless." I was determined to prove her wrong and spoke very little, replying only when questioned and then in the most maidenly and decorous way possible. I took only tiny sips of the weak tea and small bites of the crusty tarts, and yet still, when we left, her handclasp was cold and imperious. Sir Henry lingered behind while I waited in the hall, studying the medals won by the brigadier, all displayed alongside his uniforms and his sword in a glass case. I believe she would have had him stuffed and on display if she could have.

After a long delay, Sir Henry came bounding out, rubbing his hands together. "She agrees to present you," he said.

"How gracious," I answered with sarcasm. He missed the sarcasm.

"Yes, she is a most remarkable woman. Very well connected. Her sister is Lady Holly. She has quite an entree, and I think she will do nicely, Lady Molliton." He seemed quite pleased with himself.

In the carriage, he took advantage of our proximity to take hold of one of my gloved hands. I withdrew it and turned my head so only my profile was visible: There was a moment's silence. Then he began again in the formal tones of a man about business.

"Of course, the presentation must take place at Grover Square. As you can see, Lady Molliton has little room to spare. That means it must be a reception. I shall have to consult with Miss Finch as to the best date and arrangements."

I ignored him as much as possible. I knew I should be presented by Lady Throttle at a grand ball in an elegant ballroom and all the top Five Hundred families would be there.

Alas, I could not escape from Sir Henry to call upon my friend, Lady Calverley. He stayed for dinner, and the evening was soon spent.

18 May, Wednesday

Kept in by the rain and by Finch, who wanted to decide upon the menu and make up the invitation list. it was one of the few times I've felt any sympathy for Finch. She knows as little about what is served at a reception as I do. She was in an oddly girlish mood, fluttering about, agitated and vivacious. I found myself becoming cool and detached, as she usually is, by contrast.

The invitation list presented an even more formidable task. Ordinarily, I suppose, one would invite close relatives first, then those related to the family by marriage, and finally friends. But my father had no family to speak of (not that we would want any of them at an elegant gathering anyway) and my mother's family is strictly interdicted. We discussed inviting the Grover Square families, but ran into endless snags. We could not invite Gabriella Edwards, of course, nor her poor daughter, banned forever from entering polite Society because of her mother's sins. Nor Mrs. Carter, who is separated from her husband and was involved in a crim con case. Nor the former slave from Jamaica with his English wife. Nor Miss Peacock, who, though she is rich and well connected, hosts gatherings to which prominent scientists and thinkers come without their wives.

At last we could contrive only a few names: Mr. and Mrs. Tiffin, Mr. and Mrs. Asshe, the Dowager Countess of Evershire, Colonel and Mrs. Garrison, and Mr. and Lady Tuttle.

"Of course, Lady Molliton will have her own party," put in Finch. "I must ask her to call and help us arrange the details." The only bright spot in the dreary day: a note from Franklin. He has arrived safely in Yorkshire.

19 May, Thursday

Finch and Sir Henry are fast becoming friendly. I don't like this since keeping them apart has been my greatest triumph so far. I found them together in the drawing room this afternoon. Sir Henry was helping her move the furniture against the walls so they could ascertain the condition of the carpet.

Finch was glowing, her cheeks pink, her hair pulling away loosely from her usual severe braids. Is she developing a *tendre* for Sir Henry?

She is still in mourning for my father. I asked her if she would be in black at my debut. She said she thought it best.

I was going to call upon Lady Calverley and so made some excuse about shopping. Sir Henry, the fool, insisted on going with me. So I had to invent a number of articles I needed, and we spent several hours in the Burlington Arcade. He is completely beside himself when I express a desire for any little thing. It took the greatest willpower for him to resist the parure of pink topaz and gold that I admired in the window of a jeweller's. I'm sure he told himself that it was far too costly and showy a piece of jewellery for a young lady. We returned, loaded with boxes, but too late for me to go to the Marchioness of Calverley.

20 May, Friday

Lady Molliton here all day. She added some more illustrious names to the invitation list, drew up the menu, and criticized the arrangement of the drawing room. I think Finch has met her match. She literally quailed before Lady Molliton's brisk manner. I was merely in the way of the fierce battle that raged between these two matrons. Lady Molliton wanted to see my gown, so in compliance I first put on the pink silk one with the black lace overskirt, followed by the white muslin gown with the light blue ribbons. Well, Finch expressed a liking for the muslin, so I am now to wear the pink silk-Lady Molliton's choice.

"Everyone is so tired of young girls in that same old white muslin," declared Lady Molliton. "It is so easily soiled. No, you will wear the pink. Mind you, you have your maid make the alterations I recommended."

I merely bowed my head. I think if I had my choice, I would have preferred Finch's selection. But then I have none.

21 May, Saturday
Terrible nightmares. I roused the house with my screams. I thank God I don't remember much of them. I was escaping from someone who pursued me. My father stood by and watched.

23 May, Monday
The butler said Lady Calverley was not at home. How can this be? His manner was extremely icy and emphatic, or am I imagining this in my disappointment?

No further word from Franklin. My debut is only a fortnight away. Pray God he arrives in time!

25 May, Wednesday
The same message at the Calverleys. I fear something is wrong. The invitations are done and being sent out.

What a dreary day! I am slowly becoming used to the idea of a small and shabby reception held in unfashionable Grover Square under the dragonish auspices of Lady Molliton and attended only by a sorry handful. What does it matter, after all, how I am launched? The great thing is to launch me, and then I might call upon people as I please and soon attend all the great social events of the Town.

27 May, Friday
I have seen no one except Jenny since my return. I had Jenny draw all the draperies in my bedchamber until it is as dark as night but for the faint glow of light around the edges of the windows that the curtains cannot quite repress. I want no bright sunshine tormenting me with its bland cheerfulness. I have need of shadows and gloom. The candles are lit on the dressing table, and I sit before the mirror studying my face in their flickering light and the shaded mysterious smile of my mother in her frame. We are nearly twins now I have my hair loose down my back; my eyes are clouded with the tears I sense she was holding back. But my tears will not fall either. I have

been sitting here in the dimness for nearly an hour, and still I cannot weep. Will they never fall?

I suppose I am grateful that Lady Calverley was the one to tell me. She was certainly sympathetic. She cried abjectly throughout the entire interview. One would have thought she was the young girl being informed of her family's hatred for her mother's wrongdoings and I, cold and impassive, the cataloguer of the catastrophe!

Perhaps I don't believe it even yet. Of course, I don't believe it. There is something overly theatrical in holding a mere elopement accountable for a death and a broken engagement.

I suppose I was fortunate that the redoubtable Lamp actually takes an afternoon off and I chanced upon it. The well-groomed maid who answered my knock evidently had no orders to prevent my admission, so she went to ask. There was an interminable pause, an argument that continued to be debated as the maid descended the stairs, and suddenly Lady Calverley's pale and pleasant face appeared peering down from the railing.

"Oh, Melton, I've changed my mind again. Do send her up to me! Miss Farraday, is that you? Oh, please come in quickly. Don't let anyone see you. Pray, hurry. This way!"

Between her and the maid they hurried Jenny and me into a quaint little back room. I assume it was Lady Calverley's own sitting room. It was a bower of delicate laces and floral bouquets; the flowers were both real and artificial: painted on silk, worked on pillows, adorning trays, and festooning the draperies. The covers of the chairs were of gay chintz sprinkled with pink, green, and blue flowers.

The Marchioness of Calverley had not yet been delivered of her maternal burden. She wore another dainty morning gown of yellow, trimmed with green and pink, which, though it sought to disguise her condition by means of a clever apron, paradoxically emphasized it. She did not seat herself immediately, though she seemed to be drooping with fatigue. Instead she came to me and clasped my hands in her own moist ones.

"Oh, Miss Farraday," she began. "I don't know how I am to tell you. George said I was not to do so. I should simply refuse to see you and that would be that!" At this point she dropped, as delicately as possible, onto the chintz sofa, and I wondered how my uncle, oh, cruel monster of an uncle, could dismiss his own niece so! "But I could not make so little of it," she continued, as breathless as before. "It is not in my nature. I have felt so wounded whenever I asked Lamp if you called and he said, 'Yes, ma'am. I informed her you were not at home.' I could not bear it another moment, so I gave Lamp the afternoon off. Melton will never tell him or George of your visit."

"But what is it you must not tell me?" I asked coolly. My voice seemed to come from very far away. I had a premonition that the person asking the question was far removed from the person whose very life hung on the answer.

Lady Calverley sighed. She was really not very pretty at the moment with her large mouth drooping, her eyes looking gaunt, her skin pale and her brow wrinkled.

"It is about your mother," she said with peculiar emphasis. She sighed again, quite heavily this time.

Chapter Eleven

I think it was at this point that Jenny suggested we sit down. Or perhaps it was later. The whole episode unfolds like a dream to me now. I know only that I found myself sharing a small sofa with Lady Calverley, who retained my cool hand in her own warm one.

"You see," she explained, "there was a great deal of family trouble because of what your mother did."

"And that was?" Really, I was quite icy and regal in my own way.

"Why, my dear" —Lady Calverley lowered her voice to an intimate whisper— "she ran away with her cousin, and she a married woman with a young child. I guess it was quite a *cause celebre*. And then they never married. He married someone else—an heiress—I believe it was Lady Harriet Bendle, the last of the old line of the Gammages. Of course, George didn't tell me this. It was Cynthia, my sister, Lady Throttle who did. She was fascinated in a sort of horrified way when I told her of your visit. She knows only a few of the details. But, did you realize—I certainly didn't—that Cynthia would not have married Lord Throttle if your mother had not eloped as she did, for he was engaged to your aunt Rosalind, who broke off the match because of the scandal. This is what George has against your mother. That she caused his family such great pain."

I stiffened and was filled with a wild, searing anger. How could it be my mother who had inflicted pain when she had only escaped from a loveless household into the arms of a man who then apparently spurned her (or was persuaded by his family to do so, no doubt) in favour of money rather than love? How she must have suffered, alone in the world, without reputation or the support of her family. And they nourished this as a grievance against her. How cruel!

"It seems," my hostess went on, apparently unconscious of the damage she did, "that George's mother, who was never well, died shortly after the whole sorry affair, and naturally her death was blamed on all the excitement. And then Rosalind felt duty-bound to give up her betrothal to a quite eligible peer. She never received another offer of such magnitude. She's now Mrs. Clavicle, the wife of an old and scholarly prelate in Yorkshire. We've met him—more's the pity, too. A dried-up old stick of a man and a saint of the worst sort. He is above all earthly concerns, including notice of his wife's existence. But I go too far, do I not? Poor Rosalind. Her greatest sorrow, according to George, is that she has no children."

With the prettiest lack of self-consciousness, Lady Calverley laid her other hand upon her swollen stomach. "George seems to feel this was your mother's fault also, that Rosalind would have been married younger or to a more prolific man but for the scandal. Certainly, the Earl of Throttle has proved himself more than capable, though he is nearly as old as Reverend Clavicle. He is quite bitter on the subject. I gather it is a sore point to the whole family."

I intervened here with amazing self-control. "Lady Calverley," I said it is very good of you to trouble giving me all of this very sad news." She coloured a little; I think she caught the sting of my remarks. "But you have neglected one small fragment of the story."

"And that is?"

"Why, what became of my mother after her…her—" there was no discreet word "—her cousin deserted her and her family disowned her. Did they not take her in and shelter her from the jibes of the world and the pangs of conscience?" I knew they had not. "Did they see to it that she was not forced to roam the streets, penniless and ruined?" I was becoming a little vehement; Jenny sensed this and stood up.

"You must not think George a monster of heartlessness, Miss Farraday!" cried his wife, obviously chastened by my condemnation. "There was more, much more than just the elopement! George wouldn't tell me, and Cynthia didn't know what it was, but something occurred afterward, something that was quite shocking and disgraceful! And they didn't repudiate her. Oh, no! You must not think so! No, she was well cared for. I believe she was sent somewhere under someone's care."

"And they have not troubled with her since," I remarked contemptuously, rising. Lady Calverley, still seated, clung to my hands.

"I don't know, Miss Farraday. I have never heard her mentioned. Oh, do say you'll forgive me for having to tell you this dreadful story. Oh, I should have listened to George. He tells me I quite tear myself in two when I become so involved in other people's problems. But I do, oh, I do feel for you, Miss Farraday! We seemed just on the brink of becoming fast friends, and now I have spoiled it all in my usual careless manner. Please say we can be friends again. Once you have thought this all through and realize that it is not my fault, will you come to me again and let us resume where we left off?"

I did my best to promise, but my voice to my own ears seemed as hollow and grim as a ghost's. I could do nothing but flee. There is no other way to describe it. I felt as if a pack of Furies were pursuing me.

"I shall never enter that house again," I told Jenny shortly afterward. Those were my last words to her on the subject. I don't think I shall ever speak of my mother again. She shall remain mine, inviolate, pure, treasured, alone in my heart. Even Franklin, when he at last extracts these pitiful lies from his family, will he remain uninfected by the family penchant for blaming my mother for all the ills of Fortune? I suppose they blame the Reform Bill upon her—that happened a few months after the elopement; surely that is an obvious connection. Or what about the cholera epidemic?

I must avenge her! I must learn the true story and make it known! I shall have no other purpose in life but this one: to absolve my mother of the crimes alleged to her, to release her name from the confines of disgrace and free her, if she yet exists somewhere in this godforsaken world, so that she can hold up her head again with pride and dignity!

31 May, Tuesday
The Queen is all right! Thank God! She went to the Opera despite

being fired upon this evening. How brave she is, our good Queen, and her devoted husband. Shall Franklin love me as much, I wonder.

7 June, Tuesday

Oh, dear, sometimes I detest this journal! A week has passed, and I haven't written a word. And so very much has happened. I have time to note only a few things, for I am on my way to a musicale at the Hollys.

There was quite a skirmish between Finch and Sir Henry last night when he gave me the pink-topaz-and-gold *parure* for my reception. Finch said it was unsuitable for a young girl and too costly a gift to be received from a man. Sir Henry responded that he thought my father would have made such a gift to me on this momentous occasion and that he considered it appropriate for him to use the trust funds for such an investment in my future. Miserly old beggar, to give me a present purchased with my own money! I was quite put nut really.

Franklin did not come; he has such scruples! He felt it would be unseemly to come into a house where he was in an ill-defined position. He arrived in town last week and engaged lodgings near St. James's Street, but we met only once. I took Cotton, the little Pomeranian puppy Sir Henry gave me at Christmas, for an outing in St. James's Park. While Jenny trotted Cotton up and down, I sat on a bench with Franklin, and chattered away. Despite appearances, I am sure my true love is a romantic under that moderate, cautious exterior.

Tonight I shall see him at the Hollys, and after that he can call at 19 Grover Square for one of my Wednesday afternoons At Home's. I believe there's no happier young woman in all of London—no, the entire Kingdom!

8 June, Wednesday

The household is all topsy-turvy because Franklin happened to call. He was part of a throng; I am gathering about myself quite an entourage. There is young Jack Croydon, a somewhat sinister and earnest youth, but oh, so handsome, of pale complexion, dark curly hair, Byronic in the extreme! There is Lionel Holly, a gangly, awkward, shy fellow, and his cousin, Henry Molliton, Lady Molliton's son, a captain in a cavalry regiment and overly puffed up with his own importance. Picture me, if you will, in the centre of this circle of admiring men, laughing at their compliments, making a great show of whose flowers I should put at my waist and whose I should consign to the vases, when Jenny (who has been pressed into service as the downstairs maid) opens the door and, with a saucy wink, announces, "Mr. Franklin DeWinx."

Our eyes meet. The whole room is spinning around me. I rise to greet him, and when our fingers touch, a galvanic current passes through me. Meanwhile, he is smiling into my eyes, his gaze seeming to say, "Remember last night!" when I doubtless would have spent the entire evening conversing with him were it not for Lady Molliton's astute chaperonage. I gave him the seat of honour beside me on the purple settee, consigning Lionel Holly to a footstool instead. Franklin said hardly a word, but every phrase he uttered meant more to me than all the compliments pressed upon me by those other young coxcombs. It was one of his flowers that I pinned onto my belt.

Alas, there is always a serpent in Eden! Sir Henry came bouncing in and insisted upon an introduction to each of the young men. At the sound of *DeWinx* he paled, and his hand trembled when he clasped Franklin's. There was an awkward pause, and then Sir Henry reminded me of a totally fictitious engagement I had that afternoon. I tried to put him off, but it became clear in the most awkward manner that the guests were being asked to vacate the premises, and they did so like leaves being driven before the wind. In this case, a gust of hot air.

As soon as they did, Sir Henry called a conference. I insisted on being present even though he and Finch intended to have me sit it out. As my chaperone, Lady Molliton was, of course, asked to join our little *tête-à-tête.*

"Ahem!" said Sir Henry, calling the meeting to order and pacing back and forth before the hearth. "I regret to say that one of the young men who was present this afternoon is one of Miss Arabella's—er—Farraday's maternal relatives."

"Which one?" asked I, feigning ignorance.

"I was given to understand the family was not in Town this Season," said Sir Henry, his eyes shining abjectly like a dog's eyes.

"Well, so I, was told," said Lady Molliton, drawing herself up to full height. "You know I would never willingly have gone against your expressly stated wishes, Sir Henry!

"It is not your fault, Lady Molliton," said Sir Henry appeasingly. "I don't even know the nature of his connection. It was just the name—"

"What name?" I asked.

"I shall have to make some inquiries as to his presence here," pronounced Sir Henry importantly.

"Surely any young man who wishes to has the right to go about in Society," I said.

"But this young man has no business calling here," said Sir Henry sternly. I have never seen him be quite so emphatic.

"Surely he is unaware of the restrictions—" I began.

"I don't know how we are to handle this," Lady Molliton mused to herself. "Once having admitted him, how can we deny him entrance and admit others?"

"Perhaps we should go back to Pittlesbury Hall," suggested Finch. My blood ran cold at those words.

"No, no, out of the question," replied Sir Henry. "That would defeat the whole purpose." He mumbled to himself.

"Why, it was Mr. DeWinx!" announced Lady Molliton suddenly. "Of course, DeWinx is the family name of the Drumlands."

"Yes, yes, be quiet. We must ponder this carefully," said Sir Henry, still pacing. "We must handle this discreetly and—"

"I have something I wish to say!" I proclaimed, rising to my feet. It was necessary not to exhibit too much fervour and yet to be quite firm. "I will not have you turn away anyone to whom I have been introduced and with whom I have danced, and further I will not abide any restrictions made upon those with whom I shall speak at parties when there is no blame attached to the gentleman's behaviour but merely to his being connected, however distantly, to a family whose name and blood he cannot repudiate, no matter if he chose to do so. If you inform me that such is your intention, I will see no one and go nowhere." And with that, I left the room.

It was a bold stroke. I must wait now to see its effect.

17 June, Friday
I did not dress but remained in bed. Finch was nonplussed but said not a word about the scene last week. I am sick at heart—I was to see Franklin at the Mivens tonight—but for his sake and mine I must go through this Hell.

19 June, Sunday
I would not go to church today, and I decided to stop eating. Jenny, of course, is smuggling up food on the side—a ham-and-veal pie, some cold cutlets. Finch is becoming distraught. Jenny says she and Sir Henry were in conference for nearly two hours.

There was a note from Franklin. He hopes I will soon be better (they are giving out that I am ill) and missed me at the Mivens. He left a bouquet. Finch put it in her room, says Jenny.

22 June, Wednesday
It is all over. Finch announced today that if I do not spend more time than seemly with this one young man, they shall permit him to call. I have won! I am jubilant! I put on my most becoming at-home dress: blue-and-white striped silk scalloped over a double-flounced skirt with bishop sleeves. Cotton and I presided over the usual circle, with the addition of the Hon. George Grasston, Chloe's old suitor. Sir Henry and Lady Molliton were both present to see that I did not lavish my charm on Franklin. To please them, I relegated him to the farthest corner of the room, among the potted palms in the bay window, and encouraged Cotton to worry at his feet. He seemed puzzled and a little hurt. I think this will be good for him. He has been too cavalier of late.

23 June, Thursday
Dance at the Beverwils. Henry Beverwil, the oldest son, and his younger brother, Augustus, are both head over heels for me. Poor Franklin! I would not speak to him. Lady Molliton is very proud of me for my graceful handling of the snub. Oh, the hypocrisy of these people!

103

There are a great many more entries in this vein, cataloging parties and callers. I have chosen only those I believe are important in view of later events —Jenny Steward

29 June, Wednesday
Both Henry and Augustus Beverwil were here mooning over me. Franklin looks sadder and sadder. I had Jack Croydon write in my album and accepted Henry Beverwil's flowers. One defection, the Hon. George Grasston. I suppose little Miss Farraday is too common for the noble Mudlarks.

Franklin tried to entertain with an anecdote about the bald men he sees going into the wigmaker's shop beneath his lodgings who emerge with full heads of hair hours later. He imitated their furtive gait as they enter and the way they shoot rabbit-like out the door when they depart, pausing in the street to adjust their attitude, and then marching off with a swagger. Sir Henry was not amused. I wonder if he will avail himself of these services.

30 June, Thursday
This afternoon Jenny and I walked Cotton near St. James's Park. I saw the wigmaker's shop and my dear Franklin's windows above. Was he there? He did not emerge. Perhaps he is baffled by my apparent change of heart.

1 July, Friday
Franklin was being pompous, as usual, about my cavalier treatment of my suitors. I teased him about his jealousy, and he went off quite miffed. So I followed him into the library—we were at the Beverwils— and confessed that I had been ignoring him only to mislead my guardians.

"But surely you did not need to seem so cold!" was his complaint.

"Please, believe me. It was for the best," I replied. "Their suspicions have been allayed. They need never know the nature of what exists between us." I turned to him, my hands trembling, my eyes fixed to his own. For what seemed an eternity we were frozen, our gazes locked. Suddenly he shook himself. "I almost kissed you," he muttered hoarsely, freeing his hands from mine.

"I want you to," I said.

He stared at me stricken. For a wild moment, I thought he might turn and run. Then he crushed me in his arms and smothered my lips with his. It was magic! I could have remained so forever!

When we returned to the drawing room, I was afraid that Lady Molliton could see that I had been kissed, but I had forgotten her total passion for card playing. She did not emerge from the whist room for several hours. She has become increasingly lax due to my good behaviour.

2 July, Saturday

Sir Henry pressed me again to make our engagement public. I think he is becoming afraid that all the adulation I am receiving will turn me away from him.

I put him off by saying that I still felt unequal to the social challenges involved in being his wife.

He seemed flattered by this, but asked again for a lock of my hair. I gave him a flower from my corsage instead. He placed it gently in his buttonhole. He thought I did not see him bring it to his lips first.

3 July, Sunday

A great adventure! I visited Franklin at his lodgings. He seemed terrified when he opened his door to see me on the threshold.

"My God! You cannot come here!" he cried.

Chapter Twelve

"Why not?" I asked calmly, stepping around him. "No one has seen me, and I have Cotton here to protect my virtue."

Cotton, to demonstrate his ferocity, licked Franklin's boot.

"If you were seen—your reputation—you must leave!" stammered Franklin.

"A fine way to greet your lover," I said calmly, sweeping the books off an armchair and settling in.

"But, Miss Arabella, you know I have never indicated—"

"Do you think I cannot tell how you feel about me from the way you speak to me, the way you kiss me?" I answered, my eyes shining.

He ran his hands through his hair like a man tormented. I guess my mere presence was enough to drive him to distraction.

"What a pretty view!" I said, getting up and going to peer out of the window over the desk, strewn with papers and the remains of candies. "One can see just a little corner of the Park."

"Stay away from the window!" he shouted, dashing over to propel me away. I turned and fell straight into his embrace. His arms trembled; his face was drawn as if he were in pain.

"My God, you must leave at once!" he said. "You little know what sort of man, what manner of temptation—good Lord!" His speech was broken. "That I should even mention these things to you. I am not worthy of you, of any woman. You cannot trust me to behave as a gentleman ought."

"I trust in our love and the Lord who has guided us to it," I said. "He could not have brought us together if love was wrong!"

Franklin sank down in the armchair and buried his head in his arms. When he looked up his eyes were full of tears.

"If I could believe in love..." he said with great difficulty. "I don't think I have ever known it."

I understood in an instant. My darling, with his usual thoughtfulness and sensitivity and introspection, was holding himself back for fear that his love would cause me great harm.

"I will show you how to love," I cried, crossing the room in a flash and enfolding him in my arms. He wept and struggled like a naughty child until at last he fell quiet in my embrace, his cheek wet with tears against my bosom.

"I want to believe," he said fiercely. "I have wanted to believe all my life, but it has been taken from me." Now his hands gripped my arms like pincers. I exulted in the pain. "Will you teach me? Will you show me the way?" And then he kissed me, a man's kiss for a woman, a kiss full of passion and blood and fire.

"You have made me yours," I said after that fierce kiss. "I am yours forever, to do with what you will."

I saw the doubt cross his brow again. He dropped his hands, and I kissed him then, the kiss of a woman for the man she loves, a kiss of gentleness and succour, of hope and trust in the power of love.

4 July, Monday
I saw him today at the Mivens. What a world of difference! From across the room I could feel his presence as if I were still in his arms! When he spoke, it seemed the merest nonsense, but it contained all the hopes and joys of a lifetime!

I am taking great care not to arouse Lady Molliton's suspicions. I drove Henry Beverwil nearly mad with my flirtation.

3 July, Tuesday
Franklin and I laughed at the bald men scuttling into the wigmaker's shop. Oh, wouldn't it be a lark if I saw Sir Henry going in and he didn't know that I stood above him in the arms of my lover.

Jenny wants to know where I was this afternoon. She says my gown smells of tobacco. I couldn't tell her that I lit my Franklin's pipe for him and made him show me how he sits and smokes it in the evening when he is all alone. I am determined to be a dutiful little wife to him. I smuggled home one of his shirts and am going to sit up and mend it once Jenny goes to bed. Oh, how I wish I was better at plain work!

6 July, Wednesday
Henry Beverwil made a great fool of himself this afternoon, showering me with lavish compliments, writing the most sentimental nonsense in my album. Franklin and I could barely take our eyes off each other, but no one seemed to notice.

This evening we had a little *tête-à-tête* supper in his lodgings with food sent in from the pastry cook's. I was at the Hollys, but I left a message for Lady Molliton—affixed to her whist table—that I was taken with a headache and had gone home. Franklin and I ate by candlelight. I carved the mutton and poured his wine for him. In the midst of it we were struck with the giggles, and I nearly choked myself on a piece of meat. How would he have explained my death in his rooms, I wondered. "You should have to kill yourself, too," I said, "so they would think it a tragic suicide: two lovers kept apart by foolish family prejudices who decided to die together rather than be separated for even a moment."

Franklin became rather melancholy, and not all of my coaxing would lighten his weary heart. His kiss when I left lacked its usual ardour.

9 July, Saturday
A party of us attended a dance given by Henry Molliton's regiment. Who should be there but Philip Vandeleur! I tried to ignore him, but he showered me with the most marked attentions despite my refusal to dance with him or let him bring me some refreshments. I fear he was in his cups.

At last I asked Lady Molliton to take me home. I am curled up in bed with the windows open. The night is warm, and the sky full of stars. Oh, if only I could be with my Franklin in his lonely room!

10 July, Sunday

All is chaos! Apparently, Philip Vandeleur said something to Henry Molliton, who spoke to his mother, who went straight to Sir Henry and then washed her hands of me. Sir Henry arrived here, purple in the face and absolutely bloated with rage. He took one look at me, sewing quietly in the sitting room, and said, "Young lady, go find your so-called guardian, that Finch person, and send her to me in the library at once! And make yourself scarce! I have no desire to see you in my present mood." He was sputtering. He could barely deliver his words.

I guessed what had happened and fled upstairs to drag Finch away from her sermons. I could not resist listening at the door. It seems that Finch is to take the blame for my misadventures of the spring. Sir Henry accused her of not taking her duties seriously, of undermining my moral upbringing by her laxness and, paradoxically I thought, of sending me flying into the arms of adventurers because of her repressive practices and lack of sympathy for my sensitive nature. Finch was not proof against his vehement denunciations. She shortly gave up explanations and gave herself over to tears, which seemed to enrage him even more.

"How she is to finish the Season, I don't know!" shrieked Sir Henry. "Without a chaperone! Subject to the depredations of fortune hunters and cads! You are not fit to take her into decent company, not that I could trust you to do so." Finch snivelled away. "Thank God, Lady Molliton is a respectable woman and would no more spread this story, which would bring discredit upon herself, than I. But what of her son? No, we must make some excuse. Say that she has been taken ill. You are all to go off to Pittlesbury Hall at once! I will not have her exposed to the corruptions of London life without adequate protection. You must prepare to go immediately!"

I wandered away from the door in a daze. What was to happen to all of my suitors, to pathetic Lionel Holly and the ingratiating Jack Croydon? What was to become of my Franklin? I poked my head into the drawing room, full of floral tributes to my charms, and turned over the pages of my album, reading the paeans written to my eyes, my grace, my wit.

A door slammed upstairs, and I knew where I must go: to inform Franklin of this dreadful turn of events, to ask his advice. Without pausing for a mantle, I fled and was soon hammering on the door of Franklin's room, sobbing and out of breath. Thank God, he was there!

He opened the door and drew me tenderly in, settling me in the armchair, drying my tears with his hands, and waiting patiently for me to speak.

I hardly knew where to begin. I could not confess the sordid story of Philip Vandeleur, but my grief made omissions plausible; I merely indicated that someone had spread a vicious rumour about me (I hinted that it was Henry Molliton, chagrined at my lack of response to his overtures), that Lady Molliton chose to believe it, and that I was to be sent to the country at once.

Franklin was magnificent. He sent away for tea and, clearing a space on his desk, fed me like an invalid, spooning the refreshing brew between my lips. He chafed my trembling hands.

"What am I to do?" I moaned. "I cannot live without you, Franklin!"

"It is difficult, my dear Bella," he said, "but we shall be able to see each other next Season, and till then we can correspond."

I was shaken to my very core. Could he really put me off so easily? I think it was then that I realized what I must do. I must put his love to the test. I must make our love as sacred and awesome to him as it was to me.

I did not know quite how to proceed, but then I considered I could make good use of my practice upon the blacksmith's apprentice and Philip Vandeleur. I pressed myself full against him. I allowed my skirts to become discomposed so he caught a glimpse of my trim, stockinged legs. I breathed softly in his ear, as Philip Vandeleur had done in mine.

All of these gambits affected him. Throughout that long dizzying embrace, I could feel his excitement mounting. But still he strove to exercise his self-control. He pushed me away and turned his back, pressing his head into his hands.

"My dear!" I cried, all unconscious. "What is wrong? Have I done something to hurt you?" And I crept back into his embrace. The long struggle began again, on my part to vanquish his misgivings, on his to resist his growing desperation. His breath was coming quickly now, and for a time he buried his face against my shoulder and gave way to his urges. But then once more he broke loose and cried hoarsely, "Lord God, give me strength!"

I was sorely vexed. Only a minute longer and perhaps…. Then I had a happy thought. I threw myself down upon his bed and gave quite a good impression of a hysterical fit. I had little need of my usual flair for dramatics; I was quite close to actual hysterics from the gnawing tension and discomfort I felt.

He came to me then, all solicitude and eagerness to help. It was as if we were magnetized to each other, and every touch only brought us nearer to our need for closer constellation. In a moment, we were in each other's arms, kissing each other, calling each other Dearest, fondling each other, and surrendering all thought of self-control.

I was a little afraid at the last, but I refused to show it for fear he would pause and, in his hesitation, reflect on what deed we were about to commit. So I bit my lip and gave myself up to him completely. And in a moment what had seemed the strangest thing on earth seemed the most desirable and miraculous.

He cannot leave me now, for I can say that I am truly, in name as well as spirit, my Franklin's wife.

All is ready for our departure. I write this as the trunks are being hoisted in the carriage. I saw Franklin once more, and we renewed our sweet contract. He gave me a ring he has always worn, a ring that was his father's. I have it now on a chain around my neck, the chain that used to bear Sir Henry's locket.

Oh, God, how I love my love! I would tear out my heart and give it to him on a platter, still quivering and bloody, if he requested it. I cannot bear this separation, though he is to follow us to Sussex in a few days. My nerves are shattered; I see every mishap, every cold glance, as a dagger aimed at me. I could not bear the pain of separation, and so I burned my fingers in the candle flame. I told Finch it was an accident. Who would believe I could do such a thing deliberately? But I did! It eased the pain of my heart a little with all the fuss of doctors and the bandaging and the partaking of laudanum. Even now my fingers throb as a reminder of my commitment to Franklin and my willingness to suffer anything for him!

He has written me the sweetest of letters. They are models of discretion, but I read between the lines and see there the secret knowledge that we share.

I hear the last call. Tonight I will be at Pittlesbury Hall again, and soon my darling will be there. He has vowed never to leave me again!

18 July, Monday

How shall I bear it till Franklin is here? He writes, but I cannot feel reassured by mere words. I need his arms, his lips…

Another nightmare last night: A woman in white was pursuing me with a long, bloody carving knife. She had already killed my mother and my father and Franklin. I saw their bleeding corpses lying in the snow. And now she was after me, cackling and howling, her long black hair flying behind her.

I hate Sussex. There is nothing to look at, no one to talk to.

25 July, Monday

How delightful is the countryside when I am with my husband. I have taken him to all my favourite places; how they are transformed by his presence! The miracle of our love makes even the meanest bower a palace! It is a magic that's indescribable; suddenly there is a sparkle to the world!

He was most concerned about my burned fingers. When I tried to explain that I had done it deliberately, he seemed horrified and uneasy. I fear my love is greater than his! Ah, well, love is always unequal. I quickly dissimulated and said that it was purely accidental, the result of carelessness occasioned by my dreamy state of mind.

He has rented the vacant cottage belonging to Widow Morrison, close to the old mill and the river. She is aware of my visits, but she believes he is a poet working on a new volume and that I am his sister, the new governess at the Hall. Everyone knows of Finch's serious illness.

The Widow Morrison stopped me this afternoon when I was leaving and said she was worried about my brother and his late hours. I told her this was how all poets worked and that if she would see that he was well fed and his rooms kept clean, I would visit him daily and attempt to lift his spirits.

"That's very good of you, miss," she said, "seeing as how you must be kept right busy up at the Hall. I hear that Miss Arabella's a handful."

"Oh, she's no trouble to me!" I said airily.

"They say she's wild," she went on eagerly. "There was talk about her and that no-good scoundrel of a soldier—"

I frowned as sternly as I could. "Your sordid little tale," I said, "only illustrates the contemptible nature of gossip. That particular rumour was completely unfounded in fact. I hope you don't worry Mr. De—my brother with such nonsense. He requires absolute peace of mind while he's creating."

"Oh, I don't, miss: I don't," she said with a curtsy. I had a good laugh about this afterward.

28 July, Thursday

Dr Potter told me that Finch is dying of consumption. She needs the sun of Italy or the clear air of the Alps to clear her lungs of the fluid.

I forgot to mention that she collapsed shortly after we arrived in Pittlesbury. I, of course, have not seen fit to complain about this. I write to Sir Henry and convey the impression that she has been most vigilant as to my welfare.

Of course, Finch cannot afford to seek a cure in the South on her small, though generous income. I assume she would lose it entirely if she left my employ. (How ironic that I am her employer and yet her slave!)

Dr Potter suggests that we go abroad for the autumn. This I will not do unless I am with Franklin on our honeymoon, and then why would we want Finch along?

Still her eyes were most beseeching when I went up to see her. She looks terrible; her face is waxy, her lips dry and cracked. When she coughs her whole body is convulsed. I know she fears that she will die unless I agree to travel.

It made me quite cross. What an unpleasant position in which to find myself. If I refuse, they will call me a heartless monster and perhaps I shall be held accountable for Finch's death, though Heaven knows she will die anyway, and if she were employed more conventionally her employer would simply turn her out. If I do agree to go, I shall lose my only happiness, the point of my existence.

I told Franklin my dilemma.

"There is no question," he said. We were in a boat on the Cuckmere. I wore my straw hat with the green ribbons and my green tarlatan gown. The sun beat down unmercifully, and the only sound was the splash of the oars in the water and the occasional noise of some water creature surfacing in search of food. "You must go. You cannot have that woman's death on your hands."

"But, Franklin," I protested. "How do you suppose I could leave you? I would rather die."

He put down the oars and rubbed his shoulders. "You know, I haven't been in a boat since I left Oxford."

"Franklin, you are not attending to me!" I said flinging a handful of water in his face. He threw back his head, gasping and laughing, then eyed me maliciously, one hand in the water.

"Don't you dare to splash me in return," I said sternly. "You will quite spoil my new gown. Now, answer me! What am I to do?"

"When are we to be married?" he asked seriously, bending forward a little. "Tell me the answer, and I will help you solve this other problem. You must realize we cannot go on like this."

"Why not?" I wanted to know. I find I have a great need for secrets. This life of intrigue and clandestine passions suits me. I feel alive as never before! I am acutely sensitive to every nuance of tone and gesture. I view the people about me with a clear and discerning eye.

"Because your reputation would be ruined if it were known," he said solemnly.

"And so what?" I asked lightly. "I should be condemned to marry you as you would be the only man who would have me, and that is just what I wish."

"Then let us marry," he said. "I cannot abide all of this sneaking about and lying and disguising our true feelings. Why can't I call at the Hall? Why can't we post the banns? My dear," he tried to make a joke, but the solemnity of his voice made it fall flat, "I long to make an honest woman of you.

"There are still a few obstacles to be gotten over," I said, "but I promise you it will not be long before you can call me Mrs. DeWinx!"

He blanched a little bit—I wonder if he thought of his mother, who had recently remarried and was no longer Mrs. DeWinx—and I splashed him again. In the subsequent frolic we upset the boat, and he carried me out of the chilly waters laughing and spluttering. We had to retreat into a willow grove and put our clothes out to dry on the riverbank. Oh, I shall never forget that afternoon! It was like being in the Garden of Paradise, both of us so innocent and free and so deeply in love!

2 August, Tuesday

Sir Henry has said all along that once London is empty he will join us here. Now he writes that he will be with us in about a week's time.

It means the end of my idyllic paradise with Franklin, but perhaps just the commencement of one that will last a lifetime.

I have begun preparing Sir Henry in my letters. There is something most important that I must discuss with him, I am afraid it will hurt him who is my dearest friend, *et cetera, et cetera*. His responses are becoming more and more disjointed and dictatorial. He demands to know why Finch has not yet given him any account of our days.

8 August, Monday

A last picnic with Franklin. We walked up to the top of the Downs. It took hours, but the view was worth the effort. We could see clear to the sea.

"Soon we will be on the other side," I said and began to cry. We had a silly quarrel. Franklin is so very jealous of Sir Henry. He was so affected by the fact that we were fighting that he actually became physically ill. I spent nearly the entire night caring for him.

A sudden thunderstorm came over shortly before dawn. How sweet it was to lie in my husband's arms and listen to the rain beating on the roof overhead and the wind howling at the panes!

10 August, Wednesday

Storms of a different nature. Sir Henry was furious at Finch's illness and the fact he had not been informed. She is much worse; Dr Potter was here for hours.

During dinner Sir Henry demanded to know my urgent problem. I said I would discuss it over tea in the drawing room. I made sure that he was well supplied with wine throughout the meal and given a generous serving of brandy after I withdrew.

I had arranged things perfectly. I had only a few candles lit and a fire burning on the hearth. I was wearing my pink silk gown and the topaz necklace and earrings that Sir Henry had given me and was sitting on the footstool gazing into the flames.

Perhaps it was not so well thought out after all.

He came up behind me, and when I turned around, he went down on his knees and pressed a kiss upon my lips. How different it was from being kissed by Franklin! I was aghast, and I guess my countenance reflected my shock.

He apologized and went to stand in front of the fire, his favourite position.

"It is just that you are so beautiful, my dear Arabella," he said humbly, "and I have been waiting patiently for over four years."

"Sir Henry, that is what I wished to discuss with you," I spoke up. It was the time to face the matter squarely. "I have given your… your offer the most careful consideration and I fear…I regret—" my voice grew softer "—that I cannot become your wife."

He stared like a man dealt a death blow.

"You cannot…" he said hoarsely. "You have promised me! My God, you cannot mean it!"

"I am afraid I do," I said gently, going over and putting my hand on his arm. "It is not that I am unconscious of the great honour you bestow me."

"What is it then?" he asked. "What possible reason could you have?" I had never dreamed he would be so desperate. I hesitated. "It is not that you don't care for me?" he said pathetically, abjectly.

"Oh, no, I do care for you," I said.

"Or that you fear you are not equal to the position you would hold," he went on. "You handled yourself quite well in London.

Lady Molliton gave the most glowing reports as to your assurance and affability."

"No, it isn't that," I confessed.

"Then, there is nothing!" he said triumphantly. He was the eminent lawyer again. Having proved his case, he stood beaming, legs apart, face glowing.

I turned away. How was I to tell him?

"What is it?" His voice worried me and disturbed the mazes through which I pursued my thoughts. "There can be no other reason. We can set the date tonight. That is the reason for my visit. I brought you this." He fumbled in his pocket and brought forth a gleaming topaz-and-gold ring, which glowed sullenly by the light of the fire as if lit from within.

"It is beautiful," I said.

"It is yours," was his reply. "Put it on. We will post the banns next Sunday in the Pittlesbury church. We will be married in three weeks time, will go abroad and take Miss Finch with us. I have finished all my work in London. I can afford to be gone until Michaelmas term."

For a moment, I was sorely tempted. Oh, if only I could substitute Franklin for this middle-aged solicitor, I would happily agree.

I began to cry. Why was I doomed to handle this horrible scene by myself? Why did I not have a loving mother to shield me from the tumult I knew would come, a mother who would simply inform Sir Henry that her daughter's interest was already given elsewhere?

"I cannot love you," I said defiantly, spitting out the words. Oh, that was not how I planned to deliver the fatal blow. "I cannot love you because I love another. I have given my heart to him and need only your permission to marry him."

"You will never have it!" thundered Sir Henry, his eyes blazing. He did not even pause to reflect; how unlike him! The veins on his neck stood out, and his hands clenched convulsively.

"I will marry him without it!" I retorted.

"Then you will lose your fortune," said Sir Henry with greater self-control. "You will lose this estate and the house in Grover Square."

I felt as if someone had knocked the wind out of me. I stood gasping like a fish out of water.

"Who is he?" asked Sir Henry in a dull voice. "Some one of the young men you met in London? That scoundrel soldier?"

"It is someone I knew before then," I said with quiet dignity.

"Who is it? By God, I will know!" He approached me, hands upraised as if he would choke the truth out of me. I considered screaming for help, but what was the difference? He must know sometime.

"My cousin," I said dully. "My cousin, Franklin DeWinx. We have pledged ourselves to each other."

There was a long silence. We were both breathing heavily as if we had been locked in mortal combat. I suppose that, in a manner of speaking, we were.

"He shall not have you," he said at last. "You are mine. Your father gave you to me on his deathbed. You have been meant for me since you were quite young. By, God, I should have married you then."

I said nothing. What could I say?

"He has mesmerized you," Sir Henry went on. "He has flattered and misled you. Being young, you don't recognize the wiles of a fortune hunter. Can't you see what the attraction is for him? What does he have? No income, a paltry allowance, no future, no connections, a mere hanger-on in Society! How can you consider such a…a detrimental when I stand before you, offering my heart to you, my maturity, my good sense, my stable career, my unsullied name, my impeccable connections, my sound understanding of business and financial investments?"

"He is not interested in my money," I said stubbornly. "We have never discussed it." Unwillingly though I remembered the times we had discussed Franklin's dreams for the future, all of which seemed to require an initial outlay of a substantial sum.

"Of course, he would not let you see it!" declared Sir Henry triumphantly. He was rapidly regaining his usual arrogant air. "His plot would be ruined if he did so. It is the way with all such parasites. Only inform him that you will not inherit more than a pittance if I do not give my consent—and I will not—and watch how fast he runs!"

"Miss Finch has given me her consent," I put in quickly.

"Which is worthless," Sir Henry pointed out, "without mine. Miss Finch is a poor, deluded old woman, and so I shall inform her as soon as I have an opportunity to speak with her about this matter.

If I discover that she has been at all remiss in her duties—and I suspect there must have been gross negligence in order for you to have formed this attachment for your cousin—then I shall see that her income is stopped and another guardian appointed. That annuity she receives represents a great drain on your estate."

"Sir Henry," I pointed out indignantly, "we are discussing love, not money. I love Franklin, and I don't give a damn for my fortune." Which was not entirely true.

He flinched at my use of profanity.

"Miss Arabella," he said, moistening his lips with the tip of his tongue, "such language is execrable in a young woman. I trust it is an aberration due to your present mental state. As for love and money, they are much more closely allied than you believe. Your heart, or rather your fancy, can mend, but you cannot regain a fortune by wishing it so."

There was no answering him. I turned and left the room. Now I am shivering and shivering, unable to stop. What am I to do? Oh, if only Franklin were here! I am so miserable!

Chapter Thirteen

11 August, Thursday

I could not resist. I said I would not go to him until matters had been settled, whereupon I would send a message telling him to call at the Hall. But I could not stand firm. I went to Franklin.

He quelled my tears with sweet caresses. "What is wrong? What is it?" he wanted to know.

In broken words nearly obscured by sobs, I related my conversation with Sir Henry. He went quite pale. This frightened me even more. Could Sir Henry be right?

"You cannot abandon me now!" I cried.

"But what are we to do?" he asked.

"We can elope," I said. "Yes, let's elope. Let's leave tomorrow."

"But, Arabella." He was all seriousness. I hate him when he goes into this mood. "It would not do. I have only the smallest income, a trust from my mother's share of my father's estate, and it is not enough for me, much less two. And...and any children we might wish to have. My grandfather supplements it now, but I am afraid he, too, would cut off any assistance if I married you."

"You can take up some profession," I said abjectly. "I would help you."

"And what profession do you have in mind?" he asked grimly. "I am unsuited to be a clergyman. Once I thought to take orders, but that is beyond me now. I cannot go into law; I have tried it, and the effort was too much: the hypocrisy, the cant, the toadying that goes with it disgusted me. And as for a clerical position in the Government, I could not put my mind to it. I was dismissed. Can you imagine the disgrace? Dismissed!"

"The Army," I suggested.

"I have no money for the commission," he said bitterly. "No, without money there is no honourable profession I can enter. I am afraid you have chosen badly. You should have fallen in love with a man. I am only half a man."

"What is it that you do with all of your books and your papers?" I asked, grasping at straws.

"I study," he said flatly, "different subjects that amuse and interest me."

"You could write!"

"Do you think I haven't tried?" He turned on me as if I were the enemy. "My poems were sneered at; my extended work following in my father's footsteps was condemned as cheap plagiarism. Oh, God, how could I have led you into this? Will you forgive me? Can you begin to forgive me?"

"There is a way. I know there is a way," I said. I was the calm one now. "Sir Henry must be brought to give his approval. I will kill myself if he will not. Never fear, Franklin, my beloved husband, we will be married."

"And I shall be your pet husband, a sort of useless appendage, like the tailbone in a man," he said sardonically.

I slapped him. "Never say that!" I commanded. "I hate you when you are sarcastic! Wait here for some word from me."

My God, my God, what am I to do?

12 August, Friday

I am determined to make Sir Henry realize that he is killing me. It is not difficult. I burst into tears every time he looks at me. I refuse to eat. He is becoming quite agitated.

I went up to visit Finch. I told her that I would marry Franklin soon and take her south to the sun. She seemed so grateful. She asked if I could read to her from the book of sermons by her bedside. I began to weep while reading a passage on God's Love and Mercy, and she touched me, ever so gently, with her dry, timid hand. I kissed her brow and left, to stand staring out over the fields from the window of my mother's room. From this vantage, I can see Franklin's cottage. There are no lights in his windows. Can it be that he has fled, as Sir Henry predicted?

14 August, Sunday

I would not go to church. I said I was feeling unwell. In fact, I almost fainted yesterday while at dinner with Sir Henry. He had to help me lie down on the sofa in the drawing room. Sir Henry went to the services alone.

Jenny came scurrying into my room like a frightened rabbit. "Franklin was in church this morning!" she said. "Sir Henry saw him. They almost came to blows afterward."

Oh, Franklin, why did you go? I know you are not a believer. Did you hope to see me? How could you take such a foolish risk?

Sir Henry was, of course, livid.

"Are you aware of that man's presence in this district?" he said, bursting into my bedroom.

"Who? What?" I said, looking up wanly from my pillow.

"That DeWinx rascal!" he spluttered. "He had the effrontery to appear in church. I told him soundly that if he was not gone by tomorrow I would notify the local authorities that he is here plotting to abduct an heiress."

"I did not know…" I murmured.

"Well, no matter," said Sir Henry. "He promised me he should leave."

I could not disguise my terror.

"You said you did not know he was here!" declared Sir Henry, frowning. "Does he have such a hold on you?"

I guess I swooned. When I came to my senses, Sir Henry and Jenny were waving scorched feathers before my nose and pinching my arms.

"I'm sorry," I said. "I feel so weak." And I burst into tears. The doctor was coming to see Miss Finch, and Sir Henry had him look at me.

"A broken heart?" I heard him say to Sir Henry in the hall. "It will heal. She needs rest and time. A change of scene will do her good."

Later that horrible day, Sir Henry suggested that we go to the South first and get married in London at Christmas. I tried to protest, but he fondly put my health and Finch's before any practical considerations.

15 August, Monday

Now I have done it! I thought for a moment Sir Henry would kill me, then that he would kill Franklin! But when I threatened to poison myself, he stopped all of his angry threats and tried to soothe me.

Last night I could not sleep, remembering what Sir Henry had said about Franklin leaving. Could he have meant it? Then Jenny brought up a note. It said only,

> Arabella,
>
> I must go for now. My presence here is only a torture to both of us. I will be in touch with you shortly.
>
> Your cousin, Franklin

I tried to conceal my shock from her. When she had left, I dressed myself and ran all the way to Franklin's cottage.

It was true! He was leaving! All of his belongings were packed. His engravings were gone from the walls, his books vanished from the table. He was feeding some papers to the fire.

"Franklin, you cannot leave me!" I cried, bursting across the room. "You cannot. I will kill myself. I shall throw myself into the river! I will take poison! Oh, God, I cannot exist without you!"

He was not the same. He looked at me as if I were a different person altogether. He even trembled a little when I came close to him.

"You must see," he said, "that it is impossible. Sir Henry will not give his consent. We shall never be married. I have ruined you and cannot redeem you or myself. Oh God, oh God!"

"Franklin!" I pleaded. "Remember our love. It will carry us through this if you believe in it. You promised you would believe. You said you would trust me."

"I think," he muttered brokenly, "that it is impossible for me. Some defect in temperament! Some constitutional malady! I cannot give myself up like you! I cannot believe! I tremble on the brink…

but I never…quite fall! If I could—oh, God, what I would give to do so…even for an instant!"

"But you have! You surely have!" I protested.

He looked at me, his blue eyes full of misery and self-reproach. "I have deluded you and myself," he said with a sigh. "Can you forgive me?"

I was frightened as I have never been frightened before. What had we meant to each other? What had happened to our troth, our love, if he insisted on denying it?

"I will make you love me!" I said fiercely, and smothered him with caresses. I was quite unaware at first that he was completely unresponsive. I stopped and looked up into his face, which appeared bland.

"Is it over?" I asked wildly. "Is there nothing left?"

He shook his head mutely.

"No, it cannot be so!" I snatched up the wineglass that sat on the table, went to the fire and smashed it against the fender, then held up a large jagged shard to my throat.

"There is nothing left for me but death!" I announced, watching his eyes to see if any spark of concern, of caring would surface.

"Arabella! My God! Don't!" he exclaimed. "You are mad!" And suddenly he began to shake all over, and he was overwhelmed with sobs. What was I to do with my weapon? I wondered. I did not really wish to cut my throat, but he would not stop me.

He looked up through his tears and saw me, poised, brandishing the sharp fragment, and in a flash, he scrambled back, knocking over the chair, holding up his hands as if to ward me off. How could he act as if I would hurt him, my beloved? His terror enraged me. Not having had any intention to do so previously, I then stalked him like the madwoman he believed me to be. It was a wordless battle, a sort of silent minuet. He stumbled over the fallen chair and lay sprawled on the floor, babbling in fear. His very fear was what drove me on.

And then the mists cleared from my eyes. I threw away the glassy dagger. It tinkled and shattered as it fell to the floor.

"My own husband!" I said. "Do you think I would hurt you? You are more to me than life itself!" He shuddered like someone waking from a bad dream.

"You must leave!" he said harshly. "You will be missed. This is madness!"

"Not until you say you love me!"

"I love you!" he replied tonelessly.

"Then prove it to me!" I declared.

"Good Lord, Arabella. You cannot mean it!"

"I do. I will not leave until you prove that you love me!"

He took me in his arms, trembling a little, and kissed me timidly.

"That will not do," I said. "Must I teach you again?" But there was nothing in it. He was as cold and limp as a fish floundering on the bank. I tried to awaken some of the old fire in him, and when I could not I began to weep. While I was huddled on the floor in a sodden heap, crying my eyes out, he fell asleep. He snored a little. The new day began, birds chirped outside. The chill new light fell upon his flesh, making it appear grey, as if he were a corpse.

I got up and, in a fury, tore apart his suitcase. I tore up his engravings, slashed his books with his razor. I threw his clothes, his brush and comb, his boots down the hill in back of the cottage. Finding his writing set, I scratched out a brief note:

> You shall not leave! Our love is real and terrible. Any slight to it will be avenged by me!

Then I started home, weeping with fear and exhaustion, stumbling on the gravel drive. But I was too late! Sir Henry was waiting for me!

I cannot even repeat the things he said. They ring even now in my head. Somehow, he got the notion that Franklin had convinced me to elope and that suffering from apprehension, I had turned back. This seemed as likely, an explanation as any so I did not contradict it.

"I did come back," I said, "because I saw I could not go through with it unless I had your approval. You are my dearest friend, the only parent I have in the world. If you will not give me your permission, I will not marry, but I will not live either. I cannot bear my life if I cannot be with him."

Sir Henry's response was to send me to my room like a wayward child. I asked Jenny to fetch me some rat poison from the chemist in Taunceton. She refused, stupid girl.

"I don't mean to use it, Jenny," I said shaking her "I just want to frighten Sir Henry a little!"

But she continued in her defiance. She had the temerity to suggest that Sir Henry is right, that I should allow the heated emotions of the moment a chance to die down before I choose any course of action.

She shall not prevent me. I know that Finch keeps the poisons in a locked cupboard in the housekeeper's room.

18 August, Thursday

I have been very ill. I meant only to frighten Sir Henry, but I took too much of the paregoric. It was Finch's medicine. I could not find the key to the poison cupboard.

They could barely rouse me. Luckily, Jenny checked on me before she went to bed and knew immediately what had happened. Dr Potter prescribed alternate hot and cold baths and an emetic. I did not want to emerge from the pleasant dreamland in which I wandered. My mother was there in a castle made of ice, crooning a strange lullaby with no words. I wish I could remember the melody.

19 August, Friday

Victory! I cannot arise, but I sent a message to Franklin! We can be married! Sir Henry has given his consent.

It was not without a struggle. Sir Henry wishes me to go abroad with him and Finch, and then Franklin and I shall be married upon my return. He has been up to London this morning and has gotten names of physicians. He wishes us to have a personal doctor along to help build up my shattered strength and to make Finch's last days easier. He also has some qualms about the terms of the will. He thinks that if we draw up a paper saying that I give my fortune over to him, he will be able to divert it to my own needs through his personal account. I have already signed the paper that says that upon my marriage to Franklin the money shall go to Sir Henry Warder-Mull. I suppose he plans to take a generous commission for himself, indeed he wants me to give him Pittlesbury Hall *in toto*, but what do I care? I have my Franklin to be with through eternity.

Sometimes I wonder if I went too far in my endeavours to have things my own way, but now that I see it is all as I wished, I feel proud and triumphant! My Heaven is here, right now!

My mind is busy with images of velvet wedding gowns, brides-maids, our first nights together as man and wife in a cosy hunting lodge surrounded by falling snow. During my travels, I will read up on all the histories of the places we visit so that I can discuss with my husband all of his pet passions. Oh, how wonderful to be able to call him that before the world! And my mother shall come to the wedding. She will be my guest of honour, and all of London will know her as she really is!

Where is Jenny? I sent her to Franklin an hour past. Surely it should not take this long!

Voices. I hear voices in the hall, strangers' voices. They are discussing me! What new torment is this? I cannot bear another one! I am not able to survive!

Are they keeping Franklin from me? Have they sent him some-where? No, that is surely my imagination. I can sort this out if I con-tinue writing. Somehow my dreams form a pattern, which, if I could unravel them, would reveal the truth to me. Or is it that I must put them together like a puzzle?

Could Finch have died? Is that the undertaker? Oh, my poor governess! She tried so hard to be good to me, and I have never liked her. I cannot apologize for my feeling. There was nothing in her that was pleasing to me, what with her religious. enthusiasms, her other-worldly striving, her rigidity. And yet she was a good woman. Per-haps this is why I despised her so, for I am not good and goodness is an affront to me. An insult! I will not bear it! Her death is a release for me like my father's, not a further prison. She believes she goes to God! I guess she knows by now her Fate. And I? Where shall I go? Oh, I must be married to Franklin before I die, or all would be lost.

It is so hot in here. Am I becoming ill again? My mind is so acute, I cannot put down my pen, it races along the page. I am aware of the linen on my skin, the hair growing from my scalp, every blink of my eyes.

Where is that wretched Jenny? Has she stopped for some flirtation on the way? I think she has her eye on that young widower who holds the farm next to the Widow Morrison. Can't she understand my very existence is at stake?

The voices go away and then come back. It's as if they are in the room with me, but I cannot distinguish a word. It is nonsense! Are they evil spirits?

A step on the stairs. A scraping sound. Finch's coffin? No, it can't be. I imagined that. My God, will this not end? Am I doomed to sit here forever scribbling away, awaiting a word, a sweet acknowledgement from my Franklin?

Here it is—No! A rustle out in the hall. Is Pittlesbury haunted? What ghost walks here? Is it my mother?

They say he is gone, the cottage is empty. Only some broken glass remains. The floor is strewn with mutilated books. I will not believe it! He must have left some word for me! Perhaps he is hiding in the house and those were the noises I heard. Perhaps he will come to me this night while I lie here staring in my bed. Perhaps I should have killed him and then myself. At least we would be together.

My God, why have you forsaken me?

At this point Arabella's journal ends. This letter from Mr. DeWinx, which arrived the following day, is pasted onto the next page.
—*Jenny Steward.*

Southampton
15 August 1842

My Dear Arabella,
I did not tell you the whole truth when I said I was only half a man, when I said that I was not a believer, when I said I was not a gentleman, when I said I was a failure. No, the truth is that I am a coward.

It is my cowardice that prevents me from embracing something with conviction. It is my cowardice that holds me back from devoting my energies to any one pursuit. It is my cowardice that refutes the existence of Heaven and, with it, Hell. It is my cowardice that influences me when I pretend to return the love you so ardently feel.

It is my cowardice that dictates that I should be writing to you rather than speaking to you face-to-face, as a man would.

When you read this, I shall be gone. I have booked passage on a ship departing on the morrow for the West Indies. Maybe somewhere in that foreign land I will be able to determine the truth of this matter.

I cannot leave you with the words you wish to hear. I do not know, even now, if they are true. I know I believed I loved you for sometime.

I doubt that you can forgive me. However, I hope and pray that you can forget—

a miserable coward,
Franklin DeWinx

PART THREE

Mr. Franklin DeWinx:
Letter to Mr. Charles Lindley
22 August 1842

~ ~

Alas! the fearful Unbelief is unbelief in yourself.

Carlyle,
Sartor Resartus

Chapter One

R.M.S.P.C. *Tweed*
Atlantic Ocean 22
August 1842

My dear Charles,

As you may see by the superscription, I am no longer among the inhabitants of the "right little, tight little island," but rather fleeing as fast as this noisy creature, the *Tweed*, will carry me, in the face of monstrous headwinds and heavy seas, in the direction of Barbados. "Why Barbados?" you may ask, and indeed, it is an admirable question, one deserving, after due consideration, a thoughtful reply. Alas! Despite all due consideration, there is no thoughtful reply, merely the intelligence that on the day on which I found it imperative to leave England the Royal Mail Steam Packet Company's ship *Tweed* was the only vessel departing. "Then, why fleeing?" you probably are wondering. Another logical inquiry, and if I know you well, my friend, you are, as ever, logical. Will it seem too fanciful if I say I am being pursued by the *Erinyes*?

Do you remember when we read Aeschylus together at Eton, shortly after you became my tutor, how I complained of the peculiarly grim satisfaction the Greeks took in the principle of revenge? Well, it is no longer an academic question to me, to be argued with schoolboy vehemence and overblown rhetoric, for I feel myself, in truth, to be harried and hounded from my homeland. Perhaps like

Orestes I must endure a year's exile in order to expiate my sins. For if I were to define the forces that haunt me in terms more familiar to the British mind, I would have to say that I am being tormented by my conscience, my sins, my own self-doubts. It has been true for a very long time, and I think I believed that with this headlong pell-mell flight I should elude my pursuers. But instead they are more gleeful.

Dear friend, will you be, as you have been so often in the past, the mirror in which I can see myself and thereby regain my perspective? That way, instead of looking in the glass and seeing a monster dripping with gore, I will be able to gaze instead on a man—merely a man—sadder and wiser.

Of course, that is a rhetorical question, as you would take pleasure in pointing out to me if we were sitting in your chambers. You have no choice, except to put down this letter now and perhaps consign it to the fire that no doubt lights your domestic hearth. I hope all is well with Mary and the two girls. As for me, I shall continue nonetheless, since to pause does nothing but invite the black goddesses to fly at me again, shrieking and clawing at my flesh.

In your last letter, which has gone unanswered for so long, you asked how, my courtship of my cousin Arabella was proceeding. Did you mean to call it a courtship? (For I believe I had only mentioned that I had met a long-lost cousin and then, in another letter, that I saw her occasionally.) Did you guess that it was this acute question that has so discomposed my thoughts that I was unable to reply? For at the time I did not think of Arabella as a potential spouse (indeed the thought of marriage at all was abhorrent to me) and yet shortly thereafter we became husband and wife to each other in all but name.

I suppose I must go back a little in time to my first meeting with Arabella. I have given you no details as to her character or circumstances.

I first met my cousin Arabella in May 1841. Sometimes I wonder what would have been my response to that first meeting if I had been granted the power to see into the future and glimpse the misery that lay ahead. Surely, I would have taken the only sensible course of action open to me at that time. I would have gone back out the door of my grandfather's house and hurled myself into the howling fury of the rainstorm outside. Or would I? It is one of the most puzzling aspects of human nature that a man, spying a path that he knows leads to darkness follows it yet, perhaps in a vain attempt to prove that he can descend into the Stygian depths of Hades and emerge triumphant. But what if he fails? What an enormous price he pays, the price of his own Soul!

At any rate, Fate was not so kind to provide me with a vision of the future. The door had closed behind me, and I was helping my mother remove her rain-soaked mantle, when I noticed strangers in the hall. They were apparently being ejected by my aunt Portia, whose character I have previously delineated for you. One was a fair-haired, timid, lady-like girl, Lady Chloe Shale; you may recall her brother, Henry Fenton-Shale, Lord Temmary, who was, I believe, an Eton man. The other young woman was dark-haired and her eyes gleamed boldly; she glowed as if an inner fire consumed her. Somehow, she seemed more fully alive than anyone else in the room; her presence was awesome as if she were some pagan goddess suddenly incarnated in our midst, demanding an unspeakable obeisance and sacrifice.

At the outset, this elemental quality in Arabella simultaneously attracted and repulsed me. Having for years, as you know, felt my Soul to be a wintry landscape, frozen over with the ice of scepticism and despair, I longed to warm myself at her fire, to endeavour to learn the sources of her passion. I could then adopt them for myself.

But there were two great dangers in this strategy, the first being that the more captivated I became by her incandescence, the more acutely I felt my own dispassionate and cold nature.

The second problem was no less difficult. Think of a child who has never seen a fire, who knows not its composition and beholds for the first time a blaze in all its crackling cacophony, its splendour of motion and vivid colour. What would be the natural reaction of such a child? Why, he would run forward, heedless of the consequences, and be burnt, perhaps repeatedly, until he learned that it is the nature of fire to consume those who carelessly approach too close. What a thoughtless child I proved myself to be! For even though I knew the dangers, I was indefatigable in my attempts to immolate myself.

These thoughts came to me much later and after much bitter intro-spection. At the time I knew only that I wished to see a little more of this vital creature, and so, feeling no compunction, as you know, at opposing my aunt Portia, I spoke up:

"What! Such pulchritude allowed to languish in the hall! Come, this will not do. Ladies, if you will follow me into the drawing room, I assure you we will be able to provide a more suitable setting for your beauty."

Lady Chloe blushed, but my cousin merely nodded her head imperiously, as if I were appeasing her with the proper rites.

I recall very little of our conversation that day. I do recall that Arabella spoke of her mother. I had always vaguely understood that I had an aunt about whom no one would speak, but not being intrigued by such matters, I never inquired further, and if I had, I sup-pose it would not have mattered, for I would have received the re-sponse my mother gave me that night when I broached the topic to her.

"It is a subject we do not discuss," she said firmly. It was most unlike my mother to state something so plainly, without equivoca-tion, without hesitation. I suspected she was parroting words pro-vided her by someone else.

"I shall badger old Aunt Portia about it," I declared. "She will know."

"Oh, no, Franklin!" My mother became most agitated. "Oh, no, you must never mention the subject, particularly not to Portia. We are quite dependent on their clemency, ever since your poor father died." She dabbed at her cheeks with a handkerchief. "They have given us a home, quite beyond the bounds of anything we could expect."

My mother never expected anything, which was the only reason I could conceive that she would be grateful for such shelter—I scorn to call it a home—as we received from Lord Drumland.

"If you pursue this matter, Franklin, and all at the insistence of that forward little minx," I was surprised that my mother, who is usually the most tolerant of women, had taken such an instant dislike to Arabella; perhaps she feared, as mothers do, that she should lose me, but she knew that I would never contemplate marriage until I had achieved some position in the world, "we shall be turned out into the cold," continued my mother, giving way to muffled sobs. My mother never permitted full vent to her sorrow I think it was the result of attempting for so many years never to cause offense.

"Mother," I said, putting my arm about her quivering shoulder, "you need not fear. I only wondered. I would not dream of pursuing this further if it troubles you so."

"You are such a good son," she said, laying her head upon my shoulder. I hated this praise of hers for it always reminded me of my failures. I have been such a bitter disappointment, first to my father and then to her. I long to be all the things she thinks of me: a brilliant scholar, a noble Christian, a moral exemplar, a successful professional man. My mother deserves so much, and I have given her nothing, only regrets and griefs about which she never speaks.

I realize that I have written this much without giving you any description of my cousin, only my impressions and the response she evoked in me. Perhaps my perception of her derives only from my particular hopes and dreams and has nothing to do with the real Arabella; certainly, her notion of me as a romantic Hero was false from the start. But no, after she made her debut, I watched the effect of her presence upon the young men who flocked about her. She is one of those rare women who exude vitality, like a fire around which men gather to bask.

As for her appearance, she is somewhat below medium height—the top of her head comes up to my shoulder—with extremely thick, glossy, curly dark hair. Her eyes are also dark, so dark I could barely distinguish the pupil from the iris. I found this disturbing, for though, when I looked into them, I could see myself, I could never guess at her thoughts. I suppose they are what a novelist would call inscrutable eyes.

Do you suppose I should become a novelist? It is one of the few endeavours at which I have not yet tried my hand, nor yet failed.

When we first met, Arabella had the rounded, plump appearance of a very young girl, especially evident in her cheeks and shoulders, where her skin was so sensitive that if you pressed your fingertips to her flesh, the touch would leave red marks. Later she thinned out somewhat and became more womanly in appearance. Add to this an instinctive flair for drama in her choice of costume—

she has a love of vivid colours and striking contours—and you have a portrait of my cousin.

Unfortunately, even I can perceive how inadequate it is to convey the force of her presence. So much for my career as a novelist, blissfully short, I must say, in comparison to some of my other aborted careers. I shall have to limit my writing to correspondence.

As for Arabella's character, she is petulant, wilful, impulsive, reckless, affectionate, selfish, vain, proud, and occasionally cruel. Surely, without any irony intended, you can understand the attraction for me who has ever been forced by circumstance to be reasonable, cautious, reserved, self-effacing, and tolerant. I suppose we saw in each other the two severed halves of oneself. No wonder we tried so desperately to form a union.

The effect of this disjunction upon the two of us was disastrous. She waited, at first eagerly, then impatiently, and finally angrily, for the emergence of the passionate, strong, and heroic lover she imagined me to be, but her scorn and contempt for what I am drove me further into introspection and timidity. While I, envisioning from our contact a growth of understanding and patience in her, found, to my horror, that she grew daily more vehement and wild.

I might add that this insight, which came to me quite clearly several months past, did nothing to alter my behaviour or the course of our downward path. If only it were true that men act according to their thoughts. But not all of my intellectual analysis could transmute the desperate desire to be different, which kept me clinging to her.

You may wonder, if you still recall that episode described several pages back, how I came to know Arabella so well after my sincere promise to my mother not to pursue the matter further. To understand subsequent events, I must ask you to recall a little of the characters of my father's family, whom I have sketched in previous letters.

My grandfather, Lord Drumland, is an invalid due to the excesses of his appetites. He is also the most irascible, coarse tyrant imaginable. My aunt Portia has, since the death of Lady Drumland many years ago, been his only nurse—bathing, dressing, and feeding him—despite the continual abuse he heaps upon her. One would pity her for the waste of her youth, except that she has one of the bitterest natures imaginable. Her glance, her words, would curdle mother's milk.

I have never been in charity with either one of this gloomy pair. My grandfather delights in taunting me with his wealth and threatening to leave me penniless in the same breath; I have long since given up hope of any mention in his will. As for Portia, she smiles at my failures and becomes sullen at news of any success. So when I realized that they did indeed share information about Arabella's mother I took a grim satisfaction in defying their wishes to keep it secret.

I have forgotten to tell you about Arabella's circumstances. She is the only child of a wealthy merchant and heiress to a great fortune. Her mother, who is one of the daughters of Lord Drumland, ran away with a cousin when Arabella was small. The cousin later married another lady, and nothing is ever said as to the welfare and whereabouts of Arabella's mother since then. As I think you can well understand, Arabella earnestly desired to locate her mother but was free to do so only after the death of her father, who repudiated his wife entirely. But when she came to my relatives—our relatives I should say—she received an even more brutal message. Portia insisted that her mother was dead.

I suspected this was untrue and quickly had my suspicions confirmed when I overheard my grandfather and Portia arguing about Arabella's mother. Apparently, she is maintained on an allowance someplace; later I learned the exact nature of the place and wished I had never begun my quest, but that will come later.

At any rate, I went to my cousin with this glad news.

I hope you will not think worse of me when I tell you it was a secret meeting. I do not believe my cousin knew the ramifications of such an act. She had been brought up motherless, after all, and had never been allowed to go out much in Society. Besides, she has a young girl's love of drama and secrecy. As for me, I merely consented to such a rendezvous because she pressed me to it convincing me that her governess, an excellent woman by the name of Miss Finch, would not allow her callers. Perhaps this was so, I do not know; I do know only that the following spring I was accepted quite cordially by both Miss Finch and my cousin's guardian, a pompous solicitor named Sir Henry Warder-Mull. I wonder now how much of the almost Gothic picture of oppression and tyrannical brutality that Arabella painted for me was actual and how much a product of her feverish and often distorted imagination. It is difficult to distinguish her lies from the few, if any, times she spoke the truth.

Should I have consented to this secret meeting? By anyone's standards of morality and practicality, I should not have, but I did and relayed my hopeful news and was favoured with a girlishly impulsive, yet disturbingly womanly embrace.

Now, Charles, you know of the great troubles I had at Oxford, which ended in my being sent down. Women have ever been attracted to me—I trust you to understand this as I mean it and not in a vainglorious way—yet I seem unable to reciprocate with the heartfelt response that they deserve. If only I had not reciprocated in any fashion, but at the time I was a young man and the demands of my body were urgent. Well, I can make no excuses for my actions; other young men have done the same, yet I acknowledge now that I was wrong.

I cannot be grateful for the shame and humiliation of that past disgrace in my life. But it was a crisis, followed as it was by the news from India of my father's death, a conversion, if you will, though you and I understand the term to mean two entirely different things. When I gave up my belief in an all-seeing, all-forgiving God and accepted instead the personal responsibility for determining my Duty to others, I acquired a strengthened resolve not to inflict harm on any other human being. I have managed over the years to hold myself quite aloof from women. There have been temptations, naturally, but my careful self-examination and self-discipline have kept me from error.

Thus, it was easy—well, not precisely easy, but familiar—to ignore the implications of that embrace and my response to it. I met her on one other occasion before I left for that continental tour as Lord Cant's tutor—I should say "keeper." There was nothing between us other than my promise to relay any subsequent news I might learn regarding her mother, and her gratitude.

I wrote to you quite frequently during those months abroad and, I am sure, disgusted you with my accounts of the vicious habits of Lord Cant, as well as delighted you with descriptions of the scenery and people of the countries we visited. But I never mentioned the letters I was receiving, nearly daily, from Arabella. Why? Because she was divulging her heart to me, and what was in her heart was an idealistic, romantic concept of our perfect love for each other. You may ask why I did not simply write and inform her that she was labouring under a misapprehension; I asked myself this all the time. I think I know a few of the answers. My unease about her state of infatuation grew gradually; with each new letter, it swelled ever larger. At first, I had supposed she was an extraordinarily friendly and frank young woman. Then I began questioning myself. Had I done something to encourage her in this view? Were my carefully circumspect letters somehow ambiguous so that she read a secret message I was not even aware I sent? Finally, I became afraid to speak out too bluntly for I feared she would be mortally wounded by the realization of my deception, so I trusted to a face-to-face meeting with her to clear the air. Perhaps, I even thought, she was indulging her romantic fantasies in this correspondence with an unknown man who could be trusted not to take advantage of her innocence and she knew all along that her "love" was a chimera.

I copied this passage from Samuel Butler into my journal at the time; it seems to speak precisely of my thoughts:

> She was too kind, wooed too persistently,
> Wrote moving letters to me day by day;
> The more she wrote, the less could I repay.
> Therefore, I grieve not that I was not loved
> But that, being loved, I could not love again.
> I liked; but like and love are far removed;
> And though I tried to love I tried in vain.

So, when I returned to London in May, we met again, secretly, though this was not of my choosing, and it became apparent that she believed herself to be fully in love with me. Her correspondence had not been a mere exercise in writing courtship letters to someone "safe." Fearful of doing her any harm, I took myself up to Yorkshire, where my grandfather and his household were residing, and there found my mother remarried—her husband my old and hated tutor from my boyhood in India, Reverend Trout.

I never wrote to you about this because I felt I was unable to be calm and sensible about this matter, which I felt, and still feel, as a betrayal, though I recognize that such a feeling is irrational.

I had just arrived at Darton Abbey (my grandfather's estate) after a pleasant walk through the Dales, marred only at the end by an unexpected shower, one of those sudden storms that are common to the area. As I stood in the drafty hallway, drenched and spattered with mud, my mother came out of the warm, lighted drawing room.

"Franklin!" she exclaimed. "What have you done to yourself?"

I mumbled something about taking a walk to admire the countryside.

"Oh, how thoughtless of you!" she declared. "Now how can I show you to Thomas, with you looking like a bedraggled farmer?"

"Thomas?" I said. I believe my voice became cold. I was beginning to realize that my mother had changed in some subtle and discomfiting way. She wore an old blue velvet gown, one that I remembered from festive dinners in India but had not seen since then. Her hair was dressed in many tiny curls. But this was the least of it. Her voice had an artificially gay, almost hysterical quality to it; she moved with a restlessness akin to, but not the same as, her former timid and agitated manner. Her hands fluttered and gestured incessantly as she spoke, now patting her hair, now straightening the lace at the edge of her bodice.

A man came out of the lighted drawing room.

"Sophy!" he said nervously. "What has become of you?" As soon as I heard him speak, I recognized that hated voice.

"Oh, Thomas!" said my mother. "My foolish son is wringing wet. I'm afraid to have him in for fear he'll spoil the carpet."

"Reverend Trout," I said.

"Just think, he recognized you at once!" my mother put in quickly. "I certainly did not. Why, he had to come up and introduce himself to me, despite the fact that I was looking for him."

"If you wish to put on something dry, I am sure you will fit in some of my things," said my despised old tutor. "The maid can show you to my room, second from the left on the next floor."

This was my old room, adjoining my mother's. I stared at her. I don't think she missed my expression of horror and disgust because she winced.

"I suppose it is best to tell him now," she said uncertainly, glancing back at Reverend Trout and putting out one hand as if to clutch him for support.

"Yes, I think so," I replied, my voice thick with sarcasm, or so I thought.

"Sophy and I—your mother, that is to say, and I—myself we have …" began Reverend Trout. He always had difficulty speaking when he was nervous.

"Let me, Thomas," said my mother. "We were just married, Franklin. We wanted to wait until you had returned, but then your plans kept changing and well, we…" she looked at him again and blushed "…we decided not to wait any longer, and so we went ahead and did it."

"Married last Saturday at St Stephen's church by the Reverend Timothy Toffle," my new stepfather stated, folding my mother's hand in with his own. "Very nice ceremony. All that one could expect."

"I do hope you're not angry that you missed out," said my mother uncertainly, peering at my face.

"Oh, no!" I replied mechanically. "Congratulations! Most amazing news!" And other similar nothings.

Somehow, I extricated myself from their solicitations, went upstairs, then down the backstairs and out into the storm in a sort of pain-filled trance. All the memories of that miserable time in India came back to me. My mother's incessant complaints; my father's growing, sometimes savage, irritation and annoyance with her; the cold, unfeeling tutelage of Reverend Trout with his floggings for lessons done poorly and his smiling contempt for my schoolboy errors. And I was caught amidst the three of them, trying to avoid my father, placate my mother, and please the impossible-to-please Reverend Trout.

I stayed at a local inn that night, attempting to ease my anguish by drinking and also to numb myself so that I might be able to walk back into that house and face them with equanimity. My mother found me there the following morning, and when I expressed my displeasure at her choice of a husband, she told me calmly that I would not be welcome in their company until I changed my opinion and then related a string of filthy lies that Reverend Trout had told her regarding my father. He also had told her, the sneaking little cur, of the reasons I was sent down from Oxford, for he had opened the letter meant for my father.

I wonder if this information (you remember, my mother was told at the time only that I was ill) had so disgusted her that she wished to have nothing more to do with me. She did not touch me as she usually did nor use any endearments in her speech.

My mother also told me that my father had been losing his faith, that he was questioning the biblical concept of Creation because of the geological and biological evidence he found in his researches. So the manuscript over which I laboured for a year, the manuscript pieced together from the notes he left upon his death, the manuscript that my mother burned, had been a true extension of my father's thought. This, at least, was of some comfort. It was a validation of all my solitary months of work and the healing of the wound that had opened when my mother accused me of polluting my father's memory. It was as if he had spoken to me from the grave and blessed me with his understanding. As soon as I had absorbed this through my vinous stupor, I went sneaking to Portia to ask if I might have the boxes of my father's notes so I might reconstruct the destroyed manuscript and truly build a monument to him. She told me that Reverend Trout, the fiend, had consigned them to the furnace.

My mother also turned over her income from my father's estate to me; she considered it soiled money, and my grandfather had presented Reverend Trout with a lucrative living. It was little enough but enough for me to return to London, establish myself in lodgings, and plunge myself into a reckless and frivolous round of activities. I know you were discouraged by my letters during this period of time. You warned me, in your gentle way, that I seemed to be intent on proving or disproving the efficacy of such philosophies as Cynicism, Epicureanism, Hedonism, and Sophism. I will tell you now, friend, that certainly none of them salved the pain in my heart. I was a man attempting to lose himself, and I explored many avenues, among them excessive drinking and gaming.

Alas for my cousin that she became the most absorbing! I saw a great deal of her at this time. She was receiving considerable attentions from the somewhat unsavoury (gentle?) men in the social circle in which she moved, and I thought myself to be merely one of many. I kissed her once, at her request, in someone's library, but I thought little about her infatuation for me as she seemed to alternate between coolness and warmth.

Then she came to my lodgings, alone. I know you are going to wonder how a well-bred young girl could do such a thing.

So did I. At the time, I made excuses for her, based on her innocence. Knowing what I know now, I wonder why I chose to overlook the possibility that she knew precisely what she was doing and that she seemed wanton and reckless because she was. At first, I struggled with my own conscience and her dismissals of it to persuade her to leave, but I was looking for a cause, any cause for which to immolate myself, and she offered me one—love—and I accepted it.

I can see you now, dear friend, putting aside your spectacles and thinking of your Mary and wondering how I could be so self-deluded as to consider such a liaison love. I can only say that I felt differently, more alive, more powerful, more alert than I had ever felt in my life, and having no experience of love, I could only assume that this was it.

Not that we fell into sin immediately, but I suppose, though I chose to ignore it at the time, that the outcome was inevitable. She came to my rooms one day in tears because her guardians were sending her off to the country due to some ugly gossip regarding her and a certain dissolute lieutenant in the Sixth Hussars. She managed to convince me—I was not hard to convince—that there was nothing to this rumour, though later I heard differently, and in the midst of my endeavours to comfort and soothe her, she asked that I would make her my wife, and I did.

Now what can I say of this that would help you to understand, my friend? It was wrong; I knew it at the time, and I knew it forever afterward. My only excuse, paltry though I confess it to be, is that we considered ourselves man and wife already, had pledged ourselves to each other before God, and thought we would soon marry. I knew that I could not yet support a wife, but I believed that with her fortune she could help me establish myself in some career. She concealed from me the fact that the disposal of her fortune was entirely in the hands of her guardians and that there were strenuous stipulations regarding whom she could marry.

Arabella went down to her estate in Sussex near Pittlesbury, and.
I followed her there, leasing a small cottage and meeting her secretly. All of this time I was miserable with shame and guilt, though
I concealed it from her, who seemed to feel none. I thought that our
marriage would end my discomfort, that the only obstacle between
me and the vision of happiness I had seen others enjoy would be
swept away once our union was solemnized. Yet Arabella had a
thousand excuses why she could not yet broach the subject to her
guardian. And then there were the lies. I learned soon after I arrived
in Pittlesbury that Arabella had indeed known the soldier she
claimed never to have seen before. He had resided in the area the
previous summer; there were lurid tales of his having been found
in her chamber during a fire and other stories of her having gone to
seek him out at his mother's house and destroying some valuable
furnishings in a fit of temper. Of course, the gossip of villagers is
suspect and usually highly exaggerated, but there must have been
at least a kernel of truth to the stories. And then I soon discovered
that she had concealed from me the truth about her circumstances,
and I wondered if perhaps Sir Henry lived, as I did, with the hope
of marrying her in the near future. I had myself witnessed, the few
times I saw them together, how she wheedled and charmed him and
wrapped him around her little finger; I thought her attentions to him
excessive and disgusting. She said she must appease him because he
was her guardian, but I saw that she was encouraging him, by her
behaviour, in whatever foolish hopes he cherished.

I was right, of course; when she finally approached him for his
permission for our marriage, he refused. It was then that she revealed
to me the disposition of the will and the fact that without Sir Henry's
permission we could not marry for eight years.

I was aghast. I think it was at this time that the few remaining
shreds of hope to which I clung slipped through my fingers, but I
continued to act as if we would still be married throughout all the
awful revelations that followed. I went down to consult one of the
solicitors in the law firm that has served my family for generations
about the breaking of such rigid clauses in a will, and he, guessing
at the identity of my "young heiress," let slip the information that
her mother was maintained by the family in an insane asylum. A

payment was made every quarter through the family's solicitors. I then journeyed to the place he described.

It was an exquisite August morning, one of those crystal-clear days one sometimes finds this time of year. I remember the sun was so hot that I had flung my jacket over my shoulder during the walk from the nearest town; the scent of jasmine from the hedge bordering the lane was heavy in the air. Above, white clouds drifted silently through the blue sky. What a glorious backdrop for such a vision of Hell as I was given that morning! To think it's been only two weeks. Two years would not erase the images of events that transpired.

The fence was the first warning: It was of iron, extraordinarily tall and finished at the top with wickedly sharp spikes. Once I was within its boundaries, having gained entrance by attracting the attention of a gardener, I found the fence an omen for all within. No shrubbery grew against it; its barred shadow fell grimly on the expanse of grass upon which no one walked.

The house itself was equally grim. The iron gratings upon all of the windows, except those of the ground floor, altered its appearance so much that, whereas without them and that foreboding fence, one might have fancied Slow Banning Retreat just another tall, rather stark country house, it assumed the aspect of a prison. There was no sound within those walls except for my footfalls as I approached the front door along the stone courtyard that surrounded the house. I had left far behind the hum of the bees and the rustle of leaves in the wind.

There had been no time to send a letter or announce my arrival in any way; in fact, I had no wish to do so, fearing that James Marble, the solicitor, whom I had finally helped into his bed in the early hours of the morning, might have recalled his indiscretion and done something to prevent my visit. A sour-faced maid answered my knock and showed no reluctance to permit me entrance. She left me standing, trying to warm myself before a small fire, which failed to brighten its cold and damp drawing room, while she went to "fetch the missus."

The "Missus" was a large, broad-shouldered, dark-haired woman with an exceedingly artificial smile. It could have been pasted upon her face, for there was nothing else about her posture or her glance to indicate welcome. She introduced herself as Mrs. Wicklow, widow of the well-known Dr Wicklow, famous for his treatment of the unfortunate insane.

"How can I be of assistance to you, Mr. ...?" she asked. Her voice was as false in its gaiety as was her smile.

"Mr. DeWinx," I bowed. "I believe my aunt, Lady Perdita Farraday, is one of your patients."

"Ah, yes, Lady Perdita," she said, smiling even more broadly, but there was a certain increase of rigidity in her facial muscles. "There have been no visitors previously," she observed pleasantly.

"That is true," I replied. "But Lord Drumland, my grandfather, is beginning to soften in his attitude toward his—ahem—daughter. He wished to have some personal report as to her welfare—" I saw Mrs. Wicklow stiffen "—rather, her condition."

"He has certainly been most generous to our humble establishment." Mrs. Wicklow unbent a little. "I trust he is not considering a change in her care. I assure you I am fully capable of carrying on her treatment despite Dr Wicklow's death."

"Oh, no, there is no question of a change. He is very ill and, you understand, wishes to be easy in his mind about his daughter."

Mrs. Wicklow sniffed, as if to say it was ludicrous that anyone should expect to have his mind eased, but said with false graciousness, "We are always happy at Slow Banning Retreat to accommodate the wishes of relatives, and, I might add, our patrons. You understand that a keeper—ahem—a personal attendant must be present in the room during the interview. I believe you will get little out of her. I will send down her maid also."

"Her maid?" I was puzzled.

"Yes." Mrs. Wicklow paused at the door. "We allow all of our patients to maintain as much of a semblance of normal life as possible. Perhaps you are not aware, Mr. ..."

"DeWinx."

"Mr. DeWinx, of the high tone of this establishment. We are known as the *crème de la crème* of—ahem—shall we say 'Retreats?' Every one of our—ahem—family members here is permitted to bring along his or her own servant, and Lady Perdita, when she arrived—let me see, it was ten years ago—brought her maid, a young woman by the name of Puffer. This Puffer has made herself very useful to us, I might say, and also, I hasten to add, to her mistress."

I bowed, unable to respond to this, and Mrs. Wicklow departed in a rustle of silk. I had been afraid that I would hear the anguished howls and gibberish of raving lunatics, but when I was alone there was not a sound to be heard except the ticking of the mantel clock and the soft, crumbling noises of the coal in the grate. No sound, that is, until I heard heavy footsteps outside the door.

In a moment, the door was thrown open and a strange trio entered. My attention went at first to the woman in a grey, shapeless wool dress, evidently Lady Perdita. My God! Even now I recall the shock at seeing her, for though she was much older, the resemblance to Arabella was striking. She had Arabella's dark, thick hair, though hers was matted and left loose to flow down her back; her eyes, though blue, had the same intensity, the same way of turning to glance at you as Arabella's.

She was being forcibly pushed into the room by the other two: a coarse-looking man with a heavy black beard and a frail but composed woman, who wore her brown hair plaited neatly on the top of her head and who, by the evidence of the calico gown and linen apron she wore, was the lady's maid. The two of them positioned Lady Perdita directly before me. Her head lolled somewhat as if it were too heavy for the fragility of her neck; she looked at me sullenly from beneath that thicket of dark hair.

Suddenly she spoke.

"He has the look of Geoffrey about him, don't you think, Annie?" She turned to her maid. I had been startled by her voice; it was low, flat, without any intonation.

"No, ma'am, not at all like Geoffrey," replied the maid patiently. Evidently this was a frequent topic of conversation.

"Oh, yes, indeed, he has the look of Geoffrey," she said to herself, running her fingertips along my jaw. I shivered; it was so like Arabella's touch. Could such things be inherited? "Who are you?" She lifted her face very close to mine.

"Your kinsman," I replied. "Franklin DeWinx. Son of your brother, Frederick."

"There, Annie, I told you!" declared the madwoman. "He is a DeWinx. And so was Geoffrey. He was my cousin, you know. And Frederick was my favourite brother. Why did he not come to my aid when I was so vilely accused?" Her voice rose in a shrill plea, containing a note of hysteria that seemed exaggerated and assumed, not genuine; it was as false as Mrs. Wicklow's manner.

"My father died in India some years ago," I said. "He had been abroad for over twenty years."

"I am not mad, you know," she said quite suddenly and fiercely. For the first time, I thought I discerned a note of real passion in her voice. "They wanted to be rid of me, so they put me here. They didn't know how else to do away with the embarrassment that I had become, so they called me insane. Such a convenience!"

"A common delusion of the mad," grunted the keeper quickly. I looked from him to her. Despite her dishevelled appearance and strange way of speaking, I could see no sign of insanity. For a moment, I believed her and began thinking about inspectors and Commissions of Lunacy.

"They all wanted to be rid of me, she continued sadly. "My father. My husband. Portia. Geoffrey. No." Her face grew troubled. "No, not Geoffrey. Geoffrey loved me. Yes, Geoffrey loves me." Her gaze went inward as if she had closed the shutters. With her hands cradling her elbows, she rocked a little back and forth.

There was a long and painful silence, broken eventually by a few feeble questions that I posed to her about the length of her stay and the care that she received. She did not answer or in any way indicate that she heard me. At last the maid suggested that the visit be terminated; only when the keeper went up to Lady Perdita and grasped her above the elbow with his thick paw did she wake out of her trance.

"Say farewell to your visitor, ma'am," suggested the maid.

Arabella's mother looked at me, at first dully, but then the coquettish look I had often seen in Arabella ignited in her eyes. She tilted her head to one side; a smile meant to be seductive but seeming more sly crept upon her lips.

"Oh, you do remind me of Geoffrey," she said. "You are so very, very handsome." She came up to me, twining one arm around my waist and pulling herself close to me so that I could feel her body, through the thin gown, pressed against the full length of mine. "I believe you want to kiss me, do you not?" She held up her lips expectantly.

I thought—hoped—that she meant a kiss of farewell and so bent my head to give her the dutiful peck of custom. But she meant a full-blooded, passionate kiss. When I felt her wet lips fasten upon mine and her tongue attempt to intrude itself into my mouth, I remembered she was Arabella's mother. Disgust flooded me. I jerked away from her with a start and tried to fling her from me, but she had that extraordinary strength that I believe is common with the insane. She clung to me with both arms, lashing out with her feet at her keeper, who sought to remove her from me.

It was an ugly scene, and when he had finally managed to subdue her and drag her from the room, I was shaking.

"I am so sorry, Mr. DeWinx," said the maid softly. "She has never had a visitor. We did not know how she would behave. Pray, do not think too badly of us."

"I do not," I replied. "It is not your fault."

I sat down heavily on the sofa and put my head in my hands. I could feel the nausea rise in my throat. I swallowed it down.

"Do you have any questions I can answer?" asked the maid. "To satisfy yourself or Lord Drumland?"

"No, oh, yes, that is…" I struggled to regain some clarity of thought "Is she…is she difficult to care for?" It was the first question that came to my mind.

"Oh, no, she is generally as docile as a lamb," replied Annie eagerly. "You must not judge too much by what happened just now. She does not ever meet many gentlemen—strangers."

"What do the doctors call her condition?" I asked dully. "Dr Wicklow said she was suffering from moral insanity," put in Annie quickly. "It means that the natural feelings such as decency and modesty are perverted while her reasoning power remains unaffected. She does not suffer from hallucinations. It is just that, though capable of the most revolting acts, she has no more awareness of their evil than would a very young child."

"And there is no cure?"

"Oh, no, sir." Annie paused and added in a shy manner, "You know, it is my observation, having so long been in attendance upon her—nearly twenty-five years it is now—that she was always deficient in that area, that is, the moral conscience. But no one ever paid it much heed until after her cousin jilted her and her family and husband disowned her. She was mad with grief and terror and shame, and it was then that Lord Drumland called in the doctors, who certified that she was insane." There was a bitterness in her voice as she said this, and she glanced toward the door as if to be certain she was not overheard. "Once she was here, what hope was there of improvement? She knows no one cares for her or would be waiting for her on her release. She has gradually become more and more like the others here."

I guess I was staring at her, for she put in quickly, "Not that I am complaining of the treatment here. She has her own private room and a walk every day around the courtyard. She is seldom confined like some of the others. The food is adequate. The character of the men who are keepers leaves much to be desired, but then what sort of man would take on such a position? And she has a way of coz-ening them..." She realized she had said too much and stopped abruptly, her eyes downcast.

"Pardon me," I said gently, "but what of you? What chance have you had for a normal life, shut up within these walls for all of these years?"

There were tears in her eyes when she looked up. "Excuse me," she said, brushing them away impatiently with her hands. "No one has given me a thought since I came here with her ten years past." She sighed heavily. "What else could I do?" she asked, uncon-sciously holding out her hands to me a little as her mistress had done. "She was all alone, and we had been so close for all that time. I was, when all is said and done, her only friend. I have been well fed and well provided for, due to the generosity of your grandfather. Per-haps I have missed somewhat of life..." Her voice trailed off, and suddenly I was afflicted with a sorrow so deep and profound I could not bear to be in the room a moment longer.

"I must be off," I said, rising. "You may assure Mrs. Wicklow I shall give Lord Drumland a good report of my—er—aunt's care. Good day."

Once outside the forbidding fence I could compose myself no longer, but strode along the linden-shaded lane, kicking at the stones beneath my feet to give vent to my anger and self-loathing! So many women with their arms outstretched to me—my mother, Arabella, Perdita, Annie—and what had I ever given them? Reassurance? No! Love? No! Understanding?

So wrapped have I been in my own petty problems and cowardice that they have only seen in me a reflection of their worst doubts, their secret fears, their deepest longings.

You may think this a peculiar response. Surely having seen the resemblance between my cousin and her lunatic mother, having heard that chilling description of moral insanity and having seen how easily it could be applied to Arabella, I should have realized there was no hope for us.

But I found excuses. After all, I was as guilty as she of the sins of the flesh we had shared; did that mean I, too, was morally insane? And what daughter does not resemble her mother? If it came to that, I must confess that I resemble my father in more than just appearance, for one of the filthy stories that Reverend Trout had related to my mother was that my father had taken on a native woman as a mistress and she had borne dusky-skinned children for him. So I reasoned, and then forced down the panic of my instincts.

I think I believed during the interminable course of my journey back to Pittlesbury that love should redeem both of us. But, God forgive me, it did not.

When next I saw Arabella, after an ugly scene in which her guardian took a walking stick to me outside the village church, she had never looked more mad. Her hair was unkempt; she wore a soiled silk gown; her feet were bare. She was unnaturally pale except for two red patches high on her cheeks. I felt all of my hope ebbing out of me and an icy coldness taking its place.

I realized then that neither faith nor love could be willed into existence, and that I had neither.

Having faced, at last, my moral bankruptcy, I was unmoved by Arabella's pleas, her tears, her attempt to frighten and then seduce me. Once she had left, I packed a few of my belongings (I won't even describe the confusion she made of them while I slept) and took myself off to Southampton, where I found the *Tweed* preparing to sail.

My friend, my patient friend, for I do apologize for the length of this letter, my forgiving friend, for I hope you will find some compassion in your heart to absolve my sins, can you advise me? Was it my duty to stand by this young woman from whom I had taken the most precious offering any woman has to give?

The *Erinyes* taunt me, saying, "Yes, yes!" that it was my duty to stand by her, through infatuation and loss of love, through madness and through health, through eight years of chaste betrothal until we could marry. I am so bedevilled by these tauntings that, like Orestes, I pull the blankets around my head and refuse to eat.

Sometimes I quarrel with my harsh judges and insist that, no matter how faulty my judgments, no matter how weak my moral conscience, binding myself to Arabella for life because of my mistakes would be to condemn both of us to misery. We would slowly destroy our Souls. But the Erinyes insist this is the price of human involvement.

Is it my friend? Can you help me with this moral dilemma? Is my conflict as vividly black and white as I have painted it, or is there some alternative that I am unable to see?

I often stand at the stern of the ship, watching the foam slide beneath me and leave a wide track in the ocean. Against this tide I struggle with the urge to throw myself into the waves and swim back to shore. The fact that I could not possibly survive does not seem to matter to me in this fevered condition; I think only of the anguish Arabella must be enduring, of the shame that gnaws at me, and whether, if in Jamaica I find another ship to carry me home, we can both endure the two-month–long return journey.

I know, of course, no matter what your answer, it shall probably come too late. My decision must be made before any letter from you will reach me. Nonetheless, I feel an easing somewhat of my pain and guilt in the act of sharing it with you; I only hope (and sometimes fear) that my recitation of these unhappy events will not depress you.

Though I cannot do so for myself, I beg you, my friend, to pray for—
the ever-constant friend of your heart,
Franklin DeWinx

5 September 1842
Postscript: I have just reread this letter, for a ship has come alongside that is carrying letters back to England. They might, I believe, take me, but I feel the fogs of my confusion somewhat cleared by the brisk ocean breeze. If I could, I would add some minor touches of compassion, and perhaps even humour, to the words above, but I have not the time. Just enough to ask you, if you would, to carry out one undertaking for me.

Though I know you are far removed in your Devonshire rectory from all the scenes and people I have described, would you, through correspondence perhaps, find out for me how my cousin is faring? You may write with perfect confidence to her governess, Miss Tirzah Finch, whose direction would be Pittlesbury Hall, Pittlesbury, Sussex, or perhaps, since Miss Finch (who lapsed during the summer into a mortal illness) may even now be beyond the reach of words, you might want to address yourself to Arabella's lady's maid, Miss Jenny Archer at the same direction. She is exceedingly sharp and very literate and would, I think, be capable of keeping any confidence you share with her. She would also be a good judge, quite accurate, of the condition of her mistress's heart.

All my warmest thanks for the benison of your friendship, which is with me in my thoughts daily.

PART FOUR

Miss Tirzah Finch:
"The Penultimate Judgment,"
written during her last illness
September 1842–May 1843

~ ~

When the evening of this life comes on,
you will be judged on love.

St. John of the Cross

Chapter One

I had always believed that death would be a pleasure, that I would glide joyfully from this life of sorrow into the enfolding arms of God. Then why is it so hard? Why do I fight so fiercely for each breath I breathe? Why do I grieve so piteously over every act of kindness? Why, my Lord, am I assaulted by doubts? My faith, which has been my fortress, my bulwark, is suddenly shattered when I need it most Is this a test? If so, this is the most cruel and pointless of tests. It must be the last attempt of Satan, but how can my God permit him to torment me so? What if I am not proof against these temptations?

I was born into this vale of tears in God's benevolent Judgment for a purpose. There was some task He wished me to perform for Him. Until this last and most serious trial, I thought I knew my Duty—to raise up Miss Arabella in the path of honour and righteousness—and I strove valiantly to apply myself to this vocation with all due obedience and singleness of purpose.

Yet now when I have no opportunity to correct my errors, I see that I did not succeed. Not only is Arabella living in the state of dreadful sin and in daily disharmony with her lawfully wedded husband, but I have had the temerity to foolishly grant her my human forgiveness.

Then again, I sometimes wonder was there something more for me to do, something I have entirely overlooked? Dear Lord, my God, what was it?

Jenny, seeing how I am chafed by these worries and knowing how fatigued I become when I try to speak, suggests that I write down my thoughts. She called it jokingly a Penultimate Judgment. She has ever been irreligious and whimsical. And yet, while I am clothed in despair and spiritual agony, I see in her, who has not a tithe of my accumulated knowledge or unswerving service to the Lord, a contentment in the performance of her duties, even a humble pleasure in living, which has always eluded me. Why should this be so?

It pleased the Lord to place me on this earth as the fourth daughter, seventh child of Simon and Sarah Finch. My father was a clergyman of the old school, which is so evilly being swept aside by the fanatic Puseyites with their mania for ritual and lace garments and clouds of incense. My father taught his parishioners that they must surrender their lives to the Lord and that only then might they receive the Grace that would save them from eternal damnation. Any sign of self-interest, any evidence of worldly absorption, was a black mark against them; such tendencies must be immediately extinguished.

We were brought up, all eight of us who survived infancy, in this manner, my mother taking on our upbringing as her most precious task, her most unrelenting duty. My earliest memory is of being locked up in a dark cupboard for some minor transgression, the exact nature of which I have forgotten. But the blackness, the awfulness of that cupboard! From beyond the door there was only silence where I would normally have been surrounded by the sounds of family activity, but within, the darkness was filled with sounds, rustlings and creakings that filled me with a nameless dread. There was not an inch I could turn without scraping the sides or top of the cupboard even though I was a very small child. It seemed as if with every passing minute the walls drew imperceptibly closer until I feared I should be suffocated. My lungs struggled to draw in air, and what air there was, was choked with dust, making me feel more stifled than refreshed. I dared not cry out, for my mother had informed me that any protest would mean my sentence was extended. Rather than receding with familiarity, my terror grew greater as the hours passed, and when my mother released me from my punishment, I was nearly incoherent with fear.

She sat me down gently in my little chair before the fire and rubbed my ice-cold fingers in her own warm ones; even then I had difficulty keeping my feet and hands warm.

"Now, Tirzah," she said gently, "you must strive to keep in mind the connection between your sin and your punishment, for the Lord has prepared a punishment for every sin and His are the model for all of our earthly attempts, so they—are mightier and more awful in every way. You have heard your father speak of Hell?" I nodded my head mutely. "Hell is a vast pit full of darkness, not unlike our closet but the blackness is a thousand times blacker. You could not even see your hand before your face. And it is populated by demons whose sole task it is to torment those whom the Lord has confined there."

I connected the demons with the noises I had heard, and ever afterward, when I lay at night in my little cot with Abigail, my eldest sister, I could not sleep if I heard the slightest unexplained sound, for I feared it was the demons coming to carry me off.

"And do you recall how long the time seemed that you spent in the cupboard?" my mother asked. Again, I could do no more than nod. "Hell," she replied, "lasts for eternity. That is forever and ever. When a Soul has offended the Lord and is banished there, she is cut off forever from the vision of God. She languishes in that awful darkness, never to be released."

I sobbed bitterly at the thought, and she nodded her head, well pleased with my comprehension of the lesson she strove to teach me.

There were many and worse punishments, for I fear I was a naughty child, but this earliest discipline is still the most vivid in my mind, for it was when I first made the association between my sins against my parents and God's relentless Judgment.

If only I had been able to convey a similar lesson to Arabella Farraday, I am sure she would never have wandered so far from the path of Virtue. I often wonder, as I lay here confined to my bed, what I could have done differently. Should I have begun with kindness first and wooed her to the Right Way, teaching her to love the Lord and then to fear Him? But that would have been the rankest of deceptions such as nurses employ when they try to conceal a distasteful medicine in a spoonful of honey. The child inevitably develops a loathing for honey as well as the dose needed for health.

The Lord's message is clear: If one is to follow Him, one must be willing to forgo pleasure. To pretend otherwise would be to blaspheme.

Arabella was the wickedest child I have ever had to teach. Despite her father's warnings about her wilfulness and the failures of her previous governesses, I was totally unprepared for the many defects, in her character. Vanity was the most pleasant of her vices. She lied, she had tantrums, she was hypocritical, she was abominably selfish, she was contemptuous of the servants, she was rude, she was spiteful, she was disrespectful, and she was as completely irreligious as an inhabitant of some tropical jungle. Furthermore, she persisted in unclean habits that should have been eradicated in infancy; I employed all manner of remedies from floggings to tying her hands to the bedpost, but I doubt I ever succeeded in uprooting a habit so long established. I have no doubt that this practice lies at the base of her later immorality.

I did my best—but, ah! even as I write, I question whether I did indeed do my best. How many times did I prefer to overlook some fault because I could not face her black anger? How many times did I absorb myself in the management of the household rather than provide her with the guidance she needed? After her father died, when she needed me most, I was selfishly luxuriating in my own grief. And later, when I became aware of her clandestine romances, that was when my truly grievous fault began. For I concealed this information from Sir Henry; it matters little whether I did this out of shame that such things occurred under my guardianship or from fear of losing my generous annuity or even from misplaced affection for Arabella. Now he has married her, and he does not even guess at the depths and treacherous currents underlying her nature. And yet, sometimes, it is not for him I feel the most pity, but for Arabella. Would she have married him if I had been able to be the source of comfort and maternal advice she so required? Did he somehow, through his influence over her and his position of authority, bully her into a loveless marriage just so that he could have full posses-sion of her fortune?

I can still recall the day they came into my sickroom to announce their marriage. It is one of those clear memories granted to the dying. It was, no doubt, a blazing hot autumn day, but the heavy draperies at my windows obscured any glimpse of the outside. I knew only that my room was choked with a thick stifling heat, which seemed to lie on my chest like a hundred-pound weight. My sheets and my nightgown clung to me. From weeks spent in a perpetually darkened room, my other senses had become extraordinarily acute, and I could hear their footsteps from far away. There were few visitors in the part of the Hall in which my room was located. Only Jenny, who always came up the backstairs.

Sir Henry tapped at the door and peered around its edge into the gloom.

"Yes, she is awake, dear," he said, drawing Arabella from behind him.

I knew at once something had changed between them. He kept her hands in his, and his whole demeanour was different, possessive rather than paternal, in place of his usual fawning friendliness there was an obsequious sort of humility, which bathed his waxen face as if in sweat. Arabella was pale, her eyes dark-ringed, her mouth forlorn. I had never seen her look so sad, and involuntarily I rose to hold my arms out to her. But a paroxysm of coughing overcame me, and I fell back upon my pillow where, clutching my handkerchief to my mouth, I tried not to retch in agony.

"Good Miss Finch, be calm," said Sir Henry. His face seemed to glow in the dimness. I could see and hear his thumb moving restlessly along the length of Arabella's fingers. "We have come to share with you the most delightful news."

He turned to Arabella, who looked at him with the absolute obedience that she had never displayed as a child.

"We are to be married," he said, "the fifteenth of September."

I must have shown my surprise in some way, though I remained supine on my pillows, my handkerchief still pressed to my mouth.

"Yes, you may well be startled," he said. "None knew of it but we two. We have been secretly engaged since last Christmas. Do you remember those happy days when we were all together here? And my sweet child has at last consented to name the date on which I shall become the only man in the Kingdom possessed of an angel for a wife!" There was no mention of the plans Arabella had so blithely described to me only a month before regarding her love for and plans to marry her cousin, Mr. DeWinx.

A tear trickled down my cheek. I could feel my eyes filling with tears, but I was helpless to prevent them from spilling over my cheeks. I saw the young girl who had been my child for so long about to assume the solemn responsibilities of a wife. She would be forever beyond my care and company, immersed in a strange new life whose duties she must learn alone.

Then, again, I wept for myself. I realized that I would die, unbeloved by any man, never taken to wife, the full flower of my femininity withered before the bloom. Arabella and I were no longer to travel the same paths. Hers, if successful, would lead to a home blessed with the faces of little children and the love of a husband. I was embarking on a dark, uncharted journey, and I was finally, irrevocably alone.

My tears were self-indulgent, but they touched off an answering sorrow in Arabella. Perhaps she, too, was aware of the rift opening between us and the peril inherent in both of our travels. She wept silently, her dark eyes burning out at me from her pale, gaunt face.

Sir Henry did not at first notice, so rapt was he in the pleasure of his news. He went on and on, babbling about wedding arrangements, a honeymoon in Leicestershire, their plan to arrange my transport to warmer climes in the hopes of improving my health, the prodigious amount of work required to make the wedding a reality. All the while Arabella wept silently until the shaking of her frame alerted Sir Henry to the problem.

"My dear," he cried, turning to her, oh, so tenderly. "You are overcome with the excitement. Let me help you to your room." I would have died right then if it could have been me upon whom he turned that adoring gaze, if it had been my shoulders he had enfolded and my head that he pressed against his coat.

Arabella attempted to say farewell to me, but her words choked in her throat. I wonder now if she wanted to tell me about the circumstances in which she found herself, if she wanted to consult me as to what she should do, if she wanted to throw herself on her knees beside my bed and ask me to pray with her for forgiveness for her sins.

But she did not; she just looked longingly back at me from the door, with a piercing gaze that is still etched upon my heart. It was not for some time that I learned she was in a condition that made a quick marriage imperative.

Chapter Two

When I set down my pen last night, I was exhausted; so much physical and mental exertion after such a long period of inactivity was too much for me. I lay trembling, unable to sleep, and then that black shroud of loneliness descended upon me again. I had written of it so casually. I had dismissed it with a few lines—the Enemy of my life and faith, which, as if for revenge, surrounds me in a thick, choking cloud of misery.

I realized, as never before, with a speechless panic how utterly devoid of human contact and solace my life has been since my mother's death. Now I am dying, and I face my death alone. There is no one who will be with me, who will walk by my side, who will choose to ease my pain by taking some of it on him or herself. Every breath is agony, every minute an eternity, and yet no one feels this as I do. Their eyes are kind, their touch is soothing, yet it is my death, and daily I struggle to escape my Fate.

If I could believe only for an hour that they were all waiting for me on the Other Side—Esther, my mother, Miss Hoop—clothed in light, their hands outstretched, their faces bright with love, my loneliness would be eased. But all I can imagine—God forgive me— is a blackness akin to this that surrounds me. I envision myself stepping forth from the grave, my eyes searching for my Saviour or an angel messenger, and suddenly I shriek, an unearthly, chilling wail, for there is nothing about me but the Void. I am alone for Eternity.

I read one of Mr. Franklin DeWinx's poems long ago. I had found him a charming and intelligent conversationalist, this before I knew how he had seduced Arabella. But before then, I asked to see a copy of his volume of poetry. I was appalled by the bleakness of his vision and his obvious rejection of religious answers. I returned it with some kind but general remarks, which I fear conveyed my disapproval, for he did not question me further.

Yet last night as I lay there horrified by my despair and loneliness, a fragment from one of his poems came unbidden to my mind and tumbled restlessly there. It was after a line from Pascal: "The eternal silence of these infinite spaces terrifies me."

> Like silent stars flung out in endless space
> So do we drift unthinking through our days,
> Helpless to fly from our appointed orbit,
> Revolving, never reaching, never ceasing,
> Until our death can hold for us no terror
> Who have in life been dead.

He was wrong, of course. Those who are living speak glibly of death. Those who are dying cannot make so sure a pronouncement. I had lived my whole life in preparation for this moment, in the faith that my unstinting effort in rooting out the secret sources of my pleasure and eradicating them might bring me greater merit in God's eyes. But what if I have been wrong? What if there was some hidden joy, such as the joy of righteousness, which I now acknowledge to be mine, which is far more heinous to God than all my petty sins of envy and sloth? What if I was to be held responsible by my Maker for the downfall of His creature, Arabella? What if this gay, pretty child with all her selfishness and foolishness was judged to be more desirable in His sight than I, so full of bitterness and grimness as I am? And, what if, worst possibility of all, I had deluded myself in believing that God could care for me, a weak, misguided, joyless being? Suppose He turned His back on me and let me drift through infinite space like one of Mr. DeWinx's revolving stars?

I fear these scruples torment me like a pack of demons because my Lord wishes me to examine my life before it is too late. I sense there is some defect in my character that is most evident in relation to other people, a lack of charity, envy perhaps.

Esther! My beloved sister! She was everything I ever wanted to be. I was christened Tirzah, a practical, dull name that condemned me to ridicule and laughter. She was Esther, a Queen, young and beautiful, beloved of her husband and saviour of her people. How I longed for her name, as I longed for everything about her! For her brown eyes (mine are grey), for her easy speech (I have taught myself to speak well; in childhood, I stuttered), for her pretty manners (I was shy), for her easy friendships. Esther was the hope of my family. She was quick to learn because she had native intelligence; I acquired knowledge through plodding application. To be chosen to go with her to Mrs. Banks's school after my mother's death was a privilege so divine that I never spoke of it, but I also shrank from being too much in the company of someone whose mere presence brought me such pleasure. It seemed so contrary to my religious upbringing. When she took ill a year later, I prepared myself to die, for surely the Lord would choose me. But I, never got even a mild case of scarlet fever while Esther died of it.

I turned from God completely until Miss Hoop, the best of the teachers there, saw my abject misery and guided me gently but firmly back into the fold. And yet once I had given up my anger at a God so cruel and arbitrary, I was struck by a more horrific thought! Had it been my envy that had hastened Esther's death? Had God chosen to punish me for worshipping an earthly idol rather than a heavenly one? In a frenzy of expatiation, I eschewed all of those qualities that had made Esther so lovable: her prettiness, her sociability, her lightness, her curiosity about the world and people. I would leave her place vacant to demonstrate that I had not meant to step into her shoes. That way I would not feel guilty of having caused her death.

My love for Miss Hoop found far more expression than my unspoken adoration of Esther, for it was based on spiritual affinity and therefore could not be blasphemous, or so I thought at the time. When we spoke only of religious things, what did it matter that I loved to brush her hair and plait it before bed? When she insisted that I be brought down from the isolation of the attic and allowed to share her room, I excused my joy as mere pleasure that we would now be able to continue our discussions on God and His inscrutable ways far into the night. Because she was my elder, my teacher, my spiritual guide, I saw no harm in our intimacy. Surely if our fervent conversations as our heads lay side by side on the pillow, our soft embraces before we fell asleep, our fond glances exchanged during the day, surely if these were wrong, Miss Hoop would know and eschew them.

I drifted along, content to revolve around this bright light, without heed or suspicion of wrongdoing, until the new curate arrived. After his first sermon, she went up to thank him for the spiritual wisdom she had derived, and I saw that her eyes met his with the same softness and tenderness with which she gazed upon me. Jealousy struck me like a thunderbolt!

Mary and I prayed together over what we termed my covetousness, and still she continued to gaze upon the young curate with favour, so much favour that within three months they were engaged and within six months married.

I hated him, and yet there was nothing despicable about him. He had not Mary's intensity of devotion, but he offered her the opportunity to act upon her beliefs.

"You must see, Tirzah, she told me, "the enormous potential for good I shall have once I am his wife. I shall be able to make spreading the message of the true Gospel my only task in life."

How could I deny this? I watched her marry him, the whole school turned out, and I was chief bridesmaid, tears streaming down my face. Though others did not know it, the tears were not tears of joy. It was not until her letters began to speak of the dampness of the new rectory or the teething problems of her firstborn that the vague sense of disease that had been fermenting in me for years burst forth.

I had deceived myself once more, excusing my infatuation for my teacher, because it was covered with a veneer of religiosity. Once it was gone, I saw the dire truth. I hated her husband because he took her away from me. I hated each of her children as they were born because I was thus one step farther removed from the source of love that once more was incarnated in human form.

Again, I eschewed all profane and earthly attachments. Yet God sets man– and womankind difficult tasks. For I fear I often erred over the ensuing years by adhering so rigidly to the opposite extreme. I developed an aloofness and distance that alienated me from my fellow sinners. With my superiority and severity, I set myself apart as some sort of judge.

My shell of imperviousness had become so thick that for many years nothing worthwhile or otherwise penetrated to upset my peace of mind—until I met Arabella and her father. It is foul to be contemptuous of others when that contempt is borne of an inner purity and transcendence. But what of smugness, which is nothing more than a defence against envy and adoration? There is no room for deception, self or otherwise, in a document such as this.

And that is why I fully confess that I loved Arabella Farraday from the moment I first saw her, loved her completely and miserably. I, of course, labelled her liar, hypocrite, savage. This was all nonsense. For who could know Arabella and not love her?

I never met a being so full of life, so vibrant with beauty, so graceful in movement. She was as wild as a tigress, and I must admit, in my folly, I thought I could tame the tigress and have her for my pet, to admire with my eyes, to stroke her soft fur, and deep inside, to cherish my power over the wild beast in her. She was all feminine grace in those costly dresses Mr. Farraday liked to see her wear. She treated the servants, including me, like so many mice with which she toyed in her pretty, teasing way. And when she felt something, she felt it deeply. Sorrow made an invalid of her, joy set her dancing around the room. "High animal spirits"—I have heard that said of many children, but for no one was it more true than for Arabella.

I had all the weapons of a lion-tamer: the whip, the withholding of food, the banishment to a dark cupboard, and even a few ploys a lion-tamer could not use: endless pages of Scripture to memorize, sarcasm, depictions of Hell. These were all to no avail; her will was greater than mine. She snapped and snarled at me no matter how often I beat her and no matter how many days she had been denied everything but bread and water to eat.

Once on my way to a store to purchase some thread, I saw a strange spectacle. A raggedly dressed man stood beside an enormous cage containing all different types of small animals, above which had been painted the legend "A Happy Family." I stood to the side of the small crowd that was forming around him, but soon found myself pressing forward as eagerly as the urchins, because the cage contained five canaries, three cats, two small dogs, ten mice, and a ferret, all in separate corners but without partitions of any kind. The man would speak softly to the animals, and they would leap forward to the middle of the cage and perform some pantomime — the dogs danced about, the mice made a little pyramid, the canaries sang on cue. The other animals; their natural enemies, looked on unconcerned. Then, even more remarkable, he had them perform together. The birds climbed into miniature wagons, and the cats pushed them about; the mice ran up and sat on the backs of the dogs, who carried them around in circles.

When the show was over, the onlookers were most generous. I had only a few shillings with which to purchase my thread, so I grasped them tightly in my hand as I approached the keeper.

"How did you do that?" I asked.

"Hit's all done with kindness, mum," he replied, as he lifted the cage onto the back of a handcart. The animals all continued to sit contentedly in their various places.

Some of the urchins had been whispering that they must be drugged.

"Do you give them something?" I asked.

"Only kindness," he answered.

"But I don't understand." The other people had moved off, darkness was settling upon the streets, and I was close to one of the more unsavoury parts of London. But still I lingered before that old man and his tiny miraculous circle. "What do you mean by kindness?"

The man paused in his labours and regarded me as if I were an imbecile. He raised his eyebrows, took off his hat, and scratched his head.

"Kindness is kindness, mum," he replied.

"Do you really mean—" I fear my voice was sharp "—that you do not punish these animals in order to train them?"

171

"Oh, no, mum. Why, what good would that do? If I kept them under like that, why, I would only have to turn my back and they'd be at each other in a moment."

"Then what do you do?" I was near tears. "When you want to teach them a new trick, what do you do?"

He thought about that for some time, continuing to scratch his head lazily. Doubtless, he had lice. "Well, I plays with 'em a bit first, just petting 'em and romping a bit, you understand, and then, if they seems ready, I shows 'em what it is I'd like 'em to do, and if they seem agreeable, well then, they do it, and if they ain't, we waits for another day. Hanimals 'as their bad days and good days just like us. Usually though, they're eager to please. Why, that cat there, the one that washes the mice with his tongue, he learned that in one afternoon!"

"Are there never animals that you just can't train?" I asked.

"Oh, yes. Some. That ferret, he's my second one, and I'm still not sure of him. The first killed a fine batch of trained mice. The ferrets are more naturally wild, you see. Besides, you 'as to get 'em when they're babies. If they become accustomed to hunting for their food, then you're through."

"Thank you. Thank you," I said, pressing my shillings into his hand. I scurried down the black streets, my thoughts racing. Kindness, pure and simple kindness—what a startling thought! But then children are not animals; they have the capacity to reason, to know when they are doing wrong. And I fear I also compared Arabella with the first ferret. I had not had her training since she was a baby; she had already learned to hunt.

Chapter Three

Jenny just came in to bring me a pot of fresh tea that she made for me. I know she believes I dislike her; how could she guess that I cannot bear her tenderness, her thoughtfulness, her friendliness? When I think of all the wrongs I have done her, of the evil I have wished upon her, the fact that she returns love for malice is intolerable. I suppose it is my just punishment.

I tried to dismiss my antipathy for her at first under the guise of concern for Arabella. They were too fond of each other, they spent too much time together, a girl of Jenny's class and background could only be a bad influence upon a young woman of Arabella's station. Yet I did nothing directly to separate them. I sensed that to do so would lay bare my own heart and that it would be broken. In fact, I went out of my way to be nice to Jenny; I arranged for her to have lessons with Arabella, hoping that the disparity between their educations would become apparent to Arabella and she would see it for what it was, contemptible. Instead, Jenny quickly displayed a livelier curiosity and a more acute intellect than her mistress. I am reminded of the forlorn student at Mrs. Banks's school who tried to curry the favour of the more popular girls by giving up her boxes of treats to them, mending their dresses, and writing their compositions. All of these kindnesses were gratefully accepted and yet she remained friendless, as much outside the circle of warmth and companionship as ever. So it was for me with Arabella and Jenny. How humiliating for me to be wooing a maid in order to win the heart of her mistress!

If outwardly I was Jenny's champion, surreptitiously I plotted her dismissal. I was aware that she had a soldier lover and had already reported such to Mr. Farraday.

"Find me a maid who isn't walking out with a soldier," was his sarcastic comment, "and you can hire her instead!"

Twice on her afternoons off I had followed Jenny in his company in the hopes of garnering some evidence that would result in her dismissal. Once they went into a tavern that provided some sort of low entertainment. I could not enter such a haunt and turned back. The other time they went for a stroll, hand in hand, along the river's edge in Chelsea. It was a sultry summer's night. The moon was full and low on the horizon, a dusky orange-red. The stench from the Thames was overwhelming, but the air was cooler than in the stifling streets of the city and the lights of the ships gliding by silently on the river were strange and wonderful. There I was, a solitary figure in my grey cloak, darting to and fro to avoid recognition, tripping and stumbling on the uneven path, and all around me were scores of couples. Feminine laughter and low masculine rumblings sounded everywhere. Couples locked in embraces. Couples pressed up against lampposts and railings. Couples silently watching the moonrise, the female leaning against her male partner, her head on his shoulder.

A great, rasping grief rose up in me, and I suddenly lost my resolution and bolted for 19 Grover Square. There I found Katie leaning against the area railing, talking to a footman from a neighbouring house and bullied her back inside with a series of desperate blows and pushes. Poor child! She was baffled by my sudden frenzy.

If I was to successfully draw any conclusions as to Jenny's moral character, it was necessary to eliminate the intrusion of any of my own personal feelings. I realize, of course, as I record this, how unpleasant was my behaviour, how full of envy and bitterness and unacknowledged loneliness. Yet I was also motivated by a sincere concern for Arabella, by a desire to protect her from all evil influence, and it was this that I kept in my mind on the night when I saw Jenny slip out of the kitchen door to meet her tall soldier, a dark figure leaning against the front wall. There was a furtive embrace and an exchange of words, and then they were off. I rose up, donned my cloak, and slipped out after them.

One of those strange summer fogs had come up, and I almost lost them. I had gone on down the street when I heard the clink of the Square garden gate as it closed. In an instant, I was up against the bars, the cold metal against my cheeks.

Yes! There they were hurrying up a path, talking softly and laughing. How had they gotten in? Had someone left the gate ajar? I had a key on my belt with my other keys, and when they had gone off some distance I used it to open the gate and admit myself. But I had lost them during the interval, and the Square garden was vast and enshrouded in fog. I wandered along the path, the moisture from the trees dripping onto my cloak, and paused from time to time to peer about and listen for sounds. There was nothing but the white curling cloak of fog around me. It clung to me, dimmed my vision, baffled my perceptions. Somewhere in this strange grey world were two lovers, pursued by me, alone, shut out, as ever the perpetual observer. These were the sort of bleak thoughts that enshrouded me as I trod the lonely paths. The Greek temple loomed out at me from the mist, but it, too, was empty, upon closer inspection.

Twice I made my lonely circuit of the garden and was just thinking that they must have gone out again when I heard a soft feminine cry from beyond some shrubbery. I crept cautiously along the wet grass until I was close to the hedge and carefully parted the branches to peer through them. What I saw so shocked me that my breath caught in my throat.

Jenny had spread her cloak on the ground to make a sort of rude bed for them upon the grass, and there they lay, entwined in an embrace. The soldier was beside her, his back to me, so I could not see his face. One hand was beneath her skirts, and as he fumbled there, I could see her face clearly through a sudden clearing in the fog. She did not even look like Jenny. Her eyes were shut, the contours of her face were strange, her head drifted slightly from side to side like a flower in the wind.

The fog closed in again, and for a time there was nothing but murmured words and rustlings and sighs. When they became visible again, her skirt had been partially displaced so that her stockinged legs were revealed. The man was kissing her; I could see her hands moving up and down the back of his jacket, clutching at him, pressing him more tightly to her.

My fingers trembled, and with a sharp crack, the slippery branches slid from my hands and snapped back into place.

"What was that? Daniel, stop! What was that noise?" It was Jenny's voice. I panicked and ran and not knowing where I was, floundered into bushes, nearly collided with a tree, and finally, coming up against the iron railing of the fence, felt my way along it until I reached the gate. I was sobbing in terror and shame.

Mr. Farraday, when I burst into his bedroom, accused me of hysteria.

"My God, woman, calm yourself!" he said. He clutched the bed sheets around his shoulders and stared at me horrified.

I must have been an object to inspire revulsion with my hair glued in wet ringlets to my face, the hem of my dress damp and hugging my legs. I had lost one shoe in my flight, which I only then realized.

He raised his hand, as if to ring his bell pull, and then his eyes narrowed. I could guess the thoughts running through his head. He was going to summon me as he always did when faced with any problem and suddenly it occurred to him that I, his ally in the battle for order and placidity, was the problem.

I did not care. Something was flickering within me, an agitation I had, never felt before.

"It is that Jenny, Arabella's maid," I babbled. "She is…she is consorting with a soldier in the Square garden. I saw her with my own eyes. It was disgusting. It was horrible!"

"Really, Miss Finch. This is neither the time nor the place."

Suddenly I was aware that I was alone with my employer in his bedchamber at a very advanced hour of the night. My concentration, which had been constricted to admit only Jenny and her sins, now widened to permit an influx of the most intimate and embarrassing details. The nightcap on Mr. Farraday's head; the full chamber pot only partially replaced under the bed; the heavy male odour in the room. I think I must have swayed a little.

"Sit down, Miss Finch," he said gruffly, moving over a little under the bedclothes.

"I cannot, Mr. Farraday!" I wailed.

"You cannot swoon in my bedroom," he said sharply, and I sat down. I was full of misery, and trembled like a frightened rabbit. He put out one of his large hands and touched my arm. I noticed the black hairs that curled on the back of it.

"Now, tell me, what was it that you saw!" he said. I looked into his eyes. They were no longer those of a man but those of an animal, greedy and burning! I was horrified and yet hypnotized. Some knowledge passed between us in those moments that I would rather not have known.

"I cannot tell you," I stammered at last.

"Surely, Miss Finch," he said slowly, never taking his eyes from mine, though his fingers moved ever so slightly on my arm, you are a woman and not ignorant of the ways between men and women." I felt my blood pounding, and my skin seemed to burn with fire.

I did not know what I wanted in those confused moments. If I said yes, would he teach me? If I said no, would he pounce upon me? If I said nothing, would he let me loose from this strange, helpless trance?

I said nothing, and in a few minutes his fingers dropped from my arm, and he said peevishly, "Well, if you have nothing to say, be off with you then. Wretched woman, wasting my time!"

I bolted through the door and, having shut it, crouched down against it, holding myself and weeping bitterly. I could not say, even now, the reason for my tears. Next minute, up the stairs came Jenny, as jaunty and unconcerned as a child. She took in my distraught condition and the door against which I huddled.

"You are up very late, ma'am," she observed with a little smile on her face. I realized, despite my confusion, the construction she placed upon my behaviour, but I was unable to speak and so had to suffer her faintly condescending charity as she helped me to my room.

Next day all was forgotten. I never broached the subject of Jenny or that night with Mr. Farraday nor did he with me. Things went on much as before. Jenny was perhaps a little more undisciplined, I was a little more shy around Mr. Farraday, and he was, perhaps, a bit more abrupt with me.

It must have been Jenny who began the foul rumour that I was some sort of paramour to Mr. Farraday. Not that anyone ever spoke directly of it to me, but did they think I was blind to their smirks and raised eyebrows?

And then I am sure the circumstance of my having become the housekeeper only added to the gossip. Servants are an ignorant lot with nothing better to occupy their time than the telling of tales. They believed, God help them in their stupidity, that I must have acquired this position by personal services rendered to the master. They could not or would not recognize the reward of true merit.

Also, Mr. Farraday and I were often alone. Indeed, I was the only one of all the household staff to whom he would speak. An occasional reprimand, command, or commendation to Cook was the extent of his interaction with them. They resented this, not understanding that it arose from his preference for solitude and privacy.

We dined together every evening except on those few occasions when Sir Henry Warder-Mull, his solicitor, was asked to stay. Mr. Farraday liked me as a dinner companion because, as he said, "You know the value of silence." He preferred that I not speak at all during those meals, and I satisfied his expectation without undue strain. It was over an after-dinner brandy that we conducted the business of the day. I would ask for approval of menus, determine what errands were required, and sometimes advise him on the grammar and spelling of the hundreds of letters he wrote and sent out to various journals and papers. This was the most delicate of my duties, for Mr. Farraday was a self-taught man and he was very sensitive to any criticism that would imply a lack of education. Whenever one of these letters was published, it was a triumph for both of us. He would order champagne to be served with dinner and bully me until I consented to take a glass with him. I hated champagne—even a glass would trigger one of the excruciating headaches that I frequently suffered—and yet he would not let me refuse.

I often suggested that he have Arabella down for dinner. I did not like to think of her dining upstairs in the schoolroom with only Jenny for company, and I thought it would improve her table manners. But Mr. Farraday did not want to be subjected to the "endless prattle of a young girl," and so she was allowed to come down only when Sir Henry was a dinner guest. He was amused by her bright chatter and her evident delight at playing the role of hostess.

I saw much more of Mr. Farraday than did his daughter, and naturally she resented this. At the same time, she drew closer and closer to Jenny.

I recall the first time I mentioned this subject to Mr. Farraday. It was also the first time he ever spoke of his wife.

"It makes our task doubly difficult," I said, complaining of Arabella's attachment to her maid. "The two of them are always talking together, and I fear that the constant proximity of someone of her own age encourages Miss Farraday in her propensity for gossip and frivolity."

"She came highly recommended," was Mr. Farraday's only response. He was always taciturn, and I understood from this curt reply that he did not wish, to discuss the subject further. I made a slight curtsy and was about to withdraw when his deep voice began reverberating again.

"Mrs. Farraday was very attached to her maid," he said painfully, as if the words were torn from him. His heavy features were contorted; he seemed about to cry.

"Her early death must have been tragic for you," I said. No one ever spoke of Arabella's mother, and it had been my assumption that she had died so painfully that no one wished to revive the memories. His next words shocked and horrified me.

"I wish to God she *were* dead," he said vehemently.

Chapter Four

Mr. Farraday never spoke directly of his wife again, except when Arabella was being especially self-willed or irresponsible or untruthful. Then he would caution me to correct her severely, explaining he did not want her becoming like her mother. From these comments, I formed a picture of a completely avaricious, depraved, spoiled woman who had, no doubt, married Mr. Farraday for his money, poisoned his household with a series of scenes and perhaps even clandestine romances, and was then repudiated by him to protect his young daughter from her evil influence. I pictured her wandering the streets, selling her soul and her body, and my one great dread was that she would appear someday at the side door and, holding out dirty, clutching fingers, insist on being given some money. I kept a small cache of coins in my room for this eventuality, for I knew I would want to spare Mr. Farraday any grief.

I was with him the day he died. He had been especially feverish for many days, sometimes calling for his parents, sometimes quarrelling with noted political figures whom he had never met, sometimes begging me not to leave him.

"You cannot leave. My God, I will do anything. Only say you will stay," he would plead, clutching at my hand.

"Hush, I am not leaving you," I would reply.

He woke from a troubled sleep that night and turned toward me with glazed eyes but a face full of serenity and peace.

"Ah, it is all right then," he said softly. "You do love me after all."

Hot tears rushed to my eyes.

"Yes, I do love you," I said, "and the Lord loves you also and is waiting to enfold you in His Love." I was quite concerned, for he had not yet indicated any desire for reconciliation to his God. My most fervent wish was that he should die with the Lord's name on his lips.

"Your love is all I need," he murmured.

"My love is a mere reflection of the glorious Love of God, our Father," I said softly. "I am but a vessel through which he demonstrates to you His concern for each of His creatures."

"You do not know how wonderful it is to know," he said with wonder, "that you have always loved me, that you love me still." I took his hands in mine; they were cold. "I can die at peace knowing you were here with me," he said faintly, "that at last you came back to me, my beloved, my adored wife, Perdita."

I started back, dropping his hands. A perplexed look crossed his face. Then he closed his eyes. He remained still for so long that I forgot the mortal hurt that my heart had suffered and reached for his hands again. They were even colder than before, and no matter how tightly I gripped them or how much I chafed them in my own, no warmth would come back into them. I touched his face; it was as cold and lifeless as his hands.

A great cry arose in me, but I suppressed it. I would wake the house and be denied this precious time alone with my love. God forgive me, I held him in my arms. I pressed my head to his shoulder where I had always longed to be I kissed his cold, unmoving lips, which I had always longed to kiss. I removed his nightcap and smoothed back his thick, waving hair, which I had always longed to touch I wept over him until his cold face was bathed with my tears. Then, like Mary Magdalen, I dried it with my hair.

I knelt by his bedside and prayed to the Lord that He would forgive this man all his sins and would, even at the expense of my own life, accept him into His Mercy. I removed his stained and wrinkled nightclothes—surely it was no sin to gaze upon the innocent nakedness of the dead—and dressed him in his Sunday clothes, just as he would have wished it, his favourite watch in his pocket, the fine gold chain across his chest. Then I knelt down again and began reading aloud the Prayers for the Dead.

I was saying softly, "In the midst of life we are in death: of whom may we seek for succour, but of Thee, O Lord?" when the curtain to the dressing room was drawn aside and the nurse who slept there to be at his call came into the room, rubbing her eyes. It was dawn. Grey light flooded the room as she drew aside the gold brocade draperies, and it fell upon his grey face.

"Well, there is nothing more to be done for 'im, poor soul," she said calmly, trying to join his lifeless hands in prayer. "He's been dead some time," she observed, looking at me.

I had continued and was beginning: "We commend into thy hands of mercy, most merciful Father, the soul of this our brother, Walter, departed—"

"You're the one that could use some nursing," she said, drawing me to my feet.

"I must remain with him," I cried desperately.

"And be of no good to anyone," was her comment. "Think of that poor orphaned girl who is still alive. You must rest yourself so as to be able to console her." And she led me meekly through the silent corridors of the bereft household to my narrow white room. I had not slept in my bed for some days, and she drew back the quilt that covered it and tucked me in as gently as any mother with her child would do.

But when her brisk steps had faded away I could not sleep. Over and over again my mind grappled with and refused to accept the notion that, in his death, Walter Farraday had wanted his wife to be with him.

A new vision of her began to haunt me. In this nightmare, she was always beside me, tall and gracious and lovely—by then I had seen the portrait of her that Arabella kept upon her dressing table— always between me and Arabella, between me and Mr. Farraday, even between me and Sir Henry, who became Arabella's co-guardian. I could almost hear her saying to me in a calm, musical voice, "You are no longer needed. I have returned."

Despite the grief of this vision, it was many months before I could bring myself to ask Sir Henry about her. It was during that

Christmas we all spent together at Pittlesbury Hall. Indeed, I believe it was Christmas night after the exchange of presents. Arabella had gone up to bed with her new puppy, a gift from Sir Henry, and he and I were left alone before the roaring fire.

There was a warm glow, bred of the punch and the holiday, the sudden intimacy in which we all of us found ourselves while walking to church together and singing carols around the tree, from the lowliest scullery maid and the stable boys up to myself.

This same companionable mood remained when the others were gone. When I asked Sir Henry if he had known Mrs. Farraday, driven to this confrontation with my fears by concern for Arabella's health, which was poor and which I feared she might have inherited from her mother, he became expansive, even sentimental.

"Oh, yes, indeed I did," he said thoughtfully. "I drew up the marriage settlements, you know, for Walter. It was our first professional association."

"What was she like?" I asked.

"She was lovely," he said, his face softened by the firelight so that I caught a glimpse of the serious and earnest young man he had been in those days. "Everyone loved her. She was as gracious and friendly with a cabdriver as she was with a duchess. She had her faults—she was always late, she was always forgetting something or some event but it never mattered. Her presence was the greatest gift. I recall how Arabella adored her. When her mother was in the room, she had eyes for no one else. But then, it was the same for all of us."

"Was she of a delicate constitution?" I asked. "Was she frequently ill?" I wanted to turn the subject away from her charms.

"Yes, she was, after the marriage began to suffer," Sir Henry said meditatively. It was as if he were going back in time, his posture changing, his expression changing. "Poor Walter! He was so jealous of her, and he could not hide it! He could not even bear to have the doctors come to see her. I often stopped in to visit her when I came to see Arabella. No matter how ill she had been, Perdita was always charming and gracious—and lovely. She adored flowers. I always brought her flowers. Her room was always a bower of them. I used to bring her lilies. They were her favourites. One day…"

His voice trailed off, and as he gazed into the fire, the subtlest changes of expression passed over his face. I could almost believe it was my imagination and the flickering light cast by the flames, but I fancied I, saw adoration and sorrow and humiliation, each succeeding the other. He shook himself from his reverie and was able to answer my more practical questions as to the type and duration of Arabella's mother's ailments, but the warm feeling had left the room. The air seemed chilly, and he left shortly, excusing himself before ascending to the guest room.

Altogether there were enough points of similarity between Sir Henry's descriptions and Arabella's frequent attacks of brain fever that I felt I must consult Dr Steward when we returned to London that spring. Although Dr Steward had been dismissed by Mr. Farraday, he was a highly reliable physician who was also familiar with Arabella's medical history, and though this was countermanding Mr. Farraday's order I felt consulting the good doctor in the best interests of all concerned. When the time arrived, I did not reveal that Arabella's illnesses usually followed some expression of illicit passion, such as the time I found her kissing a blacksmith or the night I surprised her in her bedchamber in the embrace of Philip Vandeleur, the bed hangings burning around them.

After all, I felt that it was probably my fault that these shocking episodes had occurred. I was far too busy with my household tasks and had not, despite distaste for Mrs. Vandeleur, forbidden Arabella to visit her. Of course, I knew that Arabella waged a secret campaign against me in her letters to Sir Henry, and when he insisted that she be allowed to call upon that woman, I quickly capitulated, just as I did later when Sir Henry overcame my objections to her debut and her acquaintance with her cousin.

And I still cannot bring myself to describe that scene to anyone. It lives in my memory so vividly, lit with the flames of Hell, as I burst upon Arabella on the bed, her dress crumpled, her hair loose, and the dark head of the man upon her white bosom, his body pressed against hers. It was a moment of utter horror, all confusion and chaos, jostlings and outcries before the other servants arrived and Jenny put out the fire. I could not forget the part I played in it, how I could have actually shattered the man's skull with the poker

I brandished, the names I called Arabella, the things I said to her after he was gone.

I could not forgive myself for my loss of control. Chastisement should be meted out in a rational manner that allows the sinner respect for his punisher and comprehension of the reasons for his punishment.

In the morning, my agony was even greater, for Arabella was delirious and her flesh seemed to burn my fingers when I touched her. It was the fourth occurrence of this sort of inner fire that seemed to feed upon her, or was she, rather, like a volcano, which would periodically erupt, leaving this ruined landscape behind?

Of course, I was not so fanciful when I described those illnesses to Dr Steward. I was careful to give an accurate and complete description; I did not even flinch at the possibility of madness.

Arabella wandered into the drawing room during our interview, and Dr Steward asked her a few questions When she had departed he turned to me.

"I understand your concern, Miss Finch, but there seems to be nothing out of the ordinary, and since that is so, I would ascribe her fragile health to overexcitement and oversensitivity. As I believe I informed you last year," he went on, "such afflictions are common in young girls of this age. The natural instincts of a woman have no outlet and make themselves manifest in many strange ways: religious fervour, fits, hysteria. Once she is married, these episodes will cease."

I flushed, but he did not seem to notice.

"I treat a good many young women," he continued. "The young ladies at the boarding school, for instance. Many of them suffer similar ailments. Miss Farraday, in my opinion, is very like the other hysterical patients I have treated. The same sort of repressive upbringing—"

"Mr. Farraday was an excellent father!"

"Was well-meaning," he said, as if correcting. "She has been isolated from other young people and given few opportunities for expressing her feelings. I can guarantee that you could cure her in a matter of weeks with a few parties and some outings."

"Sir Henry Warder-Mull has arranged for her to come out this Season."

"Very good," he replied. "That should take care of the problem then."

I must confess he was right. She was never once ill during the round of parties, dinners, and outings through which she danced her way, except, of course, the few days she kept to her bed and refused to eat while Sir Henry wrestled with the problem of whether or not to allow Arabella to see her cousin. I advised against it, of course, and, of course, Sir Henry overruled my objections. He was forever susceptible to her whims and blind to her intentions; even I could see that she fell in love with her cousin from the first moment he came into the drawing room at 19 Grover Square.

I only wondered that she did not make her preference for him more apparent. After my collapse at Pittlesbury Hall, while I was still recovering from that first brush with death, Jenny informed me that Mr. DeWinx had followed us to Sussex and was visiting Arabella. I was only mildly surprised; there was such a change in her, and it was like sunshine to the winter in which I found myself. She was softer, more compassionate, more perceptive; she came to call upon me daily and read aloud to me or brought me bunches of roses.

One day she came in, a little song on her lips and a cluster of fragrant scarlet roses in her hand, which she laid on the satin coverlet. I had been placed in Mr. Farraday's old room, for it was closer to the stairs. It reminded me of the time shortly after I had been engaged as governess when Arabella brought me a strange clump of hedge branches and tall grasses. She had not prepared any of her lessons for the day and thought to appease me. As soon as I understood this I made her throw them one by one onto the fire; they made a horrible stink and a vile black smoke, which nearly choked us. She had brought these roses with much the same intent, but I could not look at them, lying limply against the green of the satin, without tears coming to my eyes at their beauty and the gift they were intended to be.

"Miss Finch, I have something very near to my heart to tell you," she said, clasping her hands and hanging her head like a penitent schoolgirl. "Do you remember Mr. DeWinx, who came to call upon me at Grover Square?"

I nodded.

"Well, he has done me the honour of asking me to be his wife, and I have accepted him."

"Sir Henry…" I murmured.

"He does not know yet," she said, kneeling down beside the bed and taking my hand in hers. She glowed with beauty, like the roses. "I need your written consent, and I need you to be my advocate with him. You have always liked Mr. DeWinx, but Sir Henry has an irrational hatred for him. He must understand how important this is to me! I shall die if I cannot marry Franklin—Mr. DeWinx!"

"He would know better than I," I managed to say, "but surely such an attachment goes against your father's wishes and thus is impossible by the terms of the will."

"Oh, hang the will!" she said, getting up and walking away to stand with her arms across her chest. It was one of her father's favourite postures. "I would give up everything, the houses, the money, all of it to be with Franklin!"

"Miss Arabella, it is fine to imagine—"

"I am not imagining anything!" she declared, stamping her foot and glaring at me. "Don't you know what love is like?" The tears that had been in my eyes since I first saw the roses came flooding out I had been particularly lachrymose since the advent of my illness.

"Oh, Finch, forgive me. I did not mean to upset you." Arabella flew to my side, an eager penitent, and dried away my tears with the edge of the sheet. It was some time before I was able to stop. Arabella was then seated on the edge of my bed, her eyes full of pity.

"Did you not love my father?" she asked, so softly I had to ask her to repeat it.

"I respected him," I said.

"No, no, did you love him?" she said, with the manner of a language teacher correcting a slow pupil.

"In a manner of speaking," I said at last.

"Would you have married him? she asked.

"That is preposterous. He would never have—"

"But would you have married him? If he said to you, 'Finch, my darling, will you marry me?' Would you have?"

No one had ever called me his darling. I felt a rush of vertigo, as if I were falling from a great height into a fiery blackness. For a moment, there was only blank terror, then I called myself back from that abyss. I thought of Mr. Farraday's social position and mine, of his wife who still might be alive, of what they would have said if a governess had married her pupil's father.

"No," I said quite distinctly. "No, I would never have married him."

"Poor old Finch," said Arabella, bending over and kissing me on my parched lips.

I wrote out my consent for her that evening, and not all of Sir Henry's rages, his threats, or his accusations ever made me regret my impulsive gift of love to Arabella.

Chapter Five

Of course, there was an ugly scene with Sir Henry. He came straight up to me immediately after Arabella informed him of her desires and woke me out of one of those restful sleeps that were as rare and precious to me then as a well of sweet desert water.

"How can you have given Arabella permission to marry some penniless upstart without first discussing the matter with me?" he said peremptorily. "How is it that this calf love has been fostered right under your oblivious nose?

"I did not consider my judgment to be dependent upon your analysis of the situation," I managed to say once I understood the content of his quarrel with me. "As for the nature of the attachment between them, I believe it to be quite deep on Arabella's part, and as for Mr. DeWinx, from what I know of him, I would conclude that he would not have spoken of marriage unless he was equally sincere and serious."

"It's absurd!" declared Sir Henry. "Arabella will marry me! That is how Walter and I planned it!"

Suddenly I felt as if I were suffocating, and it was a long time before I could speak. It is painful to acknowledge the depth of my despair and dismay, for it arose from such a foolish dream: the hope that Sir Henry would come to care for me that perhaps he would ask me to marry him. Were we not often closeted together, discussing Arabella's future, so like my former conferences with Mr.

Farraday? Were we not both her guardians and thus standing in stead like two parents to her?

"Why was it that Mr. Farraday never informed me of this plan?" I asked at last, choking back the anguish I felt, determined not to invite the final humiliation of revealing my folly to Sir Henry.

"Why should he?" replied Sir Henry contemptuously. "It was a matter between men. He wished me to watch over his daughter and her estate; he trusted me as the man most capable of managing such a sacred trust. Your only role was to safeguard her from any indiscretion before the celebration of our nuptials. And only see what a fine mess you have made of that!" He flung himself away from my bedside in an impatient move of indignation and frustration. "You will withdraw your consent, of course," he said, coming back again, "or I shall see that you are relieved of your guardianship."

"My Lord and Saviour has already made those arrangements," I said quietly. I very seldom resort to sarcasm, but what right did he have to speak to me so? He had the grace to look sheepish.

"I will withdraw my consent," I went on, with dignity, "only at Arabella's personal request."

And I did so, when she appeared a few days after Sir Henry's announcement of their marriage and quietly asked me to substitute Sir Henry's name where I had once written Franklin DeWinx. She would not speak of what had happened, but I saw that her eyes were full of tears and her hands trembling. I had no chance to seek an explanation from Jenny; suddenly the entire household decamped for town and I was left alone with one maid to watch over me.

Those were terrible nights. The huge house, suddenly bereft of its inhabitants, was alive with noises of its own: creaking, rustling, sighs, moans. The darkness and the isolation weighed on me, suffocated me, terrified me. Unable to give myself over to the friendly darkness of sleep, I lay awake until dawn made its sullen presence felt in my room through the flurry of bird songs beyond my muffled windows and the liquid pools of light that lay along the floorboards at the base of the draperies. The night after the wedding was the most difficult; I pictured my lovely young pupil and the triumphant Sir Henry and the mysteries of the marriage bed. Was she proud and defiant? Was she timid and cowering? I prayed silently throughout that night that the Lord would spare her any pain or indignity. Perhaps, in light of later events, I should not have made this prayer.

By the time the household staff returned to Pittlesbury Hall, bringing with them Dr Steward, who had kindly consented to have a look at me, I was close to death from exhaustion. He was indignant about the degree of collapse I had reached.

"She should not be sinking this fast," he told Jenny, who was weeping noisily by my bed. I suppose she felt that if she had not gone to London I would be better. "I would not give her a fortnight to live at this rate."

I began choking at these words, and for a time the struggle for breath was so intense that I was aware only of a ringing in my ears, a red curtain before my eyes, and the soothing touch of their hands. Thinking that this might be my last moment, I thanked the Lord for giving me the boon of their company and commended my Soul to Him. Next moment, I was at peace, and my eyes opened in the expectation of grassy fields and celestial choirs, finding instead the dimness of the great shadowed room and those two faces, glowing wraithlike in the gloom. I think I wept with disappointment.

"You know, Jenny," Dr Steward said as I lay weeping, "I have different ideas than my colleagues about the treatment of consumption. What she requires for life is air, and yet you and I can see that the atmosphere of this room is close, stale, full of fetid odours and stifled circulation. I recommend somewhat drastic measures." He strode over to the window and flung aside the ancient crimson velvet draperies, which gave off a cloud of dust. Sunlight poured into the room like the Grace of God, flooding every corner, bathing both my companions in a heavenly light. My eyes, molelike from long exposure to the dark, blinked rapidly and had to close themselves against the glory of that light. Even with them closed the light caressed my eyelids and seemed to bring a clarity and serenity into my thoughts.

Next minute there was a touch on my skin even more gentle and soothing than that of Jenny and the doctor, a light touch infinitely delicate and caring. Dr Steward had thrown up the sashes and a thick stream of warm air, scented with grass and roses, flowed in. I sighed with pleasure, and the tears in my eyes were those of joy, not of regret.

191

"Of course," said Dr Steward from the dressing room, "she will be too cold at night. I would close the window in the bedroom but leave these open, draw the curtain between the rooms, and light a fire to take the chill off. Your country doctor will say that I am hastening her death, but I doubt that he has done anything to slow it himself with his regime. We will see." He came back into the room. "What is she being fed?"

"Beef tea, jelly, boiled eggs, toast and water—" began Jenny.

Dr Steward shook his head. I had not yet opened my eyes, but I knew his every move. How acute all of my senses had become.

"Too bland, too lowering," he said. "She requires the lightest and most tempting of morsels. Fresh fruit, whenever possible. I brought up some oranges from London." He took one from his pocket and gave it to Jenny, who began to peel it. The tangy, clean scent of the orange oil permeated the air. "Vegetables, lightly cooked in some nice cream sauce. Perhaps a little bit of chicken, poached in wine, or some fish. No heavy meat dishes."

Jenny was putting the slices of orange into my mouth. They were exquisitely sweet and juicy. The tears continued to pour down my cheeks. How could I wish to die in a world so full of delights? Why had I never truly tasted an orange or savoured the autumn air before? My hands unclenched as I concentrated on my meal.

"I will go below to tell Cook my wishes in the matter of diet," Dr Steward said. I knew that he reached out and touched Jenny on the shoulder and that his touch conveyed a deeper feeling than simple acknowledgment. Again, I knew this with my eyes closed.

When the orange was done, Jenny set about bathing me with her swift, sure touch. The warm air, the cool water, the rough texture of the linen cloth against my parched skin—all was delicious to me. I felt thoroughly cleansed, and even the fresh nightgown in which Jenny dressed me smelled wonderful, full as it was of the homely scents of starch and piquant greenery from the hedge on which it had dried.

"Am I in Heaven already, Jenny?" I asked weakly to broach the silence.

"Not yet, Tirzah," she replied. I had asked her to call me that. "We want you with us a little longer," and she kissed me softly on the forehead.

"How was…how was the wedding?" I wanted to know, opening my eyes and taking in all the familiar details of the room, now washed in the clarity of the light, both inner and outer.

"Oh, Miss Arabella was beautiful," sighed Jenny. "She was a vision. The dress was white Swiss muslin with a rounded waist, the sleeves and neck and hem all finished with pleats of the same material." I noted with amusement rather than dismay that Jenny still had a fancy for fashion. "I fixed her hair, which was pinned up toward the top of her head and crowned with a cluster of orange blossoms, from which the blonde lace veil fell down and trained on the ground behind her when she walked up the aisle. She had a bouquet of orange blossoms and a white satin-covered Bible that Sir Henry gave her to carry."

I nodded, indicating that I wanted to hear more. Jenny sat down on the bed and took my cold, weak hand in her warm, strong one.

"Miss Arabella was a storybook bride, everyone said so, even though some of us realized that her voice was filled with doubt and dread rather than maidenly timidity as the guests fancied it. Still, she went through it all like a soldier, her carriage was so erect, her head so proud, her manners all that you could have desired, Tirzah. It was the other members of the wedding party who added a comic note to the festivities. There was Sir Henry, so bursting with his own importance that a button popped off in the middle of the ceremony and he went back down the aisle, this great gap showing. And then, you know, his sister was to be bridesmaid. She's a great, gangly, mannish old spinster."

"Like me," I suggested.

"Oh, Tirzah, not like you at all," Jenny contradicted.

"No, you have a beauty she will never have, poor thing. She wore a dress of lavender satin trimmed all over with ruches of pinked rose satin, and her bonnet, of the same lavender satin, was clustered with horrid pink roses. She looked a sight standing beside Miss Arabella. She really did."

"The breakfast?" I asked.

"Oh, Mrs. Glover outdid herself. It was truly magnificent: Pigeon pies, lobster, mayonnaise of trout and salmon, garnished tongue, decorated hams, and dishes and dishes of jellies and pastries and blancmanges and cheesecakes and fruit. The whole table was decorated with those silver epergnes full of flowers, and we borrowed a set of the most beautiful china from Miss Peacock at number 21 to complete the table. You've never seen anything so lovely. Forty guests, most of them neighbours or friends of Sir Henry. Lady Molliton refused to come, and Sir Henry was careful not to invite any of the young men who used to call upon Arabella. For the breakfast, she wore the cleverest dress, a foulard with a pale lemon background. Lengths of Bruges lace rode up the back and ruching of violet and green was sewn around the front and up the third seam. She had the most wonderful coat and page sleeves trimmed with the same ruchings. The neck was finished with more ruche and lace. In her hair, she wore a violet ribbon. She was very quiet, but no one thought that odd in a bride. At any rate, she was the topic of all conversation."

"Did she seem composed throughout?"

"Through everything. The night before, the dressing for the wedding, the departure for the honeymoon. She never cried."

I felt tears sting my eyes again—unreasonable that I should cry and Arabella not.

"She needed her mother then..." I said brokenly.

"She must be her own mother now," replied Jenny solemnly.

"Are you ladies done gossiping about the wedding yet?" asked Dr Steward as he re-entered the room. "Jenny, Miss Finch requires a great deal of quiet at this point in time. She wants to be fully recovered by the time Miss Arabella—forgive me, I should say Lady Warder-Mull—returns home."

I thought him merely jesting, but it was so. During the ensuing weeks, I recovered so rapidly that on the day set for Arabella's return from her honeymoon I was able to go downstairs. There was the sound of a carriage on the drive, shouted orders to the stable boys, the scrape of footsteps on the gravel, and then the front door opened. In a minute Arabella, dressed in a faultlessly lovely violet traveling gown, was kneeling beside the couch on which I lay, covering my hands with kisses and telling me how much better I looked. She was exceptionally beautiful herself, her dark hair fastened back under her purple chip hat in a severe bun, her complexion pale but with roses blooming in her cheeks.

When Sir Henry entered the room, she underwent a dramatic change in deportment. He frowned at seeing her on the floor, and she got up quickly, like a child caught in forbidden play.

"See how well Finch looks!" she said nervously, going to stand beside him. Her hands in her purple gloves clasped his arm tightly.

"Yes, my dear, she does seem improved," he said. "Now, go upstairs. You must need a rest after that long journey. I think we shall have to order a new carriage; the suspension on this one is dreadful. Shocking!"

"Yes, dear," she said and went obediently out of the room.

Sir Henry made a few general remarks to me, including an invitation to join them for dinner, and then began pacing about the room like an architect measuring off dimensions. When I dared to ask an innocent question about how he enjoyed the married state, he started and mumbled something to the effect that it was all he could expect, and went dashing off.

I suppose that knowing the fragility of my health I should have refused the invitation to dinner, but I could not resist the temptation to see more of my Arabella. The meal was as unpleasant as possible.

Sir Henry found fault with everything: the service, the soup, the lobster, and the *salmi* of grouse. He did not like the plate and insisted on the servants unpacking the one they had brought with them and cleaning it and pressing it into use at once, which meant that the rump of beef and the venison arrived cold and nearly inedible. Marriage had made of him a petty tyrant. He commanded Arabella to eat, found fault with the way she chewed her food, would not permit her to have a second glass of wine. Throughout it all, Arabella was docile, thoughtful of his wishes, and even winning. She attempted to tease him and flatter him in her old way, but he discouraged such light-heartedness. Why was it that Arabella, with both her father and her husband, found that her very nature was despised and discouraged? Had it been different with Mr. DeWinx? I could see by her pallor and agitation how greatly she suffered.

Luckily, I was spared any further exposure to her humiliation by an attack of coughing that sent me up to my room. I never again spent more than a few minutes with her in the presence of her husband; it was too painful. But I was blessed with the pleasure of her company. She came to sit beside me often and read the Bible aloud in her lovely, melodic voice. She took over the task of my nursing from Jenny, feeding me, changing the sheets, standing at the window and describing the weather and scenery outside. At one time, Sir Henry suggested rather grudgingly that I should be sent to Italy to recover; I think he disliked the fact that his wife spent most of the hours of her day in my sickroom. I refused to go. I suppose it was improvident of me, but I could not bear to give up any one of the precious moments I spent with this new, loving Arabella.

As time passed it became increasingly apparent that Arabella was in a certain condition that should bring great joy to her marriage. And yet she never spoke of it; nor did her husband, Sir Henry. I could not fathom the reason for this secrecy and eventually asked Jenny.

"Is Arabella expecting a child?"

Jenny nodded. "In June or July," she said.

"Why does she say nothing? Why does Sir Henry not speak of it?" I asked.

Jenny bit her lower lip. "She does not wish to tell him yet," she replied. There was something about her manner—by then I knew her thoroughly—that was not right.

"Is there something wrong?" I asked. "We must send for Dr Steward at once!"

Jenny turned her face away from me and pretended to be busy stoking the fire. "No, there is nothing wrong. Pray, don't concern yourself with it Tirzah!" she mumbled. I knew then, and from the fact that she avoided looking me in the eyes, that something was gravely amiss. I entertained such wild speculations on what it could be; dear God, I was horrified at the possibilities that crossed my mind. How could I think of such wicked deeds and suspect my loving darling of such crimes?

I put such notions out of my mind with a stern reprimand to myself for even permitting such sinful thoughts. I determined to question Arabella on the matter and offer her the maternal guidance and advice that doubtless she craved and needed. I even enlisted Jenny in this plan, and she must have been disturbed herself, for she readily assented.

One afternoon when Arabella was sitting with me, Jenny came in and locked the door behind her.

Arabella rose. "What is this? What do you want of me?" she cried, distraught.

"Bella, Tirzah has guessed at your condition," said Jenny, calmly, placing the keys in her pocket.

"Oh!" said Arabella, swinging around to face me. "It is that obvious then! I did not think—"

"It is a wonderful event!" I said. "I think you must be very happy to find yourself so. But you must share your joy with your husband. It will make him very proud, indeed."

Arabella flung herself away from the bed and backed up nearly into the grate, where a small fire was burning. Her arms were folded over her waist in the age-old gesture of protection. One lock of hair had fallen loose across one eye.

"Don't you know, can't you guess why I have not told him?" she asked, addressing Jenny with a hysterical tone in her voice.

We were both silent.

"He has never touched me!" cried Arabella in anguish, sinking down to the floor. "He has never come to me—not since those first nights when he came into the bed with me and began to…began to…" Her voice broke, and she sobbed bitterly for many minutes. Jenny and I were frozen with disbelief, staring at each other, unmoving.

"He has never been able," sobbed Arabella. "I feel so loathsome. So disgusting. Trying to awaken his interest. But never would he come to me at night. Don't you see why I cannot tell him?"

I am afraid I was very stupid.

"But if he has never…if the marriage has not been consummated," I asked, "how then can you be in this condition?"

Chapter Six

Arabella flew at the door like a caged bird, sobbing and saying she could not bear to have me look at her. Jenny went quickly to open it, and she fled without a backward glance for me.

I was stricken more by Arabella's fear of me and my lack of perception than by my dawning realization of what her words meant. Jenny explained the entire matter to me: Arabella's intimacy with her cousin, her suspicion after he left that she was pregnant, her decision to marry Sir Henry.

I was shocked. I was shocked because I was not shocked. Somehow this heinous act seemed no longer wicked or inexplicable. Instead of feeling indignation or contempt or disgust, I felt only Arabella's pain and her fear and her unhappiness.

God forgive me if I erred in doing what I did. I told Jenny to bring her back to me. I told Jenny that if she would not come to me I would go to her. When she finally entered the room, face wet with tears, head bent, I held out my arms and put her head on my shoulder and held her close as she sobbed and sobbed.

"Can you forgive me, dear Miss Finch?" she asked. "I have been very, very evil."

"You only loved too deeply and too well," I said, stroking her hair: "I forgive you. God will forgive you, too."

We could not think what to do about Sir Henry. I am afraid we hatched all sorts of wild plans to have her go away and return after the birth of the child. Though I knew my strength was insufficient to the task, I offered to go with her and Jenny and raise up the child after its birth. It gave me such pleasure, the thought of having a baby in my arms whom I could shower with my affection.

Then as quickly as the crisis had come, it passed. A few days later Sir Henry came into my room and announced that he and his wife would be leaving soon for—London, that—as she was soon to bear an heir to the Warder-Mulls, he wished to consult the best doctors in London to insure the successful delivery of the child.

We could not understand this attitude of his; I could only assume that his desire for an heir was so great that he was willing to accept a child fathered by another man out of the fear that he would never be able to sire his own. I do know that with their departure I felt the will to live ebb out of me, and I was plunged once again into the gloom and despair that marked the beginning of my illness.

I know now what it is to waste away. Each day a little of my spirit leaves me, another desire is consumed and evaporates. They hired a nurse for me from the village before they left; she is a good woman, but she is a stranger. I cannot speak to her of the things that trouble me.

Jenny wanted to remain with me, but I told her that she must go with Arabella. She sends me long letters, which the nurse reads to me, describing the growth of the baby; she rarely mentions Sir Henry.

At night I cannot sleep. I am desolate and afraid in this empty house, so full of the sounds of my demons—Pride, Envy, Loneliness. Yet I no longer see these as unforgivable faults—after what I have experienced, how can I? Doubt and Fear must be as much a part of the Human Mystery as Love and Knowledge.

I begin to see now where I have gone wrong. I have lived my life in the hopes of earning the Divine Love of the Lord as my reward. I have never hesitated to cut myself off from all earthly attachments as hindrances in this pursuit. Now I wonder if it is not through such attachments that we learn how to accept and return that Sacred Love.

A messenger arrived to say that Arabella and Jenny have vanished from 19 Grover Square. Sir Henry thought they might have come here. They tried to keep it from me, but I got up out of my bed and insisted on speaking to the man.

I am afraid I have used up what little life was left to me. I would not return to my bed until I had searched the house and grounds thoroughly, hoping against hope that they had fled to me. But there is no one here with me but Death.

With my last bit of strength, I am praying that Jenny and Arabella and the baby are safe somewhere, enclosed in the circle of God's Love.

The room is dark around me, and yet there is a light here the like of which I have never seen. Are those rustlings the sounds of demons or of angels' wings?

> *The nurse records: "Miss Finch died at dawn on the day following this last great physical exertion. Her last words were: 'Is there someone there?'" —Jenny Steward*

PART FIVE

Mr. Franklin DeWinx:
Letter to Mr. Charles Lindley
30 May 1843

~ ~

Happy is the man unto whom the Lord reckoneth not guilt:
and in whose spirit there is no guile or self-deception.

Psalm 32

Chapter One

Southern United States
30 May 1843

My dear Charles,
You were right to fear that the news in your last letter would overset me. I have attempted many times to frame some sort of reply—no less to thank you for your concern and the salve of your compassion than to let you know my feelings—but have been unable to come to any peace with the events that transpired in England after my departure. Also, I must say that I am totally absorbed in my present undertaking, one of a very delicate nature that requires the full strength and concentration of all my faculties, Heart, Soul, and Mind.

While I was on board the *Tweed*, I became friendly with a gentleman by the name of James Herrod, who was sent out to the British West Indies to report back to his Society, which is centered in Edinburgh. He worked for the abolition of slavery and on the conditions in those islands since the Emancipation of the Negroes. He offered me a position as his secretary, and we travelled together through Barbados, Antigua, and Jamaica, talking to former slaves and plantation owners, ministers and government officials. It was the best of opportunities for me; not only did I have a task to which I could devote myself and to some extent extinguish the reproaches of my conscience and the pain of my heart (you see, I have given up the conceit of the *Erinyes*; this bedevilment comes from within), but we were also provided with accommodations and the most beneficent hospitality at each of our stops. The climate of these islands is very fine and the scenery very beautiful. It would seem a veritable Eden on earth were it not for the sufferings of the former slaves. For despite the undeniable benefits they have received since the Emancipation Acts, their condition is still miserable. It is based solely on the arbitrary whims of the local magistrates who try complaints against the property owners. And many of those self-same magistrates are as corrupt as the bookkeepers and the absentee landlords.

My companion was somewhat amused by my horror at the injustice of the system, for he had been on a similar journey of observation five years earlier and had become accustomed to the problems inherent within the judicial process: He insisted that the wrongs in the British West Indies were as nothing compared to the evils of the slave system as it is still practiced in the Southern United States. I determined to go and see for myself, with the thought of perhaps writing an article for publication, so ardently did the fire of indignation burn in my breast.

With the aid of my friend and companion, who gave me letters of introduction to several of his colleagues in the country, I travelled to Georgia and there saw for myself the full iniquity of slavery in practice. I will not regale you with the horrors I witnessed; I have written up some partial accounts, which I still hope to publish one day. But these plans have been temporarily set aside while I have devoted myself to a more immediate and concrete effort to diminish some of the suffering all about me. I will not give you any details of the business in which I am engaged nor mention the names of Mr. Herrod's friends, since we are involved in an illegal activity. If we were caught, we would surely be imprisoned and perhaps even receive summary death—the notion of justice here is very specious. I have at several times faced the prospect of imminent discovery and have often been lost in the wilderness when the lives of others depended on my courage and wits. So far, no lives have been lost, but this is surely an activity in which I cannot stay long without serious consequences.

I tremble sometimes at my own temerity: Who am I, who for so long have judged myself a coward and a cynic, to be engaged in acts that require constant courage and an unswerving belief in my own righteousness? But I have found a measure of peace amongst the dangers. There is no question here, as there was for me in England, of the morality of my actions. Even when I am a criminal in the eyes of the law of this land, I don't doubt my rightness. And my courage, furthermore, has not failed me but seems to grow in strength. I also enjoy the daily company of learned men whose hearts are as wide and deep as their wits are sharp—a rare combination. They have broadened my understanding of philosophy, particularly moral philosophy, and illuminated for me the sources of many of my previous doubts.

Yet there is one area that is still dark and murky for me: the determination of the precise nature of the Duty I owed (or owe) my cousin Arabella. The news of her precipitate marriage somewhat absolved me, at least from feeling the need to take action. But I believe, as you implied in your letter, that once having pledged myself to her I did owe her an unfailing commitment, no matter what the hardships involved. And I see more clearly now than before how greatly I contributed to the misery of that unhappy situation. Her lies and deceptions and wiles were no more heinous than my omissions and failures to act according to my principles. The very deeds and words that I withheld because I feared they would cause her harm were the instruments, in the end, of my wounding her. I begin to understand that one cannot refuse to act out of fear of harming another, but only move ahead, in accordance with one's own principles, trusting that the good will outweigh the harm one inflicts unintentionally. I think of Carlyle's statement in his essay on Sir Walter Scott: "No man lives without jostling and being jostled; in all ways he has to elbow himself through the world, giving and receiving offense."

I used to believe that what I lacked was the courage of my convictions; now I see that I lacked convictions. Only examine the landscape of my life, and one finds a trail of discarded passions. A cruel denunciation by my mother and a rejection from my father's publisher, and I gave up the manuscript derived from his notes on which I had been labouring for a year. One bad notice in the *Westminster Review* and poor sales for my first volume of poetry, and I stopped writing poems. One obstacle in the path of my union with Arabella (the conditions of the will), and the possibility of insanity in her ancestry, and I fled the country. Do you notice how extreme my reactions? Only a man who feared he could be forced against his will to do some great injury to himself would need to put an ocean between himself and a seventeen-year-old girl!

I suppose my weakness comes from not really knowing myself, or at least not acknowledging those aspects of my character that I do not like. I find I have been, dear friend, the grossest hypocrite! For on careful self-examination I realize I did not love Arabella; indeed, I fear I have never loved anyone. I only feigned love because I wished to feel, it, and so drove away forever, through my deception, the possibility of ever feeling it.

There is, of course, despite my ill-treatment of her and despite my honest analysis of the shallowness of my feelings, a sense of personal injury in the news of her hasty marriage, barely a month after my departure. I suppose there is a part of me that hoped she would go into a decline, would pursue me with letters or pledge herself to wait patiently for my eventual return. I hasten to assure you that I am sincerely glad that she did none of these things and that I wish her happiness in her marriage, yet I would not acknowledge my humanness were I not to admit my pain as well.

You would be doing me a great service if you would let me know from time to time how she appears to be faring as Lady Warder-Mull. I, in turn, given more leisure, will describe for you some of the intriguing philosophical debates I am presently immersed in.

Your grateful and eternal friend,
Franklin DeWinx

PART SIX

Sir Henry Warder-Mull:
Reflections
30 September 1848

~ ~

What I aspired to be,
And was not, comforts me.

> Robert Browning,
> *Rabbi Ben Ezra*

Chapter One

Sometimes I forget I was ever married. Odd, only a month has gone by. One would suppose it would take longer to shake off a habit—no, that is not quite the right word; a way of life, perhaps—that lasted six years.

Especially for one like me. I am a slow-moving man, given to much thought and analysis. My decisions, when I make them (for I prefer to allow circumstances to make them for me), are based on precedents and tradition. It is the way of History and the Law: to refuse to move from the old courses except when bumped and jostled by the flotsam and jetsam carried along in the great drift of Life.

Thus, it is as amazing to me as it is to my intimates that just a month ago I resigned my active duties at my firm. Then I sold my estate at Pittlesbury in Sussex, closed the house, and purchased, sight unseen, this residence in Devon (a place I have never been and where I know no person) and removed here with Phoebe and the child.

It must be that wild Celtic strain in my blood centuries past, the legacy of that Welsh princess who married the first Baron Warder, that suddenly overset my Anglo-Saxon imperturbability and caution. Here we are in a wild country where they still believe in pixies and pour out libations of cider to the greatest apple tree in the orchard to insure next year's harvest, and yet we are all supremely at peace as we never were in London or even at Pittlesbury Hall.

The days are grey and warm and still. A veil of mist clothes the stone walls of the ancient house. Bella has named it the Stone Castle, and so we all call it now. It mutes the shapes of the neat gardens lined by bricks that surround the house and disguises the tall, fantastically shaped yew trees that form about us a rampart of seemingly friendly giants. Bella and I sit on the, stone bench beyond the kitchen in the mornings, and she tells me stories about these giants and we invent names for them.

The mist cannot suppress the fragrances of the garden; indeed, somehow the warmth and quiet render all the scents more potent. We have the haunting smell of lavender, the pungency of rosemary, and the almost painfully sweet fragrance of the late roses. Overhead, unseen, the gulls whirl about, their sharp cries stirring the heavy air and the sounds of life all around. A cart in the lane, the bark of a dog, the distant *baas* of the sheep, a far-off church bell—all ring crystal clear.

In London, I should have never permitted it, but here we often do lessons outside on one of the stone benches set into the wall. Some days, near noon or even as late as evening, the sun finally summons the strength to dispel the mist. Suddenly there are dazzling rents in the gentle shroud of mist and, as the sun breaks through, the clouds form and reform into fantastic shapes, sailing ships, castles in the air, and at last, they are just wisps fleeing before the majesty of the sun. Then the sky is an unearthly blue, nearly the colour of Bella's eyes, and from our vantage point halfway up a long sloping hill, we can see the woods, the harvest fields, the apple orchards, the sheep meadows, and far below, along the glittering strand of the stream, the tiny village of Clonham. Beyond those far hills that rise above Clonham is the sea, and the gulls stream across their green backs to whirl about our sheltered valley; they fly out of the gold of the sun, which glints on their backs so that they seem sparks of light, not birds.

Bella is easily moved by beauty. She springs to her feet and cries out and claps her hands. I must confess that when I watch her joy, tears often appear in my eyes. She cannot understand this—to her, tears indicate sorrow—so I must quickly dissimulate.

Even Phoebe is strangely moved by the glory of the landscape around us. She will come out from her boudoir, putting aside her embroidery, for she is always busying herself with some needlework, and stand with us in the garden, smiling a little as Bella dances like a sprite along the garden path. But, as if too much joy might spoil the child, she sharply calls her back: "Bella, that is enough! It is time to wash up and dress yourself. Lord and Lady Melwyn and Reverend Troth are coming to dinner."

Our days drift the one into the other in a gentle swell of peace and tranquillity. Even the workmen coming to redecorate the house did not disrupt our domestic peace. They were hearty, good fellows and adored Bella; then again, who does not? When I left on two occasions to go to the great auction at Stowe to bid on some fine china, I felt strangely fragile, a snail away from its shell.

None of us ever speaks of my wife. Days go by when I do not even think of her. For certainly if there is a serpent in our Eden it is her. I tremble sometimes with the fear that she will return. I think we are all aware that we owe the quiet tenor of our days to her departure; it is as if her absence is the backdrop against which our present pleasures are painted.

In the early days, when the workmen were still painting and scrubbing, clearing out the drains and papering, Bella wandered through the disarranged rooms with forlorn eyes and a little frown between her eyebrows. She came out to stand by me as I watched the gardeners scythe down the weeds and grass that had overgrown the garden, and she put her small hand in mine.

"Papa," she asked, "which room is to be Mama's?"

"Mama will not live with us here," I replied, trying to maintain a calm, even tone.

Bella clutched my hand convulsively and turned her blue eyes up to mine.

"Papa," she asked, her childish voice trembling, "is Mama dead? Is she with the angels up in Heaven?"

How I longed to reply "Yes," for what other explanation would not discredit me and the child? But I had learned from my relations with Arabella the bitter fruits of deception and concealment.

"No, my dear," I answered. "She is not dead."

"Then why won't she live with us?" Bella wanted to know. I led her away from the gardeners to a secluded part of the old kitchen garden where the herbs grew wildly and the overgrown fruit trees were alive with the songs of the birds. We found a bench beneath an old plum tree, and I sat down, placing Bella upon my lap.

"She cannot live with us," I explained. "It is impossible for her. She is different from you and me. She cannot live happily the way we do."

"But, Papa, surely she will visit? Or write to me? And I can go to visit her, wherever she is?"

"No, my dear. I am afraid those dreams will never be fulfilled, and if you have your heart set upon them, you shall only have it broken."

She considered this for a long time but at least she did not cry. Bella rarely cries. Then one of the gardener's men appeared at the gate with his scythe over his shoulder.

"Should we begin in here now, Sir Henry?" he asked. I nodded, but Bella put her arms about my neck and whispered in my ear.

"Papa, will you grant me one favour?"

"Anything you wish, my dear, with all my heart," I replied.

"Then you will tell them to leave this garden as it is," she said. "I should like to come here sometimes to think."

And so we have a wild garden. Phoebe thinks it utter foolishness. When we cannot find Bella and call for her everywhere, she comes creeping out of the bushes and through the gate, her eyes shining, her dark hair tangled with leaves, her whole person imbued with the fragrance of herbs. And I go there sometimes, too, at night, and sit smoking my pipe on the bench and listening to the thrush that lives in the old plum tree. Then my thoughts often return to my wife.

What do I feel for her now? Pity, compassion, understanding? No, and I don't believe that I ever shall be able to view her thus. There is still anger and pain, and the great sorrow of rejection, but they are mingled with the most sweet, the most blessed relief. That relief springs from my present freedom, the freedom from my guilt, the freedom to do as I please, and even more surprising, to discover that there are things that please me.

I am not a philosopher, but I have often sat in that wild garden with the thrush pouring out his heart in song above me and thought of the extraordinary effect people have upon each other. Place a moderately talkative man at a dinner table. beside a witty raconteur, and the first man appears by contrast a taciturn and dull sort of fellow. Put a plain and clever woman in a ballroom with an empty-headed, beautiful young flirt, and the former is suddenly an old maid on the shelf. Bind together for life an older man with a desire for a quiet, ordered, harmonious existence out of the notoriety of the public eye with a young woman who must surround herself with constant adulation, drama, and attention, and what does the husband seem? A grim, colourless, crusty old bachelor who has wandered by mistake into the wrong play. And to whom does your sympathy as the onlooker go? Why, to the bright young thing who beats against the walls of her prison with the wings of a butterfly!

I had always believed that people honoured goodness, responsibility, and sobriety. They do honour it, but it does not interest them. They scorn flirtation, yet they follow every action of a flirtatious woman with bated breath and shining eyes. They despise immorality, yet let a woman desert her husband and child for an illicit passion and, while they murmur words of sympathy to the cuckolded husband and deserted child, don't they come really to glean the crumbs of scandal? Were they lovers? Did they meet secretly?

I suppose this is human. We all feel bound by the restrictions of convention and civilization, and while we do our utmost to strengthen these bulwarks against any breach, our eyes and hearts and imaginations cannot help straying to those bright, reckless creatures who vault over our walls as if winged.

I have two great loves—passions, really: The Past and Beauty. It is no surprise then that I am a collector. I have the finest collection of decorated snuffboxes in England. I also have an excellent collection of medieval miniatures and illustrated manuscripts.

My love of the Past and Beauty are all tangled up with my feelings for my wife. I knew all of her past, and she was as much a part of my life as the day when, at twenty-seven, I was godfather to her at her christening. I suppose I should recall what happened afterward at the reception when some infantile disorder of her digestive system loosed over me. In disgrace, I had to sneak home in a hackney cab, and even the cabbie refused to come near me. This might be the metaphor for our relationship. And yet what did I ever do to deserve it but attempt to treasure and shelter her?

213

It was her beauty that confounded and bewitched me. It is the same passion that comes over me when I attend a sale. I am browsing through a catalogue or a display table when suddenly something leaps out at me, something so exquisitely beautiful, so lovingly crafted that it is as if a sickness has taken hold of my heart. As the moment approaches when I can bid on the item, I almost cease to breathe, my heart is in my mouth, my blood is pounding madly. And then it is announced. The bidding begins. I am always too stricken at the outset to even bid, but as the price mounts, with a lurch I realize that this precious object is about to become someone else's. Then I speak up. My voice seems normal to all around me. As so often, happens in these sales, the bidding becomes a duel between two men, one parrying, one thrusting. I know that it is a duel to the death, for I will literally die if I cannot win. Suddenly the contest is over, I have won, I stagger to my feet and go out to pay the sum. I am sweating and must wipe off my brow. A chill sense of reality is beginning to settle upon me. How could I have paid such a price? Is everyone laughing at me and my foolishness? I wait in a fever of impatience as the item is wrapped, and I am in a strange, unsettled, restless condition until I have the object home, unwrapped in my study, and free to be fondled and examined. During the next days and weeks, I am never far from it; I am always wandering into my study to marvel at its beauty again and to gloat in its possession. And this charm continues until the next auction and the next object steals my heart away.

I should never have married, of course. I am not one of those men fitted for matrimony. I believe I thought a wife would be like an addition to my collection. I would provide the appropriate setting; she would sit within the frame and refresh me with her beauty. What nonsense! Yet how was I to know that marriage meant endless conflict, countless storms; enduring senseless whims and expensive fancies overlooking petty cruelties, slights, and snubs? How was I to know that the act of love itself, the act of possession, meant an acquaintance with and an ability to overlook so much that is unbeautiful: bodily fluids and bodily smells, observation of the most private ablutions of human beings, familiarity with the most unaesthetic parts of human anatomy? But worst of all, far worse than all this, was the discovery that the bonds of sacred wedlock bound me to a demented creature, a mere animal with a resemblance to my wife.

Dear God! The horror of it still haunts me. I feel my flesh crawl, and not from the cool night air. I have sworn a solemn vow never to love a woman again, never again to present myself naked, both literally and figuratively, never again to endure the mockery and humiliation experienced before one who holds my deepest confidences.

Before my marriage my friends called me a confirmed bachelor; in the latter part of my marriage, they labelled me a misogynist. Well, I suppose I am. I cannot love a woman. A very beautiful illuminated manuscript, maybe. A medieval miniature set in gold. But not a living, breathing beauty.

I do, of course, love Phoebe and Bella. But Phoebe is my sister, and Bella my child. They are my flesh and blood. My wife was that ineffable Other—a stranger. And why? Why does human society demand that one bind oneself with the most solemn of oaths to someone one can never know, to someone who can with a raised eyebrow or a little sniff suddenly pierce one to the heart with the realization that there is something hideous or suspect about what one has just said or done?

Phoebe will never marry, I think, though the parson here is showing a great deal of interest in her. But I think she is too much like me. We have been together now some seventeen years, ever since she escaped from our stepmother's home and came to London to keep house for me. There is no need for adjustments; the compromises have been made so long ago we do not recall them. She knows my tastes and my habits, and I know hers. Why throw this over for the wild uncertainty of marriage? Perhaps if my sister were younger and wanted children, but now she has Bella and is perfectly content.

I know there are some who hint that Bella is not my child. They point to the date of her birth and scoff at the notion that she was premature, caused by the great shock her mother suffered. They can trace no resemblance to me, but then she is nearly a perfect miniature of her mother except for her blue eyes. I myself have blue eyes.

But it is not these shallow assertions that breed the certainty I feel in my core. No, it is something I would never reveal to any living soul, something, indeed, that I have never confessed to my wife. It is because of the outrage that I inflicted upon her, and thus upon this innocent child who is my only joy, that I will not be free for the rest of my days from a dark shame that soils my every pleasure.

Chapter Two

Phoebe always told me that Arabella would not suit me. "She's far too young," she would point out. "She knows nothing of how to manage a household, and furthermore, she shows no desire to learn." I believe Phoebe was miffed because she had sent Arabella some books on the subject that had never been acknowledged. "She's frivolous and sure to be extravagant."

"Extravagance is hardly a consideration, my dear," I remember commenting, "when one thinks of her fortune and the estate in Sussex."

I knew that this intrigued Phoebe as it did me, for our father had left the family estate in his will to his second wife for her use during her lifetime, which would certainly exclude me from ever taking possession of it for very long. My stepmother was only some seven years my senior. Phoebe and I both felt cheated of our birth right and humiliated by the necessity of renting and entertaining at our cramped London residence while our stepmother and her children lived in splendour at Warder Hall. When August came and all respectable Londoners left for their country homes and visits, we slunk off to rented lodgings in some beach resort or lived furtively behind closed shutters, terrified that someone would notice some sign of life and report that, "Sir Henry Warder-Mull remained in town last August, can you imagine?"

Though the Warder-Mulls are proud descendants of an ancient and illustrious family, we were forced to live like any moneygrubbing City merchant. Though for some time I had thought we must struggle forever, the potentiality of my marriage to Arabella opened before me the vista of a splendid estate, a living to control, an elegant London house, dinner parties on a grand scale, and all the other amenities that should have been mine.

"I suppose when all is said and done," sniffed Phoebe, "you find me a sadly inadequate companion and hostess."

"My dear Phoebe," I replied, "you know that is nonsense. You only say it to dangle for a compliment, which you will not have. You have been too naughty I need another slice of the mutton, my dear. Surely, you are overlooking the most important consideration."

"And what is that?"

"Why, that there should be a fifth Baronet Warder-Mull! Else the title is to lapse, and all of the honors derived to our family will perish."

Phoebe flushed a little and then said stolidly, "I don't think she'll bear children easily. Really, Harry, she is always succumbing to those brain fevers; she will never survive a confinement."

I never told Phoebe my most pressing reason for my unquestioning devotion to Arabella Farraday.

I loved her. I had loved her for some six or seven years. I can remember when I first conceived of the idea. I often came to visit her, and we played a game in which I pretended to be her father and she my daughter. She would fetch me glasses of brandy and sit upon my lap reading me her essays, and I would call her "my little puss" or "my wilful pet." She adored this game as she never received such affection and attention from her father, who told me once that as he was her only parent he could not risk damage to his position of authority by appearing too soft. This particular afternoon that I recall we were reading some poems; I don't remember the poet, but they were on love and perhaps they subtly defined the atmosphere. At any rate, when I went to kiss her farewell, rather than the fresh soap-smelling young child I had grown used to kiss, I caught a whiff of lavender perfume and felt a budding female body against mine, and suddenly I was aware that here was a young woman. I left in a whirl of emotions and walked about the wet streets for hours until night had fallen and the lamps were lit. It was then that I realized the Lord had given me the answer for which I had sought for so long, the answer to my perpetual battle with sin.

I had some serious lapses as a young man; these eased somewhat with the arrival of Phoebe in my household, but still there were nights when, as I was coming home from my Club, the sight of the well-turned ankle of a lady descending from a carriage or the flash of white bosom revealed as an opera cape slipped from its clasp would drive me mad with desire and send me searching for the company of the nearest streetwalker. I felt revolted and humiliated by my weakness and was especially concerned lest I should develop some loathsome disease. The weeks after my transgressions were filled with compulsive washings. I watched closely for the symptoms of disease.

But I was able to remain chaste with the image of my innocent bride-to-be in mind.

Heretofore I had not dared to think of taking a wife, for I was not in a position, either financially or socially, to choose the sort of woman who would be a credit to my name and household. Now I was granted the opportunity to mould and form such a being as she blossomed into maturity. And my economic anxieties would at last be quieted. In one blow, I would have everything: a wife, an estate, and sufficient income to give up the endless meetings and analyses and preparation of papers that made up the bulk of my labours as a solicitor. I could prepare instead to become a barrister, as I had always dreamed, to see my name in the papers, to wear the robes of the court, to speak eloquently before a hushed public.

Because of the amount of Arabella's inheritance, I feared that her father, despite our long friendship and my pivotal position on the board of directors for Farraday and Company, might view me as a mere fortune hunter, and thus I delayed for some time informing him of my intentions. I prepared him carefully by commenting on Arabella's remarkable qualities and indicating my growing appreciation for her character. Nonetheless, I was surprised by his enthusiasm when I finally broached the topic.

"This is certainly a fortunate notion," he said, with a little more joviality than was his wont. "I have often feared that my daughter would become too much like her mother, who, as you know…" He did not complete his sentence, for I knew, as did all the world, of her adultery. "But with the guidance and firm devotion of a serious and older man, there can be no possibility of her going astray." Dear God, how I have failed him! "And you are just the person, with your knowledge of money and its value, to help her manage her income fruitfully and cautiously. Of course," he added "there can be no question of discussing it with her now. She is far too young. You must wait until she is sixteen."

And so I waited and watched her grow every week in loveliness and grace and affection, and found that once I conjured up her image temptations fell away from me.

I remember the day I first hinted at the subject with her. It was shortly after her sixteenth birthday, and we were still playing our game of father and daughter, although she had given up her perch on my lap and usually settled at my feet where I could stroke her thick, glossy curls.

"You know, my dear," I said, "suppose, just suppose, that instead of your calling me Papa and my calling you Daughter, we were to substitute other names of endearment that would signify an even more intimate and blessed union?"

She turned her head. I could see her dark eyes peeping over the tops of my knees. "What would that be?" she asked, her lips slightly parted to reveal her even white teeth.

"Suppose I were to call you wife, and you call me my husband?" I said softly. Tears began to fall, and I gathered her into my arms until they subsided. Then she looked up at me with the most touching mixture of timidity and confusion.

"Have you never thought of it, my dearest?" I asked.

She shook her head silently, the curls tossing to and fro.

"Your father approves and even wishes it," I said. I saw quickly this was an error on my part. I had lately learned that she set herself in opposition to almost everything her father wished.

"I do not know what to say to you now," she said, hanging her head. "Oh, you have spoiled it all!" And she ran from the room in tears.

The next time I saw her, everything was different. She would not come near me or resume her old teasing ways, and when I mentioned marriage, she said quite definitely that she did not wish to discuss it. I was agitated and distressed, naturally, but I assumed that she must have time to get used to the idea, and if it had not been for her father's sudden death the subsequent year and her lack of protection, I doubt that I should have pressed the issue at all.

Our courtship suffered from the usual ups and downs and at one point seemed in serious jeopardy due to my fiancée's conviction that she had developed a *tendre* for her cousin. But Providence smoothed the way before us, and on the fifteenth of September, 1842, at St. George's, Hanover Square, we exchanged our solemn vows, and Arabella became Lady Warder-Mull.

My good friend, Sir Owlston Knevle, had offered us his hunting lodge in Leicestershire for our honeymoon. I suppose it was not wise to ask Phoebe to accompany us, but I did not want my wife to be without female companionship at this delicate juncture of her life: the transition from maidenhood into womanhood.

There were endless scenes between my sister and my wife, Arabella complaining that Phoebe lectured her and made her uncomfortable, Phoebe weeping to me that my wife was trying to alienate us and would not be happy until she, Phoebe, was out of the house and left to perish in the Workhouse.

I suppose the strain of this disharmonious ménage contributed to the failure of our honeymoon. I had an exceedingly nervous stomach, which Phoebe usually knew how to quiet with various potions. But all of her ministrations failed during that first week. Before marriage I had contemplated those moments when I would close the bedroom door and be alone with my wife as hours filled with bliss and solace. In truth, I found that I was completely and abjectly terrified every time the door closed behind me.

There was my wife, seated on the edge of the bed, her whole posture resigned and despairing, her hands clenched on her skirts, her eyes staring unseeing into the fire. I would assume a brisk and jaunty air, which I little felt, and advise her to prepare herself for bed. She would glance at me dully and get up to perform her nightly rituals mechanically. I was particularly shy of watching her undress or of having her watch me. So I would usually extinguish the lamp as she was stepping out of her gown and would wait, trembling, as

I heard the sounds of rustling garments and splashing water. When I knew she had slipped under the covers, I would go about my preparations, all the while dreading, that moment when I climbed into the icy bed and warmed myself at my wife's flesh.

When I did that first week, she always lay still and sometimes wept. I, with my mind awhirl from the pain in my stomach, my fear that I should harm her, and my desire to possess her, would set about my task only to find that my flesh was unwilling at the last moment. Then she would weep even more bitterly and turn away from me. Sometimes I woke to find her sitting in the armchair before the fire, staring at the coals. It was enough to drive a man mad, and it set up our subsequent night-time pattern: she would go to her bedroom, I to mine.

The word that best describes my wife is "perverse." Somehow, perhaps from always having her will balked in childhood, she became determined to inflict the same outrage upon others. While she was cool and distant in the evenings, dampening my enthusiasm to come to her, she was as hot and fervent as a cinder during the day, keeping me in a fever of guilty excitement. It may be she acted this way to offend Phoebe. If so, she certainly succeeded. At meals, she would nuzzle me with her foot under the table and wink with delight as she did so. When she passed me during the day, she would pause for a long, lingering embrace and often fling herself down upon my lap while I sat reading, to rain kisses about my head.

Then there was that one afternoon, the events of which still make me shake. I am convinced they lost me the love and perhaps the respect of my sister, Phoebe. Arabella had been standing in the drawing room after dinner watching the leaves fall outside. Tears were running down her cheeks, and she did nothing to acknowledge them, just stood there, leaning against the cold pane. I went up to her to comfort her, but she did not respond to my timid embrace nor my heartening words, and so I went into the study to work on some papers that had been sent up from London.

Not an hour later, Arabella suddenly appeared in the doorway, wearing her most fetching gown—a morning dress of embroidered white muslin, which always made her look as fresh and innocent as a child. Ignoring my polite query as to what she wanted, she swept into the room and settled herself upon my papers on the desk and bent her head to kiss me full on the lips. I caught a scent of the lavender perfume she always wore, and my hands placed tentatively about her waist found only the soft pliancy of flesh. She had left off her corset.

"You have forgotten something, my dear," I said when her lips relinquished mine.

"I want you to see me as I really am!" she cried with a sort of desperate gaiety and a peculiar emphasis to her words. She sprang off her perch and, lifting up her skirts, revealed her exquisite, stockinged legs.

The desires that had been suppressed by my years of abstinence and that had failed me during the nights mounted up with such swift ferocity that I literally could not think. I laid my hands upon her, somewhat violently, I fear, and half dragged, half carried her to the sofa in the room. She did not seem to be afraid, but smiled at me so that all her teeth showed. In a moment, I had thrown myself upon my wife with a hunger and an exaltation I had never known. Just as I was at last about to accomplish that deed that I had so long contemplated, the door opened and my sister, Phoebe, strode into the room.

Chapter Three

Phoebe had never knocked before on coming into any room, and I suppose she had no reason to do so then. She could certainly, as she pointed out to me in tears afterward, little contemplate such goings-on in a study in the middle of the afternoon. She froze, her prominent blue eyes bulging, and then with a harsh, unnatural cry fled the room, sobbing.

There was a long pause. I was painfully aware of the ignominy of my position. Then Arabella made some movement as if to draw me back down to her, and I slapped her. It was the only time during our marriage that I ever laid my hands upon her. I got up with as much dignity as I could muster and, after straightening my clothes, went in search of Phoebe.

She was in her room crying, saying that she knew I did not care for her or I could never have subjected her to such a hideous scene, that she would leave and find employment somewhere as a governess or housekeeper. I really think she might have left the next day as she threatened to do except that she became ill—I suppose the doctors would call it a hysterical reaction—and I was kept very busy preparing delicacies to tempt her appetite and ministering to her with *sal volatile* and other stimulants.

My wife did not like being neglected on her honeymoon. She began to consume immoderate quantities of wine with dinner; sometimes when I was called away from the table to assist Phoebe through another crisis, I would return to discover that Arabella had finished the entire bottle of wine by herself. She always retired before me, as I had to make a nightly visit to the invalid, and when I looked in on her, she was always fast asleep—another reason, beside my quivering flesh, our marriage remained unconsummated.

But one night when I looked in, she had failed to undress herself and crawl under the covers. She had cast off her outer garments, which lay about the room, and, clothed only in her chemise, lay sprawled across the bed. One of her hands lay, partially opened, partially curled, upon the tangled mass of her dark curls. I thought of the child she had been; I saw the woman she had become; I realized that she was mine, and tears came to my eyes. She seemed so vulnerable, so exquisite. I had never before been able to view the perfection of her unclothed form. I stood for a while gazing upon her, then went about the room in an agony of indecision. She did not even stir while I undressed. The touch of her cool flesh against my hands was like fire. I was consumed with lust and excused my next actions on the grounds that my caresses might rouse her from her stupor. Soon it was apparent that this excuse could no longer serve, for she did not respond in any way, but by then I was unable to stop myself. I told myself that she was my wife, that this was my right, that I was only completing the seduction she had invited in the study. I even hoped that my old weakness would overtake me at the final moment. But it did not. She did not wake; she did not even murmur in her sleep. I rained kisses upon her unresponsive lips, but she did not return me one.

Thus, on that night, was my daughter conceived. I have often wondered if Arabella's indifference to her child derived from her indifference at the time of conception. In the morning, despite my conviction that I had done no wrong, I was unable to face my wife; I got up, without sleeping, and locked myself in the study.

At dinner, Arabella seemed no different. Though I knew she must have guessed what had transpired by the signs, she never spoke of it nor did she comment on any suspicions she may have had.

Several times I was on the edge of blurting out a confession, and each time I trembled on the brink. What could I say to explain? I shrank from her touch and even from her presence, for the look of her eyes filled me with shame.

When many months later she began to show the signs of her condition, I invented countless excuses to explain how it must not be so. It was Phoebe, who no doubt assumed that the sort of shameless liaison she had interrupted in the study was a commonplace in my marriage, who at last called my attention to Arabella's condition.

"Your wife should not be going out riding in her state," she said, casting a meaningful eye at Arabella's thickening figure as she passed through the hall one afternoon at Pittlesbury Hall.

"I have asked her repeatedly to stop," I said somewhat sharply and, closing my book, got up myself and departed.

I could not think what to do. I could not imagine what to say. Arabella had never mentioned the matter to me and took great pains to never let me see her in a state of dishabille, which was not difficult as we occupied separate bedrooms. So I would come upon her crying, and she would brush away her tears and give me a sickening smile. Was it possible she did not know? No, that was clearly absurd. She must have a thousand reasons to guess the state she was in. But how could she explain it? Could it be that she thought one of my early fumbling attempts had been the cause? This thought assuaged my guilt somewhat. Certainly, an innocent young girl who had no mother to explain such matters would be ignorant of the necessities of conception. I determined to be offhand about it. One morning at breakfast, I steeled myself and with a smile, remarked, "I believe we're going to have a child, my dear."

"I believe you're right, my dear," she replied, bursting into tears, and ran from the room.

I sat staring at the grilled kidneys on my plate, and a feeling of such utter despair swept over me that put my head in my hands and wept. For there was something worse, far worse than my knowledge of the act of conception, that made me dread the birth of an heir to the Warder-Mulls, something that made me wish for a miscarriage or a stillbirth, something that made me certain I would never again wish to possess my wife. And this thing, which gnawed at my stomach daily—like some beast, would never have seen the light of the day had it not been for my guilt about the advantage I had taken of my wife that night.

Shortly after our marriage, even during the honeymoon, Arabella had begun to question me about her mother. I put her off at first with reminders that her father had not wished her to discuss the subject. Later, my desire to expiate my sin led me to elaborate on my acquaintance with her mother. She was never tired of hearing my stories of how her mother looked and acted, how she petted Arabella, and how she was universally adored.

I suppose it natural Arabella was not content with this; she always pressed me for news of her mother's fate after her elopement. Somehow, I decided that if I could provide her with this missing piece of the puzzle—dear God, I even dreamed that I could reunite them, forgetting completely my obligation to Walter Farraday—I could somehow win her love and we could begin again to forge a union of mutual affection and respect.

So when we were in London during the Little Season, I began to make inquiries. At first there was no information forthcoming. I suppose the furtiveness and diffidence with which I made my requests did not encourage interest. But just after the new year 1843, I received a letter at Pittlesbury.

The correspondent, who wished to remain anonymous, had heard that I desired information about the present whereabouts of Lady Farraday, the former Lady Perdita DeWinx, and could testify that this lady had been for the past ten years confined in a private insane asylum, Slow Banning Retreat, and was considered irrevocably mad. The correspondent hoped that such a disclosure, given despite certain ethical principles that the writer held dear, merited some sort of pecuniary acknowledgment, which could be sent to such and such an address.

I burned the letter, but I could not put the matter out of my mind. I watched Arabella constantly and thought I detected many seeds of an incipient madness. I thought of my child, imprisoned within her body, and wondered if the strain of madness was being transmitted to the future Baronet Warder-Mull. I could not concentrate upon my work, but would sit for hours unseeing before some brief I had to study and be shaken from my nightmare visions only by the interruption of a clerk or a solicitor.

When I received a second letter, then a third, from my anonymous informant, I sent a request for information, along with documentation of my identity, to the asylum named. I suppose I had put off this task in the foolish hope that I would never be in possession of the facts that became mine, when the following letter from Mrs. Wicklow arrived:

> My dear Sir:
>
> In response to your enquiry, I must inform you that Lady Farraday, who we know as Lady Perdita DeWinx, is a patient at Slow Banning Retreat and has been since February 1832. The doctors have determined that she is suffering from a type of insanity known as moral insanity in which the natural feelings and affections are perverted. Despite the excellent treatment she has received here, her condition has deteriorated over time rather than improving.
>
> You are, of course, welcome to visit her, but I would not recommend it. Her condition worsened considerably after her last visit.
>
> I remain, your humble servant,
> Mrs. Thomas Wicklow

Why did I keep this letter? Why did I not burn it with the rest? Perhaps it was my natural avidity for collecting objects; perhaps it was a lawyer's conviction that no such document should ever be destroyed. At any rate, I put it in an envelope marked "DeWinx" and locked it into my desk drawer.

We were back in for the Season of 1843. Our social circle was small, but occasionally we saw Lady Holly and Lady Molliton, who had forgiven Arabella, after our marriage for the scandal of the previous year. Lionel Holly had been most caught by Arabella during her first Season, so much so that I am told he broke down after our wedding and had to be sent to Baden to recover. Evidently the attraction had not died, and they spent a great deal of time together. I would come upon him in our drawing room, seated at her feet, just as she had sat at mine in the old days, and when I came into the room, having heard the unfamiliar sound of her laughter, the light in her eyes would, die and she would become silent and rigid. I upbraided her about the foolishness of her behaviour, but she merely replied that as she was a married woman no one would think twice about her friendship with a young man. All of my remonstrations were to no avail; she could not see why I should feel humiliated by idle gossip.

Lady Holly was as concerned as I and begged me to put an end to it. How could I confess to her that my wife did not listen to me, that I was not the master of my own house? Phoebe recounted with great glee each evening every meeting between my wife and Mr. Holly as if to finally force me to acknowledge my error in marrying Arabella.

I am not given to rages; in fact, I have lost my temper only twice in my life. The first time was when I saw Mr. DeWinx in the Pittlesbury church; the second was when I took Arabella to task for her friendship with Mr. Holly.

It began innocently enough. I called her into the study and shut the door. She settled down gingerly upon the chair I had indicated; I think she was exasperated at her increasing bulk. She was constantly sighing and puffing and spent most of her hours on the couch.

I began by describing Lady Holly's distress over her son and went on to explain construction Society would place on her behaviour. If she had attempted to remonstrate with me or, had. wept or had accused me of neglect, of which, dear God, I was guilty, all should have been well. But she merely stared at me with those fathomless dark eyes, a smile of contempt upon her lips. It seemed there was no way to penetrate the barrier she had placed between us; at the time, I forgot that it was partially of my own making. I knew that she would go on about her own business without a thought for me; I knew that she was indifferent to any discomfort or mortification I should suffer; I knew that she did not love me and had never loved me, that she merely placed herself in bondage to me and felt the contempt a slave feels for a master. I think I wanted to justify her contempt, and her fear.

"What do you intend to do?" I asked coldly, coming out from behind the desk and standing over her with my arms crossed on my chest. I had an urge to strike out with my foot and deliver a savage kick as she turned her head up to me.

By way of response, she got up and went toward the door. I was after her in a moment and closed my hand upon her arm.

"You have not answered me," I said.

"Nor shall I," she replied calmly, "while you are in a rage."

"You shall do exactly as I tell you in precisely the manner I tell you to do it," I said, my voice low but simmering with anger. "You are my wife, by God, and that means you have certain duties, none of which you have ever performed."

She blinked her eyes, indolently. "We made an agreement," she said, in the same calm manner, "and I must consider that you have the better part of it: my fortune, this house, and the estate at Pittlesbury, a hostess, and soon, pray God, an heir. As for me, if I seek some small recompense for my sacrifices in the company of a charming young man, that is my affair."

"You shall not!" I said between clenched teeth, my grasp tightening inexorably. "You shall not dishonour my name. You shall not go about indulging yourself and creating havoc and misery for all those about you. My God, you are behaving just as your mother did, and if you do not look about you, you shall end up just as she did."

I saw that I had penetrated to her. There was a flicker of pain in her eyes. I was like a hound at the end of a long hunt with the throat of the fox gleaming white before me.

"Yes, your mother, the raging maniac! You did not guess, did you? Why, what other sort of woman would run off and leave her husband and child for a lover who would discard her like a piece of rubbish only a month later? What other sort of woman would see seduction everywhere? Why, she even tried to seduce me! You did not ever think of that, did you? Your mother was not too proud to scorn my love! You think I do not see what you do with Lionel Holly? I know you intend to draw him on, to flatter him so as to flatter yourself, to throw him up to me, your husband, as a mockery and insult! Then, no doubt, when he declares himself, when he wishes to do away with himself rather than live without possessing you, you will laugh in his face, as your mother did in mine! She is not laughing now! No, she is probably howling!"

Her face had crumpled as I spoke. It was like watching death. She was suddenly ugly, small and shrunken, inhuman in her agony. The fox that had, a moment before, been bright and gay with the urgency of life was now an inanimate sodden mass of blood and matted fur and blank staring eyes.

For a moment, I was tempted to stop and gather her into my arms, but I was aghast at the destruction I had wreaked, that insidious urge in my blood to go on and even destroy what remained. I flung her aside—she did not weep or cry out—and went out to my Club.

I did not return until the following evening, having gone directly to my chambers, and then taken dinner out; I wished to put off as long as possible a survey of the ruined landscape I had left behind. And yet, as I strolled through the warm, damp darkness of the spring night, in a part of my mind I allowed myself to hope that she would be waiting for me in the drawing room with my slippers and a glass of brandy already poured and that her lips would be soft with apologies and her eyes soft with love.

Although it was late, the house, as I approached it, was ablaze with light, and even before I put my key to the door I could hear excited voices. It seemed my wife and her maid had disappeared. No one had missed them until dinner, and when a quick messenger sent to my place of business revealed that she was not with me (though why Phoebe was so foolish as to even consider this, I do not know), it was discovered that my wife's bed had not been slept in and that Jenny, her maid, had never come up the previous night. So reported the housemaid with whom she shared a room. No one had seen them leave. And they had evidently taken no more than the clothes on their backs. It was I who chanced upon the other loss.

The drawer to my desk had been forced open with a priceless seventeenth-century silver letter opener, which was now ruined. The empty envelope with the word "DeWinx" in my writing lay on the blotter.

An interruption by
Jenny Steward

Be near me when my light is low,
When the blood creeps, and the nerves prick
And tingle; and the heart is sick,
And all the wheels of being slow.

Be near me when the sensuous frame
is rack'd with pangs that conquer trust;
And Time, a maniac scattering dust,
And life, a Fury singing flame.

Tennyson,
In Memoriam

Chapter Four

Sir Henry never understood the effect that her confinement at Slow Banning Retreat had upon his wife, a fact that is evident when he continues his story.

As I consider it important for a better understanding of Arabella Farraday and her actions, I have chosen to interrupt his narrative and present my account of the subsequent events as I observed them.

I was waiting in the dressing room for Arabella on the night of her quarrel with her husband. I had been out in the Square garden with Daniel O'Connell, a lieutenant in the Third Battalion of the Foot Guards. My head was in a whirl, for he wanted me to marry him and had just pressed me again for an answer. Although a year previous I would have accepted at once, now I was strangely reluctant. First, I did not trust him. His blandishments were flattering but unbelievable; his caresses were thrilling but a trifle too expert. I suspected that he wished to marry me only because I presented that irresistible challenge: a woman who had not yet succumbed to his charms. Then there was my duty to my mistress.

I was her only confidante, her only refuge in the midst of a frightening and sinister mystery. I was the only one who knew of how long she loved Franklin DeWinx and what she considered her marriage to him. I was the only one who knew the child she carried was not Sir Henry's precious heir. We rarely spoke of her current activities; she preferred to dwell on the past, on the halcyon days with Franklin, on the birth of their love, on that magic moment when the road to freedom and happiness seemed clear before her only to drop away and suddenly deposit her, forlorn, in the midst of a howling wilderness. For, no matter how we tried to dwell in the happiness of the past, we always came up against one of those grim obstacles. Why had Franklin gone? Why did Sir Henry accept her condition so placidly? Once she laughed bitterly that perhaps he did not know how babies were made. But this seemed absurd to both of us. And if he did not know the child was not his, why the pretence? Did he intend to wait until it was born to repudiate her? Why did he watch her so? Did he hope to drive her into adultery so he could rid himself of her?

Sometimes we turned from these puzzles to speak of her mother. Arabella loved to recount the stories Sir Henry had told her of Perdita Farraday when she was young and lovely and the toast of London, of the affection and admiration that she had showered upon her pretty daughter. She told them over and over again as a child will ask to hear the same story read again and again. But then would come the same terror. Why had Sir Henry suddenly dropped this topic? Why did he flinch when she asked for news of her mother? Why had he abandoned the search that Arabella knew he had begun?

She would begin to cry then, and I would hold her in my arms and soothe her until she fell asleep.

No, I could not marry Daniel and leave her alone in the midst of these dark forests. But I was impatient that night for her to come up so that I could prepare her for bed and go out again to where he waited for me and savour a little more of the lovely spring night and his warm embrace.

All thought of Daniel left me when she came slowly into the room. She walked haltingly, painfully, as if she had been crippled, and when she lifted her head and I saw her face, a wave of terror swept over me. Her eyes were dark and burning, like coals, but her complexion was the most deadly white. There was an indescribable horror about her face. I suddenly, understood the stories about Medusa and how those who looked upon her were turned to stone. I froze. Then a possibility crossed my mind, and I ran to her.

"Oh, Bella, what is it?" I asked. "Is it the baby? Are you in pain? Has it begun?" We had feared that her time would come early and Sir Henry would be forced to recognize that this was not his child. We had calculated the birth could come any time now, though the doctor, of course, had been given false information and had predicted a date in late June.

In response to my questions and embrace, she merely thrust some papers she clutched into my hands and went to sit down heavily in the chair before the fire that I had just vacated.

I scanned them rapidly, and then I understood. Arabella had been prepared for news of her mother's death; she sometimes planned how she would visit the grave, the flowers she would bring, the monument she would erect, the words she would inscribe. But this was ghastly: to find that one's mother—whom one had adored and worshiped and emulated—whom one had longed to emulate—whose path one had striven to recreate, had become a lunatic. My imagination was not even capable of grasping the impact of the truth revealed. How could anyone comprehend it?

"My dear!" I said and sank down before her, taking her hands in my own. I wished she would weep; I wished she would fly into one of her rages. Anything rather than sitting there so white and silent and feverish, as if she were being consumed by some inner fire.

At length, she said in a strange, toneless voice, "I must go to her."

"But Arabella!" I exclaimed. "You cannot. Sir Henry will not take you, and think what effect it might have upon you, and it can do naught but disturb you—"

"I must go, I will go, I am going," she said sternly and shaking off my hands, rose up and passed out of the room as silent as a ghost. I heard her footsteps on the stairs, and discarding my momentary paralysis, I snatched up her reticule, which lay on the dressing table, then reached for a cloak for her and one for me, dashing as fast as I could after her. She was already fumbling with the front door when I caught up with her.

"Arabella, don't be absurd!" I said, trying to hold her back. "You do not even know where this place is. It is the middle of the night.

Go to sleep. I beg you, give this some thought. It will be different in the morning." Good God, my words seem foolish now, seeing them on paper: How she must have felt when she heard them!

"Leave me alone!" she cried, her face a mask of hatred. Whirling around, she raced down the walk into the silent street.

"Daniel! Daniel!" I cried, running over to the railing of the garden. I could see him, tall and long-legged in his scarlet uniform, leaning against the trunk of a tree. The smoke of his cigar rose lazily through the leaves. "Oh, Daniel, come here! Help me!" I was crying, and he came to me at once and tried to gather me into his arms.

"Oh, stop! It's not the time for that!" I cried, all the while feeling grateful that I had someone to whom I could turn. "It is my mistress, Miss Arabella. She has learned that her mother is mad, and she has just gone off into the night."

I pointed to her retreating figure, now only a pale blur in the night. Daniel sighed; he thought I was much too attached and endured too much at her hands.

"Daniel, I beg you. If you love me, help me bring her back. My God!" And I ran after her, crying. Within a few minutes, I heard Daniel's strides behind me as we stalked her through the dark streets—past giggling maids hanging onto the arms of their lovers who would turn to watch in amazement as Arabella floated by; past sleeping houses, where perhaps a dog would wake to bark at that ghostly figure disturbing his sleep; across the bridge and the black Thames. We stayed close to her heels, my worst fear being that she would turn and throw herself into the waters. Luckily, she continued straight ahead, not looking to either side in her headlong flight, which took us through the shadowy, odoriferous docks where light still spilled out of gin shops, and drunken men and tawdry women roared and hooted at her silent figure. Past huge drays and carts loaded down with produce, and sometimes herds of cattle being driven to market in London, and yet she went on picking her way along the gutter, unflinching in her haste Finally we were in the countryside and the new day was beginning to dawn, so that for a time everything was grey before sharply shining with reflected light. It was only then she began to waver.

We had caught up to her many times during the course of her flight, demanding she stop. Sometimes she would hiss at us to leave her be; just as often she would not even glance at us, but continue striding on, her eyes fixed on some vanishing point on the horizon. But now, as she slowed and began to stumble, she accepted Daniel's outstretched arm and clung to it.

"Bella, we can help you," I said, smoothing back her wet hair and slipping the mantle, which she had previously refused, about her shoulders. "We can find an inn and hire a carriage. I brought along your purse. Daniel will help us. We can go straight to this place. Please, you cannot go on like this. You will kill yourself and the baby, too."

She nodded her consent and then broke down and wept, and I held her in my arms and wept, too. My tears were with relief that her strange rigidity had vanished and that she was once more able to give expression to her troubled heart.

By the time we had found an inn, we were all so exhausted and hungry that we agreed to sit down and breakfast. What a strange party we were. Daniel, sullen and taciturn because he had spent an entire night with me and what had we done? Merely walked, rarely speaking, barely touching, for some ten or fifteen miles. He fretted, for he was due back at his barracks for a drill, and yet he was loath to leave me. I think he knew that he had lost me that night and that he would never see me again. The coach for London arrived before Arabella's and my coach. He got on it, grudgingly, not even kissing me farewell, and I was left with Arabella, who merely sat before the fire in the private room, shivering and rocking herself to and fro.

I had dared to hope she might sleep in the coach, but the stiffness and tension came back to her body as we closed the miles between us and Slow Banning Retreat. I believe all of her will and strength were being summoned for the upcoming interview. And what did she believe would happen? That her mother would break down and embrace her and weep with fondness over her long-lost child? Dear Lord, I prayed, let it be so. Grant us this one miracle.

The coach set us down at the nearest town, and I scraped together the last few remaining, coins in the reticule to hire a farmer who would take us in his cart to the asylum gates. I did not have any notion how we would get home; as it was I need not have concerned myself. We were not to leave Slow Banning Retreat for several months.

There was something so desolate about the asylum; encircled by an ominous iron fence that clanged as it shut behind us. About that stark, graceless house with its barred windows, about the chill ugliness of the hall and the grim, grey, sour face of the maid who admitted us. The countenance of Mrs. Wicklow, the retreat's directress, filled me with a foreboding of some new horror to come. She had that officious oiliness, that veneer of a sickening and misplaced optimism that one sees in the faces of undertakers.

"Oh, so you are dear Lady Perdita's daughter?" she said with false cheerfulness, not missing a detail of Arabella's travel-soiled garments and muddy shoes. "I have been in correspondence with your husband, Sir Henry Warder-Mull, a charming man. And so you wish to see your mother? Well, I will see if it can be arranged. You know she was quite naughty the last time she had a visitor, that nice young man, Mr. DeWinx, who said he was a nephew." Arabella turned white and swayed a little against me. "But then she is always incorrigible around the gentlemen. I think we can attempt an interview with you."

"Franklin, here?" gasped Arabella, after Mrs. Wicklow had bowed and scraped her way out of the door. "Oh, dear Lord, what did he find? What did he think? Why didn't he tell me?"

We knew what he had found within a quarter of an hour. There were footsteps in the hall, the clank of metal, a whispered consultation before Mrs. Wicklow appeared again, smiling for all the world like a hostess at a garden party. Behind her trailed a coarse, black-bearded fellow who yanked and pulled on a chain that fastened to the bony wrists of a gaunt, dishevelled woman dressed in grey, shapeless gown. Her dark, matted hair, streaked with grey, hung over eyes that peered out like an animal cornered in a thicket. Her mouth hung open, revealing yellowed teeth.

I searched for some resemblance to Arabella and found none, despite the fact that Mrs. Wicklow had announced jauntily, "Lady Perdita, here is your daughter come to see you." So intent was I on my inspection of the madwoman that I had completely forgotten my mistress until I turned to see her reaction, and then I saw the resemblance. They were like mirror images of each other: the same burning, dark gaze; the same chalky paleness of complexion; the same spots of colour spread across cheekbones that slanted at the same angle; the same mass of thick, dark hair. Only their dress marked them as distinct: the madwoman's shapeless rags contrasted to Arabella's fashionable if soiled blue silk gown, her chains and hand-locks to Arabella's kid gloves, the matted unwashed hair to Arabella's dishevelled yet still elegant coiffure.

The madwoman peered at all of us dully. Arabella stepped closer to her, prompting the other woman to shrink back a little, holding up her hands as if she feared Arabella would strike her.

"Mama?" said Arabella in tones that nearly made my heart break. "Mama?" she repeated plaintively. "I am your daughter, little Arabella. Mama, speak to me!"

The madwoman frowned, but there was no light of recognition in her eyes. I began to weep silently, the tears pouring unchecked down my cheeks.

"Now, now, Lady Perdita," said Mrs. Wicklow in her syrupy voice. "Surely you can favour your daughter with a little courtesy. She has come all the way from London to see you. Speak to her nicely now and tell her you are glad to see her."

The madwoman shuffled restlessly, and her chains clanked. Arabella put out her gloved hands and rested them on the metal cuffs that chafed against her mother's tiny bony wrists.

"Who are you?" snarled the madwoman suddenly, in a sly voice, scratchy and gruff as if she had not used it often. "Are you Geoffrey's wife come to gloat over me in my misery? Do you think you can take Georgie away from me, too?" She stepped in front of her keeper, who was evidently the Georgie of whom she spoke. "You shan't have him! He is mine, all mine. He loves me, just as Geoffrey loved me. Geoffrey despised you! He called you a fat, rich pig. He only married you for your money. Ah, poor Geoffrey, he always needed money."

She paused, and the large, barren room echoed with the shrill vehemence of her tones.

"You killed me! You fat, rich pig!" she suddenly screamed, her face animated with hatred and misery. Arabella took a sudden step backward. "You killed me! You bitch! You slut!" She pursed her lips and spat directly at Arabella. The saliva caught Arabella full upon the face, but she did not flinch. She merely stood there, swaying a little back and forth. Then her eyes rolled back in her head. Before I could reach her, she had fallen backward upon the floor in a dead faint.

Chapter Five

There was great consternation within the room. Mrs. Wicklow dropped her pretence of gentility and swore at the keeper to remove that creature; the madwoman continued to scream obscenities; a strange woman whom I had half glimpsed in the doorway vanished and came back with a vinaigrette full of *sal volatile*. It is only in the recounting that I can recall these various details; at the time, all of my thoughts were with Arabella. She was unconscious for only a few minutes, but then she began to moan and writhe on the floor, her eyelids shut and her hands clenched into fists.

The strange woman, who knelt beside her on the other side, said something that at first I did not hear. Then I understood her words. "Her time has come!" she said. A chill ran down my back, and I stared at my mistress helplessly.

"Mrs. Wicklow," said the woman. "This lady requires a bed. Her child is on its way."

"Good God!" ejaculated that lady, pulling up her skirts slightly as she would do if faced with a snake. She studied us through narrowed eyes. "I suppose her husband will reimburse me for the expenses," she said to me.

"Of course, of course, he shall," I said quickly, not liking the piteous appeal in my voice. "Only let us make her comfortable. Peraps it is just the shock. Perhaps, it will stop. Only let us find her a quiet place to rest."

"Very well then," snapped Mrs. Wicklow. "Annie, there is that empty room on the third floor. She can have that. You'll have to make up the bed. I shall, of course, have to charge for the linen."

"And you will send for the nearest doctor?" I begged.

"As soon as someone can be spared," replied Mrs. Wicklow coolly, doubtless, to let me know who was in command here. "The asylum's doctor is away on business in London. But there's another one in the village."

Glad Arabella's baby would not be brought into the world by an asylum doctor, I immediately turned my attention to my tormented mistress.

Sometime during that nightmare journey up two flights of stairs and down a dark, filthy corridor to an even more execrable hole of a room, I learned that my angel of mercy was Annie Puffer, lady's maid to Arabella's mother.

"Never fear, child," she said to me as I stood in the midst of the dingy closet of a room, trying to support Arabella, who was incoherent with fear. "I've delivered several babies myself." Another pain assailed Arabella, and she began to whimper and clutch onto me so that her fingernails pierced through the fabric of my gown. Her sobbing chant made me feel ill; over and over again she cried, "Mama, oh, Mama. Mama!"

Once Annie had made up the bed with a tattered but clean sheet, she helped me undress Arabella and brought one of the grey asylum gowns to put on her, since her own gown was soiled with a discharge of blood. I was terrified by the blood, but Annie assured me it was normal. I was frightened, too, by the transformation of Arabella from my young mistress into a madwoman, for so she seemed in the shapeless garment, her eyes wild with pain, her lips chanting "Mama," her writhing body and her clutching hands digging at my flesh, drawing down the sides of her contorted face to leave a trail of red lines, or tearing and picking at the fabric of her gown.

"You will be of no use to her if you are as terrified as she," said Annie. "Go and compose yourself, fetch me several buckets of hot water from the kitchen, anything that will keep you busy. There is nothing wrong with her; she was just caught unawares. Her pain seems far worse than it is. Off with you and don't come back till you have gathered your wits about you.

I stumbled down the stairs in a daze. I prayed that the baby would be born soon to free Arabella of her agony. I wonder now what I would have felt if I had known then that the child would not be born until that same time the following day. I prayed that this was a false alarm and we would soon be on our way back to London so that the special doctor and the midwife engaged to attend Arabella in her confinement could be with her. I stumbled into a room containing two hideous crones, who began to cackle and point at me with their bony fingers. I fled and, finding the backstairs at last, gained the kitchen, where the cook refused to let me carry off any receptacle in which I could convey water.

When I returned to the cell where Arabella was confined, I was hardly of a calmer frame of mind but I could see Annie had wrought miracles. She had knotted Arabella's petticoat to the metal frame of the cot and placed Arabella's hands firmly upon it every time a new pain began. She crooned to her words of endearment and encouragement, nearly drowning out Arabella's refrain of "Mama! Mama!" In the intervals between pains, she chattered away brightly about how brave Arabella was and how lovely it would be to see the baby and had she thought of names for it yet? Arabella said not a word, but lay staring at me with beseeching eyes that tore at my heart.

At the time, I wondered at the wisdom of Annie's well-meaning chatter, for Arabella had shown a strange reluctance to speculate about the baby. In fact, she never mentioned it at all, only complaining about her ruined figure every time we had to switch to a larger corset and bewailing the discomforts she had to suffer. Sometimes when I bathed her I watched with fascination how the skin of her stomach rippled and bulged. I would call her attention to it. "Oh, look, Bella! The baby is moving!" And she would glance down with disinterest. "Little monster!" she would say. I asked her if I might touch it, and with a shrug, as if she considered it pointless, she consented. How marvellous it was to feel the fluid motions of the little creature within her!

After that first time, I was disappointed if the child remained asleep during the bath, and as she grew larger and I was able to feel the distinct impression of a foot, I was ecstatic. "Only feel, Arabella! A little foot with little toes! You can feel it quite distinctly. Oh, there, naughty child, it has moved!"

"I know it has feet, Jenny," she said miserably. "The wretched beast kicks me all the time. I am quite sore." And that was all.

So when Annie left the room for a time to see about the water herself, I did not mention the baby at all. Instead I reminded Arabella that it should soon be over, that she need no longer be pregnant, and during the periods of respite recounted to her all of the stories she had ever told me about Franklin. This seemed to calm her even more, and Annie nodded with approval when she came back into the room.

"Whatever soothes her most," she said. "You will know best," and she took up a seat on a chair in the corner while I knelt by the bed. Or she occasionally climbed up next to Arabella on the bed to hold her down as Arabella writhed in pain.

So it went. The hours took on an elastic form, sometimes they seemed whole years and sometimes mere minutes. Two watchers and a woman in labour alone in a room, a primeval scene. All through that wild and lonely night, by the flickering light of one candle that cast Arabella's swollen silhouette upon the wall above her bed, we sat and watched and prayed and suffered together. Though we tried to hush her, Arabella would sometimes scream out in agony and would be answered by strange, echoing wails from other parts of that sinister house. Mrs. Wicklow appeared once, a strange, grim figure, in her nightdress, the guttering candle she held making her features appear a grotesque mask.

"She is disturbing the inmates," she hissed. "You must keep her quiet, even if it means gagging her!"

Of course, we could not countenance this, but Annie, God bless her, gave Arabella a rag dipped in water to hold between her teeth, which also helped relieve her consuming thirst and her parched lips.

The doctor did not arrive until the following morning and, after a brief inspection, stated flatly that it would be a long labour and the child certainly would not be born before the next morning.

I felt that I could not go on when I heard this. To relieve the tension, Annie fetched me some of the tasteless breakfast fare fed to the inhabitants. I wolfed it down in the corridor so as not to tempt Arabella with the sight of food. She was never coherent. Sometimes she would speak to Franklin as if he were in the room; other times she held long conversations with her mother in a voice eerily like that of a young child. At one point, she suddenly struggled to her feet and staggered across the room to the window, where she fell to her knees and held out her hands, crying, "Mama! Mama! You have come back for me! Mama! Don't leave me! Mama! Mama! I have been a good girl! They won't let me come to you! Mama! Mama! I don't want to stay here! Take me with you! Oh, Mama!"

We tried to wrestle her away from the window, but she fought us like a tigress saying, "Let me alone! Don't you see my Mama there! She is crying! I must go to her!" So piteous and moving were her pleas that I looked out the window to see what it was she saw. There was only an empty cobbled yard, the hideous iron fence, and barren stretch of green hill opposite our perch.

While she was in the grip of another labour pain, we managed to drag her back to the bed, and after that she would not let us touch her but lay weeping silently between her struggles.

In the afternoon, a new transformation occurred. She began to shout obscenities at us, words I did not know she knew, some of them echoing the epithets her mother had hurled at her the previous day. She struggled to get up, saying that she was leaving, she was going to Franklin, and when we tried to restrain her, she scratched at us viciously.

"Hush, hush," said Annie, comforting me. "This is the worst. It will soon be over now. They are always like this toward the end." And indeed, within a half hour, she began to shriek that she was being torn in half, and Annie told her that the child was trying to come out and she must help push it into the world. It was a long struggle, during which Arabella insisted that she was dying, that the child was killing her, that she could not, would not do it, but at last there was a dark, wet head between her legs and then a slippery little body, and then with piteous cry, like that of a kitten, the little girl-child announced her entrance into the world. A strange entrance indeed, to be born inside a madhouse!

Arabella barely glanced at her and then turned her face to the wall and wept herself to sleep while Annie and I took turns holding the child and examining her tiny fingers and toes. Annie had gotten a basket from who knows where and, filling this with blankets she had warmed on the stove, placed the child before the empty hearth. Then she went in search of a servant to light a fire. I realized suddenly that I must make a note of the date and time of birth and calculated that it was the eleventh of May, the same day two years past that Walter Farraday had died. Later we were to learn that Miss Finch had also left this world the same day.

"She's very small," said Annie, after the fire had been lit and we stood looking down on the sleeping infant by its rosy glow.

"She is premature," I said quickly, remembering that we must hold to the story we had concocted. "She was not due until the end of next month."

"Ah," sighed Annie. "She must have had quite a time of it, poor mite, struggling this past day to be born. I've never seen a birth so difficult. Nothing was wrong and yet—" There was a pause. "Will her father be disappointed to have a girl?"

"Oh!" I said sharply. "He must be informed. Are writing materials somewhere?"

But there was no need of my carefully composed and laboriously scribed note. Sir Henry arrived the next morning, shortly after the doctor, who showed no sign of discomfiture at having missed the birth.

I had snatched a few hours of sleep in Annie's bed during the night while Annie sat up with Arabella and the babe, and had just taken her place when Sir Henry and Mrs. Wicklow entered the room together. Arabella and the infant were still sleeping.

"Here they are, mother and child, both doing very well indeed," said Mrs. Wicklow in her arch voice.

Sir Henry glanced at his sleeping wife and then went over and cast his eyes upon the infant in the basket. I think he meant only to ascertain that there was indeed a baby in that nest of blankets, but suddenly he went down on his knees and a look of such wonder and glory crossed his face that I was deeply ashamed of the deception we were using.

"A girl, Sir Henry," I said, knowing that he had spoken of nothing but the fifth Baronet Warder-Mull.

"She is exquisite," he said in hushed tones. "We shall call her Arabella after her mother." He looked at me—for acknowledgment? for approval?—and I saw that he had tears in his eyes. He brushed them away surreptitiously, but more came to take their place. I watched him reach out his trembling fingers to touch her ever so lightly. Shortly afterward, he became bolder and, tenderly unwrapping her, counted all of her fingers and toes. She awoke finally, turning her head a little from side to side and making little mewing noises, which quickly changed in tenor to a full-out wail. Sir Henry stood up suddenly as if he had been struck.

"What is wrong with her?" he asked, facing me pleadingly. "Do something for her! What does she want?"

I had to laugh; he was so innocent and indignant.

"She is hungry," I replied. "She wants her mother." And I went over to the bed to shake Arabella awake.

None of us was prepared for the change in her. She might as well have been asleep, or dead. Despite the increasing frenzy of her babe's cries, she did not respond, merely lay there, eyes fixed on the ceiling, blank and uncomprehending as if locked in trance.

Sir Henry was the most taken aback by this phenomenon, and who could blame him? With her hair matted in strings, her eyes vacant, her cheeks marred with scratches, her lips cracked and bleeding, and her body garbed in that rough grey shift that was the uniform of the asylum, she could easily have been mistaken for one of its inmates.

We tried to put the baby to her breast, despite her refusal to assist or acknowledge, but it was an unsatisfactory business, and the poor child howled piteously, finally going back to sleep when I rocked her in my arms.

Henry tried to speak to Arabella but she would not respond to any of us. "Good God, what is wrong with her?" he said. "Send for the doctor, at once!" he fired at Mrs. Wicklow. She nodded and went off, and within an hour the doctor was back. I suppose Mrs. Wicklow was anxious to please Sir Henry in the hopes he would be generous for her hospitality. By then I had quickly sketched to Sir Henry the events of the past days, and the doctor confirmed our speculation that the combined shock of Arabella's meeting with her mother and the difficult delivery had plummeted her into either a severe depression or illness. He could not be sure which. He could be sure that, in her present condition, Lady Warder-Mull was incapable of adequately providing for her child, and plans were immediately set in motion for Sir Henry to hire a wet nurse and take the baby back with him to London. I was the only one to protest this, an act that did not endear me to Sir Henry, for I felt that Arabella would have no reason to recover if her child were taken away; but I did not protest overmuch, for I had to acknowledge that if Arabella did not rouse herself, the infant's life would be in danger.

I think, looking back on the matter, that it was not for Arabella that I wanted the baby to stay, but for me. When we had first guessed at her condition, she had tried everything from long rides on horseback to scorching hot baths in order to induce a miscarriage. When these did not succeed, she was glum—it meant she must marry Sir Henry—while I was secretly thrilled. She endured the pregnancy; I enjoyed it. She suffered through the delivery; I wept with joy at the miracle of birth. And now I longed to go on living through her, to experience the pleasures of motherhood, and yet I, too, was uneasy. I think it was then, when Sir Henry carried away his precious bundle as if she were gold and I was left utterly alone, that I recognized for the first time that someday soon Arabella and I must come to a parting of the ways.

Chapter Six

I suppose it was inevitable that, with Arabella confined to an asylum for a period of months, the rumour should have begun that she had gone mad. Certainly, she was treated as if she had, though ostensibly she remained under Mrs. Wicklow's roof as a boarder in order to recover from a difficult confinement.

At times, I feared she would become insane, surrounded as she was by the sights and smells and the elusive but real sense of menace and suspicion that permeated Slow Banning Retreat. Although we remained apart from the other inhabitants, except for the occasional companionship of Annie Puffer, one could not help but hear the wild howls that shattered the night air, the sounds of beatings and of chains; occasionally a wild and furtive face would appear in the doorway. When Arabella was improved enough to take exercise, we would go out and wander aimlessly about the courtyard with its stone paving and its bleak grey walls.

She was treated by the asylum doctor, who was away during the delivery of Arabella's daughter, as if she were insane. She was purged repeatedly with calomel and confined in cold shower baths. She was given a dose of tonic with each meal and, as she would not eat at first, she was force-fed with a hideous device like a metal funnel, which was thrust into her mouth and held in place by one of the burly male attendants. Then either the doctor or Mrs. Wicklow would stand by to see that I spooned the food into the top of this while Arabella gagged and choked and struggled beneath it. Sometimes she was bound to the bed with leather straps during these sessions. After some coaxing. I was able to persuade her to take gruel and tea, which I fed to her on a spoon, and the daily torture was done away with.

Not one of these treatments made the slightest change in her condition. I could dress her, wash her, change the linens, brush her hair, and she would lie like a doll, not helping but not hindering me. I fell into the habit of talking to myself a great deal—a habit that unfortunately has never left me—just for the pleasure of hearing someone speak. I would describe the room, the weather as observed from the window, what little I knew of the routine and amusements of the household staff. I avoided mentioning her mother or indicating in any way the nature of the establishment. No glimmer of recognition or understanding ever came to her eyes, not even when I held her or kissed her.

Disturbed by her lack of progress, Sir Henry, who came down from London perhaps once a fortnight and delivered glowing discourses to all and sundry on the progress of the baby, consulted a specialist in mental diseases who recommended commitment. Not to Slow Banning Retreat, of course, which he execrated (a fact I think that influenced Sir Henry's later decision to place his wife with Dr Steward), but to the specialist's own private asylum. Sir Henry, however, with great wisdom, wavered and finally decided against signing the certificate of commitment; perhaps he was merely frightened at the public opprobrium that would, result from being married to a lunatic. At any rate, this decision of his was to prove Arabella's salvation.

Summer had passed, though little did we know it, except for the heat that poured into the tiny, unventilated room and the unmerciful glare of the sun in the walled courtyard. Now it was autumn. We could seldom go out, for the courtyard was flooded with rain, and frost often coated our one window. Arabella and I shivered together under the thin blankets provided by the asylum.

I determined that something must be done, and remembering Dr Steward's wisdom and gentleness with Miss Finch during her long illness (Sir Henry informed us of her death), I wrote him a long letter describing Arabella's condition and begged that he would come and see if anything could be done for her. I hinted that Sir Henry would be glad to reimburse him for any expense; I vowed to myself that if he would not, I should pay him back myself by setting something aside out of my wages, even if the debt went unpaid for many years.

I did not like to give the letter to Mrs. Wicklow to post because her manner had altered noticeably after the unfavourable report of the specialist. Except on the days appointed for Sir Henry's visits, we were given no consideration. The meals, which I had to fetch, were cold and tasteless; our allocation of coal was tiny. Treatment of any sort had ceased altogether.

So I went in search of Annie to find out how a letter could be smuggled out of the asylum. I found her pouring over a little knitted cap she was making for the baby by the light of a single candle in her tiny cubicle, which adjoined her mistress's room. I had seen Arabella's mother on several occasions since that first fateful night. She never again exhibited any ferocity or venom; she was the meekest and mildest of women, barely distinguishable from the other female patients, except perhaps in her doglike devotion to her male attendant. Annie had already told me Lady Perdita's history, which I will not repeat as Mr. DeWinx has recounted it earlier in this narrative. Annie was of the adamant opinion that prolonged association with the insane can easily overcome a weak nature already buffeted by the storms of life, and thus she was my firm ally in my determination to remove Arabella, promising to take the letter and give it to the washerwoman, who came the following morning.

I lingered a little in the snug room, which was cluttered with crocheted antimacassars, china fairings, and reproductions of engravings out of magazines, for I was reluctant to return to the cold comfort of my room and the cold companionship of Arabella. We began to speak of Annie's life since she had accompanied Lady Perdita to the asylum.

"It's not a bad sort of life at all," she said, as her knitting needles clicked away. "We have a little reading society that I have gotten up with the two other lady's maids. We meet every Wednesday night, and one of us gives an account of the most recent books we have read. Sometimes we read aloud to each other. I recall when Boz's little Nelly died. We were all in such tears none of us could see the words. We passed the magazine around from one to the other and each would read a few sentences and then break down and weep. Ah! That was a lovely group then. It is difficult. People come and go so. At that time, there was a lovely young girl staying here, a Chancery lunatic, and her maid, Miss Crisp—most sympathetic! But the young lady died— hung herself, I'm afraid—and Miss Crisp had to go."

I sighed. "Do you never miss the world? Would you not like to marry?"

"Oh, la, marriage!" she said airily. "I suppose association with the sort of men one finds in this place—" she referred to the keepers "— has quite turned me off of marriage. They are so thoroughly common." She shuddered and, in the pause, we heard the guttural tones of George, Lady Perdita's attendant, in the next room. He was, of course, not supposed to be with her at night, but I understood from Annie, though she never said this directly, that he was often there.

"Once there was a gentleman's gentleman," said Annie wistfully, "who came with his master. He was very nice, though, unfortunately, several inches shorter than I. I dared to hope for a while—"

"What happened to him?" I asked.

"Oh, he went quite mad," she said calmly. "It is the atmosphere of the place. And, of course, since he was not wealthy, he was sent off to the county asylum. Perhaps he recovered. They say nearly half of the patients in the county institutions are cured. At any rate, we never saw him again."

"And how many patients have been cured here?"

"Not one, that I know of," she replied. "There was an old man who was here for years. His family at last could no longer sustain the expense. They took him out; the rumour was that they, were to care for him at home. I sometimes imagine that he recovered completely after he was gone and fancy him sitting before a fire with his grand-children on his knee."

She put down her knitting needles suddenly and lifted her eyes to mine. "Jenny," she said, "if Arabella remains here, you must go!"

"I could never do that!" I protested. "I have never been with any-one else, but her. We have been like sisters to each other."

"But no longer," she said remorselessly. "If you leave, she will not even know."

252

"I cannot believe that!" I said hotly. "Besides, I could not leave her to the mercy of these people, the keepers!" Our conversation had grown increasingly difficult because of the squeak of the bedsprings from the other side of the wall. "And if a new maid should come, well, why should she care for my mistress in her present state? It would just be an unpleasant duty to her."

"Did you have a follower?" Annie asked.

I winced because she used the past tense, and yet I used it, too. We were both later proved right, for Daniel had already married a rich widow. But I would not learn that for many months, and so I began to describe him to her. Annie's eyes glowed with wonder, like those of a child looking in the window of a pastry shop, as I went on relating our walks, our quarrels, our excursions, and though at first I merely wished to give her a treat, I soon found my narrative had swept me away. How I longed to be able to go about at will, to have an afternoon off with all the glories it promised.

When I concluded, I felt the reluctance, the nagging disappointment that I used to feel as my holidays drew to an end. The days stretched before me, dreary and joyless, and Annie's invitation to the next Wednesday's reading society meeting chilled rather than cheered me.

I often considered this conversation with Annie during the subsequent days. If Arabella continued as she was, would I stay and live a while as hope slowly faded into resignation? I had gradually stopped addressing myself to Arabella or even approaching her except for the most routine of reasons, and suddenly, with horror, I noted that I was growing more and more like her. I could sit for hours unmoving. I no longer took an interest in my appearance, for who was there to see me? When my gown was too light for the autumn chill, I had listlessly accepted one of the asylum's grey dresses, and one night, catching a glimpse of myself in the dark window—we had no mirror—for a moment I thought I beheld a lunatic with dull eyes and uncombed hair. Would I go mad also?

In a frenzy, I stripped off the grey garment and washed myself and my hair with the chill water in the basin and a bar of yellow soap. The next morning, I plaited my hair in an elaborate coiffure and put on again the threadbare gown in which I had come, ignoring the fact that I shivered with cold.

How fortunate I did so! For that morning Dr Steward arrived, having received my letter just the previous day. He had the good sense to inform Mrs. Wicklow that he had come at the request of Sir Henry. She brought him up to the room, which she might not have, with only her ill-concealed distaste for this interference showing. He greeted me with his usual warmth. For a brief time, I had allowed myself to foolishly hope that he had a special fondness for me, but when he told me that I was an excellent nurse. I had to conclude that his interest was merely professional. Besides, it was a foolish dream considering the great gulf in our stations.

His examination of Arabella was thorough and gentle. At its conclusion, he took me down to the shabby comfort of the drawing room and interviewed me over a delicious tea, which he had charmed out of the downstairs maid, about what had transpired over the past five months.

"She can hear us, you know," he explained gently, "although she does not respond. When you rattled the poker against the grate as I asked you, she started ever so slightly. I did not want her to hear this conversation, as whatever it was that precipitated her into this condition must still be indescribably painful to her."

I nodded, eyes shining. So I had been right in my instinct to treat her as if she were still the mistress I knew and loved; I vowed to redouble my efforts to reach her.

"You were very wise, indeed, to contact me, Jenny," he said at the conclusion of our talk. "Of course, a specialist in such diseases would diagnose her condition at once as *melancholia* or even *catatonia,* but I think the sudden onset promises a good prognosis. The shock of encountering her mother unleashed a flood of intolerable memories, which then became intermingled with the physical pain of the birth, and now she has simply retreated from it all. It is a sort of blessed instinct for survival, and not at all a sign of incurable lunacy."

Tears flooded to my eyes. I suppressed an urge to kneel down and kiss his hands.

"Of course, she must be removed immediately," he continued. "She can never recover while confined in this place, which has been the site of the trauma."

"But I don't believe Sir Henry will have her back!" I interrupted. "He wishes her to return, of course, he often speaks of it, but only when she is fully recovered, her old self again."

"Oh, well, that can be managed," Dr Steward said with a toss of his head. "I have a large and mostly empty house, and I have often had patients come to stay with me. It works out quite well, for I can give them a great deal more attention that way. I will consult Sir Henry immediately upon my return to London, and I think we shall have you both out of here within a few days. You must leave it up to me." He paused. "You have become quite pale and thin, Jenny. I fear you have been very unhappy here."

I nodded my head wordlessly, and he stood up, taking my face between his long, gentle fingers, and kissed me upon my forehead.

I flew up the stairs to Arabella's room and could not stop chattering away to her about our coming release. I danced about the room; I sang; I kissed her again and again and petted her. Was I wrong, or did she begin to improve from that day? I don't believe it was just my imagination that I saw a glimmer of recognition in her eyes, and I think she even smiled slightly as she watched me caper about the room, holding up my skirts.

I never doubted that Dr Steward would be able to ensure Arabella's release, but I did sometimes wonder, in the midst of my mad joy, what would become of me. Was I to return to 19 Grover Square? I did not think I should be welcome there, and what tasks could I perform while my mistress was staying with Dr Steward? Then, again, perhaps I was to go with her to Dr Steward's. But would it be right for me to be alone with a bachelor in his house?

My confidence in Dr Steward was not misplaced. Within two days, I was helping him to bring Arabella out to the carriage to be driven moments later out through those ominous iron gates. I had wept over my farewell to Annie, but I did not weep as the gates clanged shut behind us. I was much too exhilarated to be free at last, to be sitting beside Dr Steward, to observe the almost immediate improvement in Arabella. A little flush mounted to her cheeks, and although she still did not speak, she looked out of the windows with interest.

When the carriage came to a stop before a pretty green-shuttered house just around the corner from Grover Square, I still had not mustered my courage to ask Dr Steward what would become of me. But after we had settled Arabella into her room, he said, "Now I will show you where you will sleep, Jenny." I felt a sudden relief. Of course, no one would think twice about my remaining alone in the house with Dr Steward; I was only a maid, after all.

Thus, I was completely confounded when, instead of leading me up to the attic or into an adjoining dressing room, he opened the door to a room just as large and lovely as that he had allocated for Arabella. I had never dreamed of a room like this, with its wide bed and satin coverlet, its velvety *chaise longue* and inlaid armoire, its Persian carpet, and brocaded curtains. I was even more perplexed when he said, "I will let you rest after our long journey, but dinner will be served at four, and my sister and I trust you and Arabella will both be recovered enough to join us."

"Ah, of course," I thought when he had left. I sank down in wonderment before the fire in its tiled hearth. "He wants me to wait upon Arabella at table. Probably he doesn't have enough servants to go around." I had often waited table at Grover Square or Pittlesbury Hall when there was a large dinner party, and so I dressed myself in my best black satin gown and white lace collar and cuffs (for I found that Dr Steward had thoughtfully arranged to have our garments brought over from 19 Grover Square and placed in the cupboards and wardrobe).

But when I had dressed Arabella in one of her favourite gowns and led her into the dining room, I discovered, to my consternation, that there was a place set for me with all the trappings of glittering china, crystal, and silver. I had little notion of how to use it. Dr Steward's sister, a young woman who asked me to call her Kitty, chatted away to me as if I were a dinner guest, and I turned crimson with confusion.

But now I am straying into my own story and so will return to Sir Henry's narrative.

Chapter Seven

Sir Henry's narrative continued...

I have said that I loved Arabella. I did indeed, but I never fell in love with her. It was a practical decision made for a practical purpose, and I found, with pleasure, that my constant affection and interest in her gradually deepened to love.

I fell in love with my daughter, however. It was magic. From that first moment when I saw her sleeping so utterly at peace in her basket before the fire, I was captured.

What a queer emotional moment that was for me! All through the long journey down to Slow Banning Retreat, where I guessed my wife had gone, I was in a frenzy of guilt about the torment I must have caused her, and when Mrs. Wicklow informed me the baby had been born prematurely, I was sick with apprehension about her health and the survival of the child. Yet when I gazed down on the sleeping face of my daughter, my agony left me and a deep spring of joy, which I had not known existed in me, welled in its place. I scarcely dared to breathe as I knelt to examine her and saw her dark lashes curled against the porcelainlike paleness of her cheek, her tiny budlike hand, with each miniature fingernail a gem of perfection, curled beside her.

My newfound peace was quickly shattered when she awoke and began to cry, and I believe I was more annoyed with my wife than solicitous of her condition when she could not satisfy the child's needs. A fount of desolation poured up in me, as profound as my earlier joy, at the thought that my child must suffer, might sicken, might even die.

Fortunately, the doctor who attended the asylum knew of a woman of excellent character in the neighbourhood who had recently lost her own baby and who, he thought, would be willing to serve as Arabella's wet nurse. I went with him to the humble cottage where she lived and persuaded her, through the promise of a truly munificent salary, to leave her two older children in the care of their grandmother and travel up to London with me. When she heard of the sudden arrival of the baby and our lack of preparation, she wistfully offered me the garments that had belonged to her own just-buried child, but I was superstitious of clothing my daughter in the dead child's clothes, and so we carried off young Arabella in a cashmere shawl borrowed from Mrs. Wicklow.

My daughter began to cry again shortly after our departure, and Mrs. Taylor took her capably from my trembling grasp and put her to her breast. The contented sound of Bella's ardent suckling suddenly replaced her frantic cries. At first, I was embarrassed and directed my gaze out the window, but at last my curiosity was too great and, from stealing occasional glimpses, I soon found my discomfort ebbing and gazed with pleasure on the peaceful picture of the mother with a child at her breast.

Phoebe's amazement at my return with a baby and a strange woman who was not my wife was marvellous to behold. She could not believe that I knew how to hold an infant and kept worrying at me and correcting me until finally she wrestled the child away and demonstrated what she insisted was the proper manner in which to hold a baby.

She was as foolish as I from that moment on, though she attempted to disguise her infatuation by reprimanding me for the same faults she exhibited. We were always in the nursery, watching the child being bathed or fed.

"You will spoil her with too much attention!" Phoebe would say, taking the baby out of my hands and replacing her firmly in the little basket in which she slept. She would pretend that she had come up to find out what I was doing, but I knew that she had really come for the same purpose she criticized me for. She excused her attentions under the practical headings of "dressing and changing the child," but surely no infant needs to be dressed and undressed ten times a day!

Neither of us could bear to hear her cry. Sometimes at night when her howls rent the air, we would both emerge from our rooms, candles in hand, only to bump into each other at the foot of the stairs.

"Taylor will pick her up in a minute!" Phoebe would say to me sharply, wagging her head.

"I'll just go up and see," I would reply. "No need for you to disturb yourself."

And then another piercing scream would drift down to us, and in a flash, we would both be in the nursery only to find that Taylor had indeed settled herself sleepily in the chair before the fire and was giving Bella the liquid sustenance she required.

Taylor was, from all I could tell, an excellent nurse. Little Bella never suffered from her prematurity but quickly blossomed into a rosy, plump baby. She suffered greatly during teething, and so did we all, but she missed most of the usual childhood diseases since we never took her out nor allowed visitors to come too near her.

I know that every parent thinks of his own child in superlatives, but I am convinced that Bella is truly extraordinary in both intelligence and amiability. Everyone who has known her loves her. Taylor had to leave after a year and return to her own children, but she never fails to send a little handmade gift on Bella's birthday and she used to come up one or two times a year on a mission just to see her.

After interviewing probably every available nurse in London, Phoebe managed to find an excellent replacement for Taylor in Mrs. Blue, who was with us until we came down to Devon.

We were such a happy household; I think all of us dreaded the prospect of my wife's return. I did not want her to remain at Slow Banning Retreat; every time I journeyed there I was overcome by shame at having inflicted this damage on her. Yet when Dr Steward came to tell me that he believed he could cure my wife if I consented to place her under his care, I must confess my heart sank within my breast. But I naturally gave my consent.

"It is important," said Dr Steward, "that I know everything that may have affected her and caused her present paralysis of nerve."

I shrank into myself. I should never confess the details of Bella's conception, especially not since I had determined from careful observation that my daughter bore no mark of my sin. Nor should I disclose the cruel remarks that had passed my lips to Arabella before her headlong flight to Slow Banning Retreat and her present condition. I invented some tale of Arabella having accidentally found the papers relating to her mother, and Dr Steward questioned me at length about Lady Perdita's sad history.

"Then Arabella had never seen her mother since the time she eloped?" he asked, after I had finished my narrative.

"No, her father forbade her to ever mention her mother. All signs of Lady Perdita's existence were removed from the house," I replied.

Dr Steward chewed on his pipe thoughtfully. "Jenny told me that at one point during the labour your wife seemed to think her mother was outside the window and was calling to her."

"Is that what is termed a delusion?" I asked. "You know, Dr Forke-Winslow advised me to have her committed. He said her condition was most serious."

"I have found," Dr Steward responded, "that there is usually a kernel of truth in even the most bizarre of hallucinations."

Suddenly an old and nearly obliterated memory came to my mind. "Oh, there was something," I said.

"Yes?"

"Well, it must have been some time after Lady Perdita went off with her cousin. I believe it was July, yes, the very end of July, for the town was nearly empty. I came to see Mr. Farraday, but the housekeeper said he had gone to fetch a doctor, because Arabella lay at death's door. It was her first attack of what they later decided was brain fever. Naturally, I asked how it had begun. At first the housekeeper said she should not tell me because Mr. Farraday did not want them to discuss it, but since I was such an old friend of the family, she would. I thought at the time that this was merely an excuse, for she was clearly overwrought and needed to speak to someone. She loved Arabella very much, you see; they all did, the staff."

"And what was it that she told you?"

"That Lady Perdita had come back."

"Then Arabella did see her mother again?"

"Yes. Apparently, Mr. Farraday would not permit his wife to enter the house, and so she stood on the front walk and called to her daughter. Arabella was in the nursery—her windows would face on the front of the house—and she heard and came to the window and began calling back. I guess they feared in her distress she would throw herself down. She had managed to open the sash and was leaning out to her mother. It was raining that night and bitter cold. Mr. Farraday saw what was happening and went up and pulled Arabella back and closed the window and the curtains."

"Was that the end of it?"

"No, the housekeeper said Lady Perdita would not go away. All night she stood there in the rain, ringing the bell and calling out to her daughter, but the next morning she was gone, and Arabella lay ill with the fever."

"I suppose," said Dr Steward, "that must have been the morning that Lady Perdita tried to destroy herself."

"She did what?" I asked aghast.

"Yes, I've been talking to Dr Ballard. He was one of the certifying doctors. She threw herself into the Serpentine. Luckily a passer-by fished her out, and the Rescue Society got hold of her. She was obviously no longer in her right mind. All they could get from her was the name Perdita DeWinx, which was enough for them to know who her father was. They went to him and got him to sign the papers for her commitment."

There was a long silence. I thought of my daughter, Bella, sleeping upstairs in the nursery, the same nursery.

"Did Mr. Farraday know of his wife's insanity?" Dr Steward asked at last.

"I doubt it," I replied. "He never mentioned it to me. You must realize that, as his solicitor, I drew up the papers dissolving the marriage settlement and I saw the letter he sent as accompaniment. He said that henceforth she was not his wife, that he was throwing her back upon the mercy of her family, and that he wished never to hear of her nor be in communication with them again."

"Harsh!" was Dr Steward's comment.

"She made him thoroughly miserable," I said quickly and then, seeing Dr Steward's acute eyes upon me, thought uncomfortably of my marriage with Arabella. But he did not pursue this topic, merely said that, with a letter from me authorizing the action, he would remove my wife from the asylum and establish her at his house under the care of his sister and Arabella's maid, Jenny.

"I think it best," he added, just before he went out the door, "that you not visit her at all until I inform you that it is advisable." I winced slightly, wondering if he had guessed after all of the disharmony in my marriage, but when the door had closed behind him and I heard his footsteps retreating down the walk, I felt merely grateful. Another period of respite. I even dared to hope that her recovery would be as slow as it was successful.

Alas, neither hope was fully realized. When my wife finally rejoined us, shortly after Bella's first birthday, she was utterly changed. She did not look the same nor speak in the same voice. She even smelled differently. It was like living with a ghost and a stranger.

Chapter Eight

I think Arabella and I both knew from the start that it was a mistake for her to come back. I suppose a divorce is inevitable now after all that has transpired; I considered it briefly at the time of her illness, but put it from me as unthinkable. It would mean the notoriety and gossip I had always feared. Already there were rumours of her madness.

Then again, my daughter needed a mother. Her aunt Phoebe adored her; her nurse, Mrs. Blue, was soft beneath her stiffly starched apron; but surely every child deserves a mother, one of those magic creatures who sweeps like an angel into the room and kisses one good night while rustling with silk and sweet perfume. And then I needed a wife. Not for the old reasons: My physical desires were slowly dying in me. Not because I needed a hostess: Phoebe, if she did not actually grace my table, at least did the honors capably: Not as a companion: I rarely went out anymore.

No, I suppose it was merely to give me definition, to place me somewhere in human society. I was a curious anomaly during that year like a widower, but not a widower; like a bachelor, and yet not a bachelor. No one knew quite what to do with me or what to say to me. Now you could say I am that familiar and pitiable character from farce: an older man jilted by his young and pretty wife. People may smile at me behind my back, I may be an object of amusement, but at least they speak to me. "Poor Sir Henry," they probably say to each other, "we must ask him up for dinner." Or "Poor Sir Henry," they must think, "left with a young girl to raise alone. We must have Nurse make up some pinafores for little Bella." They allow me to go on and on about my darling; I am sure they endure my obsession with patience because they think I, have no one else with whom to share my news of Bella's small troubles and triumphs. During that first year of her life, whenever I spoke of her, they would turn from me in confusion. It was not seemly for a man with a lunatic wife and an infant daughter of dubious legitimacy to dwell on the topic.

I no longer loved my wife. It is as if there is room for only one person in my heart; perhaps it was constricted for too long. When I fell in love with my daughter, there was nothing left for my wife. Yet I knew I owed her a great deal, not the least of which was the gift of my daughter. I had firm resolutions to be scrupulously attentive to her every wish, to never trouble her peace of mind, to treat her with all due consideration.

Alas! When have good resolutions ever been enough? From the start, we were embroiled in conflict. She wished Dr Steward to be godfather to Bella; I had just persuaded the Earl of Gammage to accept this responsibility and could not face the prospect of telling him he was to be replaced with an unknown and highly controversial physician, who had, furthermore, been the one to cure my wife of her insanity.

Dr Steward claims she was never insane. Whether she was or not is a fine point, I think. He considers that her mother was also not insane at the time she was admitted to Slow Banning Retreat. I must confess that, although I did not accede to his wishes to commit my wife, I trust rather more the experience and reputation of Dr Forke-Winslow.

It was very difficult for me to forget and forgive Arabella's lapse. I think I often stared at her; she would frequently ask me if there was something wrong with her appearance. I flinched when she was so outspoken; I cowered when she was in low spirits; I trembled when she was witty and gay. I don't recall anything she did that pleased me. She showed too little. interest in Bella to suit me. She was unmoved by the glories of my snuffboxes and miniatures.

The attitude of others did not help. I was aware that the throng of onlookers at Bella's christening had come to gawk at my wife rather than to welcome my child into the world.

Whenever we went out, people would speak to her in scrupulously polite, carefully limited tones as if she were a young child. I know this distressed her, I could see the pain well up in her face, and I witnessed her struggles to prove that she was thoroughly capable of meeting them on their level. But I must confess I thought more of my own humiliation. After a time, we ceased to go out altogether, and I allowed myself to believe that this pleased her as much as it pleased me.

She devoted herself to music and art, two hobbies in which her father had not allowed her to indulge. She became a passably good artist, I am told, and an excellent musician. Later, after several years had passed and the world had forgotten a little, she was in great demand at afternoon musicales and evening concerts.

She never displayed the slightest evidence of maternal devotion. It was as if Bella were someone else's child. My wife would smile at her accomplishments and pat her upon the head, but unless Bella was recalled to her awareness she seemed to have no memory of her existence at all. Phoebe and Nurse Blue were horrified by this, though I think they also secretly encouraged it, for it meant they had the lion's share of Bella's care and attention. Phoebe would sniff about how my wife had taken the child out into the garden and let her run through the wet grass with no shoes or stockings. Simply irresponsible! What if Bella had taken cold? She never did, of course. She was healthy and happy, which was my never-ending quest. When I would go up to the nursery, Mrs. Blue would cluck and say, "Bella's mummy has not been up yet today." Bella would make a sad face, and after entertaining her with some puppets or a story, I would go back downstairs to my wife, who was usually at the piano, and sternly command her to go up and see the child.

"Oh, forgive me!" she would say, getting up at once. "I was so absorbed, I quite forgot the time." And off she would go, in a froufrou of silk and shimmering curls. She was still exquisitely, heart-wrenchingly beautiful:

Yet so much changed from the Arabella I had known. All of it was for the better, as Phoebe would sometimes grudgingly admit. Yet it was infinitely more disturbing to have someone that one has known from infancy behave in a manner completely the opposite of what one expects.

She was attentive, thoughtful, considerate of my every mood. It made me feel guilty. She gave way to me in every point; the Earl of Gammage was Bella's godfather. I began to dread every signal of a disagreement between us for she would always accede to my wishes. I knew that she was right. But I could never feel as though I had won by my bracing arguments.

With her curious dignity, her graceful acquiescence, the cheerfulness with which she adapted herself to my every request, I felt that she was instead the victor and that I should be squirming in the dust at her feet, a humble worm of a man. I infinitely preferred the naughty, passionate child she had once been to this quiet, reserved, mature woman.

When it happened, I was grateful. I don't suppose any other man would understand that, but there it was: I wanted her to make a fool of me, I wanted her to behave with improvidence, I wanted her to disgrace herself.

They must have met at one of her musicales or concerts. I knew he was in town, of course. I think I made rather a point of encouraging her to go out during that time. His name had been showing up during the previous few years with increasing frequency in the papers and journals. He had drifted from Jamaica to America and thence to Ireland and begun to make a name for himself as, of all things, a collector of folk ballads. He had published several volumes of these quaint songs, which had been received with wild acclaim by the London reviewers and several of which had become the rage in the circles in which Arabella's talents were appreciated. I refer, naturally, to her cousin, Mr. DeWinx. I knew at once that she had seen him. She was a little more restless, a little more distracted

"Ah, I see that your cousin, Mr. DeWinx, was at the Beverwils last night," I said one morning, looking up from the morning paper.

She had the grace to blush a little. "Yes, I saw him there," she said, bending her head to her plate.

"We must have him over sometime for dinner," I said stoutly. "It will be quite fascinating to hear of his adventures."

She looked at me curiously. "If you wish it, my dear," was all that she said.

So we had him over, and I could see at once that it was not all over between them. He was shy and diffident, but could not keep his eyes off her; she was abnormally attentive to me and barely looked at him.

"That was a very pleasant evening," I said when he had gone, after regaling us with some of his new finds. "We must have him over again."

And we did. Once, when he had been invited for dinner, I sent a message saying that a sudden emergency had arisen involving a client and that I would be detained. When I arrived home, near midnight, I could not tell what had transpired. He was gone.

"Oh, you have just missed him," said Arabella. She was seated at the piano, poring over some pages of handwritten music. "He waited as long as he could. Only look, he has given me the first chance at some new ballads. No one else in London has heard them yet."

I examined her closely, but could see no evidence of a guilty secret. Phoebe could tell me no more.

"I sat with them for a while at dinner," she said. "Then I had the maid come in and tell me that Bella was unable to sleep and needed me, just as you requested. When I came down later, they were in the drawing room. She was seated at the piano, trying out the words of one of his strange songs, and he was standing, watching her. He certainly seemed to be entranced, but she was quite natural and invited me to sit down and listen. You know, Harry, you are playing with fire. I don't pretend to have the slightest notion as to why."

I could not explain it to her. But my blood was in a tumult. It was the summer of 1848. The past year had seen some remarkable events: The Chartists were gathering on Kensington Common and breaking windows and tearing up fences around the Park. There was a revolt in Sicily. Louis Philippe was forced to abdicate his throne by a blood-thirsty mob in Paris. Ireland was up in arms, and Belgium was invaded by the Republicans. There was a revolution in Milan and an insurrection in Madrid. All over Europe the old order was in ashes and blood was flowing in the streets.

One could hardly help being affected by this spectacle. For most Englishmen—my sister is a good example—it encouraged a greater Conservatism, a stronger devotion to the Queen and the country. Phoebe thought the Chartists should all be seized and executed. Well, I had very little sympathy with their absurd demands, but I think I was a little stirred, even thrilled, at the evidence of the wild beast that lurked behind the civilized man.

And it was there in me, too. I threw my wife and her old lover together and prowled about, imagining their love passages, peeking around corners, creeping silently into rooms.

One day, I realized it had happened and I felt a weird exultation. My perfect wife, my adoring companion, my uncomplaining spouse had wronged me, had betrayed me! My debts were cancelled! The last vestiges of my love were erased! I could be near her and yet unmoved by her loveliness, unplagued by my old shame.

I knew that something had happened because Mr. DeWinx never again came to the house, responding with excuses to all of my invitations. I knew that they were lovers by the indolent grace of my wife's body, by that evident satiation and well-being that follows physical gratification.

She became careless again, going out without informing anyone where she was going, coming back late at night and going up the stairs singing a little under her breath. She began to play his peculiar ballads for herself in the drawing room during the afternoon, and I would enter quietly only to find her completely unconscious of my presence, rapt in a reverie of her own.

Also, she began to seek out Bella every day. I think she was preparing herself for her departure, stocking up her mind with memories of the child she was to leave behind. This was the only aspect of the business that I did not like. It meant that when she was gone, Bella's tender heart would be grieved with recollections of her mother's attentions, of the picnic they had in the Square garden, of the time they climbed the elm tree together and I found them giggling among the green leaves.

Of course, although she left ostensibly to accompany Mr. DeWinx on his lecture tour, it was not long before the note arrived:

> I have decided not to return, as you knew I would. Pray forgive me for all the wrong I have done you and take good care of my darling, as I am sure you will.
>
> Arabella

There was also a longer sealed letter for Bella, but I threw it into the fire unopened; who knows what version of the story she wanted to leave her daughter?

I immediately transferred my remaining clients to a colleague, sold Pittlesbury Hall, and purchased the estate in Devon. I suppose in many ways I wanted to make it impossible for Arabella to find us if she ever decided, like her mother, to return. While we were preparing for the remove, I did away with every vestige of her existence. I gave away her clothes, sold the piano, dismissed her maid. It was a bloodless *coup d'état*. The only thing I retained was the miniature I had had painted of her shortly after our marriage. I keep it locked in my desk drawer. Someday, I suppose, I will give it to Bella. Until then, I take it out occasionally, even though it plunges me into the thick of painful memories.

Bella had a linnet that Nurse Blue gave to her for a birthday. It frightened Bella so because it would hear the song of a wild bird in the trees outside and then beat itself frenziedly against the walls of its cage. It was far worse in Devon than in London. When the thrush began its sweet song every evening, the linnet would go mad with grief. Last night after dinner, Bella and I took it out to the wild garden in its cage. We set the cage down among the fragrant herbs and opened the door. Bella climbed onto my lap as I sat on the bench under the plum tree, and we watched with bated breath.

At first, the bird would not move. It looked about from side to side; it hopped nervously to and fro on its perch. Then, as the sun began to set and the clouds overhead were suddenly golden, the thrush began its glorious paean of thanksgiving for the day. The linnet began to fling itself as usual against its bars and suddenly fell through the open door. It picked itself up and stood, rooted to the ground, looking at me and my daughter with unfathomable dark eyes, as if to bid us farewell.

Then it was gone, in a flutter of wings, soaring high into the sky, a dark speck against the dark blue of the sky and the golden outlines of the clouds.

Tears rolled slowly down my cheeks. I was thinking of my wife.

"Papa, don't cry," said Bella, wrapping her arms about my neck and kissing them away. "It's happier to be so free."

PART SEVEN

Mr. Franklin DeWinx:
Letter to Mr. Charles Lindley
1 September 1848

~ ~

...The passions that endure flash like lightning;
they scorch the soul but it is warmed for ever.

Benjamin Disraeli,
Henrietta Temple

Chapter One

London
1 September 1848

My dear Charles,

I must thank you and Mary again for your generous hospitality during my unfortunately too-brief visit with you in Devon. You were correct, as usual. I did need peace and some gentle companionship before showing myself in London to be feted (or should I say poked, prodded, and paraded—if you will forgive the alliteration) as the new literary lion. I had forgotten, after so many years spent alone or in the company of simple people, how strangely distorted life becomes in London Society. I am expected to patronize the very people whose talent has brought me fame; they are never tired of hearing of the "quaint Irish peasants" and their "primitive customs." I am afraid I am living up to my reputation as a lion and acquiring a reputation for savagery, since I will not accept their condescension. I never fail to disabuse them of their misperceptions. I shall be glad to make my escape from here in two days time to begin on the lecture tour which Messrs. Brown and Cotton have arranged. Plymouth may be one of the last engagements; I will let you know.

I give you the business details first, for I know I will not be inclined to return to them once I have begun on the subject that is filling my heart and mind daily with a strange joy. Do you know; I have seen my own daughter? I cannot withhold this bit of news, which should, chronologically speaking, appear later in this epistle, for I am transported by the realization of myself as a father. Not that I will, I fear, be able to reveal myself as her father to my daughter; the damage I would do to her would be too great, for she loves and even reveres the man she has been raised to believe is her father. Perhaps I shall have only the one glimpse of her in all my life, but—do you know?—that seems to be enough. My heart is full of her.

I know you are asking yourself if I have gone mad. How is it that a thirty-one-year-old bachelor can within the space of a fortnight acquire a daughter? Perhaps you have guessed already. The child that Arabella bore shortly after her marriage to Sir Henry, during the time when she was confined in the insane asylum, is my daughter. She is now five years of age, the same age as your Caroline, exquisitely lovely and far more intelligent than any child of five has a right to be. But then, of course, this is the way all parents rave, isn't it?

Now you must be wondering how it was that I came into contact with Arabella, for you will recall that when we spoke of this matter I felt that it was best, despite my curiosity and a lingering yearning, to leave that door firmly closed. That was especially true considering all of the suffering she has undergone.

It came about quite by accident, actually. Arabella has found a joy and a source of self-expression in music, a talent that was not fostered, in fact was absolutely condemned, by her father. This reminds me of my struggles to exercise my own talents while oppressed by the memory of my father's success and my mother's discouragement. Arabella is, without doubt, extremely gifted. Her voice is rich and expressive; I have seen her bring an entire roomful of people to tears with a simple ballad, and what was even more affecting, she herself wept as she sang. I have rarely witnessed a performance in which the artist was so engaged emotionally; I wondered at the cost to her, but she says she feels enriched rather than depleted. Her piano playing is equally passionate and moving. All of the old qualities that attracted me—her warmth, her intensity, her dramatic sense—are present in her music. Beside those crowded, cluttered London musicales full of pompous prima donnas, pallid renditions of classics by debutantes, and technically perfect but cold performances by musical virtuosi, her talent is awesome. I believe she

274

does not have more acclaim, because by convention she's the wife of a prominent barrister, and because her artistry is consummate, and therefore frightening.

It would seem, since we were both swept up in the same circles, that we would meet. But Arabella has confessed to me that she did everything she could to avoid me. It was not until I had agreed to substitute at a musical society meeting for a guest who had taken ill that our paths crossed. I came into the lecture hall while she was performing, and though I did not immediately recognize her, I was so impressed by her skill and so eager to convey my compliments and gratitude for the pleasure she had given me that I asked my hostess to introduce me. We went into a little antechamber adjacent to the stage, where the musicians gathered after their performances, and there we came face to face for the first time in years.

She had expected to see me eventually, so she was more prepared than I for the encounter. It was awkward enough at the first with all that remained unsaid between us and our hostess fluttering nervously at my side. Soon we steered the conversation into the safe waters of music and were still engaged in a lively dialogue on the topic when I heard myself announced as the next speaker. She was in the audience as I spoke, and I found myself speaking only to her, for in that sea of bored and complacent faces only her countenance was alight with interest and understanding. However, when my task was concluded, she was not among the crowd of well-wishers and lion-prodders who flocked about me, and I felt a lurch of disappointment.

Then came an invitation to dine with her and her husband—at their house in Grover Square. I debated, as you can imagine, at length about whether or not I should accept, but, of course, I went. Sir Henry had mellowed over the years; he was positively jovial at times, though there is clearly a great strain between him and his wife. They barely spoke to or looked at each other. The child (at the time I did not know she was my daughter), Bella, was allowed to dine with us, an unusual concession, I would have thought, for a man of Sir Henry's ilk, but perhaps it is his affection for her that has broadened his heart. And perhaps also she serves as an excellent distraction to cover up the long silences that otherwise occur between him and his wife. At any rate she was utterly engaging, and

I fell half in love with her myself before she was sent off to bed with a round of kisses for everyone, even me. I was surprised at how moved I felt when her young arms curled about my neck and she pressed her lips trustingly to my cheek. Could it have been that even then I guessed or felt our relationship to be deeper than it appeared?

I expected an awkward evening with Sir Henry perhaps baiting or taunting me with his possession of Arabella. But he seemed, on the contrary, eager to throw us together, a circumstance that was even more awkward since Arabella clearly did not wish it. We spoke a little of my adventures working with the Abolitionists in America and then about my travels in Ireland. Arabella played a little (much more constrainedly than before) and before long the evening was at an end.

Again, I felt dissatisfied, and anxious to resolve some of my feelings about the past, I set out consciously to meet Arabella. After haunting a succession of stultifying afternoon musicales, I came across her at one house and had an opportunity to witness another of her amazing performances. We talked afterward and much was settled between us in that conversation. We reviewed our ill-fated romance with honesty and apologies on both sides and with the understanding that circumstances had so distorted our perceptions of each other that we could not have chosen wisely at that time anyway. A great load seemed to lift from me as we spoke; I felt lighter than I have ever felt in my life, and Arabella described the same sensation. Yet, oddly enough, or perhaps not so oddly, once we had left each other, I desired nothing more than to be with Arabella again.

We met occasionally after that at different social events. Her husband does not accompany her as he is not fond of music and, in fact, as I saw for myself, does not understand her talent. And I was invited several times to 19 Grover Square at Sir Henry's express request. When my accompanist, who illustrated examples of the songs I had collected in Ireland—for my voice cannot uphold the dual strain of speaking and singing—became ill, Arabella took her place. Since then we have worked together constantly. It is like a romance, but such a romance as I have never before imagined. She is utterly responsive to me and perceptive, sensing instantly what will improve our presentation, which she then carries out. She has such respect for my work that her appreciation multiplies my pleasure, and the same is true on my part for her musicianship. I have watched her blossom even more as an artist during the past few weeks—I am frustrated by the obstinacy of these words! I know you understand, my dear Charles. I have seen the same reciprocity between you and Mary and how you both have been strengthened by it. I feel singularly blessed and aware of aspects of myself that have never been alive before.

I do not even feel deprived because our relations with each other are strictly Platonic, despite the strong attraction I feel. But I would never again involve myself in a clandestine affair; if Arabella comes to me again, it must be as my wife. The obstacles between us, however, have seemed to multiply rather than diminish with time: the complete loss of her inheritance, which is naturally the property of her husband, the stigma of divorce, and, of course, the loss of Bella. We have spoken of these things, but can come to no sure conclusion at this time.

I have asked Arabella to accompany me on my lecture tour, and she feels she would like to do so. Sir Henry has given his tentative approval; of course, there is no question of any illicit connection between the two of us, but is the man mad? I believe he wants his wife to leave him; he must see how she has come alive again.

I think perhaps I am mad to tempt Fortune for, as I grow to love her (and I do), I face the possibility that she will choose to return to her husband and child. I cannot deny the grief this would cause me. And she has, I suppose, equal reason to fear that I will again turn tail and desert her. I am happy to assure you that this is not a shared fear. I know that I will never turn back from where I have pledged my heart.

If Arabella does indeed accompany me, I would want her to meet both you and Mary while we are in Plymouth. Until that day, when you will be able to see with your own eyes the truth of these words, I ask only for your blessings and prayers for my beloved and for—

your devoted friend,
Franklin DeWinx

EPILOGUE

Jenny Steward: 1877

~ ~

We must never part.
Are we not halves of one dissevered world
Whom this strange chance unites once more?
    Part? Never!
Till thou the lover, know; and I,
the knower Love—until both are saved.

Robert Browning

Arabella and Franklin were given that rarest of all miracles: a chance to begin anew having learned from the errors of the past. That they were happy beyond their expectations I know from the letters I received from Arabella during the lecture tour and after their move to Ireland.

Arabella granted me the same boon of a new beginning when she refused to take me with her on the tour. At the time, I felt this as an indescribable betrayal. After all I'd devoted years of loyal, unde-viating service to her. But now that I have reaped the bounty of that fresh chance, I recognize the wisdom of her actions, the wisdom that accepts pain as sometimes a necessary step on the road to wider opportunities and happiness for all concerned.

Arabella had, after all, found the love she'd always craved in Franklin; it was the love that had been denied her for years first by her father and then by Sir Henry. Sir Henry, in his daughter, found the focus for all his attention and protective needs as a new landed baron in Devon, while Bella now had the security and love always denied her, mother. And as for me?

After months of doggedly trying to find another position, I threw away my scruples and married Dr Steward, who had been waiting patiently for me all those years. We married in December of 1848. I cannot properly convey my gratitude at the miracle of his enduring love nor of my growing appreciation of his noble character, so I will not even attempt it. Besides, it would embarrass him.

After Sir Henry's death, James and I were able to purchase 19 Grover Square and fulfil one of our fondest dreams, the establishment of a private Shelter for the care of just such patients as Arabella had been in her direst straits. We usually have three or four private patients, so it is a little crowded, what with our own five young ones, but every time we see one of our patients leave to take up his own life again, I think of Arabella and all that she gave me with the gift of her departure.

Arabella never mentioned her daughter in her letters. I think it was, at last, the one topic that proved too painful for her. But she need never have worried, as she knew, and must have heard: Bella grew up healthy and happy, the mother of her own large brood of children, living in the Devon house her beloved father bequeathed to her and her progeny.

I retain in my memory an image that gives me great comfort. I was visiting the Great Exhibition of 1851. James and I had finished strolling through the exhibits arm in arm, and he had just gone off to fetch me some refreshment from one of the stands, when I saw a familiar figure seated on a park bench beneath one of the elm trees. It was Sir Henry, a little stouter than before, a little redder in the face. At his side sat an exquisitely beautiful child in a white frock with a blue sash and blue shoes. They were so absorbed in each other and their task of feeding the sparrows that I was able to observe them for some time without their ever being aware of my watching them.

They spoke to each other and gazed upon each other with the fervency of lovers. She kept one gloved hand clasped firmly in his, and one of them could not remark something amusing about the sparrows without immediately pointing it out to the other.

I marveled at Bella's resemblance to her mother. She had Arabella's ivory skin, dark lashes, glossy curls, and perfection of form, but they were overlaid with a sweet seriousness, a maturity that one rarely sees in a child and that was so unlike Arabella that it made me wistful.

Suddenly there was a flash of her mother's vitality. The sparrows, disturbed by my husband charging heedlessly through their midst in his hurry to reach me with the refreshments, darted up into the sky like so many small brown fireworks exploding. Bella, too, darted off her bench and did a scampering little dance in imitation of their flight.

James came up to me then, and when I turned to point them out to him, Sir Henry and Bella had gone. I caught sight of them in the far distance, the old man hobbling along leaning on the shoulder of the lovely child, as they strolled along the path among the over-spreading trees.

It was my last sight of them and how I shall ever remember them.

Jenny Steward
19 Grover Square
18 June 1877

About the Author

NANCY FITZGERALD learned to write at about the same time she learned to type—at the age of eight. One saga, composed when she was twelve, grew to three hundred pages before she lost interest.

She wrote her first novel, *St. John's Wood,* while working at the Los Angeles Museum of Art, researching the book as she rode the bus, back and forth to work. She began teaching novel writing through the UCLA Writers Program, with her friend and colleague, Ellen Pall, shortly after her novel was published by Doubleday.

In 1980, she moved to Seattle with her young daughter, changed her name to Waverly and continued to teach writing, for the University of Washington and Seattle Central Community College.

After publishing three novels with Doubleday and one with Jove, she took a long break from novel writing, focusing instead on non-fiction writing about seasonal holidays and natural time. Her book, *Slow Time: Recovering the Natural Rhythm of Life*, was published in 2009.

When she began writing novels again, she took up the mystery novel. Waverly wrote one series featuring a female Seattle PI and then co-wrote a series of humorous mystery novels, featuring a talking Chihuahua, with her friend and colleague, Curt Colbert, under the name Waverly Curtis. The first book in that series is *Dial C for Chihuahua* and was published by Kensington in 2012.

She currently teaches online for *Creative Nonfiction* magazine and Hugo House, the literary arts center in Seattle. Her most recent novel, Queen of Shadows, is also set in Victorian London.

Learn more at http://www.waverlyfitzgerald.com.